ROCK 'N FIRE

ALSO BY MARK STALLARD

ROCK 'N FIRE

A NOVEL

MARK STALLARD

Kaw Valley Books LLC
Overland Park, KS

Cover design and formatting by Damonza.com

Published by Kaw Valley Books LLC, Overland Park, Kansas.

ISBN: 978-1-7358675-0-2 (paperback)

ISBN: 978-1-7358675-1-9 (eBook)

Library of Congress Control Number: 2020918167

First Edition

Visit *Stallardblurb.com* and **facebook.com/RocknFire28** for blogs, event news, and other information from the author.

People are trapped in history and history is trapped in them.

— James A. Baldwin

Baseball is a game for louts.

— Ernest Hemingway

Night and the day, when united,
Bring forth the beautiful light.

— Victor Hugo

To Kathleen

ROCK 'N FIRE

CHAPTER 1

October 17, 1963
Cooperstown, New York

Baseball was dead—again. Stacks of magazines, small packages, and poorly marked cans of film were piled haphazardly on a gray-metal desk and the floor around it, conclusive evidence showing the complete and final demise of the recent baseball season; or as Frank Aldridge liked to think of the material, the stuff of life *leading* to death.

The other side of the slightly dusty, medium-sized room—more storage chamber than office—held poorly organized photos, game programs, boxes with autographed baseballs, and other non-descript items collected throughout the season. A bent and dirty folder marked "Dead players '63" was sitting atop one of the piles, the holder of poorly-written obituaries and photos of mostly long-ago ballplayers who had perished sometime during the season—baseball death that was real.

For the part of the office that had a small semblance of orderliness, clipped newspaper articles and relevant memorabilia from the highly-significant events of the season past had been carefully set aside on a table next to the desk, the most noteworthy being the stuff belonging to Stan Musial, the great St. Louis player who had finally, and some would argue sadly, retired. A jersey, a couple of bats, a glove, and other Musial items were carefully arranged on the tabletop, soon to be preserved for the "The Man's" inevitable induction into the Hall.

Standing somewhat slouched in the dim morning light of the doorway to his cluttered office in the basement of the red brick building that was the Baseball Hall of Fame, Frank gingerly clutched his full coffee cup and glanced around adoringly at the mess of the room as if he were flirting with it. He finally honed in on the photo of Ted Williams hiding behind a couple of books on his desk, a great shot of the Splendid Splinter in the middle of his beautiful, effortless swing.

"Good morning, Ted, and good morning baseball," Frank whispered quietly to himself as a slight ache in his head from last night's beer reared up. Then he looked at the picture of his family on the other side of the desk next to the over-flowing ashtray—wife, children, and himself—and with a warm smile, nodded lovingly to it. A strong caffeine craving pulled hard on him, and as he took a long sip of the drab coffee, the previous evening's big news swept over him; his wife Peggy thought she might be pregnant.

"I'm late, Frank," she told him the night before after the kids were in bed. And then in a low, partial tone of happy sorrow, "Late."

"So? You've been late before." Frank touched her shoulder, grinning and frowning at the same time.

"We're not having sex tonight," and she pushed him away.

"Okay," Frank had said, and finishing his Ballantine with a big gulp, grabbed for her butt.

"Frank. No." She pushed him away again, but it didn't matter. They still had sex, good sex. As for the possible pregnancy—he just knew she was—he didn't care last night, and didn't care this morning, either. They had even tossed around a few names after they finished screwing, deciding that if it was a girl, they were going to name her Molly. She would be Aldridge child number four. They fell asleep in a warm cuddle before going over boy names.

"Molly, Molly, little girl, by golly," Frank sang to the office as he began making mental notes about what he needed to get done that day; the list was long.

Hell, it was always long.

Frank wasn't exactly a curator at the Hall, wasn't really a registrar, either. He did parts of both jobs—and many others it always seemed—while reporting to the director. It was, in every possible aspect, a perfect setup; he would give items an unofficial "official" authentication, deem which pieces of writing would be entered into the Hall's research system (basically everything he could get his hands on), and occasionally he would put forth a small effort to track down specific items he felt would greatly enhance the library and museum—usually a game ball, a glove, a photo, or special magazine. And while he enjoyed piecing together the information the library kept on ballplayers, "biographical detective work" wasn't exactly his forte or expertise. Frank was a historian, curator, archivist, and librarian—in that order—and whatever else he wanted to be within the confines of the Hall. Whenever separate and unusable pieces of history fell into his capable, baseball-knowledge-sized hands, he attacked their relevance as he would a giant jigsaw puzzle, expertly squeezing them together into a perfect-fitting baseball narrative.

For today, Frank planned to rummage through the correspondence scattered throughout his office and hand off most of the items he had already decided were going to stay in the building to the different departments and archivists. It always seemed as though the accumulation of baseball memorabilia was never-ending, and while that was a good thing, for every diamond-type of "relic" that was donated, loaned to, or acquired by the Hall, there were at least ten pieces that were worthless. Over the years, Frank had filled the Hall's storage warehouse with valueless old equipment, phony autographs, and fake items. But some of the guys who worked at the Hall thought everything was valuable.

"They're really artifacts ¼ artifacts," Registrar Larry Johnston liked to say of the items in a double-deadpan voice that wasn't supposed to be expressionless at all. "They're the pieces of greatness, pieces of great history. It doesn't matter what the value is." An overly-serious type from the Midwest, Johnston's co-workers constantly ragged on him for being an Iowa hick who liked sticks—Johnston loved game-used bats more than any other type of memorabilia. He had been caught more than once lovingly caressing the Musial bats during the last month of the season.

Tippy-toeing his way through the chaotic mess on the floor to his sloppy desk at the back of the room, Frank cleared off a spot for his cup and plopped into the old swivel chair, staring up at the ceiling. Did he need another doughnut? No, just a cigarette.

There was also the matter of carefully going through and cataloging around 2,000 items recently donated by a wealthy New York City family, a collection that was supposed to be a veritable treasure trove of baseball history. Frank was saving it for when his end-of-the-season wrap-up work was complete—a dead-of-the-winter project.

Many times, when he was alone and looking through the objects of baseball's past in his office—a scorecard from a 1934 New York Giants/ Boston Braves game, a pair of shoes worn by Bob "Fatty" Fothergill, an Athletics' souvenir stuffed elephant from the 1920s—he usually felt them to be nothing more than meaningless things in the great, overall scope of baseball's majestic history. But he liked baseball jackets, the sweaters and coats worn by players to stay warm in the spring and to fight off the brisk cold in the late games of September and early October. Frank's favorite was the one the Dodgers wore in the early 1950s, a blue wool zipper jacket with leather sleeves and a script "Dodgers" across the front—he had one. It was a cold, gray morning in Cooperstown, and he was wearing it that morning.

As he took off the jacket and hung it on a wall hook behind his desk, it hit him like it had almost every morning for the past ten days—where in the hell did the time go? Frank never grasped how the baseball season, which would move with the creeping slowness of a slug, and absent any kind of seminal flow throughout the summer, could explode into the final weeks with the speed of a soaring F-8 Crusader, and in a great flash of lost time, the World Series would be upon him and done, and with it, the season. And with the end, a sad, perplexing notion of 'no baseball' would settle over Frank's brain as quickly as the gray shroud of autumn enveloped upstate New York.

He was a teenager the first time the end of a baseball season filled him with melancholy angst. The Dodgers lost the 1947 World Series to the goddamn Yankees, a defeat that left him depressed for… hell, it still made him depressed.

For the last several years, Frank tried the same tired remedies to shake his end-of-baseball funk: a lot of beer, a lot of cigarettes, a lot of sex with his wife. But time, not drunken orgasms and hangovers, was always his best healer. A couple of weeks or so after the conclusion of the Series, his mental "snap back" would usually hit, and instead of mourning the recently passed season, Frank embraced the pleasures of the freshly completed campaign, remembering that the just-finished season could never really die because of the infinite amount of recorded history that lifted the game to his imagined level of poetic and mythical immortality. The best part was that he got to fit the pieces of the deceased campaign together, his way of leaving a personal mark on the game.

Today, regardless of the slight hangover, Frank finally felt like himself. Baseball was waiting for him: the collecting, categorizing, and cataloging of the game's recent past, plus a future that was already happening. The hot stove league—a stupid name for the off season, how in the hell did that ever stick?—with all its crazy, unsubstantiated columns, trade rumors, and feature articles, was about to start. Why did any of that matter?

Ron McMasters, Frank's top assistant in the archives, had piled the newest arrivals of magazines and newspapers on Frank's desk chair the night before—*Sports Illustrated, The Sporting News, New York Times, Chicago Tribune, Los Angeles Times*—all the good stuff on the just-completed World Series.

Dodgers four games, Yankees zip.

The fuckin' Yanks had been swept—*swept*—by the Dodgers, still Frank's favorite team, defection to Los Angeles notwithstanding. The series had ended almost two weeks earlier, and despite his end of the season mood, he still felt the same giddy, 'The Yanks lost' rush he got as a kid. Watching Koufax and Drysdale, Davis and Howard sticking it to the New Yorkers in the series had been glorious.

But Dodgers or not, Ted Williams was, and always would be, Frank's favorite baseball player. The Splendid Splinter—The Kid. He had traveled to Boston more than a few times to see the great hitter play, and even when Williams went hitless, Frank never felt cheated and kept the scorecards to help savor the memories of watching his magnificent swing.

The best was when he saw Williams hit his 400th home run, a nice shot against Kansas City's Tom Gorman in July of 1956, at Fenway Park. It was the only run of the day as the Red Sox beat the hapless Athletics, 1-0.

Frank hated—no loathed—the scumbag writers who had whined,

complained, and attacked Williams with bullshit stories. He kept the worst of the lot in a special folder, his "Shitty Writers to Williams" file. It was one of his largest. Ted's vendetta with the Boston fans and faithful had always been well known because it was overly perpetuated by the Beantown scribes themselves. Frank hoped that when he finally met Williams he would show him the file, plus most of the other cool stuff the Hall had already collected for when the Splendid Splinter joined the other baseball greats in the Hall. Hidden in the stack of magazines and newspapers on his desk was a nice little piece about the baseball camp Williams started after he retired. Frank had read it twice before marking it for inclusion in the good stuff that the Hall was collecting on the Splinter.

Next to the stack of magazines and newspapers was a small pile of envelopes, plus a couple of packages—Frank's ongoing correspondence with all the Major League teams and top writers at the major newspapers across the country. After flipping through a few of the lesser-known magazines and papers—"rag, rag, bullshit rag"—he tossed them to the floor and picked up the envelopes, hoping a return letter from Cubs' coach Buck O'Neil might be in the small stack. As the first negro coach in the Major Leagues, Frank felt some words from O'Neil would be a nice fit for the library and future researchers. Slowly, one-by-one, he started sifting through the letters, but there was nothing from O'Neil.

By mid-morning his head was finally feeling 100 percent, but Frank had done very little work. He checked the time on his watch and opened a small envelope addressed only to the Hall of Fame. He pulled out a flimsy, off-white piece of stationary, a one-page note typed with what had to have been a very old ribbon. Frank stood up for no reason and looked over the note before starting to read. Some of the letters were slightly smudged, but no words were misspelled. The imprint of the capital C left a much darker, shadowy image than the other characters, giving the letter a look like an art image in a textbook instead of a simple correspondence. Frank started to read, but stopped, walked around his desk, and sat down in the chair used by the rare visitor to his office, and finally focused on the short note.

October 10, 1963

Dear Baseball Hall of Fame,

My name is Lita Lawson and I hope that you can help me. I am trying to find Raymond Cavanaugh. He played baseball in St. Louis and Washington DC 20 or 30 years ago. He was a pitcher. Do you know anything about him? I have contacted the newspapers in St. Louis, Washington, and Kansas City. They didn't help me much, but a reporter in St. Louis thought the hall of fame might know something.

It is important that I find Ray Cavanaugh because I think he is my father. I have been looking for him a long time.

Can you help? I would be grateful for anything you can tell me about him. I have never met him and want to very much.

Please contact me at 712 E. Euclid in St. Louis. Any help you can provide would mean the world to me.

Sincerely yours,

Lita Lawson

Ray Cavanaugh? Frank thought for a moment before the image of a grainy black and white wire photo floated through his head, a posed shot of a left-handed pitcher in a St. Louis Browns uniform with a hard and rugged face coupled with mean eyes. Then he turned toward the door of his office and yelled.

"McMasters!"

A 1960 graduate from NYU with a degree in history, Ron McMasters was rapidly increasing his overall knowledge of the game, as well as his knowledge of baseball periodicals, books, and other items. Never much of an athlete—he stood just 5-foot-7 in shoes—McMasters loved looking at old photos and watching newsreels. He'd been at the hall for a few years, and Frank really liked him and the way he tackled different projects. When Ron ambled into Frank's office, he was holding an old baseball and a few papers.

"What?" McMasters' voice was heavy with dishevelment.

"Ever heard of Ray Cavanaugh?" The young man started to shake his head, but then answered that maybe he had.

"Find his file and anything else we might have on the guy," Frank said. "He was a pitcher in the '30s and '40s."

"What do you mean by anything else?"

"I don't know, ask around. Some of the other guys might know a thing or two about the guy. Talk to Johnston." They both laughed at the suggestion, and as McMasters left the office, Frank called after him again.

"Make sure you find photos." McMasters grunted okay.

After lighting another cigarette and dumping a large amount of ashes from the ashtray into the trash, Frank slowly paced through and around the piles on the floor in the office, glancing at the letter, re-reading it several times as he tried to visualize the girl writing it—he supposed that Lita was a girl's name. The possible circumstances surrounding the letter writer, request, and situation were limitless; his mind surged through many different scenarios. What was the story? Every possible way he stacked it up it smacked of scandal—adultery, a woman wronged, whoring, stupidity, and alcohol. Money. Probably some other seedy things, too.

Frank walked to the lone filing cabinet in the room, opened the middle drawer and fingered through the files. He knew about most of baseball's shocking secrets and the men who held them: the drunks, drug addicts, womanizers, gamblers, and overt racists and exclusionists. He pulled out a folder simply marked "Stories," his collection of rumors and facts, tidbits, and other things on all of baseball's secrets—the homosexuals, the drug users, the drinkers, the sex stories, and any other type of society's undesirable behavior that was, for the most part, secret within baseball's world. Frank briefly glanced at the stuff in the folder, knowing there was nothing in it on Cavanaugh.

It was just after lunch time when McMasters returned with the Ray Cavanaugh folder, a couple of reels of film, and an envelope that held a few photos. "Rock n Fire" was scrawled on the folder next to the name and that's when Frank remembered; he was "Rock 'n Fire Ray" Cavanaugh, a notorious lefty in the 30s and 40s, known for beaning hitters, swearing at reporters, having few if any friends on his teams.

Ray Cavanaugh was remembered as being a real son-of-a-bitch.

"This guy was pretty good," McMasters said as he set the materials on top of a small stack of magazines on the corner of Frank's desk. "Why don't we have more stuff on him? His stats look good."

"He played for shitty teams."

"So, here's the stuff we have, and oh yeah, Johnston didn't know anything," McMasters said with a short smile-laugh as he left. Frank grabbed at the folder, began sifting through the numerous clippings and other papers that were not in any sort of order—everything looked like the routine stuff found in every player's file—game pieces, bios, profiles. As he started to drop the file on his desk, an old article slipped out, almost jumping at Frank as it fell to the floor.

The newspaper clipping was yellowed, delicately brittle, yet flimsy. Frank picked it up and carefully placed it on the desk. The name Cavanaugh was circled wherever it appeared in the article, and Omaha Bee, July 10, 1933, was scribbled across the top by the heading.

PACKERS HIT HARD, LOSE BIG

Topeka's Cavanaugh beans Sorenson, sends him to hospital
Omaha Left fielder listed in critical condition
Huddleston and Smith are also beaned
Umpire tosses the left hander from game
Suspension is possible
Topeka wins, 6 to 0

By William Stark

Rourke Stadium, July 9 --- Ray Cavanaugh isn't just the Western League's top pitcher, he's also the circuit's top intimidator. As if losing to the left-handed Topeka hurler wasn't bad enough for Omaha, the Packers also lost two of their top players. In the seventh inning, Cavanaugh tossed a fastball into shortstop Tom Huddleston's ribs, but that injury doesn't appear to be severe. If only Cavanaugh had stopped there.

The next few paragraphs in the article were underlined, more words circled, and a couple of smeared, mostly unreadable notes were scrawled on the side with pencil in large, uneven lines. Frank sighed heavily, coughed a couple of times, and lit another cigarette. He took a couple of long drags and sat down at his desk. After taking a sip of cold coffee and one more drag, he again started to read the old clipping.

CHAPTER 2

July 9, 1933
Omaha, Nebraska

Ray Cavanaugh stood slump-shouldered on the right side of the pitchers' mound, pretending to take a break while scanning the sparse crowd for a doll to screw after the game. It didn't take long for him to hone in on the auburn-haired beauty in the front row down the third base line who was sitting in the late afternoon sun like a ripe peach waiting to be eaten, staring intently at him with glassy-eyed wonder and star-obsessed lust.

She was the one.

Ray flashed a smile her way and climbed back on the mound, ignored catcher Hal Hagerston's sign, and cut loose another high fastball that the batter flailed at weakly for strike three. The small crowd of heat-soaked Nebraskans groaned and jeered. Hagerston fired the ball to Cory Smith, the Senators' third baseman, to start it on a quick journey around the Topeka infield, then back to Ray, who rubbed the ball as he smiled again in the direction of the auburn-haired woman in the stands. She was still staring at him.

The next hitter was Omaha's shortstop, Tom Huddleston, a frail-looking kid with severe acne who had somehow gotten the only hit against Ray that afternoon, a puny pop shot that Topeka's poor-fielding second baseman lunged for and missed behind the bag in the fourth inning. Ray knew what he was going to throw, rocked into his smooth, rhythmic motion, and again ignoring his catcher's sign, unleashed the fastest pitch he'd thrown all afternoon into the middle of the batter's plank-like back. Huddleston, unable to move away from the velocity of the pitch, dropped to the ground on impact and whimpered lightly for a few seconds—the crowd exhaled a breathless gasp in anticipation of an injury. Hagerston pulled off his catcher's mask and stood over the beaned shortstop, grinned briefly, picked up the ball, and trotted to the mound as the Omaha trainer ran to the field and helped the skinny kid to his feet.

"Little bastard," Hagerston said as he handed over the ball to Cavanaugh. "I knew you were going to bean his ass."

"Shut up." Ray turned his back on Hagerston and waited for the batter to take his base.

"Goddamn, throw his ass out!" Omaha's old-fart manager had ambled onto the field and was sticking his grumpy-pruned face close to the home plate umpire's nose. His left hand was jammed into the back pocket of his pants and tobacco juice dripped over his lower lip.

"Back to your dugout old man," the fat umpire said with a stern harshness to the manager's feet. "Get off the field." Then he turned to the mound and addressed Ray's back. "Watch yourself, young man. *Watch your ass.* I'm sending a note about you to the league office." The puny shortstop was the second batter Ray had hit that afternoon.

The small crowd remained somewhat quiet in a hostile way as Huddleston, getting the okay from the trainer, wobbled down the line to first, holding and rubbing his back. He sat down on the bag when he reached it, then jumped up and waved off the pinch runner that the old-fart manager had sent in for him.

"Hook this next guy," the catcher said to Ray. "You're lucky that guy can still walk."

"I told you to shut up."

Hagerston shuffled back and dropped into his crouch position and gave an emphatic "2" sign three times before finally positioning his glove on the lower-right outside corner of the plate. Ray stepped on and off the mound, glared at the freshly-beaned runner on first, then into the dugout at his manager, who was picking his nose. He looked over his shoulder and shot a smirky smile at the auburn-haired woman who was *still* staring at him. Hagerston again gave the sign for a curveball, made a fast adjustment to his cup, and waited for the pitch. The right-handed hitter, a short and stocky outfielder named Sammy Sorenson, took one last practice swing, and defiantly held his bat high in anticipation of the lefty's delivery. Ray stepped on the mound, set himself to pitch out of the stretch, and hummed a fastball toward the hitter.

The pitch rocketed to home plate and froze Sorenson like a statue in the dead of winter before exploding into the left side of his head—a resounding yet dull "thunk" rolled through the ballpark, instantly followed by long, loud fanatical shouts and screeches from the stunned fans.

Then, deathly quiet.

For the eight or nine hundred spectators who were at the game, many said afterwards that they had never heard anything like the sound of the ball crashing into Sorenson's skull, even though they could not accurately describe exactly what the sound was.

"Like a gunshot? No, and not a hitting noise, either," an overweight and balding fan said of the head beaning.

"The pitch was so fast, I only heard it," another unbelieving spectator said.

"It was like a bomb going off," a distraught woman recalled.

"I thought he was dead for sure," one of Sorenson's teammates told the *Omaha Bee*. "I don't ever wanna see anything like that again."

After the ball met the resistance of Sorenson's head, it rebounded toward third base and settled to a stop on the messy chalk line, oblivious of its crime. The force of the pitch had knocked Sorenson's cap more than 20 feet from the plate.

A dumbfounded Hagerston gasped as the batter fell to the ground. "Oh, lordy lordy fuck. Oh, sweet Jesus." Blood spilled out of the batter's ear and nose, his eyes open and rolled back as his body settled in the dusty clay around home plate. The umpire threw his mask to the side, took a quick look at the fallen batter, and started screaming for help. The Topeka team stepped slowly at first from their positions in the field, skeptical in what they saw, then ran like hell towards the batter's box, getting there just after the Omaha players, who had streamed quickly from their dugout.

Both managers kneeled over the batter as the umpire rolled the comatose man over on his back. The crowd remained eerily silent, standing, gawking, leaning forward from all parts of the park, trying to get a look while holding its collective breath.

Ray stayed on the mound, hands on hips, oblivious and looking somewhat irritated by the scene at home plate. He kicked at the dirt, popped at his glove a couple of times, squatted up and down. When Hagerston noticed he was still moving around the rubber, he walked to his pitcher, trepidly, like a man going to a bad dentist.

"What the hell? Why?" he asked sadly. Ray turned away for a couple of seconds, spit, then turned back and burned a hard glower into his catcher's eyes.

"Because," he said almost whispering, void of remorse. "Because. I don't want anyone to think I could lose my fuckin' nerve. Ever." Then he touched his catcher's shoulder.

"Holy mother," Hagerston said as he took a step backward from Ray. "I hope I never have to hit against you, you crazy son-of-a-bitch. Fuck."

The crowd was buzzing now, and while most eyes were still fixed upon Sorenson—the Omaha trainer was taking his pulse, touching and looking at his head, waiting for a stretcher—a few fans had turned their attention toward Ray and Hagerston, and the scene they were making on the mound away from the injured hitter. Quickly surveying the spectators who were watching him, Ray saw the woman was still in her seat, then turned back to Hagerston.

"Get your fat ass away from me," then he spit again. "And shut the fuck up." The burly catcher spit back and returned to the area around home plate.

They were carrying Sorenson from the field now, his arms dangling off the side of the stretcher, head cocked in an unusual angle, blood smeared across his face. Through the static drone of the crowd rose some polite clapping, and after Sorenson was gone from the field, the old umpire, flush with sweat and smelling of chalk, stomped toward Ray at the pitcher's mound, shaking his head and fists.

"You're out of the game!" the umpire screamed, and after circling his right arm, pointed wildly at Cavanaugh, and waved his arm again. "Get the hell off my field!"

Jeers, shouts, and hisses fell from the stands—"Killer! Kick him out, kick him out!"

Ray looked one last time at the auburn-haired beauty in the stands, flipped the ball to the umpire's feet, and walked slowly to the dugout. Before exiting the field, he turned and glared at the Omaha dugout, cocked his head and spit.

"Murderer! Monster! Villain! We'll get you, Cavanaugh!" The hoots and catcalls rose high in volume but fell harmlessly off Ray's shoulders. He disappeared into the dugout and headed for the clubhouse.

❧

When he began playing with Topeka at the start of the 1933 season, Cavanaugh wasn't sure what to expect. He had somehow slipped through the sights of the organizations he wanted to play for—the Cubs or Yanks or Giants—and even though the Topeka club was affiliated with the Browns, he knew he would have to play extraordinary baseball to move up from the purgatory of the Western League.

More than anything, Ray wanted to leave Kansas and the never-ending string of farms that stretched across the state's flat, uninspiring landscape. He hated his own family's farm, and while he yearned for the spoils of life in the cities and everything they could offer—women, booze, night-life, and more—he knew that baseball was the only way he'd ever get to approach what he considered was the good, grand life a citizen of a metro-politan area experienced.

Still, his first tour through the Western League offered much for the young rookie ballplayer—he found the illegal liquor, easy women, and new music that dulled the sad feelings of the Depression's stranglehold on the population of the country, especially the people of the Midwest. Joplin, Des Moines, Wichita, St. Joseph—not exactly cradles of culture, but for the farm boy pitcher, there was enough in the cities of the league to expand his urban experience. The bus rides were long and awful, and the fans of the opposing teams soon learned to fear and despise him. But Ray enjoyed the taunts and jeers from the fans in Springfield, Cedar Rapids, and the other cities more than the thunderous cheers he received in Topeka's shabby ballpark.

His first game with the Topeka Senators had been a masterpiece, a two-hit shutout with 12 K's against the Hutchison, Kansas squad, a performance so dominating that he received write ups in the *Kansas City Star* and *Wichita Eagle*. He got hit hard in his next start in Cedar Rapids, but still won the game, 7-6. After that, he never gave up more than 2 runs and lost only once.

He was, indeed, a special pitcher.

He was also a young man ready to learn about life and sow some oats. Ray explored the nightlife throughout the league, but he really had looked forward to the Omaha trip because it was the largest in the league and had many of life's best temptations—easy flowing illegal alcohol, one of the best brothels west of the Mississippi, and a lot of music—one of the best jazz bands, The Dixie Ramblers, called Omaha home. There was also the Sporting District, an entertainment area run by city "boss" Tom Dennison around 16th and Harvey Streets —gambling, burlesque shows, prostitution, and other attractions embellished the seedier side of life, keeping the Nebraska sinners happy.

One place that Ray had particularly liked was the Dreamland Ballroom, a jazz venue on North 24th Street in North Omaha. One of the older, career minor leaguers on the Senators took him there, and realizing the negroes weren't the unhuman abomination that he had been raised to believe, Ray settled in and fell in love with jazz. On his first night in Omaha, Ray had seen Duke Ellington—the jazz great performed "It Don't Mean a Thing" and "Sophisticated Lady," among others. Heavy smoke filled the space, he had a steak that melted like butter in his mouth, and of course there was the sweet, delectable music—the place erupted his senses.

A couple of the players on the team had ventured to the brothel, but Ray didn't see the point. There were always plenty of women clamoring for sex with ballplayers, even in the smallest of cities, and Ray was content to save his money for booze. He would have gone back to the Ballroom if he hadn't seen the auburned-haired beauty in the stands. Jazz could wait, he was hungry for other things.

❦

The clubhouse was empty when Ray walked in. He sat down at his locker, threw his cap on the floor, and ripped off his jersey. He was starting to pull down his pants when a reporter waltzed in. Old-looking for being just 27, the chubby scribe had a notepad in his left hand, a pencil in the other.

"Cavanaugh, did you throw at Sorenson on purpose?"

"Who're you?" Ray didn't look at him, kept his head down. He knew the guy was a reporter, but since it wasn't the hammerhead scribe from the Topeka newspaper, he didn't care.

"I'm Stark, with the *Omaha Bee*. Did you throw at him?"

"Throw at him?" Ray loved to play dumb.

"Who? Sorenson, of course."

"No, of course not."

"It sure looked like you did. What about Huddleston?"

"Nope."

"That's a bunch of applesauce, and you know it," the stout reporter said. Then he leaned in closer to Cavanaugh and asked, "What did your manager say to you about the beanings? Is he mad? Did he tell you to throw at them?"

"He said 'Nice game.'"

"More applesauce. So, tell me about the beanball pitches." The reporter was smirking, playfully. "Is that related to your nickname, Rock 'n Fire?"

Ray was already irritated with the little guy's applesauce shit comment, and the mention of Rock 'n Fire rubbed him even further the wrong way. He was ready to belt the guy.

"Look, sometimes I hit hitters." Ray made a fist, held it up so the reporter could see.

"You know, Sorenson might be dead," Stark said in a suddenly serious tone.

Dead. Killing a guy with a baseball was something Ray had thought about from time to time, but he never considered it a real possibility. Now this chubby, smart aleck reporter was telling him that he might have actually done it—killed another player.

"That's awful," and Ray looked up at the reporter, tried hard not to let the remorse and regret show on his face. "Look, I feel bad about that. Incredibly bad, but I didn't throw at him.

"Now leave me alone."

"I want to—"

"Goodbye." Ray turned his back on the reporter, who slowly—and smartly—backed away and left. Then Ray went into the manager's office, found a piece of paper and pencil, and wrote a short note.

Meet me at the front gate after the game.

Ray Cavanaugh

Then he strolled to the dugout entrance, hollered for the batboy, pointed to the auburn-haired woman in the stands, and instructed him to get the note to her.

⚜

The woman was waiting for him. Dressed in a simple blue dress with a white collar, she had smooth skin, deep green eyes, and a slender figure. Sitting on a bench close to the front gate of Rourke Stadium, she jumped up and walked quickly to him as he ambled toward her with a swagger she had never seen before from any other man. She liked watching him more than she had imagined she would.

The game had been over for more than two hours, and Sorenson was now at Lutheran Hospital. The public wouldn't know the details for another 12 hours or so, but the beaned outfielder was conscious and functioning, and while he obviously needed to be watched and screened for complications, everything pointed to him recovering. His face was bruised beyond recognition, swollen and purple-black, but the ball had not done sustainable damage, somehow. It would be proclaimed a "Miracle" in the *Omaha Bee* two days later. **He's All Right!** screamed the headline on the sports page, but for the time being, Sorenson's fate was still very much in doubt.

The injured outfielder was the last thing on Ray's mind. Sizing up the woman as they got close to one another, he saw that she looked even better than he thought, and he was pleased with himself that he'd made the visual connection with her during the game.

"Oh, Mr. Cavanaugh," she said breathlessly. "Hello. Did you really want me to wait for you?"

"Yes, I did," he said casually, staring into her eyes and glancing at her breasts. "What's your name?"

"Betty, Betty Tarkinson."

"Hi Betty. Let's go."

"Go? What are you talking about?"

"Don't you want to have dinner with me?"

"I hadn't expected to, I just wanted to get your autograph." That's when Ray noticed she was holding a piece of paper and a pencil.

"Sure, why not. But I'm hungry, and I want you to join me."

"Really? Me?"

"Come on," said Ray, and he casually took her right hand into his left and gave it a slight squeeze.

They ended up at a speakeasy he knew about, not one of the famous places he had on his list of things to do in the city, but still a decent steak house that was a few blocks from the team hotel. She ordered a KC Strip and ate like she hadn't had a meal in days. Ray made sure to order a second round of drinks, whiskey for himself, gin for Betty.

"So where do you live?" Ray asked during the meal. And he asked other questions, stuff about herself and her life. But he didn't listen to the answers. She yammered on about her mom, and friends, her job at a bank, and that she was from Lincoln, but had moved to Omaha two years earlier. Ray didn't say much, but after his second drink he decided that yes, he wanted to screw her. When they finished eating, he stood up, grabbed her hand, and said "Time to move."

This time she squeezed his hand back, and they went to his room at the hotel, kicked out his roommate, and had at it.

CHAPTER 3

July 19, 1936
St. Louis, Missouri

The blueness of the sky was deceptively cool-looking, hiding the high temperature and thick, exhausting humidity. The back of Aulette Lawson's neck was damp and annoying—she hoped the scorching sun would somehow help burn away the sweat, but the sultry air did not allow that relief. She looked over at her mother, a slender woman with a soft face aged nicely despite life's heavy burdens, and wondered how the sticky air and heat mixture was not affecting her in the same way. It had to be close to 100 degrees—the city was mired in a month-long heat wave—and normally Aulette would seek shady cover, but not today. She loved baseball, and loved watching her bother Lonnie play, so she remained sitting in the scathing brutality of the sunbaked bleachers of Stars Park. At least until she needed to quench her thirst.

"Do you want something to drink, mama?" Aulette stood up, ready to find a beverage under the stadium's grandstand. Her makeshift fan, the game scorecard, fluttered slowly in front of her face.

"I'm fine," her mother said. "When does your brother hit?" Loretta Lawson was still trying to grasp the subtle complexities of the game, and while she had been watching baseball for most of his life, she never worried about anything going on in the game except watching her son hit, something he did very well.

"Probably next inning," Aulette said as she started to walk up the aisle to find the concession stand. "I'll be right back." Her mother nodded at no one, never taking her eyes off the field. On the next pitch, the batter lined a shot down the left field line for what appeared to be a sure double. Lonnie Lawson raced to the corner of the left field wall, stretched out his gloved left hand, and with the grace of a ballet dancer, leaped and dove to snag the ball just before it hit about five feet from the chalk line, then somersaulted to a quick standing position. His throw to second base easily doubled off the runner as the heat-blistered fans went absolute bonkers.

The crowd noise brought Aulette back to the grandstand with a rush— she knew she'd missed something big. When she found out about Lonnie's great catch from an old woman sitting next to the ramp, she sadly shook her head, knowing Lonnie would ask her what she thought of it after the game. As she walked back to the concession area for her drink, the low blare of horns rang from the left field bleacher seats throughout the park, followed by a resounding "Go Stars go!" from the happy crowd. Aulette whispered to herself, "Go Lonnie go."

A franchise in the Negro American League, the St. Louis Stars were usually one of the best black teams in the country. Lonnie Lawson played left field for the club, and while his hitting was good, it was his overall speed and great outfield play that had landed him a spot on his hometown nine two years earlier. Before the Stars, he had played very little organized ball—Lonnie honed his skills on the sandlots of the black neighborhoods of St. Louis and then at his high school. Mostly, he was self-taught.

From the time he was old enough to know what baseball was, he began hitting rocks from the alley behind their small home with an old broom handle—over and over in a never-ending sequence of toss up, wait, and swing. He would spray rocks all over the neighborhood, never once breaking anything but the sticks he used to swat at the stones. Playing with his friends in the streets or empty lots, his speed was so overwhelming to the other kids that they started calling him 'Lightning' when he once raced home ahead of a dangerous summer electrical storm—Lightning Lawson.

The nickname stuck.

When the Stars held a public tryout to find a couple more players to round out their roster two years earlier, it was Aulette who insisted he go.

"I can't play with those guys," Lonnie said. "I'm nothing compared to those players." He had watched the Stars play several times and didn't think he was good enough.

"This is your chance, Lonnie. Think about mama. Think of yourself," Aulette said. "I've seen the Stars play and I know you can play with those ballplayers. Believe. Believe in yourself. Baseball is in your blood."

❧

Aulette and Lonnie's father, Leonard "Lanky Lenny" Lawson, had been a decent ballplayer in the South 20 years earlier, a light-hitting outfielder who played for a couple of Negro League teams—first the Montgomery Grey Sox, then the Birmingham Black Barons—before ending his playing days with a traveling team based in Mobile. He and Loretta married a couple of years before his break came with the Grey Sox, and by then they already had Aulette and Lonnie. Baseball, it seemed, was providing the break they had been waiting for, giving them the chance to line up a storybook life. Loretta was crazy about her husband, and the two children were everything she ever wanted—except more children—and Lenny's baseball talent was their ticket to good times. Black ballplayers, with the right team and league, could make a decent living, and with barnstorming trips to play games against local teams around the country also a possibility, it could make for a nice life.

But Lenny's dick ruined everything.

By the time he joined the Grey Sox, the lanky ballplayer had discovered he had a powerful proficiency for womanizing, a vice that would quickly become legendary around and across the black baseball world. While Lenny wasn't quite good enough to stick for more than a couple of seasons with either team, there were some things—not baseball related—that he was very good at. Women flocked to him as if he were a movie star, a never-ending line of females waiting to take a turn with the tall, handsome man.

There was a reason. Lenny had the "stuff"—the women always seemed to know about his penis, and they wanted to see it. Of course, it was reported to be a lot larger than it really was, but that didn't matter—Lenny "used" it at a record pace—and he always tried to have a different partner every night.

Lonnie was let in on the story of his dad's perpetual philandering years later when an old-timer casually asked if Lonnie's dick was as big as his dad's. Lonnie politely declined to answer, and then heard the stories.

When he was on the road, Lenny's legendary philandering also included drinking—a lot of drinking—and that was more than he could handle in addition to playing ball or caring for a family. It never mattered what kind of alcohol he drank, Lenny loved and craved all of it.

Since the stuff was illegal in the 1920s, he usually ended up with some sort of rot-gut, homemade hooch, or bootleg beer—on occasion he was able to find a bottle of Canadian whiskey. He also had a few regular speakeasy spots in Montgomery and Birmingham, as well as the other cities around the south where his teams played, back-alley nightspots for negroes that accommodated his never-ending need for a booze buzz. Ballplayers always helped business, even the drunk ones, and he was welcome, regardless of his behavior, which was usually obnoxious and crass. More than just alcohol to Lenny, the clubs were where he found his women, and while he had a few "regular" girlfriends across the league, his hunt for something new was constant.

"You never know what you might be missing," he laughed to his teammates.

When Loretta finally found out about his prolific womanizing, it wasn't from the tattle-tale words of another player's wife or girlfriend, but by catching Lenny in the act in the women's bathroom of the Early Bird club in Montgomery as he was enjoying a wanton woman on the toilet.

"Baby, baby, baby," the woman panted loudly, and when Loretta recognized the sound of Lenny's grunting, she pounded on the stall door, screaming.

"Lo, get out of here!" Lenny yelled back, and she ran from the room.

When he found her an hour later, sitting in front of the bus station— she had purchased a ticket to Atlanta—he tried to laugh it off, but Loretta had none of it. She was devastated; her heart had exploded like a bomb when she heard him with the other woman, especially since she had always been more than willing to have sex with Lenny whenever and wherever.

"It is what it is," Lenny said for an apology. "It means whatever I want it to, which is nothing."

"It means more than nothing, for sure," she said, sobbing uncontrollably. "It does. It does. I hate you."

He walked the sloppy walk of a drunkard, somehow following her back to their small apartment that was just blocks from the station, and tried to have sex with her before passing out.

Loretta was never the same after that, but for whatever the reason, she stayed with him, trying to make do for herself, Aulette, and Lonnie, leaving the emotions of love behind. The church became her anchor, and she prayed daily—it seemed to her that she never stopped praying—not just for Lenny, Aulette, and Lonnie, but more for herself, to have the strength to sustain staying with her wayward husband and endure the pain of his adulterous, alcoholic sins.

The church had always been a staple within her life in Alabama. Her father had been a pastor in the Baptist Church for a short time, but his own predatory, adulterous ways caught up with him and after he was caught with the 15-year-old daughter of the congregation's wealthiest member, he was quickly defrocked. Loretta's mother, also shamed by the sins of her man, endured the lingering effects of the scandal for several years and eventually died of pneumonia, spiritually battered and broken.

After his release by the team in Mobile, and having no other baseball options available, Lenny said goodbye to his girlfriends, loaded his family into their makeshift auto, and followed his brother Johnnie to St. Louis in hopes of catching on at one of the several factories that were hiring negroes. He initially landed a nice assembly line job in the St. Louis Truck factory, attaching and fastening two tires to the trucks on the line. But his drinking got the best of him—missing work or puking on the job—and he sputtered along on the line until he was finally canned six months after starting for passing out on the toilet after throwing up at ten o'clock in the morning.

"I ain't the only colored man drinking on the job," he told his wife after being fired. "I know the bosses are doing it, too."

After that, he found few offers. He kept drinking, but because of a friend of his brother, Lenny eventually got a job driving a delivery truck for one of the many local breweries in St. Louis. That's also when Loretta began working as a maid and cook, putting in long days and leaving her two kids by themselves. Lenny never worried about the children as much he worried about his next drink. Somehow, despite the drunken binges and lost days, he held onto the delivery job.

A little more than two years later, he went out for a delivery, drank a lot of the onboard beer, picked up one of his regular girlfriends—a white woman—and drove across the Mississippi River into Illinois.

He was never seen again.

Lenny occasionally didn't come home, but he always showed up after a couple of days. His worst binge was the previous year when he stumbled into the front room of their home after being gone for five days, fell to the floor by the front door, and threw up on himself.

The last time was different. When a week had gone by, Loretta didn't panic. She knew he wasn't coming back, and she felt horrible praying for his safe return because she didn't want him back. The speculation about his disappearance always came around to murder—murder by the police or murder by his own hand. Aulette loved her father and had found a way to look beyond the boozing. She never knew about the many women he bedded, she just wanted her daddy. Lonnie knew, and hated him for it. But for all his lying, drinking, whoring, and dishonorable traits, Lenny was still a man who was easy-going with a warmth that came naturally, a way that endeared him not just to women, but also to the men in his life. There were a few remembrances of Aulette's with her dad, tender moments of father-daughter chatter, sweet hugs and kisses, holding hands on long walks. But there were never enough of them, at least when he was sober.

For Loretta, the loss of her husband was only devastating in a financial way. It was also when she found her inner strength and resolve not to let her children down. Aulette was just 11 when Lenny vanished; Lonnie was 12. A third sibling, Coretta, had died shortly after the family arrived in St. Louis from Alabama. She was three when pneumonia took her.

Loretta did everything she was allowed to do as a black woman to take care of her children, but it was like pushing a two-ton truck up a steep hill. When Lenny disappeared, she began a full-time domestic service job for a family in University City. She also did laundry on the side and worked for a neighborhood florist whenever possible. If she wasn't working, she was sleeping—or thinking about working—but occasionally she would stop everything and go to a ballgame, especially after Lonnie started playing for his high school team. Short of turning to prostitution—which at one time was a very scary and regrettably, a real option—she had been resilient in finding ways to make do.

The church—the United Baptist Church of St. Louis—was a big part of her strength, and the congregation rallied around her. One of the first all-black congregations in St. Louis, the church was more than 100 years old, dating back to when Missouri was still very much a slave state. The pastor was a big, burly teddy bear of man with premature gray hair and bad breath, and while Loretta always suspected he was trying to bed her, she never allowed the remotest of possibilities for that option to happen. Lenny refused to have anything to do with the church—"I'm going to hell no matter what anyone says or does for me."

Aulette and Lonnie usually went to the Sunday service with their mother, but even at a young age Aulette, while enjoying the social aspects of the church, never felt the spiritual connection to God or Jesus that her mother did. Lonnie simply prayed for baseball agility and talent.

Putting together a makeshift baseball uniform—he had an old pair of gray pants, an undershirt with black sleeves, and a used pair of spikes that were a half a size too big—Lonnie signed up for the tryout with the Stars. Three swings, three throws, and a run around the bases. Despite the minimal tasks, Lonnie put on a show and was signed to a contract before he left the park. The owner and general manager of the Stars, William E. Ruggles, couldn't believe his luck, landing a young, promising star from his own backyard—that was something he never thought would happen. Ruggles fell in love with Lonnie immediately and made sure he got the best of everything the team and the city could offer. He was constantly asking the *St. Louis American*, the negro newspaper in St. Louis, to promote Lawson as one of the top players in the league.

"Lightning Lawson. The kid is better than Pepper Martin, for Christ sakes," Ruggles was often heard saying, and the comparison was a good one. Lonnie *was* better than the popular Cardinals' player, better than a lot of players in the majors—but he would never see a major league field, at least not while wearing a major league uniform. Knowing that was the lay of the baseball world, Ruggles was determined to keep the young outfielder in St. Louis and away from the other big-time negro league teams.

"When 'Lightning' strikes, the Stars will shine!" Ruggles belted out his corny slogan whenever he was asked about Lonnie. The St. Louis fans, the white fans for the Cardinals and Browns would have loved him, if only they knew who he was.

Back in her seat and slowly sipping her cold drink, Aulette looked around the stadium and felt the pureness of joy from the crowd, which was still buzzing after Lonnie's catch. There wasn't a white face among the sweaty throng of happy fans, save a couple of older men sitting close to the Stars' dugout. They stood out among the crowd like accidental specks of white icing on a chocolate cake. The out-of-place men both held scorecards, notebooks, and pencils, their heads covered by brown fedoras. When the next batter grounded out to the shortstop, both men slowly scribbled in their book and made a couple of marks on the scorecard. They said some-thing to each other before turning their attention back to the field. Aulette thought for a moment about why the men might be at a Negro League game, but when the next batter popped out to the second baseman to end the inning, they got up and swiftly left.

Baseball "crazy" was a good way to describe St. Louis in the 1930s— the fan base for the Cardinals was one of the best in the country. The city's other big-league team was the Browns, and because they were perennial losers, their following was best described as poor. But for the negro in St. Louis, Major League baseball was not a welcoming venue, especially at Sportsman's Park where the Cardinals and Browns played—the city itself was not a good location to be black in America. Was any place? Most white fans in the city didn't know that there was a Negro League team in St. Louis, and the collective thought of white people supporting a black baseball team was considered ludicrous and stupid. The blacks in the river city—almost 100,000, which was 15 percent of the metropolitan area's citizens—like everywhere else in the country, were on their own. The good thing was that most of them didn't mind—what other choice did they have? As long as they were left alone to conduct their business and live their lives—most of the time they were anything but. Which was why Aulette pushed Lonnie into the baseball tryout that changed his life, as well as her's and their mother's.

Fighting the struggles all black women fought during the 1930s, Aulette's chances in her early adult life to find a place to thrive and grow in St. Louis were dim. She had always dreamed of attending Sumner Normal School, a negro teachers' college—it was relatively close to the Lawson home and as it happened, the ballpark—to become an educator. A couple of her teachers at Sumner High School had encouraged her to pursue her dream, but the money was never there.

Lonnie playing for the Stars changed that—he made enough money to help with her tuition—and the dream was now within reach. Aulette would be starting classes in the fall. Lonnie had baseball, and despite the absence of any real coaching, he excelled as a teenager, being even more athletic than their father. Aulette also fancied jazz—she loved Duke Ellington—and many of the arts, especially painting and drawing. Joe Jones—a local St. Louis painter—and his brilliant images spoke to Aulette across the darkness of segregation, gave her hope that someday she too would realize some of her dreams. It was a longshot, at best. Unless their talent was extraordinary, negroes were *always* discouraged and kept from pursuing anything other than menial labor jobs or domestic service. If she could become a teacher, a way out of the segregated neighborhoods, or at least a better way of life in St. Louis, might be possible.

Lonnie had a fragile level of confidence, and he would inevitably fall into a mini depression, which usually led to a skid on the field. Whenever he hit a rough spot with his play, it was his sister's guidance and knowledge of his overall skillset that helped him out of the slump.

It was the bottom of the fourth, and Lonnie was the lead-off hitter. He took a couple of pitches, drove a shot down the right field line, and seconds later was standing on third. Loretta went crazy with the rest of the crowd, and when the next pitch got away from the catcher, Lonnie strutted home, scoring his second run of the day.

"That Lawson can run, for sure," said a man sitting in the same row as Aulette and Loretta. He had no idea that Lonnie was Loretta's son.

"He sure can," grinned Loretta.

The rest of the game played well for the home team as the Stars won easily, 7-1, and it was a happy crowd that left the stadium. When Aulette and her mother attended home games, they would wait for Lonnie, get something to eat, then head back to their modest home in the Ville district of the city. But today was Sunday, and Lonnie was headed to Kansas City on the team bus after the game. Aulette and Loretta were going straight to the church, which was also close to the ballpark, ending their day where they started it.

As the two women left the ballpark, Aulette again saw the two white men who had been inconspicuously watching the Stars. That's when it hit her—they were cops. The men were closely watching the fans as they left the game, and when two men dressed in almost matching pinstripe suits appeared with a woman in a blue-green dress, the fedora twins walked up to them, quickly pulled out their badges, and ushered the three people into the back seat of a dark sedan that was parked across the street from the main gate of the stadium.

Aulette breathed a quick sigh of relief. White policemen at a Negro League game was never a good thing. Her mother seemed oblivious to the encounter and quickly talked of normal things.

"Have you seen Harold recently?" Loretta asked her daughter as they started the walk from the stadium to their church. Harold was the latest boyfriend of Aulette's, a taxi driver and sometimes bartender.

"Not for a couple of days." Aulette didn't really like him that much. "He's been busy."

"Busy with what? Planning on not seeing you?" Without looking, she knew her mother was also rolling her eyes.

"Mama—" Aulette crossed her arms and stiffened her back.

"What about the ball player Lonnie introduced you to?"

"Skeeter? He can't do anything but baseball. A bit of a fool, if you ask me."

"Hmmm." Skeeter McGee was the Stars center fielder, and a good friend of Lonnie's. But he was too happy-go-lucky for Aulette's taste, and his conversation skills and education level were minimal at best—he was not a smart man. The world was more than baseball, but not to Skeeter. Mother and daughter walked on, saying little for the rest of the way, and that was fine with both of them. Neither seemed to mind.

It had been an especially good day for Aulette—she and her mother had not been called niggers on their walk to and from the ballpark, and while that happened infrequently, when it did it stayed with her for days. There were also no whistles, catcalls, wolf-like behavior from the few white men they encountered. The big plus of the day was that the Stars had won, Lonnie was terrific, and now they were headed back to the church where they would feel the warm glow of spiritual friendship and well-being within its old, revered walls. Aulette's life, laced with horrific racism and hate, misogyny and ignorance, and the daily beat-down of denied opportunities, had a temporary reprieve from the normal emotions that constantly swallowed her as she entered the church with her mother, and she smiled at herself.

The feeling was almost good.

CHAPTER 4

February 25, 1964
Cooperstown, New York

It had been a couple of months since Frank had done any kind of research on Ray Cavanaugh; the assassination of President Kennedy had thrown the entire country into a massive, grief-riddled depression—Frank wasn't immune to the nation's sorrow. A large, splendidly-framed print of JFK throwing out the first pitch at a Washington Senators' game now hung in his office—the handsome president surrounded by other dignitaries, flashing a great smile, his right arm slinging forward in the photo. The Hall was trying to figure out if there was some sort of tribute that baseball could appropriately make on behalf of the slain leader—a special day, commemorative souvenirs, even a uniform patch. Eventually, the powers that be within the two leagues and the commissioner's office decided to do nothing distinctive. President Johnson threw out a ceremonial first pitch for the Senators on opening day—nothing special about that—and JFK's brothers, Bobby and Teddy, did the same at the Red Sox home opener.

Frank had hoped baseball would somehow tie together Stan Musial and the slain president. The recently retired star had vigorously campaigned for Kennedy during the 1960 presidential election. Musial's presence helped in a couple of hotly contested states, and the JFK campaign acknowledged that he was, indeed, "Stan the Man" when it came to campaigning.

Americans didn't much like Catholics in 1960 (Frank always grumbled to himself how America didn't like anybody) and since JFK was very much a catholic, he needed help convincing the protestant public that he would not be answering to the whims of Rome and the Pope. In an impressive effort to show the citizens of the U.S.A. that JFK was likable, trustworthy, and presidential, his campaign assembled a team of celebrities to canvass the country extolling the Democratic candidate's virtues. Musial, along with Byron "Whizzer" White (who, by coincidence, was later selected by Kennedy for the Supreme Court), author James Michener, and actors Jeff Chandler and Angie Dickinson, made up a team of personalities that toured the country, looking for voters who identified with baseball, reading, and the movies. It was, at least according to Michener, "as grueling a tour as could have been devised."

Stan the Man was the true headliner of the group, and the goal was to send the group where Kennedy might still be considered as nothing more than a catholic trying for a massive world power grab for the Pope. Would anyone at a campaign rally dare to yell things like "You're a goddamn fish-eater" or "No Catholics in the White House" in Musial's presence? The baseball star was counted on to put a common-man window around JFK, and his overall popularity across America paid off.

"I was constantly astonished at how the men in the cities we stopped at would crowd the airports to see Stan Musial," Michener wrote of the traveling campaign caravan. "He seemed about 15 years younger than he was, and men who were now quite old remembered him as a beginner in the big leagues."

Frank admired Kennedy and had cast his vote for him in 1960. The young president had inspired Americans across the country, Frank included. And while Frank was non-political on almost every level, JFK had instilled in him a will to do better, at least in his realm of baseball. The 1960 campaign had made Kennedy a fan of the popular Cardinals' star, and the president made a point to let the Redbird slugger know he was liked and respected.

"A couple of years ago, they told me I was too young to be President and you were too old to be playing baseball. But we fooled them," Kennedy said to Musial at the 1962 All-Star Game. The Man agreed.

Now, JFK was gone.

While the assassinated president had been a baseball fan, his father, Joe Kennedy, absolutely loved and adored the game. The senior Kennedy had a small portion of playing time for the Harvard nine when he was in school, but it was what he did as the United States Ambassador to Great Britain that fascinated Frank.

After Joe moved to Britain with his family as the new Ambassador, he wanted to make sure he had some of the comforts of home—baseball was one of the things at the top of his list. But baseball is like a foreign language in England and keeping up with the game's skinny and other goings on at home was going to be difficult, damn near impossible. In a request of sheer American gall, Joe convinced one of the local London newspapers to publish the daily baseball scores from America. Frank envisioned the scene at the newspaper as the new ambassador made his request to the editor.

"Can you get the baseball scores for me every day in the paper?" Kennedy likely asked. "I'm sure we can make some arrangement to help the paper."

"Baseball?" the London editor said incredulously. "Baseball?"

"Good then." And Joe would hand over the contact information to have the scores wired in every day, take out a subscription to the paper, and maybe promise to curry a favor down the road for the periodical—or so Frank imagined. However the scene played out, Frank had recently gotten his hands on a couple of the newspapers from London with the baseball scores listed, and while they would probably never be displayed in the Hall, having them was like having a small piece of gold with huge historical importance. It was one more item to add to the never-ending list of things that baseball influences.

The other new stuff wasn't near as interesting, at least not to Frank. As the slow cataloging process of correctly placing new items—not just 1963 stuff, but all the other new pieces—into the Hall's library, research, and collection system moved forward, Frank was able to push a lot of the work onto McMasters. He did so reluctantly, not because he didn't trust the kid, but because he enjoyed it so much. When he rooted around in the new items, it didn't take much—maybe a game program from 1939, a set of baseball cards from 1948, or more microfilm of old magazines. The new stuff would conjure up the echoes of the past, turning up their volume—the resonance from last fall was making sound again—and Ray Cavanaugh was calling to him, or at least his presumptive daughter was.

After receiving the initial letter from Lita Lawson, Frank sent a quick, curt note to her a couple of days later:

> Dear Miss Lawson,
> I received your letter. Thank you for contacting the Hall of Fame. I have looked over the materials that we have in our research library, and while we have no evidence that Ray Cavanaugh had children, nonetheless I will see what I can find out. I'll contact you soon with any details or information I can get my hands on. In the meantime, please let me know if you find anything as well.
> Sincerely,
> Frank Aldridge
> Baseball Hall of Fame

A week later, he received confirmation from Lita that yes, she would stay in touch. The hunt was officially on for Rock 'n Fire Ray.

It was official: Peggy was pregnant. Frank and his wife were in the prep stages for their fourth child, which was due sometime in May.

"April showers, May flowers, and baby poop," sang Peggy, rubbing her belly and arching backward. She was in the throes of some awful hemorrhoids and swollen ankles.

"Shit," Frank mused back. "A lot of shit."

The pregnancy had also unloaded a massive level of nausea on Peggy—when she wasn't puking, she felt like she had to throw up. It made for hard days, harder nights, and a lot of parenting of the kids by Frank that he wasn't prepared for. She always wanted to nap, and that meant when he was available, Frank was in charge.

"Daddy, where's my jacket?"

"Dad, I'm hungry."

"No!"

"I need to potty."

"No, no, no!"

And of course, the killer, "I want mommy." That one always hurt.

When Peggy would finally return to the fold of motherhood, Frank would gratefully relinquish his duties and hope upon hope that the new baby would be easy. More diapers and less baseball—the thought was not pleasant, but the thought of a non-pregnant wife was.

❧

The lingering, basic question first formulated by Frank weeks earlier was now stronger than ever and firmly placed at the front of his mind, and he constantly turned it over and over, hoping to figure it out without doing any real work. One simple question.

Where in the hell was "Rock 'n Fire" Ray Cavanaugh?

The thing was, Frank knew that he was not a detective. A missing person search wasn't something he ever contemplated doing, even if it was a hunt for an old ballplayer. He had a couple of people he could contact about starting possibilities in the search for the old lefthander, but that was it. He was just as much at square one as his letter writer, Lita Lawson, had been. His beginning point, at least from a baseball research angle, would be to pull something from the articles in Cavanaugh's folder, and perhaps find a tidbit or two out of whatever biographical information he could find.

He had considered taking out an ad in the *Sporting News*, or at least lobbying a couple of the writers for the magazine to see if they might do a piece on the hard-to-find man: Missing – Rock 'n Fire Ray Cavanaugh. After talking it over with McMasters, they deemed the requests to be too dramatic and nixed the idea. But Ron kept brainstorming for ways to jumpstart the search.

"Frank, have you thought of contacting some of the older sportswriters? Who was that guy in Washington you used to know?"

"He died."

"Oh. The other guy?"

"Dead. Very dead."

"What's the guy's name at the *Sporting News* in St. Louis? Will he help?"

"He hates me. Remember last season when I told him we didn't need anything else on the stinking Cardinals? It seems he's a big fan." Frank lit a cigarette, handed one to McMasters. "But the bastards at *Sports Illustrated* might help. They seem to think we're important, so I'll check them out." The two smoked in silence for a couple of minutes, then Frank decided he wanted to watch the 1939 All-Star Game movie footage again. McMasters put out his smoke and left to set up the reel.

So, it would be a letter campaign, Frank had realized, to start the search, letters sent to the newspapers across the country where he had some sort of connection, paying special attention to St. Louis, Washington, and Kansas.

᪥

Frank waited to contact Lita Lawson again until he could make a well-substantiated and educated guess that the girl could, indeed, be the offspring of Rock 'n Fire Ray. He found nothing in the Hall's files that even remotely suggested the ballplayer had children. He decided to send her an update anyway.

> February 25, 1964
> Dear Lita,
> My apologies for taking so long to get back to you following my first note last year. I want you to know that I am trying to track down Ray Cavanaugh. I've done a couple of preliminary things, and what I have discovered so far is that it might take some time. I have found nothing to give me a clue as to his whereabouts. The good news is I'm pretty certain he is still living, I just need to hone in on possible locations.
>
> I'll send you periodic updates, and hopefully I'll know where he is soon. As I work to make progress in this search, I again urge you to send me an update if you find any information on your own.
>
> I found this extra baseball card of Cavanaugh, from 1950 I think, and thought you might like it.
>
> Stay in touch, Lita.

Sincerely,
Frank Aldridge
Baseball Hall of Fame

❧

Their music was everywhere—the Beatles. The pop music radio stations seemed to play their songs on a never-ending loop—"She Loves You," "I Want to Hold your Hand," "Please Please Me," "I Saw Her Standing There." Frank had had a hard time with the British band at first—the long hair and music that was like nothing else he had ever heard or seen. Their sound engulfed the airwaves across America, and with the birth of Beatlemania, he decided that like a lot of other men his age, he hated them, *hated them.*

That changed, and quickly.

The constant barrage of their music took hold of his senses, and he was okay with that—suddenly he liked them and forgot about the hair. The songs were catchy in a way he had never experienced music before, but more importantly, they were fun. He also liked seeing the news footage of their concerts—girls crying, screaming, yelling—begging! And weeping with hysteria, stomping and pleading, pleading with the young men from Liverpool to take them, to do anything, but for god's sake, *keep singing.*

Soon enough, he realized just how incredibly talented the Beatles were (like the rest of America), and the group gradually became a part of him, something that he felt almost as strongly about as baseball. He listened to them whenever he could, purchased their albums and 45s, even brought a record player to his office so he could listen to them while perusing the history of baseball. Sometimes when he was alone, Frank would sing along, croaking out the words with his monotone voice—"Tell me that you love me baby, I wanna be your man!"

❧

One of the best pieces that Frank pulled from Cavanaugh's file was an article from the *St. Louis Post-Dispatch* about his first major league game. He had read it several times, but today as he re-read the old clipping he found a prescience from the article he hadn't noticed before, and that writer had somehow captured a nice window into what and who Ray Cavanaugh was, at least on the baseball diamond. After carefully finding the clipping among the pieces in the file, Frank closed his office door, stretched out behind his desk, sipped a cup of fresh coffee, lit a smoke, and pretending he was at the game, returned to 1935 to watch Cavanaugh's first big league win.

CAVANAUGH SHINES IN DEBUT

Rookie Twirler K's 10
Browns' Losing Streak Ends
Southpaw Hurler also gets a Hit in Win

By a Special Correspondent

Washington, D.C. --- July 15. This season might already be gone for the Browns, but the future looks to hold better things. Fresh from the farm, Rookie Lefthander Ray Cavanaugh made his debut here today, tossing speedballs with great ease, teasing batters with hard breaking curves, and even hitting a couple of batters just for good measure.

It was, needless to say, a gem of a pitching performance. Ten times young Cavanaugh sent the Senator hitters back to the dugout with a K on their belts and easily won for the Browns, 3-2. The lefty showed that his nickname, Rock 'n Fire Ray, was not a misnomer, tossing the ball with the guile and nerve of a veteran. If he maintains his poise, Cavanaugh could be the long-sought-after ace pitcher the Browns have been searching for.

CHAPTER 5

July 15, 1935
Washington, DC

As he walked to the mound in the bottom of the first, Ray tried not to think. His heart was pounding faster and harder than he could ever remember, and as he picked up the ball resting peacefully in the brown-green grass, thoughts of Hagerston and Topeka, hitting Sorenson in Omaha, San Antonio—even his high school team at Hillman—surged through his brain.

And, of course, his dad. Always his goddamn dad.

An insignificant ache from the long trip to Washington shot through his body, then disappeared. The ball felt funny in his hand for some reason, and as he fingered it around in his palm, he stopped to read the printed label; *Official American League Ball, William Harridge, Pres.*

It was true. He was here, he was in the Bigs.

Ray stepped off the mound, and leaving the ball in his mitt, slowly moved his fingers across the brown 'St. Louis' lettering on the front of his gray-flannel jersey as he stared at the center field fence. The field was starving for water and overall care—the infield dirt was baked and burned, the blades of grass brittle and hard. The outfield walls were also weathered and dreary looking, in need of a good paint job.

Here he was, at Griffith Stadium, about to pitch for the Browns against the Senators. The god-awful, last-place stinkin' St. Louis Browns. The catcher—Ray couldn't remember his name—yelled at him to start warming up.

"Come on, Rook!"

Ray begin whipping the ball at the nameless hulk crouched behind the plate. A slow toss, then faster and faster, a couple of hard curves, then a final fastball. After the catcher's toss down to second, the squatty backstop rambled out to Ray.

"You got the signals down?" He spit, caught the ball from the first baseman, and handed it to his pitcher. Ray turned his back on the veteran.

"Just catch the ball."

The catcher spit again, this time at his pitcher's shoes, and waddled back to the plate. Ray rotated back around and glared at the number 14 on the back of the catcher's jersey, turned to look at the first baseman, then up at the press box. He rubbed on the ball as he surveyed the sparse Monday afternoon crowd, turned back to home plate, and readied himself to face his first-ever major league hitter, the Senators' left-handed first baseman, Joe Kuhel. Ray got the signal for a hook on the outside corner, nodded at the catcher, and then drilled a fastball in Kuhel's back.

The train ride from San Antonio to Birmingham and Atlanta, and then north to DC, took two days and then some. The Browns were in need of a starting pitcher—hell, they needed just about everything—and Ray's masterful dominance in the Texas League could no longer be ignored by the big club. St. Louis had won just 21 games so far in the season—pathetic. They were, in every sense of the baseball definition, wretchedly bad, almost like little boys playing with men. Just dreadful.

Ray was sitting in the dugout by himself as always at Tech Field, San Antonio's ballpark, when the Missions equipment manager, a small man with balding hair and an enormous rear end, called his name to come into the clubhouse.

"Now?" Ray didn't feel like getting up.

"It's important. Come on, come on."

Ray stood, and as the clicking of his spikes on the concrete floor of the dugout tapped out a little tune, left the dugout and saw the little man standing by a table and holding a yellow piece of paper.

"Telegram, Ray. From the Browns." He was smiling.

"Did they finally trade me?" Ray asked. He had been hoping against hope for some time that the Browns would sell him off to the Yanks, or maybe the Giants.

"Trade? No, no. They bought you out. You're going to the team."

"The team?"

"The Browns!" the big-assed man said. "You made it! You're going to be a big leaguer!" He was overly excited, giddy almost, and Ray could only imagine it was because he somehow thought he had a hand in the success of the players. The man handed Ray the piece of paper.

"What's this?" Ray asked.

"The telegram. Here ya go, congrats."

Ray took the piece of paper, looked at it. Addressed to the general manager of the San Antonio Missions, Ray wasn't sure if he should read it or not. The smile on the attendant's face told him to go ahead. With a big, bold heading of Western Union at the top of the sheet, sloppily arranged strips of all-caps type filled out the paper.

AS OF TODAY, THE BROWNS ARE PURCHASING THE CONTRACT OPTION OF RAYMOND CAVANAUGH. GET HIM ON THE NEXT TRAIN TO WASHINGTON DC AS SOON AS POSSIBLE. HAVE WIRED 500 DOLLARS TO GIVE CAVANAUGH. WIRE BACK WHEN YOU HAVE AN ARRIVAL TIME. HE WILL PITCH FOR BROWNS ON MONDAY.

BEST, STANLEY HARPER, ST. LOUIS BROWNS GENERAL MANAGER

"And here's this," big ass said, and he held out an envelope to Ray.

"What's this?"

"The $500 for the trip, and also to help get you set up in St. Louis, once you get there." Ray took the money, threw his cap on the floor, and started to take his uniform off. He only had few belongings at his hotel room, and if he didn't need the suitcase, he would have left San Antonio without his meager belongings.

"A lot of the guys take their uniform with them," big ass said. "Kind of a souvenir."

"I don't want it," Ray said as he dropped the jersey to the floor. He turned back to the locker, grabbed his glove, and stuffed it into his traveling duffel bag. Turning back to the equipment manager, he asked, "Would you get my bats?"

"Sure, sure. I can send them down to the station."

"Okay." Ray turned away from the man, pulled off his pants and the rest of his uniform. He decided not to shower, quickly dressed in his suit, and high-tailed it out of the clubhouse, then the stadium. When he reached his apartment—rented to him through the Missions—Ray quickly grabbed his clothes, the two books he had, his bathroom items, and threw them into his oversized suitcase. The few things he left in the apartment included a few magazines, dishes, and non-perishable food.

He also had a couple of girlfriends to consider—Cathy was expecting to see him after the game for dinner and sex. Susan was slated for the next day. He briefly thought of writing them each a note but decided it didn't matter. He was never returning to San Antonio and ending it this way was the best bet to not have either one of them search him out. They could read about his promotion to the Browns in the newspaper.

He gave the small space a final, somber look and left for the San Antonio train station.

❧

Ray's train journey through the south proved uneventful. He snagged a couple of newspapers along the way to read up on the Browns and their woeful play—they were routed by the Athletics, 9-0, on the day he left Texas and dropped a doubleheader the next day to the Senators. Scheduled to arrive in DC on an off day, Ray hoped to get a feel for his new team, find out something about his manager, and learn the on-the-road mannerisms of his new teammates.

He would also pick out a jersey number. Ray had always worn number eight, but he knew that digit was taken by Ray Pepper, the team's light-hitting right fielder. No one on the Browns wore a number higher than 25, and no one had 13 (the bad luck number). He thought about choosing 26, 28, 31, and even 13. After pairing the selections down to 13 and 28, Ray flipped a coin, using heads for 28—that was the winner. He liked the pairing of 2 and 8, and was suddenly anxious to make the number famous.

The other thing he wanted to get started on was his day-before-pitching routine, which consisted of alone time—a lot of alone time—stretching out his muscles and pitching arm, and eating a meal of steak and eggs. Some-times he would do sit ups and pushups, take a late morning nap, read the newspaper. Ray never shaved the day before or the day of his pitching turn, a habit he picked up by accident when he forgot his shaving kit on a road trip during his first season with Topeka. He liked the look of the stubble on his face with his uniform, imagined it gave him the rugged look of a railroad or construction worker, though it never did. It did enhance his self-conceived ruthlessness on the mound, boosting the fear factor in at least a few hitters.

For batters, there was a lot about Ray Cavanaugh to dread.

In his minor league career, Cavanaugh beaned more than 80 hitters in two-plus seasons—a phenomenal amount. But he racked up more than 500 Ks, also extraordinary. He was the most feared pitcher in the Western League during his time with the Topeka Senators. The whole of the Texas League had to be sighing in a collective breath with his departure to the Browns—his dominance over the Lone Star state was masterful, and the beanings were a big part of that.

What Ray never fully comprehended was how close he was to a full-season suspension following the Omaha incident when he was with Topeka. His manager had lobbied hard for him, citing his lack of control as the main culprit in all the hit batters, and the league president bought the story. The miracle recovery of Sorenson played a role as well, and even though Cavanaugh plunked a few more hitters in the head after Omaha, there was never another player on the doorstep of a near-death experience.

❧

Joe Kuhel stood at first base with a pained look on his face, but he never touched the spot on his back where he was hit. On the mound, Ray stared at the Senators' leadoff hitter with an angry smile. The crowd was buzzing after the beaning, and a hesitant John Stone, Washington's left fielder, baby-stepped into the box.

"Watch your ass," the catcher said to Stone. "This kid is wild as hell." The hitter looked down at the pudgy catcher, then spit in front of the plate. Once he was set in the box, Ray went into motion, hummed a fastball under Stone's chin, then struck him out on the next three pitches.

The next batter K'd, too, and the third out was a weak grounder to second.

When Ray took his place in the batter's box to hit in the top of the second, there was a runner on first with two outs. The Senators' pitcher, Earl Whitehill, looked into the dugout, then at the runner on first, twisted around and glanced at the shortstop. He waited a couple of seconds, went into his stretch, and threw a fastball into Cavanaugh's ass.

The plunking set off a wild cheer of shrieks and hollers from the stands as the Browns' and Senators' dugouts quickly emptied onto the field. Ray rushed the mound and got a shot to the face of Whitehill before being pulled away. A couple of Senators tried to get to him, but the catcher intervened, saving his young pitcher from a punch or two. There were a couple of other scuffles in the dust of the dry infield, but when the skirmish ended, both teams returned to their dugouts and Ray trotted out to take his place at first base. No one was tossed from the game.

After giving up a run in the second inning and another in the third, Ray ran into a real jam in the fourth—a single and two walks filled the bases with no outs. He scuttled around the mound, kicking at the dirt for a couple of moments. Wanting to ask the catcher about how to pitch to the next hitter, Cecil Travis, he motioned to the catcher, who didn't move. Instead, Rogers Hornsby, the Browns manager, came trotting out.

"What's up kid?" he asked. "Does your arm hurt?"

"Nope. I wanted to know if there was anything special about this guy. Does he have an out pitch?"

"Not really," Hornsby said. "He's a good hitter, so don't give anything to hit." Then Hornsby slapped him on the butt and strolled back to the dugout. One of the all-time great hitters in the history of the game, Hornsby's managerial career was all over the place. He won the pennant as a player-manager for the Cards, but the Browns were his fourth team in the last ten years—since he left the Cards his teams always finished out of the money.

Ray rubbed the ball in his hands and tried to find a pretty woman in the stands. He hadn't made his usual surveillance of the crowd at all—the intensity of the first big league appearance had stifled his in-game libido. As much as he wanted a nice setup after the game, winning *this game* was more important. He focused back to the left-handed-hitting Travis, who stood ready in the box. Ray started him off with a low outside fastball for a strike, then a high changeup that Travis couldn't lay off—he popped out to the third baseman.

The next two hitters struck out and Ray made it hold up the rest of the game, easily cruising to his first big league win—Browns 3, Senators 2.

✧

The team gave him some triumphant congratulations afterwards, threw him into the showers in his uniform, played slap ass with wet towels, and took him on a victory drinking bender. Never a real lover of alcohol, Ray indulged his new teammates more than he wanted, but still enjoyed himself. He wanted to go to the Club Caverns, a small establishment in the basement of a drugstore that was famous for its floor and variety shows—Duke Ellington and Cab Calloway played there.

"Club Caverns?" a new teammate said when Ray asked about the place. "No way. That's a nigger joint. Why would we go there?"

Normally he would have gone off on his own, but this night was different—Texas was in the rear window. Ray Cavanaugh, "Rock 'n Fire Ray," was now a major league pitcher. He knew it wasn't necessary for the other players to like him—or for him to like his teammates—but on this night, he decided to let them think he did.

CHAPTER 6

August 3, 1938
St. Louis, Missouri

The signs always sent a burn up the back and across his face.

No Coloreds. Whites Only. No Colored
Allowed. Coloreds Must Sit in Balcony.

The reprehensible hate Lonnie Lawson encountered daily filled him with a rage he never thought he'd feel when he was young—now he dealt with the fuckin' crackerheads, the goddamn motherfuckers, *the malevolent white devil*, on a daily basis, and that was more than any decent man should have to endure.

"Hey boy! Boy! Get out of the way!"

Many, many times Lonnie wished he could run the racists through their own horrific bullshit, make them use inferior facilities, sit in the back of a bus, turn them away from a restaurant or hotel. Better yet, use colored toilets.

Call *them* a nigger.

When the anger subsided, disappeared temporarily, Lonnie was able to re-focus, re-adjust to the white world around him. And that was when he played great baseball. That was when he was at his best, when he hit, when he stomped on his opponents' throats and pushed the Stars to victory.

He loved baseball, but he really loved the game when he wasn't feeling like a victim of racism, wasn't feeling the beatdown of the white world on his shoulders. How many times had he heard the term 'nigger ball'? How many times had he been called a coon by a hillbilly farmer in a small town in Indiana or Kansas or Iowa? That was the easy stuff to endure, easy because he knew, as all his teammates did, that with the slurs came dollars, dollars from the ignorant racists themselves who had paid for the privilege to watch their team get thrashed on the field by the Stars.

The barnstorming games and travel that went with them was something he didn't relish—it never felt like real and meaningful baseball. The Negro League games felt fantastic, they had a genuine feeling of importance. They were playing for something. The other Negro League teams respected them, and best of all, the hotel accommodations in the cities they played in were always prime—even though they were always colored only—and usually the food, music, and women were there for the taking. Lonnie always wished that there were more league games. Some teams in the league might play as many as 80 games, others barely 40. The number of games that the Stars played each season always fell somewhere in-between, and while the money Lonnie made with the club was decent, he always wanted more.

That's where the barnstorming came in.

The touring games were just for money—sometimes a lot of money—but they were never much fun because of the white fans, even when they hid their racism with a forced, over-polite congeniality.

"Just another crackerville, only in disguise," Lonnie said as the team bus pulled into Lincoln, Nebraska. The Stars were set to play a quick couple of games against the Lincoln Links before returning to St. Louis for more Negro League action and the finish of the season. The Links played their games at Landis Field, a typical covered-stands stadium that held up to 8,000 people—the Stars might draw a couple of thousand spectators to each game. The payout to the players for the two games might be as much as $300 or as little as $100—either amount was good. Since he wanted to buy his mother and sister some new clothes and other items, Lonnie was hoping for the highest possible amount. Too many times, though, the team was cheated by the local promoters, especially if the Stars dropped a whooping on their hometown boys.

It had been a long trip from St. Louis to Nebraska, and the Stars were restless in a tired way. Most of the players also deplored the traveling show—white customers expected a certain type of play.

"Time to pull out the nigger ball, boys," Lonnie liked to say. The team would ham it up, do a little shadow trickery, run the bases with gusto, and hopefully thump the Links. But first, a little relaxation and real rest.

The Lincoln Hotel wasn't much for fancy amenities, but it was still a nice hotel. The best of the local negro establishments, the Lincoln had housed traveling baseball teams for several years, as well as other negro entertainers. The hotel's owner also happened to be the promoter for the baseball games, so most importantly, the Stars were sure to get paid. Lonnie and his roomie, Skeeter McGee, checked into their room and then hit the pavement. The first game wasn't until the following afternoon, and Lonnie wanted to get a look at Nebraska's capital city.

Once they left the hotel, the surprise of the Lincoln's mean, unfiltered racism startled both players. They knew of no true colored restaurants where they would be able to sit down. They found a small bar close to the hotel and after asking, were told of a tourist home a few blocks away that would provide them with a decent meal. The hotel also had a small café, but it was only open for breakfast and lunch.

"Wanna look for a woman?" Skeeter asked after their meal was finished. His infatuation with Aulette was finally gone, much to Lonnie's relief.

"I heard there's a jazz club around here somewhere. Maybe one drink."

"Or more." Skeeter liked his hooch and was pretty good playing with a hangover. Lonnie always drank very little, preferring to look out for his teammate's friendly drunkenness. The two men found the small club, had several drinks, took in some mediocre jazz, and then stumbled back to the Lincoln Hotel to sleep it off and get ready to play ball the next day.

"Nebraska? Why would they go there?" Loretta Lawson worried—fretted with grave anxiety, really—every time the Stars hit the barnstorming road.

Knowing the ins and outs of St. Louis' white racial and racist policies was one thing, but she always imagined the worst for all places that weren't her home. Aulette had heard the uneasiness of her fears many times.

"Momma, it's fine."

"I know they don't have very many negroes there," Loretta said. She was pacing around the kitchen.

"You want a new chair for the living room? Lonnie told me this trip will buy that."

"Why can't they play the games here? I'd go to the games."

"He'll be back in five days or so. Do you want to listen to the radio?" It was early evening, and Aulette knew her mother's favorite program was coming on soon.

"Can we listen to the game on the radio?"

"They only do that for special events like the All-Star game. Your show will be on soon."

"Your father could have played in an All-Star game, maybe," Loretta said. Aulette frowned at her mother, and while her memories of her dad Lenny Lawson were few, she knew he was a devil of a man, a horrible husband, and father.

"Sure, Momma."

"Do you think Lonnie is okay in Nebraska? Will he get hurt?"

"He can take care of himself." Aulette turned on the radio, twisting the tuning knob back and forth until she finally stopped on a station playing Benny Goodman's "Don't be That Way."

"Is this my show?" Loretta loved *Kay Kyser's Musical Klass & Dance* show, one of the most outrageous, over-the-top and entertaining programs on the radio. Kyser always had top celebrities on his show, and he performed regularly with Ginny Sims, Harry Babbitt, and Sully Mason— Loretta loved it all, and when Goodman's song ended, Aulette tuned in the NBC station just in time to hear Kyser's lyrical, fun voice.

"There he is," Loretta said.

❦

The writer's name was Stanton Walters, a young reporter for the *Pittsburgh Courier*, and he wanted to write an article on Lonnie. The Negro baseball world had been buzzing about Lawson's running speed for a couple of years (Is he faster than Cool Papa?), but no one had done a piece on the Stars' outfielder. Walters, who wrote frequently about the Pittsburgh Crawfords and other Negro League teams, decided he was the one to write about the star on the Stars—*Negro Baseball Magazine* wanted to run the piece before the season ended.

When the Stars returned from Nebraska—it was a financially successful trip that saw the team win all three games—a two-game set against Pittsburgh was waiting for them. Walters came in with the Crawfords, and while he hadn't sent a preliminary notice to the Stars about talking with Lawson, he figured an interview would be easy to set up.

He was wrong.

"I ain't talking with a reporter," Lonnie told his owner when he met with him at the team's office. "Why now? I've been playing good ball for a couple of years."

"Talk with him, he's a good writer," William Ruggles said to his prized outfielder. "It'll be good for you, good for the team."

"I don't like it. What's he going to ask me?"

"A lot of things, but I know he'll ask about your dad. Is that something you can do?"

"My dad? Shit. No, no I won't do that." Lonnie was visibly upset.

"I'll keep that off the list, but I know he'll write it up that Lenny is your dad."

"Fuck it." Lonnie stood to leave the room.

"Son, do this for me. Do it for yourself," Ruggles said as he lit a cigarette. "Tell this guy anything you want. Tell about the plight of the colored ballplayer—hell, tell about how hard it is to be a negro!"

Lonnie nodded and left. He was supposed to talk with Walters before the game in about an hour, and while he had heard of the writer, he'd never seen his work, mainly because he didn't read much.

The last time Lonnie saw his father was an uneventful, unmemorable day, one like all the others. He was playing with Aulette, running around the neighborhood with a few of their friends when Lenny walked out of the house in his usual pace, waved at them, and left for the bus to go to work. It was more than a week later that Loretta told him and Aulette, through solemn tears, that Daddy might not be coming back.

At the time, Lonnie shrugged it off—Lenny's presence in his life was less than minimal. He had a few decent memories of his dad, but as he grew older, the truth of what his father did and was, the awful way he treated his mother, and the over-exaggeration of his baseball talent came fully to light. But by then, Lonnie was on the verge of his own manhood, expanding and improving his own baseball talents. He was close to his sister, loved his protective mother, and while he had had several girlfriends by the time he embarked on his career with the Stars, he was not, by his own admission, the marrying type.

Comparisons to his dad were few since Lenny had played mostly in the South, and only for a few years. But the Lenny "Dick Tales" were now legendary throughout the world of negro baseball and time had added much to the stories—conquests, showings, etc.—but to Lonnie, they were nothing more than distressing and humiliating. When asked about his father, his standard reply was, "I didn't really know him."

But of course he did, at least through the anecdotes from old timers— all the drinking, whoring, philandering, awful things his father did. He also pried a few things from his mother, but almost every time he would carefully ask about Lenny, Loretta would simultaneously get angry and cry.

He finally stopped asking.

By the end of his second season, Lonnie was casually telling people that he wasn't sure Lenny was really his father, and while he knew how that made his mother look, he didn't care—she would never know what he told people about his dad. The only legacy Lonnie wanted to have was that of a great player, not as the son of Lenny Lawson.

The writer didn't show before the game, but Aulette and Loretta were in their usual seats. Lonnie waved at them when he took his place in left field, they looked splendid in hats and blue dresses. He was supposed to have dinner with them afterwards—Loretta promised to make her fried chicken. It was a fast-paced affair that the Stars won easily, 8-2, but Lonnie was hitless and made an error on a poor throw to second in the fifth. When the game ended, his manager told him the writer was waiting for him in the back of the clubhouse.

"Now? I thought I was talking to him before we played. I'm going to meet my mother."

"He had problems getting here, couldn't get a cab. Give him a couple of minutes and say something nice about Ruggles."

Lonnie showered and dressed slowly, and after almost an hour, motioned to the writer sitting and waiting patiently on the other side of the room to come to his locker. Short and slightly overweight, Lonnie figured the scribe was around 30 despite how young he really looked.

"I'm Stanton, call me Stan," the writer said as he walked to Lonnie, his hand extended. "I'm looking forward to talking with you," and he pulled out his notebook.

"Sure," Lonnie grunted. "Will this take long?"

"Long enough," Stanton said with a smile. He had been told that Lawson might be a bit standoffish, but he was a pro at getting people to talk. After a couple of explanations about what he wanted to talk about, Walters jumped into some simple questions, hoping to ease back Lonnie's stale attitude.

"How long have you been playing ball?"

"My whole life." Lonnie thought to himself that maybe this would be okay after all.

"The game grows with you, doesn't it?" Walters said. "What were you doing when you hooked on with the Stars?"

"There were a couple of neighborhood teams I played with, a lot of older guys. All of the negroes in town wanted to play for the Stars, and that was always my dream, too."

"So, dreams can come true for talented ballplayers."

"Not yet. I want to play in the majors. I belong in the majors."

"A lot of negroes do, and I think you do, too," Walters said. "I don't see it happening any time soon, though, if ever." He scribbled down the quote along with a few of his own thoughts for the article.

"Yeah."

"Let's talk some about the Negroes Leagues. Give me your full story, how it feels, the fans, everything."

Lonnie thought for a moment, then gave some standard quotes about opportunity, fun, and being grateful for Ruggles giving him the chance. He told Walters about what a great baseball town St. Louis was, and how he was lucky to play there. He decided to hold back on the city's racial problems.

"What about your speed?" Walters asked. "Did you always know you were fast?"

"Oh, yeah," and Lonnie smiled for the first time in the interview.

"And how fast are you?"

"I've been told I'm the fastest ever, but I don't believe that," Lonnie smirked a little, did a little hop for the writer, moved his arms up and down like he was running. "Cool Papa is the king of speed, but I'm up there, too."

Walters then moved in for some personal information, sensing the time was right.

"What about you mother. A lot of help?"

"My mother is the best, my sister, too," Lonnie said. "I wouldn't be where I am without them. Aulette, my sister, gave me the biggest push, the most encouragement."

"What about your father?" Walters asked cautiously.

"What about him?" The smiling was gone.

"Well, any help from him?"

"He left us. Abandoned us. Disgraced my mom. I don't want to and won't talk about him. I thought you knew that."

"But he was a ballplayer, too. Did you get anything from h…"

Lonnie got up, snarled at the writer, and headed for the exit, the surprised and startled Walters running after him, apologizing profusely as he also asked to finish the interview.

Lonnie stopped, turned back toward the man, and growled at him.

"I'm done with you."

❧

The article came out in *Negro Baseball Magazine* a month later—Lonnie was on the cover, a posed shot he did for the club at the beginning of the season. Ruggles came into the clubhouse, beaming with a grin that covered his face, left a couple of issues on the trainer's table, and put one in Lonnie's locker. The piece was everything Walters wanted it to be—Lonnie never read it.

A MERCURIAL METEOR ON THE BASE PATHS – LONNIE LAWSON

The Fleet-Footed, Do-It-All Outfielder is the Pride of the St. Louis Stars and a Big Drawing Card Throughout the Negro Leagues

By Stanton Walters

The mere mention of his name makes Williams Ruggles, upright owner of the St. Louis Stars, puff out his considerable chest a little bit more.

"Lonnie Lawson? A real ballplayer, a real *fast* ballplayer," Ruggles said of his speedy outfielder. "I can't tell you how happy we are that he plays for us, and not for some other team."

Lawson burst upon the baseball world almost three seasons ago, blazing around the bases and in the outfield with as much zesty gusto as that other famous Star player, Cool Papa Bell. But unlike the other great Negro League stars—Josh Gibson, Buck Leonard, or even Satchel Paige—Lawson has hung low, wanting to earn his place among the other stars.

"I just want to do my best and make

> my family, teammates, and Mr. Ruggles
> proud. St. Louis had been great, and
> since this is my hometown, well, it has
> been special. But my mother and sister,
> they're the ones who made it possible
> for me to play ball."
>
> "You bet he's a star," Ruggles said
> of Lawson. "One of the best, and let me
> tell you, he's only going to get better."

The piece went on and on about Lawson's place in Negro League Base-ball, and it was only toward the end that Walters inserted a couple of sentences about Lenny Lawson and small acorns growing taller and stronger than the trees they came from.

The first time Lonnie came home to see his mother and Aulette after the magazine came out, Loretta had purchased five copies and had the cover framed. She thought about getting him to sign one but thought better of it.

CHAPTER 7

April 18, 1929
Hillman, Kansas

Ray wasn't ready to play baseball, and he certainly didn't feel like pitching. His left shoulder was a little stiff, but he knew that as soon as he started winging the ball the standard movement of his arm would return, accompanied by the normal, minimal soreness. Most of the time he liked how his arm felt when he was throwing, but today he didn't want to start. It was one of those cold days at the end of spring in Kansas; 47 degrees with a gray sky, and it seemed like it had been raining nonstop for a week. It was also windy, and everything was wet and chilly. Big Jack Cavanaugh, Ray's father, stomped into the kitchen of the small, two-story farmhouse, and barked at his son.

"Get your glove and cap," commanded Big Jack. "Time to work on that arm of yours."

Ray grumbled quietly to himself. He was sitting at the table and listening to the *Aunt Jemima Show* on the family's Philco 511 radio. A strange-looking contraption, the 511 had a round speaker centered on the top of a casket-shaped body, earning it the name "Coffin" radio. Big Jack had won the receiver in a contest at the Emahizer-Spielman furniture store in Topeka the summer before and it had changed the entire dynamic of the Cavanaugh family. Big Jack rarely listened to the modern monstrosity, but the rest of his clan loved it. And while the *Aunt Jemima Show* wasn't a program that particularly enthralled Ray, it was something to listen to. Aunt Jemima was passionately singing "Carolina Moon," on the program, and he kind of liked it.

"Now, Dad?" he asked quietly.

"Get your ass out here."

Ray's mother, a robust woman with sad, striking features and half-gray hair, was standing by the sink, peeling potatoes. She liked the *Aunt Jemima Show*, and ignoring Big Jack, turned, and nodded at Ray to go practice ball.

"Now," Big Jack grunted again.

Ray left the kitchen, grabbed his glove out of the mud room at the back of the house, and headed outside. The wind was whipping in gusts, and even though it wasn't raining any more, droplets from the trees sprayed through the air.

The high school baseball season was underway—because of Ray, the Hillman High Hawks were one of the best teams in the area—but the squad couldn't practice every day for various reasons. For Big Jack, that was great. It allowed him time to run his oldest son through his made-up, rigorous pitching regimen—he had devised the workout specifically to strengthen his son's left arm. Whether or not that was really happening was never debated, but Ray refused to argue. Even when the team did practice, Big Jack wanted to make sure he got his input to the advancement of Ray's baseball talents.

"That coach of yours is nothing," Big Jack said of Ray's high school baseball coach. "What did he ever teach you? Nothing. He's a good coach because of your left arm. Remember that." Again, Ray didn't argue and simply nodded at his dad.

"Let's go, son."

Maimie Cavanaugh, Ray's mother, was never a big baseball fan—she didn't have too many things in her life that she was a fan of. The never-ending chores on the farm—feeding the pigs and chickens, cooking for Big Jack, making clothes for her children, washing, cleaning, washing some more—produced no joy. As the years rushed past her, the beauty of her face gave way to a hardened somberness, and the perceived promise of happiness that the first couple of years on the farm might have held disappeared with the sudden quickness of a torrential spring thunderstorm. Consequently, there were times when she felt the hard pull of the farm was going to kill her, but then the local paper would run another baseball story on Ray and that small light of hope would sustain her being for another few days, sometimes weeks.

Maimie married when she was just 16—Big Jack, who was 21 when they tied the knot, had fallen for her stunning beauty and ample bosoms. He couldn't believe his luck when she agreed to go on a simple dinner date with him at the downtown café, and after forcing himself on her following their second date, Big Jack proposed. Scared that she might be pregnant, Maimie accepted.

The nuptials came fast—they ran off to Kansas City and married—but she wasn't pregnant.

Eleven months after the hasty 'I do's,' Raymond Jackson Cavanaugh was born, tipping the scales at nine pounds and two ounces, complete with a canon-loaded left arm. Big Jack was ecstatic—in quick succession, two girls and another boy were added to the family. A young mother and wife, Maimie was just 22 with four children, and she said no more. And while Big Jack was already visiting the local brothel, he now made it a part of his permanent routine.

For Maimie, it became nothing more than the lonely life of a farmer's wife.

❦

It wasn't so much a makeshift baseball diamond as it was just a dirt field next to the family's rundown barn. A group of boards, connected by nails and rope—and maybe some of Big Jack's spit—were positioned against the west side of the gray building—Ray's "catcher." His dad had fashioned a makeshift strike zone on the weather-beaten boards with black paint, and the small area inside the lines was battered, chipped, and splintered from the pounding it had taken over the years from Ray's fastball. A poorly constructed pitcher's mound was positioned about 60 feet from the wall ("If it ain't perfect, so what?" Big Jack had said), and an odd-sized slab of wood was used for the pitching mound rubber. Ray hated the makeshift mound, but he never made the mistake of complaining about it to his dad.

On the other side of the barn Big Jack had hung up an old tire from the biggest oak tree on the farm, another target for Ray to work on when his dad felt he needed to "shrink down" the zone and learn how to manipulate a smaller area. Ray thought it was a stupid drill, throwing through a tire, but again, he had learned to keep his mouth shut. The tire throw was more of a cooling down activity when everything else was done.

Big Jack had put together a grueling baseball workout routine for his son's left arm, a series of stretches, exercises, and throwing drills. Ray never liked it, never tried his hardest, but would always strain his face and groan, occasionally spitting and blurting out a swear word or two.

"C'mon, Raymond!" Big Jack yelled after the stretching exercises started. "I know you ain't trying.

"Bend! Bend your legs. No!

"Work your arm! Faster! Slow down!" After twenty-five or thirty minutes, sometimes longer, Big Jack would stop the warmups and command his son to start playing catch with him.

"Soft toss, Raymond. Soft.

"Throw the goddamn ball.

"Okay, fast.

"Faster," Big Jack snarled out the order, and Ray hurled the ball at his dad, a high hard one, hoping that he would miss and take it somewhere on his face. But Big Jack caught the ball. He always caught the ball.

"Dad, my arm is starting to hurt." Ray shook his arm, strained his face in mock agony.

"Good, that means you're doing something."

After completing the "normal" baseball things, Big Jack went inside the barn and came back with his bags of rock balls, four taped up sacks of rocks that were a little bigger in size than a baseball but weighed about three times as much. The burly farmer had carefully made the strange balls, thinking that the heftier ballast would help to increase the muscle size, endurance, and tone of his son's arm. Ray hated the awkward hunks of tape and rocks, and was convinced that whatever good the makeshift balls might be doing, they were also bad for his overall balance.

Like everything else concerning this special workout, his dad didn't care.

"Here, go to it," Big Jack said to his son as he dropped the balls to the ground. "Start

throwing 'em." Ray started with some slow tosses of the clumsy bags, then worked into a slightly faster rhythm, battering the marked spot next to the barn with loud cracks. When he reached 100 tosses, he stopped, ready to quit the workout. Before he could hightail it back to the house, Big Jack appeared out of nowhere, pushing for more exercise.

"Time to run," Big Jack barked at his son. "Get a drink now if you want." Ray grunted, went to the side of the barn for a drink, looked back at his dad, and started to jog out toward the end of the closet field to the house, around a third of a mile away. The sun broke through the clouds and gave a momentary shine to the wet grass and leaves, and Ray took the energy of the instant light and ran faster. Big Jack slumped down next to the south wall of the barn and took a few slow swigs from his jug.

⤚

Hillman, Kansas, existed as most small towns in the Midwest did in the months before the start of the Great Depression. By all indications, the municipality was thriving, growing, almost booming. There were three banks in town and nine churches, including a small Catholic parish that persisted to exist despite the bigotry and prejudice against it.

"Goddamn fish-eaters."

The high school mascot was a Hawk, the daily paper was the Gazette, and the primary street that ran through the center of downtown was named Main.

The town also loved baseball, and it loved its local heroes.

It really was *America*. And it was an America that Alvis Cavanaugh was searching for when he left his home state. He purchased and moved to the farm outside of Hillman some 40 years earlier from the backwoods of Kentucky, intent on finding a better life for himself and his pregnant wife. The land was good to him, and soon he was producing profitable crops every season, pitching for the local town team, and enjoying the fruits of his land labor. His son grew into a stocky man like himself and also became a baseball player. His wife Mae, who almost died during Jack's birth and was left barren for the rest of her life, sought out religion to comfort her from the outrageousness of her wayward husband. The local brothel became his haven of comfort. For Mae, religion was her relief and she found that prayers, while never answered, left her with enough strength to carry through each new day on the farm.

❧

When Ray finished his run around the farm, Big Jack was waiting for him.

"Let's go to the ballpark."

"My arm is tired, a little sore. I thought you wanted me to finish up the chores."

"Forget 'em. I want to see you throw at the park." Ray grimaced, knowing there was no getting around going to the ballfield. He helped his dad load the baseball equipment into the truck, grabbed a quick drink of water, and they headed to Hillman.

It was a quiet drive into town—Big Jack took a couple of pulls from his jug and said nothing. When they got to the diamond, the field was still wet and muddy.

"Go on out, the mud will dry," Big Jack said. Ray grabbed a ball and trudged to the pitcher's mound, hoping this unannounced part of the practice session would be short. Holding the baseball tightly in his left hand, Ray moved his arm back and forth, up and down, and then side to side, followed by a few circling motions. He loosened his grip, moved the ball around his palm, fingered the laces, then tightened the grip again to a comfortable feel—his arm was tight from the earlier work, but he knew better than to complain. The mound at Hillman Park was also wet with mud, but that wasn't going to stop Big Jack from making his son pitch some more. Ray kicked at the sloshy mud around the rubber, spit a couple of times, and tried to concentrate once again on the task at hand—pleasing his dad.

"Come on son, goddammit, throw the ball," Big Jack said impatiently as he squatted behind the plate. "Rock 'n fire, Ray, rock 'n fire!"

Rock and fire. Shit. Ray was never a fan of the common pitching phrase his dad had been yelling at him for his entire baseball life. He again looked at the ball and wondered why it was so easy for him to throw it faster than anyone else in the county, maybe the whole state. The funny thing was that Rock and Fire wasn't even his style—his was more of a pure, steady motion with a low kick and lunge merged together as one. A lot of pitchers rocked backward before beginning their delivery, but Ray didn't.

The fire, however, was something else. He always had a lot of fire.

Ray's fastball, when it was moving just a bit, was virtually unhittable. The velocity, while never truly measured, was the fastest ever seen in that part of the state, maybe the entire Midwest. Maybe. The only time he ever saw his dad truly happy was after he struck out a batter. A sly grin would ease across his grisly face, and as the batter trudged back to his dugout, Big Jack would holler, "Way to go, Ray." Then Ray would strike out the next guy, and Big Jack would puff out his chest a little bit more.

When they returned home, the *Hillman Gazette* was placed prominently on the table—there was a new story in the paper about Ray. Big Jack glanced at it, scoffed a little, then headed to the barn to get drunk.

CAVANAUGH STARS FOR HAWKS

By Howard Turrell

Swanson County has not seen anything on the baseball diamond like Ray Cavanaugh since his father, Big Jack Cavanaugh, tossed the ol' horsehide for the Hillman Hawks more than 20 years ago. The younger Cavanaugh, known throughout this part of the state as "Rock 'n Fire Ray," pitched his second no-hitter of the season last week against Martin City, has the whole county buzzing about his baseball talents.

The winner of seven games for the Hawks against no defeats, Cavanaugh is averaging more than 14 strikeouts a game, while giving up not more than one run. His strong left arm has the town thinking about another regional tournament championship, something that Hillman hasn't won since before the Great War. The Hillman fans are talking about him, and the popularity of baseball has never been greater in the city.

"He's the best I've ever seen wearing a Hillman jersey," said Mayor Alvin Dankler of Rock 'n Fire Ray. "And I saw his dad. But let me just say, that in my opinion, Ray has the chance to be a great one." The mayor should know, since he himself was once a pretty good baseballer.

"It's been a pleasure watching the young

man throw the ball. I'm sure glad he's on our side," said the Hawks' second baseman, Howard Jones. "I've tried to hit him in practice, and he is good!" Jones knows a thing or two about baseball, too, as he has played many games at Hillman Park.

Ray Cavanaugh has lifted the town up with his impressive pitching, and while there are still games to be played and won, the prospect of taking on one of the top teams from Topeka or Kansas City is something all the players want. With Cavanaugh twirling the ball from the mound, the chance to make this a memorable season remains high.

"I really like pitching," said young Cavanaugh. His father, like the rest of the town, is as proud as he can be, and Ray has been quick to give his dad a lot of credit for his success.

"He helps me a lot," Rock 'n Fire said of his father's baseball coaching tips. "I'm a better player because of my dad." The Hawks' next game is at 3:00 p.m. Saturday against the Tonganoxie Tornadoes at Hillman Park.

CHAPTER 8

June 5, 1964
Cooperstown, New York

McMasters found some lost film highlighting Cavanaugh's pitching motion and Frank was mesmerized with the footage, watching it over and over again, analyzing Ray's form, pitch placement, and guessing at the velocity of his fastball that left many hitters wailing at the breeze long after the pop of the ball in the catcher's mitt. The lefty nearly always looked almost unhittable, but then a Browns' or Senators' fielder would botch an easy grounder or drop a popup, and Ray would lose it for a couple of batters, allowing two or three runs to score.

Or he would just hit a batter.

Still, watching the lefthander pitch on the old film was amazing. Frank especially liked the Movietone newsreel snippets—there were five such pieces that showed and mentioned Cavanaugh, including his no-hitter. Lowell Thomas' commentary was priceless:

"St. Louis' superb southpaw hurler, Rock 'n Fire Ray Cavanaugh, tamed the Tigers with a real pitching gem as he kept the Detroit boys hitless," the famous announcer said in the segment. "Here, Tiger slugger Hank Greenberg doesn't know what to do with the speedy pitcher's offering and punishes the air as he strikes out. Rock 'n Fire Ray walked two and hit two batters as he rang up the no-hitter win for the Browns."

Frank watched the Greenberg strikeout clip so many times he could recite the dialogue by heart, and he was also good at mimicking the hard-line look on Cavanaugh's face. The other clips were also good, but none of them had the same amount of panache Lowell Thomas put into the no-hitter.

"This guy was incredible," Frank said to McMasters after watching the clips one more time. "I wonder how he felt playing for the Browns." But he knew. Anyone as good as Cavanaugh had to have had his guts eaten alive many times watching inept teammates repeatedly lose—the team lost more than 100 games twice, plus more than 90 two other seasons. The team had one winning season, 1942, the last full year Cavanaugh played for them. In Washington, only the '43 team was any good.

"It's not like he could pitch in more than 40 games a year," Frank said as he looked at the records of Cavanaugh's teams. "Man, these teams were awful."

"But he wasn't," Ron said. "Do you think he was hiding something, some horrible secret?"

"Who knows. But if he was, I'll find it. I always do."

When Frank first learned about Rube Walberg and Big Ed Delahanty—a couple of famous drinkers in baseball around the turn of the century—baseball's drunks, derelict-like players, and all-around bad apples grabbed at him, a strange fascination to be sure. He was constantly looking for new pieces of information about the otherwise unprintable reputations of seedy, lowlife, addicted-addled ballplayers. The daily grind of the baseball season easily lent itself to the drink, of course, but a constant, day-in-day-out drunk was something Frank could not fathom. Sexual antics were always at the forefront of bad behavior, and the illegitimate children of ballplayers sprinkled across the major league cities in the country was not uncommon. With his great love of the game, the statistics, memorabilia, and the lesser heralded parts of baseball, cradling the sordid and sleazy human parts weren't something that Frank talked about much. But he was always surprised when a piece of juicy historical gossip fell into his lap unsolicited.

After watching the film of Cavanaugh again, Frank pulled out his

"Stories" folder, the file with his researched and recorded baseball debauchery information, the stuff of rumored facts and inappropriate hearsay. Over the years, the file had grown—it seemed that a lot of baseball players also had a good amount of cretin in them. Most of the information recorded was tittle-tattle garbage, but that didn't make it any less true.

At the top of the list was Hal Chase, long considered the greatest fielding first baseman of all time—he was also the greatest game-thrower. In addition, he was known to be a bit of a lady's man. Chase was called Prince Hal—Frank always assumed Prince as in Prince of Darkness—and for the duration of his career, was allowed to gamble on and throw games. When the Black Sox scandal hit—the White Sox threw the 1919 World Series— baseball finally shut the door on Chase. Many other players wagered on the game, Ty Cobb being the most prominent.

There was one player in particular who fascinated Frank—Benny Higgins—a journeyman outfielder who played mostly for the Phillies in the 1910s. Higgins was not a very good player, but by all accounts, at least from the information gathered by the Hall of Fame, he was a helluva gambler, drinker, and womanizer.

"Triple-crown winner," is what Frank called him. An incredibly handsome man, Higgins was rumored to have children in every major league city, a hand in unsubstantiated gambling scandals during the 1913 and 1915 seasons, and the capacity to drink unlike any other player before him. The gambling—game-throwing is a better description—afforded him a much better lifestyle than his paltry salary with the Phils should have allowed, which made the numerous women he sought easily accessible. When the little talent he had finally disappeared during the 1918 season— the Phils dropped him when his batting average sunk to .122—Higgins slinked off to the West coast—he was from the Bay area—and tried to start a gambling ring concentrated within the Pacific Coast League. A couple of years later he died in a fiery car wreck while driving along the coast.

Frank had a posed picture of him holding a bat hanging in his office.

"Do you think this Cavanaugh is anything like Higgins?" McMasters asked, pointing to the photo.

"Nope, I'd already know about it if he was," Frank said through a small cough. "No, Cavanaugh is a different type of story. I don't think he had the vices of guys like Higgins," and he lit a cigarette.

"The funny thing is that there isn't much written about him after he was traded to Washington," and McMasters dropped a couple of pages on Frank's desk. "Here's the list of papers and writers you asked to put together. If we can't find out anything from this group, I give up."

Frank grunted, took a drag and looked over the pages, scanning for names that he knew. A couple of well-known writers jumped at him, and he knew they should have something. Since his first couple of years at the Hall, he had worked hard to foster relationships with the newspaper and magazine men who covered the game. He would occasionally get requests for information, photos, or just a pick of his brain about certain Hall-of-Famers. Frank liked helping, but he was constantly reminded that most writers—sportswriters—were, in their hearts, assholes.

Frank had been waiting—categorically procrastinating, in reality—to write to the newspapers, which is why he was never in a hurry to get the contact information. He wanted to get more of a firm grasp on what kind of information he wanted, but it was apparent now that he had nothing, and anything anyone could offer him would be helpful.

The requests to the writers, it was decided, would not mention a possible "daughter." Frank did not want the slightest hint of scandal—too many times in the past he's seen writers run with a bullshit story just to make a name for themselves. Frank also knew that a newspaper's morgue— its archives and such—was a fascinating place for a researcher.

At the top of the list was Sal Sampoli, one of the New York writers who covered the Yanks. Frank had never disclosed his hatred for the Bombers to Sal, instinctively knowing that someday, whether Sal was a "fan" of the Yankees or not, he wanted to be in a good place with him to curry a favor if one was ever needed. After inserting and positioning a sheet of paper in his typewriter, Frank rattled off a note to the famous New York writer.

New York Times
Salvador Sampoli, Sports
Hi Sal,
I'm currently updating some the lesser documented
non-Hall-of-Fame players for our research library.
I've run into a bit of a snaggle trying to piece
together some background information and current location for "Rock 'n Fire Ray" Cavanaugh.
Do you have anything or know where I might
look? Anything in the morgue of the Times? Possible people I might be able talk to?
Any help you provide will be greatly appreciated. When you make it back to this part of the state,
hopefully to cover the induction of Miller Huggins,
let me know and I'll buy you a drink.
Sincerely,
Frank Aldridge

Next on the list was Bill Battles—Frank had heard many stories about the
writer, what a nice man he was, a true encyclopedia of knowledge when it came
to baseball. Battles had been with the *St. Louis Post-Dispatch* for more than 15
years—maybe he knew something about the lost player. And maybe he would
be courteous and cordial with that information and share it with Frank.

Bill Battles, Sports Writer
Hi Bill,
Once upon a time the Browns had a pitcher named
Ray Cavanaugh—ever heard of him? Of course you
have. I'm trying to fill up my research file on him
for our library, and believe it or not, I have almost
nothing on the guy after he left the Browns.
Can you help?
I'll owe you one, and thanks.
Frank

Next on the list was Kansas City, and since it was so close to Cavanaugh's hometown, Frank thought there might be a good possibility that the

newspaper would know something, too. He wrote to the *Kansas City Star*, even though the paper had never officially covered the pitcher during his playing days. The Sports Director was supposedly a bit of a bastard—Frank gave him the soft touch with his request.

> Jonathon Harden, Sports Director
> Kansas City Star
> Hello Jon,
> I'm Frank Aldridge, Research Director and Historian at the Baseball Hall of Fame. We're updating files right now and I'm hoping you can help us out.
> I'm working on our research library, which is never an easy task. I'm trying to get some information on Rock 'n Fire Ray Cavanaugh, especially about what he did after he quit playing. Do you know anything about him, and is it possible that the Star has run an "after baseball" piece on him in the last few years?
> Any help you can provide will be greatly appreciated. Let me know if you're ever in the area and I'll give you a personal tour of the Hall.
> Sincerely,
> Frank Aldridge
> Baseball Hall of Fame

The rest of the list included famous writers, a couple of editors, and the communications managers for the two franchises Ray pitched for—they had both moved to new cities, and while that usually meant the purging of old stuff, Frank wanted to give it a shot. This was the rest of the list of people he contacted:

> *Sports Monthly* – Larry Smith
> *Baseball Monthly Magazine* – R.J. Crenshaw
> *Sport Magazine* – Lancaster Johnson
> *Washington Post* – Bob Meridith
> *Hillman Gazette* – James Stoddard
> *Omaha World-Herald* – Leon Larson

Topeka Capital-Journal – Carl Compton
Chicago Tribune – Harold Titus
Baseball Digest – Allen Anderson
Baltimore Orioles – Michael Dodds
Minnesota Twins – Jackson Smith

For good measure, Frank decided contacting a couple of the radio stations could lead to nuggets of information—he sent letters to the stations that covered the Browns and Senators when Ray played.

～

Waiting for Frank and Ron was the great party of the summer, the inductions of the newest members of the Hall of Fame, scheduled for the end of July. Seven players were going into the hallowed Hall—Luke Appling, Red Faber, Burleigh Grimes, and Heinie Manush were the players still living and set to come for the induction ceremonies. The four men had had great careers and all of them, at least by Frank's standards, were worthy of the honor. Miller Huggins, Tim Keefe, and John Montgomery Ward were this year's group of dead men, all worthy of a place in the Hall, but still dead.

"The worst part of the dead honorees," Frank told Ron, "is playing nice with their family members. We'll have to pretend that Tim Keefe and Ward are a couple of our favorite old timers."

"What about Huggins?"

"Yankees or not, he was pretty great," Frank admitted. "And his death was kind of tragic. Should have been in here a long time ago." Frank kept thinking that sooner or later the writers and veterans committee members who voted for induction would figure out which long-gone players deserved the honor of being in the Hall and then get them in all at once. But seven was a good number, a lot of research and memorabilia to put together, and enough living men to make for a good induction ceremony.

Frank turned on the radio in his office just in time to hear the start of "Love Me do," the Beatles' latest number one hit—he had to stop thinking of Huggins and hum along to the tune. Simple and satisfying, it wasn't the group's best, but it was still better than the other music on the radio. And unlike anything else that Frank allowed into his world of baseball—music was never a thing to him before—now it was needed.

After again thinking about all the things Benny Higgins had been— could that be all there was to Cavanaugh—Frank left the induction stuff to McMasters for a while and sat down at his desk to write a quick note to Lita Lawson. He hoped that this wasn't some wild chase, some joke an old buddy was pulling.

> Dear Lita,
> I hope this note finds you well. I've been hard at work trying to find a connection somewhere, somehow, that will lead me to the whereabouts of Ray Cavanaugh. I've had no luck. I'm contacting several writers at newspapers across the country and should start hearing back from them soon. Have you heard anything or found something that might help in our search? Anything will help.
> We are also working on the upcoming inductions for the newest members of the Hall of Fame. We'll have a couple of visitors here who played against Ray, and I'll be sure to see if they know anything.
> Stay in touch,
> Frank Aldridge

Frank carefully folded the letter, addressed the envelope, slid it in, and dropped it in his mail basket to go out the next day. He knew she'd think there was something in the correspondence, some hint of where the missing man might be, and that disappointment would be large. Frank was disappointed, too. Ray Cavanaugh, it seemed, even all the years after the best of his playing days, was still throwing high hard ones, making his opponents swing and miss.

CHAPTER 9

September 17, 1939
New York, New York

From the moment he arrived at Penn Station with the team, Ray felt the anticipation that only New York could elicit. The city was filthy and reeked of stale death, yet to Ray, nothing was more vibrant, exciting, and gorgeous in its concrete-steel way than this city-of-American cities. He loved pitching in Yankee Stadium, loved the screams of hate from the Yankee fans as he moved effortlessly through their great lineup, loved their over-reactions when he beaned a Yankee hitter.

As he stepped out onto the field to begin his pre-game warmup, Ray took in the atmosphere that was gloriously illuminated by the fall sun—the stadium smelled of beer, hot dogs, mowed grass, and just a touch of urine. It was a wonderful place to pitch for a lefty, and it was his favorite.

"I love playing where the champions play, I love beating them in their place," Ray had told one of the St. Louis newspapers earlier in the season after pitching a three-hit gem at Yankee Stadium. It was the feel of the stadium, more than anything else, that Ray liked.

"I always knew that, no matter how bad the guys were playing behind me, that I could do well. I'd hit a couple of Yanks, then strike out DiMaggio or Dickey, and I'd be on my way to a win."

The Bronx Bombers were already assured of going to their fourth straight World Series, the Browns were once again on the verge of losing 100 games. But the Yanks were going to feel the fury of hell this afternoon—Rock 'n Fire Ray Cavanaugh, the best pitcher in baseball in 1939, was on the mound for St. Louis. As one New York writer had put it, "Cavanaugh would be a god if he pitched for a team in the Empire City. Instead, he's just a lucky bum for a last-place ball club."

⌘

Because he played in St. Louis—even with the lowly Browns—baseball afforded Ray the opportunity to climb the ladder of local celebrity, even if he was with a last-place club. He began to pitch local products in the papers and make appearances at events, and even landed a national magazine ad hawking *Coca Cola* ("Relax…Take it easy"). A couple of cigarette companies also came after him, but smoking had always left him feeling nauseous—he turned them down (chewing tobacco also spurred puking). A little uncomfortable with the attention at first, he soon found that he wanted it, craved it, at least on his terms, and that meant all the women he could possibly handle.

He began to frequent the Castle Ballroom, the premier jazz house in St. Louis. Count Basie, Fletcher Henderson, Miles Davis, and Duke Ellington played the Ballroom, which was nestled comfortably within the black, midtown neighborhood of the city. The music floated into him, kept him relaxed—Count Basie's "Oh, Lady Be Good," "Jive at Five," and "Evil Blues" were new favorites. Ray's time in the minors had prepped him to keep company with the negroes—his enjoyment of the music also afforded an affable manner with the other customers. After his first couple of seasons in St. Louis, Ray's presence in the clubs, especially at the Castle, was not only accepted, it was almost expected.

But it was the trips to New York that excited Ray the most.

Jazz found its place in the big city—any and every great musician and singer gravitated to New York—and as Ray progressed in his baseball career, the trips to play the Yankees were always his favorite. He got to hear his music and usually, at least when he pitched, beat the Yanks. On this latest trip to the Big Apple, Ray was hoping to experience Count Basie's latest music at the newly opened Lenox Lounge in Harlem. The

Club featured jam sessions—it quickly became popular—and because it was open from 11 p.m. to 7 a.m., many musicians would hit the Lounge after two in the morning to play. To jam. Ray was planning on hitting the club after he pitched.

Another favorite spot for jamming was the Rhythm Club, and it was frequented by the likes of Chick Webb, Johnny Hodges, Sonny Greer, Benny Carter, and Jelly Roll Morton. Ray hit it the last time the Browns were in New York, and he was going back. Morton was supposed to be there—"The Crave," "Black Bottom Stomp," and of course, "Tom Cat Blue." Or if nothing else panned out, he would go to the Kentucky Club and see the Duke. If he was lucky—and he always was—Ray would have a date on his arm when he scoped out the clubs.

His Rock 'n Fire stuff was with him as always, and Ray breezed through the Yankees lineup easily and won, 4-1—his 20th win of the year. New York had filled their lineup with right-handed hitters, but it didn't matter. The only run he gave up was when Babe Dahlgren tripled after Ray beaned Joe Gordon. He also hit Joe DiMaggio, the fourth time he clipped the Clipper this season. It was a satisfying win, and when he saw a redhead he'd met the last time the Browns were in New York, it was doubly so. After the game, Ray and Red had a steak, took in the Duke, and finished off the night together at his hotel room.

When the season ended a couple of weeks later, Ray was in possession of his best season ever—he was the starting pitcher at the All-Star game, fanned 291 hitters, won 21 games, beaned another 35, and posted a career-best E.R.A. of 2.77. The national publications—*Baseball Monthly* and *The Sporting News*, were writing that he could become one of the best left-handed pitchers ever—high praise for someone on a really bad club. Ray took it in and hoped that somehow it would equal out to the raise he felt he deserved the year before—he wanted $40,000—and while he knew in his heart he wouldn't get that much, he figured it was a good starting point. The highest paid players in the league were DiMaggio and Hank Greenberg, both making $35K.

"I pitch for the money," Ray told his only real friend on the team, his personal catcher Sam Harshaney. "This is the season I stake it out." Ray's contract for '39 was a respectable $17,000—with his other dealings, ads, and appearances, he was making pretty good dough.

"We play for the Browns," Harshaney said with a snarky laugh. "If they pay you, they won't be able to pay anyone else. And there's no way you'll get that much."

"Not when I win—they'll pay me. Besides, I want you on the team, so they'll pay you something, too."

⟋

A few weeks after the season ended, after the Yanks had swept the Reds to win their fourth World Series in a row, Ray loaded up his 1937 Chevy Coupe, drove west out of St. Louis and headed for Kansas. The blue auto had become one of his favorite possessions and going back to Hillman would be a pleasurable ride. The route along US 40 was a nice enough drive—Ray would always stop in Booneville for gas and food. After topping off his tank at one of several different gas stations in Kansas City, Ray would pull into Hillman about 45 minutes later.

He usually headed straight for the farm, but this time he stopped, parked his Chevy on Main Street, and waltzed into Mother's Restaurant, walking tall and looking dapper in a gray pinstripe suit.

Heads quickly turned in the eating place, followed by loud whispers.

"It's Rock 'n Fire! It's Cavanaugh!"

"Ray! Hey Ray! Rock!"

After grabbing a spot at the front counter, Ray quickly shook hands with everyone there, ordered a pop, and tried to acknowledge the fast-paced well wishes coming at him from all angles and directions.

"What a season, Ray," an old farmer said.

"We've followed you all year, even made it over to St. Louis for a game," the manager of the First National Bank said. "What an arm."

"Good to see you Rock, how long will you be here?" asked Mayor Dankler, who had made a career out of leading the town—he was in his fifth term. A couple of other folks wandered into the restaurant, eager and happy to see the baseball star—his success, many felt, was also theirs. Ray took a sip of his Hi-Lo Grape soda, turned around in time to see the editor and publisher of the *Hillman Gazette* walk through the door. The man, Howard Turrell, had run the paper for more than 15 years, and published stories on Hillman's baseball star many, many times.

"Back in the old town, I see," Turrell said smiling as he extended a hand to you Ray. "I think maybe I should do another piece on you, Rock. Something about your great season."

"Sure Howard, sure." Ray knew he'd have to do an interview with the paper and was actually looking forward to it.

After talking with a few other old acquaintances, he looked up in time to see Myra Hooper—his former girlfriend—open the door and step tentatively inside. She stopped abruptly when she saw Ray, stared hard at him with sad eyes, and then quickly left the building.

Ray gave a little sigh, paid for his drink, and headed out for the farm.

The farm looked better than it had a right to, set off in a brilliant rural aura of light from the afternoon November sun. The trees still had most of their leaves—the reddish orange and yellow colors were faded—and the grass was half green and brown. Ray parked the Chevy on the gravel driveway, grabbed his bag from the back and walked slowly to the side door off the back of the two-story house. Sissy was standing at the door and gave him a half-hearted hug as they walked into the kitchen. Her husband, Allen Neeter—a former Hillman teammate of Ray's—was sitting at the table smoking a Lucky Strike.

"Ray," he said taking a drag, nodding.

"Allen."

"I've got a little stew left from last night," Sissy said. "You want it?"

"Where's mom?"

"Upstairs, probably sleeping. I didn't tell her you were coming; it would've worried her something fierce, trying to get ready for you. Want the stew?"

"Nope, and let mom be. I'm going to look around outside." He took off his suit jacket, dropped it over a table chair, and pulled an old coat out of the back closet.

Ray stepped outside and looked around at the farmyard, across the desolate fields that ran in the back of the house, then over to the left where the empty pigpen stood barren with baked and dry dirt. The farm was dilapidated at best—nothing had come from its once fertile soil for a few years—and Ray felt a twinge of regret at the emptiness of the unused countryside. There were still a few chickens wandering around, but they were there for Sissy and Allen's daily eggs, nothing more.

The old barn looked worse than ever, long past the need to be repaired or painted, and when he walked around to the far side, Ray saw that the old pitching marks on the wall were barely visible, burned away by the scorching summer sun and blistering winds of the Kansas winters. He stopped at the spot of his dad's makeshift mound, did a little pantomime windup, and whipped his arm toward the gray wall.

"Strike three," he said to himself.

Inside, Maimie was coming downstairs, looking hungover and smelling of vomit, surprised to see both her daughter and husband at the kitchen table.

"Ray's here," Sissy said. The haggard-looking woman took on a distressed look but didn't say anything as she turned and went slowly back upstairs.

"Mom? Don't you want to see him? Mom?"

Ray sat on top of a fence surrounding one of the fields and saw a tractor moving slowly in the distance on what was once one of the family's larger pieces of acreage. Squinting his eyes, Ray also thought that the tractor used to belong to the family, too.

He jumped from the fence, took another look around, and headed back to the house. David and Ruthie were supposed to come by for dinner, but he wasn't sure he'd stick around. If he left the farm by seven o'clock, he could be in Kansas City in time to catch most of the night's jazz action at the Reno Club and other spots. When he got back in the kitchen, Ray grabbed his suit jacket and left without saying goodbye.

When he hit Main Street in Hillman, he turned off on Third Street and parked in front of the Gazette Building, went inside, and gave a quick 20-minute interview to Turrell, telling the newspaper man about the glories of the season past and the hope he had for next year's version of the Browns.

"Always good to see you," Turrell said as Ray left. "Don't be a stranger."

Ray left town, and as he turned toward the highway to go to Kansas City, he glanced at the sign on the other side of the road, just catching a glimpse of Hillman's warning for negroes to stay out of their fine city.

CHAPTER 10

October 11, 1958
St. Louis, Missouri

Anew day always brought fresh opportunities, or with a more realistic point of view, unrealized disappointment. As Lita Lawson had moved through her school days, the more she fell to a very real comprehension of just how much the deck of the world was stacked against her. Keeping an optimistic view of everything was getting harder. She wanted to play sports, but there was nothing available for her—women were pretty much relegated to cheerleading and field hockey, and black women were allotted even less— she wanted to play baseball, basketball, or even run track. Lita also began to think about higher education—she was close to being a straight A student— but that also presented severe limitations for negro women.

"I wish," she told herself constantly, "and I will continue to."

Making good grades came easily to her, much easier than they should have.

"Just like your mother," her grandmother would say with each excellent grade card.

The process of disseminating complicated information ran through her thought progression very fast, something she was proud of. But Lita was not good at making friends—the other girls she'd tried to run with always had an ease of natural movement, airy confidence, and outright obliviousness to the world around them. Lita lived in the reverse moments; once something entered her brain it was ingrained—fixed within the gray cells to bewilder and torment her for days, weeks, months. Her natural introversion came across to others as a snobbish, a 'too good for you' attitude, the opposite of what it really was.

Sumner High, her school (and her mother's and uncle's), was still all-negro, and it did afford some prospects to advance forward in the whiteness of the world. But opportunities, or rather the chance to have opportunity, seemed to Lita to be beyond her reach most of the time. Loretta had always been a solid rock of love, encouragement, and support, but she was old. She was also devoid of hope, forever seeing the world through her 1920s-negro eyes.

"You can't change things," Loretta told her granddaughter many, many times. "Just because a black woman sat in the white section of a bus a couple of years ago doesn't mean anything is going change."

"I know, grandma."

"Know your place and move from there," Loretta said. "If you try to do something that is impossible, bad things can happen."

"Okay."

"We have to endure, that's what makes us good."

Lita had heard that speech many, many times. 'Know you place' had been preached to her not just from her grandmother, but also by a couple of her teachers, and especially the pastor at the church. Lay low, don't ask the white man for anything, lest they punish you and your family.

For the most part, unfortunately, it was good advice.

The line of history, slow-moving as it might be, shifted slightly in St. Louis following World War II. The tall, long, and unpenetrated walls of segregation in Mound City finally began to show small cracks of change, but it was, in most cases, much too late. The negro population decided collectively that enough was enough. Starting in the 1950s, black families began to vacate the city for more welcoming places in the country, places where the racism was well hidden, cities and towns in the country where minor advancements didn't need to be made, where everyone peed in the same restrooms and ate at the same establishments. It was dream-like, fantasy stuff. But it was real. Places like Los Angeles, Seattle, and New York. Chicago. And that was Lita's dream—leave St. Louis and move to a place that would give her a better chance at a life her mother missed, and one her grandmother couldn't conceivably believe existed. That was Lita's biggest hurdle—Loretta. She did not want to hurt her but knew that someday she would.

There was also the matter of her father.

She knew virtually nothing of the man—Loretta had closely guarded the secret of who he was, what he was, and whether he was still alive. It was around the time she was seven or eight when Lita started asking all the questions, and with each unanswered inquiry, several more followed.

"How can you not know anything about him?" Her young voice was always filled with a combination of sorrow and frustration.

"Don't you know his name? How could he not have a name?"

"Where is he from?"

"What did he do?"

"Did he know Lonnie?"

"Did he love my mother?"

Loretta would cringe with each query, never fully looking at her granddaughter straight on.

"Honey babe, I know you want to know, but I don't know the things we need to know."

"Why?"

"Oh, Lita honey, I wish I could tell you, I do. I just don't know," and Loretta would let go of a small sob, which was the cue for Lita to stop asking, at least for now.

Lita secretly started calling her father 'I don't know,' and one day, she hoped, the answers would come, and with them, a fullness and completeness to her life that was still unrelenting in its dour sourness and loneliness.

≈

Every so often, someone—even her few friends—would drop the word "mulatto" on her, always as a question.

"Is that what you are?"

"I guess so, I don't know that I am," she'd answer, "I'm just a negro."

"Why aren't you darker?"

"I dunno," but it ripped at her chest, and a slight panic would rush to her head, blast at her heart like a giant string of firecrackers, a quick and long succession of subtle explosions capped by lingering anxiety.

Because of her striking looks—Lita had inherited the best and perfect combination of her parents' physical traits—she was spared a lot of verbal abuse. Still, the name calling would rear up on many different occasions.

"Hey, mu-lat-to, mu-lat-to!" The taunts never lasted because of her beauty, but they were there, always at the forefront of her mind, and she wondered if people, when she first met them, weren't thinking the word.

It always hurt, even when unspoken. Nigger never hurt as much.

She liked to retreat to the aloneness of her room at home after hearing the slur, be it intentionally hurtful or not, and there Lita would release tears, crying more about her parents being gone than the ugly feel of the transmuted moniker society had so callously left to her "kind." It never seemed fair—she received a double-whammy of bigotry and racism. The whites certainly didn't want her and the negroes, well she wasn't one of them, either. Light caramel in color, Lita's skin was magnificent in its contrast to her shoulder-length, black hair. Coupled with facial features that mirrored her mother's and a strong, athletic build, the only word to use when describing her was stunning.

When she recovered from the stain of the word again being dropped on her, Lita would gather the courage and like she had done numerous times before, confront her grandmother.

"Was my father white?" and Lita would stare at Loretta, eyes sad and searching.

"Did someone call you a mulatto again?" Loretta stung hard with her pronunciation of the word.

"I hear it all the time."

"You do?" Loretta scowled, as always, at the thought of everyone knowing her granddaughter was a mulatto.

"Grandma, yes. All the time." She turned away from Loretta, then back again. "Was my dad white? Just tell me. I know he had to be, so tell me."

Loretta thought of Ray, remembered the first time she met him, the last time she saw him. It was painful, it was almost unbearable to conjure his rugged, sun-stained face into her thoughts. Teetering on the truth, Loretta finally decided on the answer of "maybe."

"Whatever I tell you," Loretta said to Lita, "whatever I say, you won't believe me."

"So, you're going to lie to me?" Lita was visibly angry, on the verge of crying. "I'm called that awful name and you don't care. If I knew about my father, at least I could feel better about who I really am. Grandma, who am I?"

Loretta sat down, rubbed the back of her head, and sighed with a sadness that only the regret of past things—things uncontrollable—can place on a person. She couldn't control her granddaughter, not anymore, if she ever did.

"It's time for me to go to church," Loretta said suddenly. "The pastor is waiting for me. Would you like to come?"

Prayer was always the answer for Loretta, prayer for surviving the horrors of Lenny's abominable philandering and drunkenness, prayer for the well-being of her granddaughter, prayer to find and keep the goodness of life, prayer for strength in all things through sweet Jesus.

Prayer to get through and beyond the unbearable.

The church had a hold on most of Loretta's neighborhood, providing comfort and cover from the brutality of St. Louis' overtly racist atmosphere. For a price, a steep price. The pastor fancied himself a lady's man, and while Loretta was too old for his tastes, Lita was not too young. For most of the previous year, he had slowly worked his way to getting closer to her, positioning himself to make a move—"Know your place, don't make waves, I'll help you." And at the last weekend function at the church, a youth celebration and dance for the end of the summer, his calculations complete and patience used up, the pastor pounced.

"Lita, can you come back to my office?" he asked at the side of the punch table. No one else heard him.

"OK," she said. The lack of a father—her need for something she knew nothing about—had moved her closer to the pastor. She saw the middle-aged man as a true father figure, and she held him in high regard.

He walked in front of her as they strolled to the side of the building to his working office. When they reached the room, he locked the door behind her, grabbed her quickly around the waist and forcibly kissed her hard on the mouth. She instinctively spat back at him.

"No, what are you doing?" Horrified and panicked, Lita tried to open the door, but he pushed her down to the floor. Then he unzipped his pants and pulled out his penis.

"Have you ever seen one of these before?" He was erect, and he was smiling—he didn't plan on her screaming.

"No, no, get away, no! No!" Her voice was high and shrill, and when she turned her head away, Lita screamed even louder.

"Quiet, be still, be still!" He raised his right arm to strike her, thought better of it, and then moved away from her, stumbled on his pants, zipped up, and unlocked the door. He grabbed at Lita then, and opening the door with one hand, he pushed her out of the room with the other.

"Goddamn mulatto, apple bottom girl," he whispered. "You're a half-breed like the rest of them." Lita ran from him, ran down the hall of the old spiritual building, and left, almost jumping off the steps leading up to the front entrance, ignoring all calls to her from the other people who were worshipping. She didn't stop running until she was home.

For whatever reason, the pastor never approached her again, but a couple of weeks later Lita saw him walking with another girl from her class, and he was smiling, a big grin that vanished quickly when he saw her staring at him. He turned then with the girl, took her into the library, disappearing into the sanctity of the church's religious and academic resources, no doubt to explain the proper way to pray. Lita ran to the bathroom to hide her tears, thankful she had busted loose of the pastor's powerful, controlling grip. She would feel the effects of his demonizing trance for many more months, indeed, years.

For her part as a victim in his criminal dalliance, Lita never told anyone about the attempted rape. She cried herself to sleep the night it happened, cried herself to sleep many times—never again did she try to believe in Jesus, God, the church, and certainly not in the blessedness of all that was supposed to be good.

❧

What was it like to have a father? As much as her thoughts of family fantasy and togetherness filled her with a hopeful warmth like nothing else ever did, the dreams also left her emotionally empty with a lingering sadness. Lita loved her grandmother, but she longed for the thing she couldn't have—a father. On the good days, she imagined that he'd been killed in the war, a hero who saved countless lives, killed hordes of the enemy, and received many, many medals. Or maybe he was stricken with a rare disease, cut down in the prime of life, dying a sad death, full of regret over leaving Lita behind.

The other, un-ending questions ran non-stop through her thoughts—was he nice, good-looking, smart? How tall was he? How did he meet my mother? Did he know my name? Sometimes she would imagine sitting at a nice table, little snacks and candy arranged in a circle, drinking soda, and just talking to him, telling him about the other girls at school, how the boys said lewd and disgusting things to her, how she loved her grandma, but sometimes hated her.

Of course, there were also numerous questions about his parents. Where were they from, where was he from? Why did he come to St. Louis? College? Jobs? What kind of food does he like? Fish? Steak? Then she would get up, kiss him on the cheek, hug him with all her energy and love. After the snack they could take a walk together, she would hold his hand and feel special. The feelings were sometimes so overwhelming that she had to stop herself from attacking Loretta, from threatening her with bodily harm and more. She wanted to know everything she didn't know.

And then there were the other fantasies about "dad."

On the darkest of days, when her inner-most solitary existence fell into the empty void, Lita allowed all aspects of human evil to invade her mind. A sinister, ugly face appeared in her consciousness, and as it hovered about, the other questions—the awful probes in any search for the truth—eerily floated into the darkness of the night air. Was dad a murderer? Executed for crimes against the state, or locked away forever? Was he just a petty criminal? Maybe the man was a drunkard, always wallowing in his own urine and vomit. What kind of menial work did this man do? Garbage collector? A school janitor, or maybe he cut the heads off chickens. A street cleaner?

Lita ran through a hundred different occupations, low-paying non-esteem jobs, but in the end, she always ended up in the same place.

Her father must be a rapist.

The imagined scenarios were always different, but always the same— this monster of a man, the person she would never know, this "dad," had raped her mother, brutally attacked and violated her being beyond any type of known depravity. Lita decided that no matter what she dreamed of or hoped for, that rapist was the only real possibility for what her father had to be. And the visions of her mother being attacked would stay with her, and then the blame would fall back to Loretta, and when she had no more tears to cry, sleep would reset her being, allowing her to move forward the next day with the strength to shrug off the catcalls and nickname slurs.

"Lita honey, time for dinner." Lita could smell the pork chops and potatoes but wasn't in the mood for either one. She sat up on her bed and crept slowly to the bathroom to wash her hands.

"Coming," she said meekly after Loretta called at her again.

It was another lonely Saturday night, and tomorrow would be another meaningless morning at the church, listening to words from the would-be rapist, the revered pastor. Lita imagined a spiritual talk centered around space exploration, the boundaries of which had barely been broken. The pastor had touched upon the evil of Sputnik the year before, talked about how the devil was trying to send man beyond the reach of God, looking for answers in places that had none.

Lita thought the possibility of space exploration was neat.

That morning, the United States and Soviet Union had each launched satellites that were intended to reach the moon. Both would prove to be failures—the Soviet's rocket, Luna E-1 (No. 2), disintegrated less than two minutes after launch, while the United States' failure, Explorer I, didn't have enough fire power to break free of the Earth's gravitational pull. The botched attempts were sure to put a little fire into the pastor's talk, perhaps again focusing on the hand of God punishing man for trying to break the bonds of earthly limits—he was very good at putting evil meanings on good things.

As she ate her meal in silence, Lita thought about her own improbable chances of finding a man that didn't exist—her father—at least not in her world. She looked across at her grandmother and silently made a promise to herself to never give up once she was able to start looking for her real father, rapist-nightmare be damned.

CHAPTER 11

March 6, 1930
Hillman, Kansas

The news spread at a furious pace—there was going to a lynching, and the aroma of frenzied bloodthirst wafted throughout the northeastern part of Kansas, filling the hearts and minds of the citizens with a fever of holy hate and vengeance. The "killer" of Abigail Jones, an 18-year-old school girl who was raped and murdered three weeks earlier, was going to be lynched that evening somewhere in the vicinity between Topeka or Hillman, depending on where the condemned man was being hidden, and how fast he could be purloined from the authorities.

"Hell, who doesn't want to see a nigger hang," Ray had heard an old man say to another old farmer outside Mother's Restaurant on Main Street in downtown Hillman, the words punctuated with a stern-sounding chuckle. Hearing that word—his father said it constantly—always punched at him a little. Ray had said the word himself too many times—it never felt right, never felt wrong in a "good" way. There were days when he might hear it a hundred times, and usually it wouldn't affect him, but this time he felt the old man's hatred fall over him.

After picking up the needed supplies for the farm—wire, a new pair of cutters, and a couple of boxes of two-inch nails—Ray cruised off Main in the family's 1924 Dodge/Graham Brother pickup, turning south toward the farm nestled on the other side of the Kerland bluffs a couple of miles outside of town. He wanted to get the repairs done to the pig pen, but the buzz of the pending lynching still rang loud in his mind. The jailbreak was definitely in the works, and with the unnamed, notorious vigilante group from Topeka running things, it was a good bet the lynching would be a big-time event.

At Hillman's city borders— entry points east, west, north, and south— small, visibly-aged signs were posted with the simple, yet terrorizing statement: "Whites Only Within City Limits After Dark." Ray had seen the signs many times, never thought much of them, until today, with the speculation of the forthcoming lynching.

A gang of about 100 men assembled the previous evening near the Kaw River on the North side of Topeka and hatched a plan to take the accused killer, 27-year-old negro William James Smith, to his death. Identified by the girl's father, Smith was quickly arrested and charged with the murder, even though the evidence against him was circumstantial at best—the man had made the mistake of being in the vicinity of the grieving father's flivver, parked about five blocks from where the girl's body was found in the town of Oswald, which was about 15 miles to the north of Hillman. Under the cloak of darkness, the group was planning to steal the prisoner from his safe location, transport him to a not-so-secret spot, and carry out the special form of "justice."

Ray knew his dad would be going to the immoral spectacle, and after staying away from the house for most of the morning, he finally saw his dad in the afternoon as he was replacing the wire around the pen.

"Raymond, the lynching is tonight." Big Jack was in a drunken state of giddy excitement as he moved close to his son.

"I heard."

"You're coming with," Big Jack said with a slurry slobber as he wiped at a dark stain on the front of his mud-coated overalls. He smelled of pigshit and bootleg whiskey.

"I don't know." Ray didn't look at his dad and stepped back to get away from the smell.

"You coming. I woulda took you to one-a-these years ago, but they haven't strung up a nigger in a long time."

"I don't want to," Ray said. What he really didn't want was to be in public with his plastered father, feeling the shame of Big Jack's outrageous behavior burned onto his face through the eyes of everyone else. It was a scene he had had to endure many times in the past—he vowed the last time it happened, watching his dad puke on Main Street, that never again would he be seen with him.

"There's things that you have to do, things to see," Big Jack stammered on. "A lynching is a part of our rights." He waved his dirty fingers in the air.

Ray didn't answer. Part of him wanted to go, wanted to look at the otherwise decent citizens of the town who prayed on Sundays and then lived life their own way the rest of the week, the same people who wildly cheered him on at the baseball games. And like it or not, the entire town—if indeed the event graced the downtown streets of Hillman—would be there to watch the negro die. Ray also wanted to watch someone die, he just didn't want to be there with his dad.

"Dad, I don't think I'll go," and Ray flinched a little, expecting a drunken rage and a slap to his face—Big Jack started walking toward his son, raised his fist to the gray sky.

"You're going."

"No," Ray held his hammer sideways in the air and stared hard into father's gray eyes, "I will not."

"Hmmm, bastard son of mine," Big Jack muttered and he backed off, again wiping his hand on his overalls. He spit at nothing and Ray relaxed, knowing that the old man didn't have it in him to fight this time, and went back to working on the wire on the pig pen.

In the shadows of the late afternoon, Big Jack came back once more to make Ray, who was sitting at the kitchen table, go to the lynching. Ray's youngest sibling, eight-year-old David, stood next to their father, eyes red and wet, adorning an otherwise smiling face. Big Jack was holding his jug in the other hand, and after taking a swig, swallowed loudly, and grunted at Ray.

"It's-a time. The thing will start at dark." Big Jack turned and looked at David and smiled.

"I ain't going," Ray said. "I don't need to see this stuff."

"You'se are going," Big Jack slurred out. "You need to see this, it is the way things are done. Davey wants to go, don't ya?" David nodded.

"I play ball dad, baseball. The last thing I need is to see some dumbass negro criminal get murdered."

"Negro?" Big Jack almost laughed, glaring at his son. "It ain't murder, you going to see a nigger hang," and he lurched toward his son, but slipped and fell, hitting his left arm on the kitchen table.

"Goddamn nigger, shit." The drunken man rubbed his arm, then pulled himself up, and left the room, David running after him and asking if he could still go. Big Jack smiled back at the young boy.

"C'mon on, Davey. Let us leave the disappointment of your brother at home," and Big Jack spit on the floor of the kitchen.

Ray heard the pickup begin to move outside, walked to the window, and watched as his dad and brother left to watch the public murder. They returned hours later, Big Jack so drunk he could barely walk, little Davey traumatized, scared, and cold. The lynching had gone off without a hitch, and the accused negro's body was hanging forlornly from the old, solid Oak tree positioned just off the square that was close to the courthouse in Hillman.

Big Jack had been to one lynching, as a young boy, and Ray had heard his father's story many times—too many times—about the *glorious* night in Hillman almost 30 years past, when the good citizens of Kansas had repelled the Governor's wishes and lynched a "murdering nigger." It was an infamous lynching, not just in the state, but the entire country. The ease of the killing had shaken the state, and the reminders and signs of lynching were always around to intimidate the non-whites.

When he was ten, Ray had stumbled upon a makeshift wooden box at the back of the top shelf in the kitchen pantry, and thinking it contained maple sugar, Lifesavers, or some other type of hidden candy, pulled it down, eager to steal a small treat for himself.

What he found instead were collected memories of murder. Big Jack had saved newspaper articles about the lynching he saw as a young boy when his father, Ray's grandfather, had taken him to watch the unlawful spectacle. There were also a couple of photos of Jack with his father and mother. Under the clippings were an assortment of other items: a marriage license, Ray and his siblings' birth certificates, insurance papers, an envelope with about $500, and the deed to the farm.

After Big Jack and David left for the lynching, Ray went to the pantry, pulled down the old box, sifted through it, and pulled out the clippings of the lynching from three decades before. He had read it several times, but this felt like the first, and so he sat on the floor of the pantry, and slowly moved his eyes across the text on the yellowed newsprint.

BURNED AT THE STAKE!

**A NEGRO IN HILLMAN
CLAIMED INNOCENCE TO THE END**

Suspected of the murdering Emily Gladstone last year—Also attempted assault on another woman—Father of slain girl lit the fire that burned the negro—Huge crowd watched and cheered the horrible spectacle—Negro professed his innocence to the end—Crowd grabs relics from fire

Hillman, Kan., February 23.—A suspected killer, negro John Anderson, who on Saturday past attempted to assault Amy Hardesty of Hillman, and who is supposed to have killed Emily Gladstone last year, was taken from the sheriff's guard by an unruly mob and burned at the stake near the scene of her murder. It is estimated that as many as ten thousand people witnessed the lynching.

> The negro, taken from his cell at the
> County Jail in the middle of the after-
> noon, was placed in a hack, and under the
> guard of at least 50 deputy marshalls,
> brought to the edge of downtown Hillman,
> where he met his unlawful demise.

The story went on and on, describing the accused's crime, the details of his death at the hands of the mob, and even included a quote from the Governor of Kansas. Ray left the pantry with the old newspaper and walked to the kitchen table, sat down, and started to re-read the horrible story again, and read it several times before his father returned with his little brother from the latest successful lynching to take place in Kansas.

CHAPTER 12

February 23, 1901
Hillman, Kansas

Jack Cavanaugh came running in from the cold—again without his coat—through the back door of the two-story farmhouse, a dead chicken in tow.

"Momma, we got another one," the boy yelled with a high level of stress. His mother didn't look up from the kitchen table where she was sitting, and Jack knew something wasn't right. The broad-shouldered woman's head was lowered with her hands clasped tightly on top of the table. Her head was moving slightly up and down in a rhythmic, silent manner.

"Momma? Skippy got one again. I know dad's gonna kill him this time. Momma?" Mae Cavanaugh looked up, and Jack saw that her eyes were red with tears.

"Son?"

"What's wrong, momma? You won't let him kill the dog, will you? He can't kill Skippy," and then again, "What's wrong?"

"Nothing," she said, looking at him with an unforgiving sadness. "Nothing is wrong. Nothing at all." Then, almost as an afterthought, "I think your father needs you." She paused for a moment, then said, "Go find him."

The boy didn't answer. He turned and left the house with the dead chicken, took it to dump area with the other accumulated trash from the family on the back side of the barn. When he came back to the house, his father was sitting at the table with his mom, who was now openly weeping.

"I don't want him to go," she said in a low tone to her husband.

Alvis Cavanaugh, a big and round man, was wearing a dirty, stained coat on top of his brown overalls.

"Jack's going," and then he glanced over at the boy, a calm, ireful look across his grimy face and stood up. "Get your coat, Jack, we going into town." His voice was strong and authoritative, despite his visible level of intoxication.

"OK, father," and then, "Did mom tell you about the chicken?"

"I'll take care of the goddamn dog tomorrow. Now get your coat."

Jack never questioned his father—the result was always welts on his backside, or worse. The boy ran to the closet off the front room of the house and pulled out his winter coat, a dark-cloth workman's jacket that was two sizes too big, a black cap, and a large pair of old gloves.

"I want you to see what justice looks like in this state," his dad said as they walked out the door.

"Justice?" Jack was confused. "Dad, what about Skippy? You won't hurt him, will you?"

"Forget about that dog. We're going into town to see what happens to niggers that break the law, niggers that kill."

Jack remained silent and followed his sozzled father outside. The wagon was all set to go, and the boy jumped up and sat on the right side of the seat, grabbed a blanket to keep warm. His dad climbed up gingerly, dropped into an awkward sitting position, grabbed the reins, and yelled at the old horse.

"Get it, go!" The dusty-colored mare started slowly, and after a couple hundred feet, moved into a steady pace that suited the drunk driver.

The ride into Hillman was blustery cold, but Jack noticed his father didn't mind. He kept taking swigs from the jug he always carried on the hack, and occasionally he'd whistle a non-descript tune. Jack remained silent for a while and huddled under the scratchy, grey wool blanket. Finally, his curiosity got the better of him.

"Daddy, what are we gonna see in town? How long will we be there?"

"A nigger killed a girl and the cit-zens are going to lynch him. Death penalty," Alvis said with a cough. "We call it justice."

"What about the judge?" Jack picked his nose, looked at the bugger and thought about eating it before wiping it on his pants.

"We the judge," and Alvis took another swig. "I think you'll like it. It ain't baseball, but what is?"

⁖

John Anderson, 25-year-old negro, was accused of raping and killing a young woman named Emily Gladstone some three weeks earlier. It was a gruesome, highly-publicized murder across the state; the 19-year-old girl had been abducted, raped, sodomized, and murdered. Her throat was cut, and the monster rapist had also inserted the knife into her vagina and ran a jagged slit all the way up to her breasts.

An utter, unimaginable depravity.

The crime was beyond any type of comprehension the citizens of Hillman could fully grasp within their small-town worldview. Blood was everywhere at the murder scene—more blood, the local paper reported, "than anything ever seen at a Kansas City slaughterhouse." After the body was discovered—the girl's skin was a pale white and the blood around her was so plentiful that she looked to be bathing in the deep, black-red liquid—it didn't take long for the police to determine that Anderson, who played baseball for a negro ballclub in Topeka, was the killer. It seemed almost a miracle—the "deranged" negro was identified by the girl's father—and the man was quickly captured and arrested. Talk of lynching had begun as soon as Anderson was apprehended. The horrific crime was more than the good people of Kansas could endure or fathom, and their collective, raging anger was quickly and substantially directed toward the negro. Like any concerned group of citizens might do across the country, a lynching was quickly organized.

Once under arrest, Anderson was placed in protective custody at the state penitentiary in Lansing. A day later he was transferred to the city jail in Topeka, and for good measure, back to Lansing the day after that. For a full week, a large, angry crowd surrounded the fenced-in structure at the penitentiary, waiting, hoping for a chance to bust out the accused and kill him.

The back-and-forth façade of protection ended a couple of days later, and on the order of Kansas Governor Ronald Reynolds, the accused man was taken from his cell early in the afternoon on February 23, and brought to Hillman's county jail, supposedly to again protect him from the dangers of the ever-growing mob camped out in Lansing. As many as 50 deputy Marshalls were positioned at the Hillman jail to guard Anderson, but when a simple skirmish erupted on the back side of the square a couple of blocks from the jail—a crowd had materialized almost instantly when the word was spread that Anderson was in town—the law men seized the opportunity and left, scattering across Hillman's downtown area. Like locusts on a ripe field of corn, the horde of would-be assassins swarmed the jail, broke through to Anderson's holding cell, and jacked open the door using first a sledgehammer, then a huge iron bar.

Soon enough, the prisoner was in the killing arms of the mob.

When Jack and his father reached the outskirts of downtown Hillman, it was evident that something big and special was happening. A sizeable throng of people had gathered throughout the square area that surrounded the jail, and there was an air of great anticipation swirling in the cold wind. Faces were angry and jubilant at the same time. The rowdy atmosphere was celebratory in nature, and even though the hum of the mob was high and erratic, Jack expected to hear a band begin playing a marching tune at any moment. There was no band, of course, but only because no one thought to have one.

The fast-setting sun fashioned an ominous gray-orange sky, and the strange looking atmosphere seemed to jell the frenzied voices together into an echoing chorus.

"Kill him! Kill the nigger! Burn the nigger! Kill him!"

Jack understood the hysterical words in the high-emotion flurry of the moment, but then again, he didn't. And while he had heard his dad talk of niggers many, many times, he had never heard him speak of killing them—he thought of the difference in what his father talked about and what the crowd was yelling—but he knew the nigger who was going to die must have done something very bad.

And then the happenings and exhilaration of the pending lynching swallowed him again. Other children scampered back and forth across the town square, playing tag, kicking a homemade ball, even singing. Jack wanted to play too, but when he started to run toward the other kids, his father grabbed his jacket and pulled him back.

"Stay put," Alvis grunted, and Jack didn't try to move again.

When shouts of passionate rage circled around jail, a great eruption of volcanic noise spewed from the crazed crowd throughout the downtown square as the accused man was pulled into the now dark, cold night air. A small stream of blood dripped from his temple and nose—a smallish, dark-haired man rushed through the crown and took a swing at the prisoner with a long board, connecting a shot to the man's right ear, spilling yet more blood.

Then the chanting started again, fast and uneven, filling the chilly space.

"Kill him, kill him, kill him!"

"Kill the nigger!"

Jack tried to hold his dad's hand—wanted very much to hold his father's hand—but both of Alvis' arms were busy with the jug. Now being dragged by his shirt collar, the accused was clobbered with a baseball bat by one man, and other infuriated men fought to get a hit on the doomed prisoner with their fists or a strong kick with their boots. Many in the mob were armed with rods, boards, chains, anything that could be used to inflict pain on Anderson.

"Don't hurt him, don't hurt him," yelled a man in a blue suit who ran to defend Anderson from the onslaught. "Stop! Just stop! We're going burn him!"

Still, the prisoner was pulled at and pushed, dragged by more people than seemed possible, back through the square, across Main Street—he was hit many times—and when the group reached the yard surrounding the courthouse, they stopped. Anderson's face was bloody—his nose was broken—he tried to wipe the scarlet mess off his cheeks with the top of his shoulder because his hands were still shackled. The blue suit man and three other men quickly chained the doomed negro's torso to a pole next to the brick-paved street. After tying his feet, the blue suit stepped back, and looking at Anderson like captured prey, spit, and talked loudly at him.

"Are you going to confess, nigger?" blue suit asked, hands casually in his pockets, above the dim roar of voices. "Confess. This is your chance, confess before we harm you.

"Confess before we kill you. Before you die."

Anderson lifted his head, blood seemingly everywhere on his face, and stared out the at huge, screaming gathering. Terror bounced out of his eyes but it was not in his voice.

"I am innocent," he said slowly, blood spilling from his mouth. "I am dying for something another man did." The doomed man struggled to sit up straighter, failed. "I see many of my friends here; they know I didn't do it. If I had done it I would've said so and stayed at the prison for the rest of my life."

"You lie, nigger." Jeers all around, and then the noise dropped down.

"You have no friends here," the blue suit man said. A skinny man in overalls sprang from the middle of the mob, rushed to Anderson, and punched him square on the left eye.

"Confess," the man screamed. If it affected the negro, he didn't show it.

"My god," Anderson whispered, "I have told you, I am innocent. I didn't do it."

"He lies, he lies!"

Three men approached Anderson carrying two large, metal containers—they poured a clear liquid from one of the cans—it was coal oil—all over the negro. Then the crowd parted quickly and a man with a pot belly wearing a well-worn Carhartt railroader's cap strode toward the brutalized man. He was carrying a box of matches.

"Are you guilty of killing my daughter?" the man asked Anderson.

"I don't know what you want, or what I did," the condemned negro said.

"You killed my girl," snarled the man.

"Mr. Gladstone, if that's your name, it wasn't me. I'm the wrong man."

The crowd came to life again, "Kill him, kill him, kill the nigger, burn him!"

"You're burning an innocent man," Anderson said. And then, "Can I shake hands with my friends? Can I say goodbye to my mother?"

"You have no friends here, you wretched soul," Mr. Gladstone said. There was a shout or two from the mob for the man's mother to come forward, and a smallish woman appeared, crying. She started to approach her chained and bloody son.

"Stop there," Gladstone barked at the woman. She stopped at the front of the crowd and mumbled something through her tears toward Anderson. Another crying woman approached, and it was clear from the murmurings that she was the negro's wife. She stood next to his mother.

"Okay nigger," the Gladstone said. "Make your peace with God, you are going to die." And then, just for good measure, the second can of coal oil was poured over Anderson's head.

"Goodbye my friends, goodbye mother," he said softly, the oil spilling into his mouth. And to the woman who was his wife, "Goodbye Eunice.

"I am innocent."

Mr. Gladstone then lit the match and dropped it on the negro.

Flames burst high on the living kindling, and as the crowd bellowed loudly with cheers, Anderson let out a long gasp and began swaying back and forth as the blazes swept over him.

The surprising, rancid stench of burning flesh was suspended and unmoving in the murky air. When Anderson finally, mercifully died, the crazed and blood-lusting crowd rushed his maimed and fiery carcass to cut off pieces of his charred skin for souvenirs. His ears, nose, and fingers. Three hours later the smoke stopped floating from the charcoaled mass that was once Anderson's body and the mob was gone. The absent Hillman police finally made an appearance at the scene, and with shovels, bags, and rakes, cleaned up the remains. Anderson's widow stood off to the side with his mother, her mother, and her two children, shaking uncontrollably, weeping loudly.

"No, no," his mother whispered to no one. "I don't. No. Oh sweet Jesus, why?"

The last, lingering part of the celebrating crowd finally began to disperse from the area—Jack left an hour earlier because his father had had other things on his mind for most of the evening. As the police started their cleanup, Alvis was having sex with a negro prostitute at the not-so-secret brothel several blocks off the downtown square—he was with Jenny, his favorite. Jack waited alone in the lobby of the three-story house, afraid of the men circling in and out of the rooms who occasionally threw out unruly drunks. Thirsty and hungry, he wanted to go home, eat, and go to bed.

More than anything, Jack wanted to see Skippy.

The remaining pieces of the mob were now blissful, and when a few drunken men began to sing, a lot of the other folks joined in, more men, some women, even kids. Bound together by their sins of the night, they sang with a happy tone that infected the tune with the unthinkable death bestowed upon Anderson. It was a popular song from before the Civil War, but had recently been recorded and was played, and sung over and over across the country. Stephen A. Foster would have been proud.

Well, way down upon the Swanee River,
Far, far away-hey.
Wo, that's where my heart is yearning ever,
Home where the old folks stay.

All up and down the whole creation,
Sadly I roam.
I'm still a-longin' for the old plantation,
And for the old folks at home.

All the world is sad and dreary,
Ev'rywhere I roam.
Oh, darkies, how my heart grows weary,
Far from the old folks at home

Big, raucous cheers erupted at the end of the song, and the crowd finally began to dissolve and go home, happy that justice was achieved, and ecstatic that they got to watch.

᷍

The soft and wailing sobs of Anderson's widow remained with Jack for a long time—it was almost like she had feelings, he thought to himself, like she was a real person. The rest of the lynching, however, always came back to him in a strong rush of excitement, the glory of the crowd chanting, the swelling rise of emotions and cheering escalades as the roar of the fire engulfed the negro, swallowing him into the pit of death and surely sending him to the depths of hell. Jack had wanted to grab a souvenir for himself when the ashes of justice had cooled down, but his father had been overly anxious to leave and get at Jenny.

From the ashes of Anderson's charred flesh rose a movement within Hillman to once and for all turn the small community into a Sundown Town. The mayor called a special town meeting three days after the Anderson lynching and addressed what most of the citizens felt was the real problem facing Hillman.

"It's the niggers."

If the negroes had been banned from Hillman, argued the mayor, then Emily Gladstone would still be alive. A new city ordinance, disguised as a real estate law, was presented to the citizens—all negroes had to be out of town by sundown, and if they were unlucky enough to live in Hillman, they had to be inside and out of sight when the sun disappeared.

The ordinance, quickly voted into law, was a rousing success. Within three months of the lynching, Hillman had successfully expelled all negroes, and like many hundreds of other communities across the United States, Hillman indeed became a Sundown Town—in short, if you were colored, you better not be anywhere in the city limits after dark. The prohibiting of negroes putting down roots in the town was easily enforced by the community's real estate agents via the new covenant regulating who could buy a home or even rent property. If the real estate exclusion failed to work, a few simple yet intimidating encounters with the local police did the trick.

When the sundown rule became official and the last negro family had left the town, the *Hillman Gazette* heralded the good news of the vanquishing with a big headline on the front page:

NEGROES GONE FROM HILLMAN

Ordinance Obeyed, Last Family Removed
Mayor Patterson Makes Announcement
Legacy of Town Restored

Hillman, Kan., May 28. —The city of Hillman can take a breath of fresh air. The Real Estate Action Act, the new covenant passed last month which allows the city to determine how certain properties will be sold within the boundaries of the town, is working as intended.

"It is a great thing for Hillman," Mayor Patterson said of the new city rule. "We have advanced into the 20th century, rightly taking our place on the list of the top-rated municipalities in the state."

"If some people can't adhere to the new measures put in place to protect our fair city," James Fields of Turner Realty said of the covenant, "then they will not be allowed to live here. We will make sure who does and doesn't purchase the great homes we have in the town."

The article continued on about the dangers of the Negro race, the pandering effects of lazy negroes, and the devaluing of the fine homes in

Hillman. It sang of the virtues of attracting new white families to town, and that the economic boom promised by the Mayor two years earlier was now possible. Hillman was ready to become a top-rated city in the state.

Another black family wasn't allowed to move into the city limits of Hillman until well after the end of World War II.

CHAPTER 13

September 15, 1950
Boston, Massachusetts

Ray didn't dislike too many cities, but he hated Boston. Steeped in the traditions of more American history than any one place should be, Beantown seemed, at least to Ray, the embodiment of everything that was wrong with the country. Baseball was just one more example of that "problem." It was now the fourth season since Jackie Robinson had joined the Dodgers and the Red Sox were no closer to signing a negro than they were in the 1920s.

Not that they were alone in their slowness.

Just five of the 16 major league teams had integrated negroes onto their rosters—the Senators, Cavanaugh's club, were still four years away from adding a negro—it would be Carlos Paula—to their team. The Red Sox would be the last to integrate, bringing Pumpsie Green on board in 1959. It was an appalling lack of progressiveness on the part of the Red Sox ownership, and just one more reason for Ray to dislike the city.

The day before, Ray lost to the Red Sox, 4-3, when his centerfielder misplayed a fly ball in the ninth inning, allowing the tying and winning runs to score. Still pissed at the loss—his 13th of the season—Ray was in no mood to be with his woefully inept teammates. He went through his day-after-pitching routine quickly, stretching with a little running, then settled into the corner of the visitor's clubhouse at Fenway park with the newspapers and a mystery novel. He figured he would pitch in another three or four games as the season ground down to its end, maybe more if his arm held out. The steam was now completely gone from his fastball, the hook was sloppy most of the time, and he even fought his control. Still, he knew he should have had more than six wins.

Ray's time with the Senators had briefly been good—he snapped back to his pre-war form for his first couple of seasons when he returned from the army. But a lingering sadness enveloped him for most of his time in Washington, part of it was because his talent ever-so-slowly ebbed away, more was from the disintegration of his family. Even though it was self-inflicted, his perpetual loneliness ate him constantly. He found himself listening to his jazz records more and more—the pleasure of sound—and a new kind of solitude was realized in reading.

When the 1950 season started, Ray was hoping for a rebirth of sorts for his game—by the middle of June it was apparent that he was in the middle of a swan song finale, riding the last viable strains of his fastball and stamina. Intentionally beaning hitters quickly became a thing of the past—it seemed like every time he put a runner on base, they scored. Ray gave up more runs, homers, walks, and had less strike outs, collectively, than in any of his other major league seasons. When he started hearing the calls and insults from the stands—"You're a goddamn bum," and "quit old man, quit!"—he used the shots of angry adrenaline he got from the taunts to temporarily move his game up a notch or two. It never lasted more than a couple of games.

Occasionally after arriving in D.C.—it wasn't very many times—Ray would scan the stands and pick out a woman for after game entertainment, but that had only happened twice this season, and the results were quick and awful. He finally decided that a bad fuck was a bad fuck no matter how willing or good-looking the woman might be.

His final attempt at an after-game dinner and sex date was with a woman he'd been with a year earlier but didn't recognize—she thought he was back, maybe as a boyfriend. When the woman finally realized at dinner that he had no idea who she was, her glass of beer splashed home on his face and was quickly followed by a strong slap to his left jaw. The angry woman ran from the establishment and Ray was thrown out before his food came—he was still charged for the meal.

It had been a tough year.

On the days when he thought the melancholy would kill him, Ray turned to jazz, the slow, thoughtful blues. He had a special record for his worst moments during the summer of 1950, a song called "Kansas City Torch" by the Castle Jazz Band—he listened to it many, many times.

Ray also hit the movies to curb his feelings of despondent unhappiness—he liked going to the MacArthur Theater and the Playhouse Theater to see shows. The auditoriums were large, affording Ray the opportunity to hide among the many people, something he liked doing. Eating popcorn by himself with a drink was great therapy with the flickering images of movie stars pretending to be things they weren't.

While he saw most of the top features that year, the one that he liked the best was *In a Lonely Place*, a thriller about a possible killer destroying the relationship with the love of his life. It starred Humphrey Bogart. He went to see it several times, and if he could have found a theater showing it in Boston that evening, he would have seen it again.

"I was born when she kissed me," Bogie says in the movie when he realizes he's lost everything. "I died when she left me. I lived a few weeks while she loved me."

᷑

The excitement was almost too much to bear—Frank Aldridge was headed to Boston to see Ted Williams—oh joyous wonder—the Splendid Splinter in all his hitting greatness. Fenway Park was kind of a dump, but then so was Ebbets Field, and just thinking of watching Williams waltz around on the outfield grass was too much to bear.

The 1950 campaign was going pretty much the way all of Williams' seasons went—he'd banged out 25 homers with a .321 batting average by the All-Star break, and while the Red Sox were eight games off the pace, hope for a pennant run was still hanging around in Beantown. Until the unthinkable—at the All-Star Game in Chicago, Williams fractured his left elbow when he smashed into the outfield wall at Comiskey Park while catching a fly ball. Always a tough guy, Ted finished the game—the fracture was discovered afterward. He missed the next two months, ruining any chance the Red Sox had for the title. Oddly enough, that's when Frank got the great idea of going to see his one true baseball idol play in Boston.

The Kid was set to make his return in September—he'd missed a total of 60 games. Frank decided to cut his classes at NYU—not the first time he'd do it—and make his way to Boston to see Williams and the Red Sox take on the Washington Senators on September 15, a Friday night game at Fenway. It was a trip he'd always wanted to make, and when he couldn't get any of his pals to go with him, he decided to go it alone—a train from Penn Station in the city to Boston's Back Bay Station, then make his way over to Fenway. Instead of spending the night, he'd just hop back on the last train and be back in New York the next morning.

A real baseball adventure, complete with Ted Terrific.

If ever there was an iconic ballplayer that had a true love-hate relationship with almost everyone, it was Williams. He also had nicknames, a lot of great nicknames—The Kid, Teddy Ballgame, The Splendid Splinter—he liked to call himself Ted "Fucking" Williams of the American "Fucking" League. He was also called Terrible Ted because of his apathetic indifference and downright hostility toward his fans. Williams wasn't mean-spirited, but he came across that way most of the time. Ted swore a lot—if he was talking, profanity was usually laced within his words. One writer called the great hitter "savagely independent"—if ever a ballplayer was his own man, it was Williams.

Some of his other antics included his refusal to smile in most photos, spitting at the stands when booed after bad defensive plays, or flipping his bat into the stands after striking out. His owner, Tom Yawkey, once fined him for spitting at the press box after he homered.

Williams was a badass, and Frank loved him for it, admiring the unconventionality that only truly great players can get away with.

As the game started, Ray hunkered down in the far-right corner of the dugout and started reading Raymond Chandler's, *The Simple Art of Murder*, a collection of short stories. He had discovered the detective writer two years earlier on a long road trip, and the hard-boiled, macho-laced Philip Marlowe character appealed greatly to him.

"But down these mean streets a man must go who is not himself mean, who is neither tarnished nor afraid."

In the deep, right-field bleachers, Frank Aldridge got comfortable in his seat, scorecard and hot dog in one hand, a coke in the other. The pre-printed lineup on the card had to be altered—the Red Sox manager Steve O'Neill made a last second change, swapping out catchers at the bottom of the order, thereby rendering the cards invalid. Williams was in his custom-ary slot as the third hitter.

As the game progressed, it had the making of a pitcher's duel. The Splinter grounded out his first time up, singled in his second at bat, and by the time the game had reached the top of the sixth, the score was tied, 2-2. In the Senators' dugout, Ray was finishing chapter three of his book.

Washington scored three to take the lead, but in the bottom of the sixth, the Red Sox busted out for six runs, led by Williams' three-run homer, much to the ecstatic joy of Frank. From there Boston coasted home for the win, 12-9. Ted didn't disappoint, finishing four-for-six with the home run and three RBIs. It was a good win for Boston, a typical loss for Washington.

Ray left the dugout in the eighth inning, quickly showered and left Fenway. He wanted the relief of some live jazz but didn't feel like being in public. He ran into the hotel bar, downed a quick beer, and retired to his room to read some more.

Frank faced the long trip back to New York with a lot of happiness, and despite the exultation he felt over seeing Williams play, was able to sleep for most of the trip. He arrived at Penn Station in the early morning, weary yet energized.

On his way home, Frank grabbed a couple of newspapers from the neighborhood newsstand (*The Daily News*, *Times*, and *Brooklyn Eagle*), found the articles of the game, and clipped them out. He carefully pre-served them with his scorecard from the game, his train tickets, an 8 x 10 souvenir photo of Williams he got at Fenway, plus one of his baseball cards, a 1950 Bowman.

"Hot damn, goddamn," he thought as he slid the souvenirs into an envelope. "I saw the Splinter hit a homer."

CHAPTER 14

July 26, 1960
Cooperstown, New York

When the interview at the Hall of Fame ended and he was walking to his cream-colored, 1955 Ford Fairlane parked near Cooper Park in downtown Cooperstown, Ron McMasters felt defeated and despondent. He had been shaky-nervous at best during the meeting, unsure with most of his answers, slow when asking his own poorly-worded questions, and had even displayed a lack of baseball knowledge—it was horrible in every way possible. He stopped at a gas station on the way out of the small town, had the car filled up, and bought a soda for the road.

It was going to be a long trip back to the city, and worse, the hunt for a job he'd really like would have to start up again. It rained a little as he got closer to the Bronx, but the gentle shower seemed to wash away part of McMasters' disappointment. He knew there would be other job opportunities, and maybe he'd even get a shot to work at one of the city's museums. Besides, who would want to live in upstate New York?

Well, he would, that's who.

A position at the Baseball Hall of Fame was his dream and landing a job there straight out of college always seemed an impossible dream. But the Hall was expanding a little, and with the creation of new roles, McMasters presented his best self on paper and applied for an assistant position.

❧

Much like Frank, McMasters had tried and struggled with his overall lack of athleticism, ultimately failing in his bid to become a decent ballplayer. As a kid, he practiced alone for hours, constantly swinging a bat, tossing the ball up in the air to himself, and hitting it against the back of an abandoned building a few blocks from his home. But he knew, soon enough, that he would never have the real stuff to play into high school and he reluctantly moved his baseball drive to academics—his change of direction worked. Ron started reading sports books, Hemingway, and found a side of himself he didn't know existed when he stumbled upon James Baldwin's *Go Tell It on the Mountain*. He worked at making straight A's, and came close to perfection, recording just two B's in high school.

The long hours of study paid off, and while he didn't make an Ivy League school, Ron earned a full ride to NYU. His love of baseball and its history transcended into other areas, and using his strong, hard-earned academic prowess, McMasters began his pursuit of museum work, a desire enhanced after visiting the Baseball Hall with his parents following his junior year of college.

The game held a special place in his heart.

Ron cried when the Giants left New York, tried to like the Yankees, but it didn't take. Even though he was in Cooperstown when the Mets began playing in 1962, they quickly became his favorite, and he took good-natured ribbing from all the guys at the Hall because the team was god awful beyond all definitions of the word bad.

"The only thing worse than a *Mets* game is a *Mets* double header," manager Casey Stengel said of his '62 Mets team. "We've got to learn to stay out of triple plays."

❧

McMasters was rolling a sheet of paper into his green Smith Corona to finish up another revision of his resume when the white wall phone in his parents' kitchen started ringing. He pushed away from the table, stood slowly, and picked up the receiver after the fifth ring.

"Hello?"

"Hi. Is this Ron?"

"It is," and McMasters let out an exasperated sigh.

"Good. Ron? Say, this is Frank Aldridge at the Hall of Fame." McMasters almost dropped the phone. "Anyway Ron, I'm calling with good news. I'm offering you the position here in Cooperstown."

"What?"

"The job at the Hall. Are you still available? I sure hope so."

"Yes, sure," and Ron felt his face flush with excitement. Then he stammered, "You're offering me the job?"

"That's what I said. Hey, we both went to NYU for god's sake. So, what do you say?"

"I say...yes! I want it. Yes."

That's when Frank started talking about Cooperstown, rambling on and on about the virtues of the small town, the beauty of the area, and specifically the magic of baseball and its hold on the country.

"There's nothing else like it," Frank said with great enthusiasm in his voice.

Two weeks later Ron was in the small town—he had a small one-bedroom apartment a few blocks from downtown and his own office—a very small space—at the Hall. Within days he had locked in step with Frank—his new boss had helped him greatly with the move—and McMasters was running through the items and words of baseball's history like he'd been doing for years. The rest of the people at the Hall were unique in their own way, but Ron liked all of them, even Johnston—especially Johnston, strange as he could be. The small town was massively large in so many ways, because of the game, but still very small—also because of the game. Ron settled in, learned the ways of the area, found his place both in and out of work, and looked to Frank when he needed reassurance or information on a topic outside of his zone.

Baseball, and Cooperstown, became his comfortable home.

CHAPTER 15

November 18, 1964
Cooperstown, New York

The days had morphed into a long string of minutes and hours, not much else. Frank began to feel the pressure pinch of little progress from self-made deadlines in his hunt for Cavanaugh—nobody knew a goddamn thing about the former pitcher. It was very strange. The pitcher had had a very good career—yes, he played for horrible teams in St. Louis and Washington—but why had he vanished? What was his story? Where had he gone, and was he, like Frank had come to the reasonable deduction, hiding something by hiding himself?

One of the most striking things Frank had derived was that Cavanaugh didn't have many friends—or no friends at all, especially his former teammates—who recalled the pitcher with any kind of fondness. The same for his managers. He was still waiting for more hometown news, but no friends usually meant no current information was available. Putting thoughts of Cavanaugh on hold, Frank looked over some of the news items and collectibles from the 1964 season—the Cardinals won the Series; the Yankees fired their manager, Yogi Berra; the Phillies had a collapse for the ages at the end of the season. Frank was hoping to get his hands on their unused World Series tickets.

By the late morning, Frank was looking for a way to head home. The baby was giving Peggy fits—Molly was a handful, a gorgeous little girl already set in having her own way. The other kids doted on her—especially Debbie, the oldest—but Peggy was crazy from the stress of all the kids, each wanting more attention than she had to give. While Frank didn't want to help, the more he did to relieve her motherly stress, the more he got laid.

"I need a nap," she told him on the phone. "For one hour? Can you come home?"

"Do you remember Ray Cavanaugh? We're getting ready to look at some new stuff," he said, lying. He didn't want to go home.

"I need this. Maybe we'll have a night?" she said, hoping the little bit of added sugar to her voice would convince him. So Frank went home, and when he strolled into the house through the front, he was singing, busting it out as if he were Roy Orbison himself.

"Pretty Peggy, won't you love me too? Pretty Peggy, I cannot help but see, Pretty Peggy, there are poopy butts to be changed…"

Peggy threw a diaper at him and went upstairs for her slumber time.

Frank grabbed the baby and cleaned her up. Then he played with little Steven, read a book out loud, talked about the other two kids who were at school with them, and changed another diaper. After making a grilled cheese for himself and Steven, Frank noticed the time, and knew he had to get back to the land of baseball's past.

The lunch time was a rousing success—Peggy got a nap in, and before he headed back to the Hall, he snuggled up Steven, kissed the baby, and considered himself lucky, with or without baseball and its trappings of history. As he walked out the door lighting a cigarette, Peggy gave him a little kiss and told him to save his energy for later that night.

The hold that baseball had on the American public always fascinated Frank. The game was better documented than anything else that he knew of—not wars, elections, universities, companies, music, even the lives of the most famous, influential people in the world. If something happened in a professional baseball game, every possible aspect of it—pitches, hits, attendance, weather conditions—everything—was recorded for posterity, and had been almost from the beginning of the sport. And after that, the participants would talk about it, why they did what they did, and how the outcome was ultimately decided. Breaking down the elements of preserving each piece of baseball enthralled Frank to no end, which is why the Hall of Fame had become so important, especially its research library, and why Frank wanted to be a part of it. And because it was important, Frank felt important, too.

But Cooperstown almost ruined it before he got started.

When Frank first moved to upstate New York with his wife seven years earlier, he didn't like it—at all. The little hamlet was virtually in the middle of nowhere, and while there were a couple of larger towns within 20 to 30 miles of Cooperstown, they were also in the middle of nowhere. Buffalo was more than four hours away, Syracuse two hours. And while Frank would take periodic trips to either city, he soon found that he preferred Cooperstown, not because he didn't like the travel, but he had come to love the lake, the landscape, the feel of what the town was to him, and how only residents could really know what Cooperstown was. It was very much a small town, but very much a window for the outside world to gaze into—it really was baseball at its most basic level. As the town and people grew on him, he slid into the feel and self-importance of the Hall and what it meant to the game, the fans—hell, what the place meant to America.

He adored the place, but Peggy, a woman of the city, had a hard time. While she loved the game of baseball—and more importantly, Frank—she also wanted more culture than just baseball. And that was a problem in the middle of upstate New York in the 1950s when the Aldridge's moved there.

The answer proved to be babies. And then more babies.

Debbie was born the year before they moved, a pregnancy so easy that Peggy was willing to do it again. David came along almost two years after they got to Cooperstown, Steven two years after that—a total of 18 months of constant vomiting and swollen ankles.

"Never again, Frank," Peggy said after number three. "Never again."

Molly had been the "unplanned" surprise, and while it was easier for Peggy to carry her, it still was hard, especially with three other kids. But the significant thing about the newest baby was Frank, who finally found a way to enjoy babies, his baby, especially when grouped together with the other kids. Debbie was now nine—"Oh my God,"—David six, Steven four, the baby Molly, six months.

Frank always thought four was a pretty good number.

With the children came a settlement for both parents—the Aldridge offspring had grounded Peggy more than she ever thought it could—it was easy for her to center her life around them—and even the overabundance of baseball was more than doable. Like Frank, she soon loved Cooperstown, too, fell into the small-town life she thought she'd hate, and was glad her children would get to live their childhood in the wonderment and shadow of baseball's history.

It was the damnedest thing—the seasonal death of everything was just around the corner and Frank was looking forward to it. The winters in Cooperstown were bad—bitter cold, a lot of snow, and it seemed, like a bad movie you had to watch over and over, never ending. The absence of baseball made the cold days colder, the sometimes shrillness of the wind a bit harder, and the time it took to shovel out of a snowstorm longer. Winter was completely at home in upstate New York, and Frank had no idea how he would ever endure the harshness of the weather in the small town the first cold season he was there, let alone the many more he hoped would follow when he moved there. And then he discovered the joy of high school basketball.

Or rather, it discovered him.

With little else to do in the lightly populated area around Cooperstown during the winter months, high school basketball became highly popular, thriving in the small towns and drawing large crowds to the gymnasiums with large amounts of hometown hysteria. The games between the neighboring communities were bitterly fought contests, the tensions relentless and never-ending. Grudges ruled the rivalries—losses from ten years earlier still hurt—and any chance to stick it to a top rival was relished by the teams and the towns.

Frank fell into the hardwood heaven of New York high school basketball by accepting an invitation from Johnston to watch his son play against Milford.

"Don't you like basketball?" his colleague asked him when Frank declined the initial invitation. "It's a lot of fun."

"It isn't baseball," Frank deadpanned. "And I don't know any of the kids."

"Doesn't matter, doesn't matter. Just come to a game, if you don't like it, leave, you can leave."

"Or not go, but okay."

Weeknights in the winter, and sometimes the weekend, were never the same again. Frank, like the rest of the community, went nuts for the high school cagers, living and dying with each game. Since a silly ban was placed on New York high schools from having state basketball championship tournaments—it had been in effect since the early 1930s—winning the league title for each town was huge, raising the level of competition even higher.

Most years Cooperstown had a good team, and there were a couple of seasons when they were great. Frank found himself caught up in the flow of each season, following the other teams' scores, cheering on the Senior players to go out as winners, always hoping that the next great player for the team was in the Freshman class. Even for the one season when the team lost more than they won, it was still enjoyable—upset wins over Westmoreland and Oneida were big highlights for the town.

One of the stars of the town was the basketball coach, a former player at St. Bonaventure who learned his trade the hard way—he did it all on his own. What little Frank knew of basketball—it wasn't much—quickly changed. The coach ran man-to-man defense with a switch-out zone that befuddled superior-talent teams. A run-around offense with a lot of fast breaks was also unique, and when the team was in the midst of a ten-point run or great defensive set, Frank would lose his voice from letting loose shrieking screams.

He even talked Peggy into a game or two, and while she was okay with the marvel of the high school game as it was presented in Cooperstown and the towns in the league, she decided to relegate her attendance to one or two games a year. Babysitters were easy to get, even cheap, but she preferred baseball.

It was when Frank started going to the road games with Johnston—his son, Larry, Jr., was on the team—that the final hook for the team and games was set. That made it official; basketball fandom was a part of his life. The towns and teams became a part of the winter verbiage and banter among Frank and the other workers at the Hall, and when he was able to pull

McMasters onto the hardcourt ring, the circle of basketball was full. Trips to Sauquoit, Waterville, Tully, and Herkimer became common place. The history of baseball had somehow begat the greater love for the small towns of New York and basketball.

∽

In addition to the joy of high school hoops, Frank began reading novels shortly after his arrival in Cooperstown—it was a nice escape from sports and the comfortable sameness of the small town. Peggy had always been a reader—she fancied the bestsellers—and ever so slowly moved her husband to look at non-baseball books.

Like the rest of the country, Frank read *The Spy Who Came In from the Cold*, a thriller by John le Carré about a spy going deep undercover and getting into a large web of plots and counter plots. Frank liked it—le Carré was a good writer.

"He became a solitary, belonging to that tragic class of active men prematurely deprived of activity; swimmers barred from the water or actors banished from the stage."

It almost sounded like Cavanaugh.

His favorite book of the year, however, was by Kurt Vonnegut, a writer he just discovered. *Cat's Cradle* painted a bleak portrait of the world, as the narrator of the book describes what important people are doing the day the atomic bomb was dropped on Hiroshima. The writing was spot on and Frank read it as fast as he could.

"Americans… are forever searching for love in forms it never takes, in places it can never be. It must have something to do with the vanished frontier."

His other top read was by James Michener, already prolific in his word production and publishing frequency. *Caravans* is about a man stationed in Kabul at the American embassy who is assigned to find a young woman. As he journeys through the country on his search, a deeper understanding of the complexities and nuances of life that aren't American become clearer to him.

"We are never prepared for what we expect."

The books veered him away temporarily from what was quickly turning into a ridiculous search as his quest for Cavanaugh was unyielding with any kind of information. At this point, Frank wasn't expecting anything, and was ready, at some point, to write a note to Lita Lawson and tell her he was done looking.

⤸

McMasters pranced into Frank's messy office, smiling the smile of a crazed Cheshire cat. He held out a large manila envelope that appeared to be stuffed to capacity, clippings and papers sticking out of the open end.

"I've got a real find," McMasters said with a small amount of glee as he dropped the envelope on Frank's desk. "Really good stuff. It was almost hidden, shoved into one of those 'unusable items' storage boxes. I was rooting through 'em, and boom, it was like a bomb went off when I opened the envelope."

The package contained 8x10 photos, lineup sheets, newspaper clippings—a lot of clippings—and a few scorecards. The top photo was a posed shot of two ballplayers, each pretending to throw a pitch. Their pinstripe jerseys had "Feller All Stars" in block letters across the front, and on the back of the pic, written in perfect cursive were words that jumped at Frank: "All Star aces: Bob Feller and Ray Cavanaugh."

Frank carefully picked up the photo, gently turned it over a few times, reading and re-reading the names on the back. Then he flipped through the rest of the stuff—everything was from Bob Feller's barnstorming team that played a one-month tour against Negro League All Stars following the 1940 season. It was an incredible collection of recorded history. Frank could only surmise that it was ignored for a couple of reasons: it involved Negro League players and was not "organized" baseball.

The rest of the photos were more posed shots of the other players on both teams and game shots—players at bat, pitchers on the mound, different pics showing how many people were at the game. Frank found a couple more photos of Ray Cavanaugh, looking fantastic in the Feller uniform, even smiling.

The newspaper clippings were well-preserved, and Frank was surprised that they were from the mainstream press of the day, even written by some of the top writers. He flipped through them, looking for anything about Cavanaugh.

"This is amazing," Frank said as he lit up a smoke. "Have you ever heard about this tour?"

"I knew Feller did a little barnstorming, but I thought most of it was after the war."

"Damn. Go check Feller's file and other items. Maybe we have this jersey."

"Already started, I've got a couple of the guys looking." Frank nodded and took a drag.

"Let's look this stuff over. Maybe we can find something."

Yep," McMasters said, and they sat down together at the cluttered table in the office and started reading the articles. From the October 9, 1940, edition of the *Cleveland Press* they found this:

ALL STARS STOP NEGRO TEAM

Rock 'n Fire Cavanaugh tosses shutout
Negro Bats Silent
Johnson Homers for Major Leaguers

Cleveland, Oct. 8. - As Ray Cavanaugh walked off the field following a dominant performance against a stellar group of Negro League stars, Bob Feller had to be happy. The Cleveland ace had pitched poorly the day before, losing this long tour's opening game. Cavanaugh more than made up for Rapid Robert's outing: Rock 'n Fire Ray struck out 10 Negroes, surrendered just six hits, and, of course, beaned a hitter as well. Feller's men prevailed, 3-2.

Another clipping was from the *Des Moines Register*, dated October 15, 1940:

FELLER ALL STARS DROP GAME

Negroes Triumph, 4-3
Error leads to defeat
Josh Gibson Homers for Negroes

Des Moines, Oct. 14. – The game was already set to be marked as a win for the Feller All Stars, but it was not to be. A ninth inning throwing error by the Indians' slick fielding shortstop, Lou Boudreau, allowed the tying and winning runs to score, ruining a nice pitching performance by Rapid Robert in front of a capacity crowd at Holcomb Park.

The next piece was from the *Kansas City Star*:

NEGROES WIN AGAIN

20,000 See Major Leaguers Lose
Satchel Paige Strikes Out 11
Josh Gibson Homers

Kansas City, Nov. 2 – The hometown crowd got to see the Monarch's own Satchel Paige twirl a little magic Saturday afternoon at Ruppert Stadium as the great pitcher led his team of Negro All Stars to an easy 6-1 win. Paige pitched a complete game with 11 strike outs, and even collected a couple of singles to help with the scoring. Bob Feller

> also struck out 11 hitters for the Major
> League stars on his team, but he also
> surrendered 2 home runs.

One of the last clippings was from the November 9, 1940 edition of the *St. Louis Globe-Democrat*:

MAJOR LEAGUE ALL STARS WIN GAME VS NEGROES

Drop Paige All Stars, 3-1
Rock 'n Fire Cavanaugh Wins Game
Lefty Pitcher is Hurt

St. Louis, Nov. 8. - Stars Park was rocking Friday afternoon as Ray Cavanaugh took control early in the game and the Feller All Stars coasted to an easy win over the Negro players, 3-1. Cavanaugh struck out eight and gave up a home run to Josh Gibson before leaving the game in the bottom of the seventh. He was hit by a pitch and had to be helped from the field. Mel Harder came in to get the final six outs for the Major Leaguers.

Frank and Ron excitedly looked at the clippings, scorecards, and photos for the rest of the afternoon. One of the last pics they saw—it was stuck together with another photo—was a shot of Ray on the mound pitching to one of the negro players. The caption on the back of the photo read:

Feller All-Star Ray Cavanaugh pitches to Paige All-Star Left Fielder Lonnie Lawson.

The two historians, whose combined knowledge and research skills for the game were basically unsurmountable by everyone else in the Hall, fell back in their chairs, feeling complete disbelief and shock over what they read. Lonnie Lawson. Negro star.

Lawson.

Frank lit a cigarette, mentally scratched his head, and pondered the find, trying to decide if it meant what he thought it meant.

CHAPTER 16

September 5, 1940
St. Louis, Missouri

When Ray received the invitation to play in the barnstorming series against a Negro League all-star team, he didn't want anything to do with it. October was a month that he always used to travel around—New York, California, even Mexico—to shake off the dust of the season and relax in the rhythms of new-found jazz and women. It was an effective way for him to forget about baseball for a few weeks and ready himself for the preparation of getting the long recharge of energy he would need in the spring.

Playing more ball was not a part of his off-season process.

Cleveland's flame-throwing pitching star, Bob Feller, was the driving force and organizer of the tour, and the Indians' righty sent the invite to Ray via Sportsman's Park. The note ended up in the middle of a stack of fan mail dropped in Ray's locker, and it was a lucky break for Feller and company that Ray decided to sift through the envelopes before tossing them, which is what he usually did. Already looking forward to the off season, Ray casually glanced through the letters, but stopped and tore open the envelope that had Feller's name in the return address area.

Hello Ray,

You've had a great season, and while the Browns aren't much, you sure are. Congratulations! When the season ends in a few weeks, I will have a team of baseball stars put together to play a series of exhibition games against some Negro Leaguers, and I want you on the team. Now before you start yapping off about not playing with those boys, let me just say, they are great players and fine gentlemen. I've done this a few times, and the best part is that the games are fun, hard, and the important part, the money is good. I always make a nice amount, and I'm pretty sure, you being a headliner, that in the end your take for the tour will be around $10,000, probably more.

Not bad, huh?

So I'm inviting you to spin your pitching magic with my group of players. You can pick a couple of guys from the Browns, maybe you'll want that catcher of yours who seems to know how to handle you. It will be an eight-city tour and we will be playing in Cleveland, Chicago, Des Moines, Omaha, Kansas City, Denver, Fresno, and then head back east, finishing up with at least four games in St. Louis. We will play from Oct. 8 through Nov. 9th.

Let me know soon Ray, I want to watch your Rock 'n Fire stuff strike out those negro players. I have a contract waiting for you to sign.
Sincerely,
Bob

It was an ambitious tour, one that was designed for maximum dollars. Still a young man, Feller was already experienced at putting together successful barnstorming tours—he had paired with Dizzy Dean before, but this time he was banking on the great pitching nastiness of Ray Cavanaugh to bring people to the ballparks. What most players didn't know about the tour was that Feller would get his money no matter what kind of split was devised for everyone else. The black players would get the least, just a little more than half of the major leaguers, except for Satchel Paige and Josh Gibson, who would get as much as Ray.

The main question Ray had about the series of games was simple: when did he get his money? And who would be at the games? What if they lost? What if *he* lost? Ray also figured that his catcher, the Browns' Mike Mahoney, would love to play, and he imagined Mahoney's response would be typical of what the catcher said all the time, and he was right.

"Beating niggers? Goddamn, let's do it." Mahoney was excited, and he didn't ask about the money. He just wanted to know when and was happy it was right after the season. For Ray, the clincher was going to Omaha and Des Moines, two of his favorite cities in the minors when he pitched for Topeka, places where he expanded his personal horizon beyond the ballfield—he was especially anxious to revisit a couple of the jazz joints in Omaha, and he knew he would hear some good music in Kansas City.

Ray was also excited about going to Fresno—he'd never been to the west coast. Battling against Satchel Paige was also a determining factor. The great negro pitcher had been called the best there ever was by almost all the white hitters who had faced him, and a pitching duel—winning several duels if Ray was lucky—could only enhance his own legacy in the game.

He wanted very much, now more than ever, to be remembered and revered as one of the all-time greats.

Getting an invite to play in an exhibition series against the major leaguers was exciting, but Lonnie was hesitant. He wanted to play, knew he could perform well against the major leaguers, but the anxiety it would cause, coupled with the possibility or doing poorly, crept over him. He was going to turn it down—then he talked with Aulette.

"What do you mean you're not going to play?" Aulette was mad.

"I've got other plans. And I've heard about these tours—no fun, and for what I'd do, the money should be better."

"You're going to play, Lonnie," she said with a surprised, stern tone. Lonnie had talked about playing against the major leaguers since he was a boy. "And I bet the money is good. Why would you turn this down? You're a star!"

Lonnie didn't have an answer, but she saw it in his face, the troubled look of mental beatdowns from being held down his entire life. It was the same when he first tried out to join the Stars. As silly as it seemed to her, Aulette knew she needed to do a little building up of her brother's ego and confidence, for whatever reason.

"Don't be afraid," Aulette said, her voice softening, because she knew he was scared to fail against the white players. "You're one of the best. Did you forget that?"

"I didn't forget nothing, and I'm not afraid. I remembered, that's all."

"Do you think Satch would've asked you to play if you weren't one of the best? I know he wants to beat the Major leaguers." A slight nod from him and Aulette knew that he would play on the tour. "The best part is that you'll play some games here, you'll play in Sportsman's Park."

The Cardinals' and Browns' stadium was a venue that Lonnie wanted to play in—the forbidding rules of the major leagues kept him out of most of the best stadiums in the country. In the back of his mind he knew he could play with the white players, play better.

"Will you bring momma to the games here? I want her to see me play against the white players."

"You know I will, it will be exciting. Did you find out about the money? With all those cities on the tour, there should be a lot."

"It will be enough, maybe I can get you a car."

"A teacher with a new car, that would be something," she said. "Let's take care of mom first."

So, Lonnie Lawson threw his talents in with the Satchel Paige All Stars. He was assigned number 9, his number with the Stars. The Paige team would wear gray flannels trimmed in red with red caps, the Fellers had pinstripes trimmed in navy blue with blue caps. When the details were finalized, he was suddenly impatient to get the tour started, and left for Cleveland two days earlier than needed. His uniform would be waiting for him, and he was anxious to hit the field and prepare for the tour

The trip got off to a good start—nobody gave him a hard time for being a negro on the train.

❧

The final weeks of the season for Ray were long and torturous, the worst stretch of playing out the string he'd experienced so far in his career. Pitching his final game on the next-to-last day of the campaign, he lost at Chicago, 5-1, his worst defeat of the year. It was still a great season, at least for Ray—he finished with 19 wins, 9 losses, more than 200 strikeouts, the best E.R.A. in the league. And, of course, the most hit batters with 30. But it was a hollow feeling since the Browns were quite bad, losing almost 90 games.

Getting ready for the trip was simple enough. Ray threw together a couple of suits, sports jackets, and seven ties. Taking the train to Cleveland for the first game would take most of a day's worth of traveling. He wanted to arrive a full two days before the series began to check out the scouting reports waiting for him—he was assured by Feller that there would some decent information on the hitters' tendencies—and to get a feel for Municipal Stadium, rest up and be prepared to pitch against what he figured to be a very good team. The Negro League players and their teams were never openly considered to be a serious threat to the big leagues—the skin color supposedly made them inferior in all ways. But Ray had seen and heard enough of the black ballplayers to know that was a bunch of outlandish, bigoted bullshit. The black players had beaten the Major Leaguers many times throughout the years in these types of games, and he relished beating them more than anything.

"This is going to be bigger than some of the world tours that players have gone on in the past," Feller told Ray when they talked on a quick phone call. "We'll draw huge crowds in Cleveland and Des Moines, and we should draw well in Chicago at Comiskey Park, too." There were 17 players on each team, enough to give everyone a break when needed, and to make sure the spread of money was good.

Ray was excited—it had been so long since he had played meaningful baseball with other good players, that for the first time in years he needed to calm himself down. The negroes would be out to show the baseball world that they could beat anyone—Ray was going to make sure it wasn't him.

❧

From all angles, both on the field and in the box office, the tour was a huge success. By the time the teams rolled into St. Louis, they had played in front of capacity crowds in all cities but Omaha and Denver, and that was only because of cooler, rainy weather. Ray rocked 'em out in his games—a lot of strike outs, very few runs allowed, and for whatever reason, only two hit batters. Feller hadn't fared as well in his outings, but he didn't care.

Everyone was going to have a nice payday waiting at the end, which was why they were playing the games.

One of the things Ray gleaned from the tour was a true sense of appreciation for the talents of the black players. He'd heard and joked with the other players on his team and in the league about "nigger ball," about the lackadaisical play of the negroes, how they weren't very smart, and that their overall baseball sense was nonexistent. He'd even heard that Paige and Gibson were not good enough to play in the majors.

Boy, was that ever wrong.

After the first game in Cleveland—Paige shut down Feller's team and won easily—Ray knew that everything he'd ever heard about negro baseball was a flat out lie. Gibson was just as great a catcher as he was hitter, and the team's left fielder, Lonnie Lawson, was one of the fastest players, period. The Paige team's fielding was also excellent, their on-field baseball demeanor top-notch. He was in awe of their spirit, their overall competitiveness, and the seeming effortlessness with which they played.

Ray took a lot of mental notes during that first game, and when it was his turn to take the mound for the second game in Cleveland, he was ready. The black players hit him a little, but he learned enough about which parts of the zone to pitch to, who liked the high pitches, and who would clobber the inside offerings. He won a tough game, 3-2, and for the tour, he would lose to the Negro Stars just once. And it turned out to be a great tour. When the two teams hit St. Louis to finish off the trip with four games, the overall win-loss totals were tied. It had been a tough, well-played series of games, a great month of baseball.

Still, some things during the trip were business as usual for Ray. The ritual of finding a woman in the stands during the games he pitched held up throughout the tour, with good results in Cleveland, Omaha, Denver, Kansas City—even in Fresno. But once the tour landed in St. Louis it felt different—the four games in the River City were played out over a week and alternated between Sportsman's Park and Stars Park, the home stadium for the Negro Leagues' St. Louis Stars. It was as if his usually raging libido had been turned off. The cool weather of November dropped a pleasantness on the city, the flavor of fall taking control over it. He didn't try to meet new women—meeting up with one of his regular girlfriends when the games ended, he decided, would work just fine.

Ray was the starting pitcher for the Feller team in the second game at Stars Park, which was the final game of the tour. Most of the 8,000 people in attendance were indifferent to Ray and the other major leaguers—they were overly polite beyond any type of baseball etiquette—major league players were a new experience in the ballpark. There were white faces in the crowd, intermingled with the regular fans of the ballpark, but it was mostly a black crowd, exactly what Feller had hoped for when he scheduled the games.

He called it new and easy profits.

Ray had good control of his pitches for most of the game, but he wasn't gassing it on every pitch because his arm was not well-rested, and the travel had kept him from doing his normal routine on a steady basis. But the ball still moved all over the zone and even when it was hit hard, a fielder was always waiting for it.

When Ray sauntered up to the plate to hit in the top of the seventh with the Feller team up, 3-1, he received a small ovation from the crowd. His arm had been lively throughout the game—hitting and missing the spots as he wanted, upping his speed when needed. The hitting tendencies for most of the Negro players were now locked in his brain, and the only bad pitch he threw was a low, over-the-middle fastball to Josh Gibson that was quickly launched over the left field wall of Stars Stadium.

There was one out, nobody on, and after settling into the box, Ray was looking to hit away—that meant he'd strike out. Jimmy "Jumper" James was pitching for the Paige All Stars, a tall, lanky man with a decent curve and fastball—he played for the Kansas City Monarchs. Ray had somehow squibbed one into left field his last time at bat, and he figured James would really bear down this time and try for the K. The first pitch was off the plate, but the ump called it a strike. Ray didn't care and after stepping away from the plate, prepared for the next offering. When the pitch left James' hand, he couldn't react fast enough to move out of its path—it was an uncontrolled toss that first hit the top of Ray's right shoulder, then the upper part of his head right above the ear—a double-shot beaning. The impact noise was a muffled sound, and the crowd drew in its breath with a collective "ohhhh," as the ball careened off his noggin.

Ray dropped into the dirt, and while he wasn't knocked unconscious from the ricochet shot to his head, he also wasn't fully alert. As soon as the ball hit the skull, James ran in from the mound, visibly upset and panicking.

"Rock, Rock, I'm sorry, sorry," the pitcher said frantically as he bent over Cavanaugh. "It got away from me." Cavanaugh's teammates popped out of the dugout, but everyone knew it was nothing more than a wild pitch landing in a bad place. Bob Feller ran to home plate and looking down at Ray sprawled out in the dirt, quickly motioned for help.

He awoke in a soft blanket of darkness with small rivulets of light cutting through flower-patterned curtains that covered a small window. Ray squinted his eyes open, gradually. He liked the ease of the broken shadows on his eyes, and as he started focusing on his surroundings, he could tell his head felt abnormal, like a punched-out, swollen melon. He gingerly touched the spots on his shoulder and skull that endured the beaning— they were tender and almost hot. Then he rubbed his neck slowly, grimaced at the shallow pain, knew instinctively that he would be all right, but his head did feel strange. Sitting up tentatively, Ray scooted backward to lean against the headboard and took another look around the room. He didn't remember coming into the room or falling asleep, nothing. There was a damp towel laying on the floor next to the bed.

Throwing off the sheet that was covering him, he saw he was still in his uniform, minus his stirrups and sanitary socks. With a quick slowness, he moved his legs to the floor and sat up straight. And that's when he saw Aulette sitting across the room—he missed her before—the outline of her body cloaked in the murky grayness of the room. When she saw him move to the edge of the bed, she stood and walked toward him.

"How do you feel?" she whispered.

"Where am I?"

"This is our house. We thought you might need to go to the hospital, but then you were grabby, and I knew you were okay." Aulette said it as if she were pleased.

Ray felt a flush of blood rush over his face and turned away from her.

"Oh, grabby? Grabby? Don't remember that, sorry." But he wasn't. Looking at her through squinting eyes, he realized she was a striking woman with a soft, warm voice. Ray could still taste the dust from the field, and he coughed to try and clear it from his throat. Aulette, on cue, took a couple of steps to the table by the wall, poured a glass of water, and brought it to him. He took a sip, then another, and looked up into the dark deepness of her bright, brown eyes.

"Thank you."

"You got hit pretty good. How's your head?"

"Hurts. Who are you? Where am I?

"My name is Aulette, and this is our house. Lonnie Lawson is my brother, and since we live so close to the stadium, we brought you here." Not the best decision, probably. Aulette intervened because taking Ray to the hospital wasn't a real option by anyone at the game. How she became the star pitcher's on-the-spot caregiver had more to do with who she was and where she lived. The plan was to watch him and see a doctor if the concussion symptoms appeared and persisted.

"Lightning Lawson is your brother?" Ray was intrigued.

"Yes."

"Oh. No doctor?" Ray rubbed his head again. "Where's Lawson?"

"You were checked out at the park by the attending trainer for the teams, and he said you were okay, just needed to sleep it off. Lonnie is at his place," and she poured him some more water. "Maybe he was wrong." Then as an afterthought, "Do you want to see Lonnie?"

Ray tried to stand, but his legs wobbled and a slight push of queasiness ran up his throat. Aulette grabbed his arm and sat him down.

"I'm good," Ray said as the feeling subsided. "No, but man is he good."

"Lay back down. I'm going to get you something light to eat."

"Not hungry," he said as he closed his eyes.

"Go back to sleep, then, okay?" and she placed a fresh, damp towel across his forehead. Ray touched her hand, then squeezed it.

"Thanks," and he closed his eyes.

❧

When he woke up, she was sitting there, still.

"I think you need to stay here another day or go to the hospital." Aulette instinctively touched his head again, gave it a little caress.

"I'm fine," but even through the grogginess of the sleep, Ray knew he wasn't back to normal.

"Hungry? I'll make some eggs if you are."

"A little, eggs sound good."

Aulette got up and went to the kitchen, her mind swirling with the craziness of actual attraction. This man, this *white* man, had produced the strangest pull on her, a feel that was unknown but comfortable. She also knew that after today, or tomorrow, she'd never see him again. Aulette turned around at the sink, and there was Loretta, holding her robe tight and close around her bosom, a slight frown rolling across his lips.

"Is he leaving today," Loretta asked. "Soon?"

"Not yet. I'm making him food."

"Don't make him too much. I want him out of here."

"Momma, he's hurt. I'll take care of him, don't worry, he'll probably leave tomorrow." Loretta gruffed at her daughter and went back to her room to get ready for the day.

From the bedroom, Ray glanced out toward the kitchen, trying to get a good look at Aulette. He marveled at her beauty, her boobs, her wonderfully shaped bottom. But it was her face, specifically her eyes, that sparked him, and with the gentleness of her voice, he knew.

Ray rubbed his shoulder and head again, hoped that he could somehow stay with her a little longer. He needed to learn more about her, figure out just what it was about her that had captured him. He still couldn't believe she was Lawson's sister, and he was also in disbelief that his Feller teammates had somewhat abandoned him, leaving him with people he didn't know. That didn't matter right now, because he was happy to be in her presence.

Women had always been easy for him—easy to catch their attention, to make them feel he had special feelings for them, easy to get them to talk while he said nothing. Most of all, it was always easy to screw them. While Ray had conversed with many negro women in the jazz clubs around the country, not once had he ever thought about screwing them—he always had a date on his arm, and if not, a group of his teammates were with him. But this woman, this Aulette…

He wanted her—and he knew it was strange—really wanted her, but how would it be possible? And this want was something else, a new kind of feeling.

It's not like he was at the ballpark using the celebrity of his presence. Ray had never been very good with the small matters of getting to know someone, especially a woman. But she wasn't just a woman, this was a negro; a negro so beautiful, and he believed, sexy and full of life. She also had a strong tenderness in her manner, and a confidence he had never seen in the other negroes—hell, other women—save for the jazz stars he saw perform.

Aulette stood at her stove, making scrambled eggs the way she always did, and ready to fry a couple of slices of bacon, too. She turned and looked back toward the bedroom many times, wondering if this feeling was nothing more than a nurse thing, trying to understand an attraction for a white man that had never—and she certainly thought would ever—existed.

"Why are you feeding him?" Loretta's presence in the kitchen startled her, and Aulette almost dropped a plate.

"Momma."

"I don't like this, I don't like him being here."

"And you've said so. I'm taking care of him and he'll be gone soon enough." Loretta huffed a little, sat down at the table.

"I want him gone when I get home, okay?"

"If he can leave, I'll make sure he's gone," Aulette lied. She didn't want him to leave, not yet. When the eggs were finished, she took them back to the bedroom, fed him, and made him go back to sleep, and this time, just to test the notion she felt, gave him a little peck on the top of his head, ruffled his dirty hair, and gave him her warmest smile.

Ray looked up at her as she pulled back, gave her the same look.

≪

He left a day later, still a little dazed and very confused, but not from the beaning. Ray had promised his mother he'd come home after the tour ended, and while going back to Kansas was the last thing he wanted to do, he needed to give Maimie some money and check on his siblings, too.

Aulete missed a couple of days of teaching because of her caregiving— "You're going to lose your job," Loretta had warned—but was outwardly stoic in watching him leave the house.

She gave him a warm, strong hug as he left, again kissed him on the cheek, and as he squeezed her hand goodbye—Loretta was watching, frowning—Aulette gave him a piece a paper with their address and number on it. Ray had already given her his information.

"We'll get together soon, I promise," he said. "I want to thank you properly for taking care of me." He was also pissed off that no one— not Feller, his goddamn catcher, or other barnstorming teammates, had checked in on him. As he left and walked to Stars Park to get his auto, Ray looked back at the beautiful woman on the stoop of her home, standing with grace and a bright smile, a slight wave from her followed by a forlorn look. He walked a few more steps, turned to look back, and she was gone.

≪

The trip to Hillman was easy, the time spent there unbearable. His mother had become a shell of her former self, and while she'd never been a strong person, Maimie Cavanaugh was now feeble and meek, looking and acting much, much older than she really was.

"Ray, you look tired," she'd whine. "Ray, when are you coming home for good?"

"I live in St. Louis, momma. I need to be there all the time."

"I need you here. David needs you here." Then she'd ask him about baseball, the team, and finally, she asked why he wasn't married.

"Mother, please."

"Well, I know that's what you want."

Before he left town, Ray took her out to dinner in Topeka with his brother David and sister Sissy, gave everyone a little bit of money. After three days of impossibly glad-handing what seemed like the entire town whenever he left the house, he finally decided to leave. The goodbye to his crying mother was quick and painless.

When Ray returned to St. Louis from Kansas, he stalked Aulette like a prey in the dark, urban woods of the city—he had somehow lost her address and number between his trip to Hillman and back. After a slight panic attack, he went to Stars Park and roamed the neighborhoods in the area until he found the familiar look of the front porch and knocked on the door.

She answered, and when she saw him standing there, looking somewhat foolish and embarrassed, she knew—felt it—that he loved her. When Ray saw her sly smile spread across face, he knew he was right, and that she felt for him everything he felt for her. Aulette asked him to come in, and he did.

They had it, impossibly, together.

CHAPTER 17

August 25, 1937
Hillman, Kansas

David Cavanaugh heard the shallow discharge echo through the house while he was tying his boots at the kitchen table. It was already past nine in the morning and the rest of the family was gone. He didn't think much of the sound, and even though his head was pounding like an overworked jack hammer from last night's drinking, he thought he would try to get some chores done around the farm before his dad showed up and started yelling at him.

He turned on the radio, twirled the station knob back and forth before settling on *The Wife Saver with Allen Prescott*, a program about doing household chores and special cleaning tricks. Then he sat back and enjoyed the solace of the morning with Prescott's friendly voice—his mother was in town working at the dime store, his sister Sissy was most likely at the library, and Ruthie was probably shacked up somewhere with a drifter who promised her a buck for a screw.

A drink of water, a nibble on a couple of crackers, and David was out the back door and headed to the barn to get a couple of tools. Even though it was mid-morning the heat was sweltering—the air was stiff and sultry. He looked around the yard surrounding the house, feeling that something was missing. He rubbed his head and strolled to the barn, thinking that at any moment his dad would appear from nowhere and start screaming at him.

David pulled open the side door of the barn, and as he walked in, a bird flew across the space and toward the rafters. Startled, he glanced up at the small sparrow, and before he could look down, tripped over his father's body, fell, and smashed the side of his head on the 12-gauge shotgun laying next the remains of Big Jack Cavanaugh.

"Oh god. Jesus fuck."

The back of Big Jack's head was blown out—his fat body was prone sideways and smelled of shit. David crawled a few feet from the carcass and puked several times. Then he turned around, sat up on his knees, and looked at his dad's pale-white face. Big Jack's eyes were open, staring hard from the great unknown. The oozing blood at the back of his skull was still somewhat fresh—David realized he had heard the shot. A newspaper sports page lay crumbled next to Big Jack's legs, its headline at the top of the page screaming, "Rock 'n Fire Fans 12." Still on the ground, David scooted over to Big Jack's head and leaned in so close to the death gape on Jack's face that he could have kissed him.

"Fuck you, you son-of-a-bitch," he whispered to the lifeless body. "Fuck you." He stood and kicked several times at the eyes and mouth of his dead father. Then he dropped to his knees, held his head in his hands, and blubbered uncontrollably.

Ray was in St. Louis, scheduled to pitch against the White Sox the next day. It had been a difficult season—the Browns were, as always, terrible—and while crowds of as many as 20,000-plus turned out to watch Ray pitch, his teammates did little in the way of helping to win. Every contest was a struggle, every game he pitched turned into a one-man war, and the hard toil of pitching for a miserable team had taken a real toll on his mental state. Worn down but not-quite broken by the burden of playing for the Browns, Ray was very much ready for the season to end.

Sissy Cavanaugh, the youngest Cavanaugh sister, was at the city library where she worked as a librarian's assistant. Having barely graduated from Hillman High School, Sissy still had a great love of books, and it had led her to the library. With short, thin hair, a lot of acne, and a rail-thin body, Sissy was homely at best. Coupled with her shy demeanor, the boys only came around when they couldn't get sex from anyone else—at 22, she had yet to go on a real date.

David and Ray's other sister, Ruthie, was still asleep in Topeka the morning of Big Jack's suicide, snuggled up in the bed of a stranger—she would soon feel the effects of a bad hangover. Drinking and sex were refuge from the brutal life made for her by Big Jack's fatherly ways. Ruthie was in the final stages of electropyrexia treatment, a short-wave apparatus used to induce pyrexia or high fever in a patient to combat syphilis. She didn't care if she infected anyone else, and she really didn't care if she contracted another disease.

The dime store had just opened in downtown Hillman, and Maimie Cavanaugh was happy—happy to be working, happy to be away from the farm, very happy to be away from Big Jack. The steady flow of customers wouldn't start for a while, and so with the cash register counted out and ready to go for the day, she sat down, thumbed through the newspaper, and sipped a cup of coffee with cream.

David came busting into the store as she finished her cup, wild-eyed with arms flailing.

"Dad's dead, Dad's dead," he howled. "Dead."

"What happened? Happened? Dead?" Maimie felt a huge rush of grief, then pulsating relief wash over her, and she began to cry. A shallow, "No," came out of her mouth, and she covered it.

"He shot himself," David said. "Shotgun in the mouth." His mother said nothing then, and David reached out, pulled her up from the chair, and they fell into each other with a tender hug, softly crying.

Big Jack received the foreclosure notice two days before—he had taken out two large loans—and he was losing the farm, the land that his father's father had purchased when the family moved to Kansas from Kentucky almost 50 years earlier. The severe drought the last four years had been brutal, ravaging the farm—the land was scorched beyond any reasonable type of production state. Every crop planted—maize, wheat, soybeans—the previous two seasons had failed miserably, yielding less than five percent. Big Jack was never much of a farmer anyway—planting and harvesting was the only real work he did—so the loans went unpaid. With each passing month of non-payment, the farm slipped closer and closer to foreclosure, until finally, waiting longer by months than they normally would, the bank dropped the hammer on Big Jack's land legacy.

Like his father before him, Alvis Cavanaugh, Jr., Big Jack Cavanaugh had been a pitcher for the town team in the early 1910s. A crafty righty who could be sneaky fast, he sometimes tossed a hellacious curve, but it was a pitch he couldn't control. A star in Hillman, he dreamed of a professional career, but Big Jack never got a sniff from a professional team.

"I should have been in the bigs," Big Jack would say to anyone who would listen to him later in life, especially after he'd had more than a few pulls from his jug. Then he'd start yelling and cussing—"Fuck it, shit…and hey!" he would turn to any stranger who was within earshot and stammer, "fuck you!"

Ray's mother always stayed clear of her husband when the hooch had a hold of him, and while her life had been miserable for her entire marriage, she stayed—where would or could she go—loving her children as best she knew how, enduring Big Jack's infidelities, and praying daily, almost hourly. She finally found a small piece of happiness working in the dime store. Many a time she had stopped her husband from beating his sons or trying to see his daughters naked. He had hit her a lot—again the wonders of his drinking—and when black eyes and bruises were present, everyone knew. He would always try to make up by forcing himself on her, usually when he was again drunk.

The night before Big Jack received the foreclosure had been a make-up night—Maimie was still sore.

As the drought in Kansas started and lingered, Big Jack made his sparse fields of sickly wheat and meager maize his places of solace, chucking dirt clods and rocks to the sky, drinking whatever he could get his hands on, and dreaming the dreams of baseball that couldn't come true, at least not for him. His son was fast becoming a star for the St. Louis Browns—Big Jack could barely stomach his son's success.

"Better than that no-good son o' mine," whenever baseball or congratulations for his son's playing were brought up while he was drinking. "I was better," and he'd belch or fart, laugh, and take another drink.

Most days, however, the old farmer would just walk up and down the rows of dead wheat. Some days he would stay in bed, and when he was feeling particularly downtrodden, a day trip to the brothel would take place, where he would spend money he didn't have.

It was at the whorehouse, while in the throes of sex, that he began to scream "Rock and fire, rock and fire" before he came—the poor prostitutes. They would scatter in all directions when they saw his arrival, and even though the Madame would charge him double on most visits, he always came back.

"He is one, sick son-of-a-bitch,"

When he wasn't talking baseball, Big Jack would start in on politics, especially his hatred of the Democrats—Big Jack hated and loathed FDR.

"He's a fuckin' commie, a traitor to the American way." But he loved the government checks he got because of the Agricultural Adjustment Act, an FDR New Deal program. While he had absolutely no understanding of how or why money was coming his way, it didn't matter.

"Money for nothing, and brother, I deserve it."

With the hot wind and unbearable drought throughout the early part of the Great Depression, the farm turned on Big Jack. Over the course of two seasons worth of planting, he lost most of his topsoil. In 1934, he made nothing—the crops were non-existent and failed. After that, he gave up. But with the government's supplemental farm program, Big Jack was able to spread out the debt owed on the farm—he had second mortgages on his second mortgage—for three more years.

And then the First Bank of Hillman was bought out by a Kansas City firm—all past due accounts were put on notice, and within a month of the new ownership, Big Jack received the foreclosure. His final two days consisted of a trip to the hardware store for gunshot shells, a big drunk, an attempted last romp at the whorehouse—he was quickly turned away—and a final stroll around the farm's desolated, burned out acreage.

He pulled the trigger that morning after eating a normal breakfast and taking a couple of big, final swigs from his jug.

☙

The funeral was a quick affair, attended by most of the town folks who came to say hello to Hillman's most famous citizen. Solemn handshakes and somber greetings filled the minutes before the service started. The pastor, who had been at the church for years, was brief in his comments. Maimie, Sissy, David, and Ruth sat quietly in the front row of the church when Ray walked to the pulpit to give the only true eulogy at the service.

"I want everyone to know," he said matter-of-factly, "that despite all of my father's short comings, he loved this town, loved his family, and he loved baseball." Ray stood quietly for a couple of seconds, thought about all of things he'd planned on saying, but in the moment he couldn't.

"My dad had a lot of vices, but as I'm sure everyone here knows, I wouldn't be where I am today without his guidance. I look around this room, I see friends, I see friends and family."

He didn't say much else, he didn't need to. The gatherers prayed with the pastor when Ray finished, prayed at the grave site on the outskirts of town—the cemetery sat on a slight hill overlooking the valley that used to be the best farmland in the state—when they lowered the remains into the ground. Big Jack always hated the graveyard, always appeared to be a bit scared of the place. It seemed fitting, at least to his sons, that the son-of-a-bitch was resting with the so-called ghosts that he was afraid of in life.

Ray held his mother's hand as they left the cemetery, David walked quietly behind them to Ray's car. Sissy was the only one who cried, and she cried almost non-stop for the duration of the funeral. Ruthie was quiet—she'd been drinking before the services.

When they got back to the house, Ray said his goodbyes.

"You're leaving?" His mother started crying for the first time that day.

"I have to get back, but I'm taking care of everything in town before I go."

After tossing his suitcase into his new '37 Chevy Coupe, Ray drove to what used to be the First Bank of Hillman, and using most of his savings, wrote a check to pay off the note on the farmhouse and land.

"I want you to make sure my mother gets this paperwork," he told the loan director. Then he drove to the local realtor. After waiting ten minutes, a middle-aged man in a brown suit sat down with Ray.

"Sure, sorry about your dad," the man said. "Sure am sorry."

The two men talked for several minutes, and when Ray shook his hand to leave, the deal was done. Ray put up the farmland up for sale.

"Are you sure?" the man asked several times. "That land had been with your family for decades."

"Sell it, fast," Ray said. "My mother stays in the house, but if you need to sell it with the land, let me know."

"Well, Ray, I'm sure…"

"Sell." Ray left the Real Estate office quickly, and in minutes he was on the highway, headed east to St. Louis.

CHAPTER 18

May 27, 1941
St. Louis, Missouri

The feelings were surprising to both of them, but it was the need, the constant necessity of wanting and craving to be together that surprised Ray and absolutely floored Aulette. He had danced around the edges of love before, but for her it was a new, unconscionable sensation—it was killing her not to be with him.

At least he had baseball to pull his mind from her. He'd flip through old magazines, look for new equipment, anything to keep his mind off her face and body. She didn't have the luxury of easy distractions, so she started listening to the radio more than ever, waiting for songs that conjured his soft hands and rugged masculinity—most of all his face. One of Aulette's favorites was a popular song from a couple of years earlier—"And the Angels Sing." Played by Benny Goodman and sung by Martha Tilton, it always seemed to sooth the problems of their love for a minute or two. Aulette loved the images the song invoked—moonlight beaming, silver waves, and the face that she adored.

❧

Ray's apartment was a simple, third-floor one bedroom close to downtown St. Louis and a decent distance from Sportsman's Park—he liked the place for the convenience to all areas of the city. He assumed that Aulette would sleep with him in his bed whenever he wanted, whenever he was in town and they wanted it—not quite. The first night they tried to stay in his place the landlord appeared out of nowhere and dropped a threatening warning on Ray.

"I don't care if you're the mayor of the city, no nigger is staying in my place," and he pointed at Aulette while looking at Ray. "No niggers."

Ray held back his considerable anger and they left. The next day he started looking for another place to live, but he knew that no matter where he ended up, Aulette staying with him was never going to be an easy thing. Because he now had an easily recognizable face when in public places, finding a decent place for the two of them to couple turned out to be a lot harder than it should have been.

Rock 'n Fire Ray Cavanaugh being seen in public with a negro woman? It was a scandal that would blow up, if not in the papers, then privately among the sports reporters, his teammates, even the local businesses he pitched for. He found another place to live, a two-bedroom apartment that was cheaper, and closer to Sportsman's Park—having Ray Cavanaugh as a tenant was going to be a boon to the building—but it was going to be equally difficult for him to have Aulette as an overnight guest. And it was obvious that it would be that way at every apartment location he checked out.

The ultimate solution would prove to be a hotel.

There was one woman, a girl really, who once rattled Ray's heart, temporarily piercing it with what he thought were feelings of love—Myra Hooper. Since his earliest days in grade school at Hillman, Ray had been enamored with her pretty face, brown-blonde hair, and easy manner. Myra had always had eyes for Ray—they dated on and off throughout their school days until he left Hillman for the Topeka Senators.

It wasn't until after his first season with Topeka that they finally had sex, and the first time Ray fucked Myra he was certain she'd get pregnant. It was in the barn on her father's farm—at midnight after they shared a few pulls on a bottle of his father's bootlegged whiskey—and it was so easy, so completely his time, that he knew his father's so-called curse of bad luck was going to ruin everything. Christ. He prayed for one of the few times in his life, a prayer for the death of a pregnancy that he wasn't sure even existed.

When Myra started bleeding a couple of weeks later, they got drunk and screwed again, and this time she did get pregnant.

"Why can't we get married," she asked over and over. "I want to get married."

"No, I won't do that."

"I love you," she whispered to him sadly, and then, "Don't you love me? Don't you?"

Ray thought for a second, wanting to scream at her that yes, maybe he did, but he certainly didn't want to marry her. The fruits of the world were already a needed part of his palate, and the plain bread and water of the life she offered would never do.

After two long weeks of panic-driven hysteria, Ray finally fell to his last, desperate resort: driving to Topeka and randomly asking a pharmacy worker about abortions. It took him more than 30 minutes to get to the city on Highway 24, another five minutes or so to find the Stansfield Drug Store on Kansas Avenue. He parked the truck—he had just told his dad that he was going into town—walked in and hung out at the magazines, waiting for the two customers at the pharmacy counter to leave. Finally, after more than 15 minutes, the man was alone.

"Excuse me, sir, I need some help."

"Yes? Hello. What can I get you?" asked the man. He wore round spectacles and a white jacket. Ray had thought over and over on how to inquire about help. He had heard stories the last few years about this store providing "abortion kits," but he had no idea what they were.

"I have a problem," Ray started, "and I was told you can help." The man, with more instinct than Ray thought a person could possibly have, gave a grim nod.

"Pregnancy?" the man said.

"Yes, I need to…"

"You want to do it, or someone else?" the man whispered without looking Ray in the eye.

"I don't understand, what's the diff…"

"Twelve dollars for a kit or a phone number," the man interrupted. He pulled a pad off the counter behind him and quickly wrote a number down. "Here, in Kansas City. They can do what you need." Ray took the sheet of paper, looked at the phone number and address.

"What's the cost?"

"Just call the number. If you decide you need a kit instead, come back—$12. Good luck." He turned away from Ray shaking his head and disappeared into a back room.

Ray walked to the front of the store looking at the piece of paper. There was a name, Katherine, a phone number, and an address in Kansas City sloppily written across the sheet. He folded it carefully in half and slid it into his front pocket.

Two days later Ray called the long-distance number to Kansas City, Kansas from a pay phone in downtown Hillman. After two rings, a woman answered with a cold "Hello." Ray told her his problem and she said okay, told him to come the following day at ten in the morning.

The trip to Kansas City for the abortion was the longest car ride he'd ever taken. Myra was not happy, crying the entire trip, begging Ray over and over to get married.

"No."

The address Ray drove to was a simple house just off 30th and Campbell Streets, and when he knocked on the door, a middle-aged woman with short brown hair and a sad face answered.

"You're here with Myra," she said. "I'm Katherine."

Red-eyed and half weeping, Myra walked slowly into the house holding Ray's hand. Katherine told Ray to sit down and led her into another room. The procedure was done in Katherine's kitchen, and she had Myra remove her underpants and lie down on the table—she inserted a strange-looking rubber tube contraption into Myra's vagina. Fifteen minutes later the cramps started and the woman took out the tubing, or whatever it was. She told Myra to lie there for a few minutes, and then she moved her to a little adjoining room that had a cot in it.

"You need to stay here for several hours," Katherine said. Then returning to the front room of the house, she said to Ray, "Can you come back around seven o'clock?"

"Sure, I guess." And Ray left without saying goodbye.

When Ray picked her up, she still hadn't aborted, and was very scared.

"Go home, Myra," Katherine said. "There's nothing more I can do for you. Something will happen in the next few days and you'll be okay." It was about a week following the trip to Kansas City before Myra finally miscarried—aborted—officially ending the pregnancy.

Ray never talked to her again.

⁓

Love always eluded Aulette. She went back and forth with several different boys during her school days and after, but Loretta was always on the watch, looking out for the "bad boys," never trusting the ones she considered good. After years of her mother's controlling, critical appraisals of the men, Aulette stopped bringing them around—the one guy Loretta liked, Skeeter McGee from the Stars, was the one Aulette liked the least.

"Does Lonnie have any other friends?" Loretta would ask occasionally.

"No more Skeeters, Mother."

"I thought he was nice, and a good player, too."

"He drinks, mom. A lot." This information always surprised Loretta, and she could never fully give up on Skeeter, not even when he changed teams and moved to the west coast.

Aulette still managed to find a little romance in her early college years—and sex—away from her mother, always being extra careful when it came to birth control. It never felt the way she'd imagined, didn't pop out a spark like she always dreamed of. Sex was one thing, romance was virtually unfindable. She was damned if she'd ever put herself into a situation like her mother, married to a man who would diddle anything, at any time, as long as he could drink, too. She'd worked very hard to become a teacher, and she would never let a man take that away.

⁓

Following the horrible, unforeseen experience at his apartment, Aulette decided that if they couldn't be together as much as possible—Ray's baseball travel also cut into their coupling and physical needs—then maybe writing to one another would lessen the tensions of separation. Not thinking it would amount to anything, he agreed.

Never one to write even the shortest of notes to his mother, Ray found his thoughts and feelings just spilled all over the paper like unrestrained honey when he started a letter to Aulette. He fascinated himself with the amount of words produced simply because he wanted to let her know how he was feeling. It was a magical thing for him, and while he looked forward to getting her letters, it was returning his thoughts of love and life to her that he liked the most.

For Aulette, his letters were thrilling—Ray captured his mood and love for her in special ways. Her correspondence to him, she felt, was overly sappy, filled with a childish look at the world and their relationship—maybe they were. But through the writings and mail exchanges, they found a connection that society denied them—they were together in separate worlds, a spiritual bond neither thought was possible.

❧

"I know this is special," she said, and he agreed.

"I don't really write letters, ask my mother."

"I would, if I could meet her," she said, knowing that it would never happen, and that she didn't want it to happen.

"Do you write to your mom?"

"I live with her," and she kissed him. The notes, cards, letters, and small presents to each other started that week—Aulette was the first to pen a love letter.

Dec 1940

My Dear Ray,

Here it is, and while I just left you not more than three hours ago, I can't believe it feels like a couple of weeks. My mother is asking questions constantly, and telling me I seem depressed, happy, sad, and a lot of other things. She has figured out that I have a boyfriend, and while I so very much want her and you to meet, it can't happen, at least not now. You are, and I'm so afraid of this, nothing more than the white devil to her.

What will you tell your mother and the rest of the family? I think I know their reaction to me, but I'm hopeful, always hopeful.

As the Holiday approaches, I can already feel the constant uneasiness of not seeing you for a long period of time. Have you decided yet on going back to Kansas? Is there anyone there you want to see? What about the one friend from high school?

Mother is asking me to come and help make dinner, she must have a new set of questions to ask. I'll say goodbye for now and write more tomorrow. Until then, I'll dream of us.

As you know, I love you!

Aulette

His happiness was so high that Ray started saying "hello" to every post-man he saw, corny as it was, knowing the uniformed workers were playing and would continue to play an important part in his life.

CHAPTER 19

September 22, 1942
St. Louis, Missouri

The West End Hotel ended up being the best place for Ray and Aulette to meet and be together when he was in town during the season. A couple of the other hotels in the Negro business districts of the city weren't too keen on a white man with a colored woman, but the West End didn't seem to care, even appeared happy to have Ray as a customer since the manager knew who he was—a definite perk of his baseball celebrity instead of a hindrance. Aulette was suspicious of the ease in which they were able to make the hotel their own, but after a couple of stays she no longer cared.

They tried staying at Booker T. Washington Hotel, but the place was "somewhat" strict on the mixing of races—the couple decided not to go back. The other possibility was the Poro Hotel, but it wasn't very nice—the amenities were older, it had a run-down lobby, and their room was saturated with a slight, strange non-offensive odor.

"We're not staying at this place," Aulette said when they walked into their room and took a whiff of the air. They had sex and left.

And then they found the West End.

The hotel wasn't the nicest, but it was always clean, and most importantly, smelled fresh every time they were there. When the Browns had a home stand during the season, Ray and Aulette would stay there a couple of times, but never on the night before he pitched. Ray knew that having sex the night before a game shouldn't hurt him, but superstitions were always prevalent within his baseball mind—the one-time Ray broke from the rule and spent the night with Aulette was disastrous. Still, she always tried to get together.

"Come on, I need you," she would coo.

"Tomorrow night. What was the score that one time? 9-0? No way," Ray said with a stern seriousness.

"Last season, that was last season," she protested, but it didn't matter. He kissed her goodbye and made the short journey to his apartment to get a restful night of pre-pitching sleep.

⁓

Aulette hated the sneaking around, which is what she called it, to see her man. A white man walking hand-in-hand with a black woman meant just one thing in their world—immoral sexual behavior. While both were cognizant of how they looked to the public at large, Ray was especially protective. He didn't want Aulette to hear the calls, slurs, the coon-bunny names, and jig-a-boo shit directed at her. It happened once and the rage of his furry scared her as much as it made her feel safe.

"Stop it, Ray."

"Funny how they run when they realize I could beat the living shit out of them."

"Ray, stop. Just don't, you'll get hurt. There's three of them."

"I'm all you need. Hang on, Aully, let's get back to the hotel." The anger would fade, and the time alone in the hotel would right their world.

The nights were never long enough, most of the time the days too long. In the mornings, he loved watching her fix her hair—she did a simple and elegant looking finger wave, a look that placed a high-fashion sophistication about her that he loved. Aulette kept her dresses simple, but not plain, and Ray loved them, too—polka dots, flared skirts just below her knees, a buttoned bow at the collar. They were easy to get on, easy for Ray to take off.

And then, their days together would end—he would be off on a long road trip to pitch superbly for his horrible team or she would have to return to teaching. The letters would start up, and the art of capturing small messages—the simplistic notion of sharing words with one another—commenced.

> July 1941
>
> Dearest Aulette,
>
> It's the middle of the season, and it seems an eternity since I've seen you. It feels as if this road trip will never end and since we've only won once in 10 days, that makes the pain of being without you even worse. Did I mention the heat? Who ever thought Boston and New York could be this hot? And then Cleveland, the awful humidity, their stupid baseball fans. I keep thinking that maybe a nice rain will hit the ballparks and we can get a day off. No dice.
>
> Are you starting to get ready for the school year yet? I know it's still weeks away but get moving! And have fun. I know how lucky the kids you teach will be to have you. I'm lucky, too.
>
> I keep thinking about us, wishing the time would move faster or slow down. I seem to always want more than too much, or not enough of too little, whatever that means. I'd love to bring you on a road trip, a lot of wives do it once or twice a year, and the impossibility of it makes me sad.
>
> All of this is just a long-winded way of saying I need to return to St. Louis.
>
> Keep waiting for me, Aully. Keep waiting. I'll be back soon.
>
> I love you,
>
> Ray

July 1941

Dear Ray,

I'll start simply this time – I love you!

There, I feel better and I hope you feel better after reading it. We have much to learn about each other as we move through this wonderful romance. I think it's much like a baseball game or just the sport in general—we have to keep playing, move forward, learn as much as we can each day, and take that with us as we continue to love one another.

What is it they say about the game, you need to grow up with it?

I journeyed over to the newsstand at Union Station yesterday to pick up a Post-Dispatch, knowing you had pitched and won the game. The writeup was very nice, including things like "Cavanaugh stymied the Indians" and "After striking out Wilson for the second time, Cavanaugh took the return throw from his catcher and gestured for the next batter, Gellard, to enter the box."

Did you really do that? Sounds like something the pitchers in the Negro Leagues would do—Ha Ha! For your enjoyment, I clipped out the article and underlined all the wonderful things that awful writer had to say about you and the Browns.

My mother is still angry with me about you, and Lonnie asked if I had talked to you recently. I simply tell them that we're friends and you have problems (again, ha ha). Or maybe I'm your problem, and you are mine.

So my love, I hope this letter finds you. I always think it is amazing I'm able to get this to your hotel in the city the Browns are playing in while you are still there.

Be safe on the trip home, I'm very anxious to see and hold you!

All my love,

Aulette

It was never anything that Ray thought was real—love. He knew his dad never loved his mother, and while at times he felt that maybe she loved Big Jack, most of the time he knew she hated him even more than he did. Love. He had heard almost every woman he had ever met, talked to, or screwed, talk of love, even after he was done having sex with them, even when they had to know he never wanted anything to ever do with them again. Love.

Thoughts of Myra Hooper floated across his brain, an image of her soft face and big breasts caused a slight tinge of sadness, but then he remembered her grating voice, her empty heart, the sad confession of her broken soul as she told him her father had raped her, and how she let it go on for several years. He had always supposed he loved her, but...

No. No, he didn't.

Aulette was like no one he had ever experienced—warm and cool, soft yet firm—and fresh. An indescribable, absolute joy to his senses. When he kissed her, eyes shut and heart soaring, he felt the unmistakable rapture of a woman who loved like no other ever could, or should.

For Aulette, Ray's overwhelming masculinity seemed to melt into a basic essence of manhood—she wanted him but wasn't sure that she could ever really have him, regardless of the taboo nature of the two of them together. Sex was one thing, having one another was something else, something that wasn't supposed to be possible.

The bulb in the lamp on the nightstand was burned out, so Ray left the light in the bathroom turned on. Aulette was standing next to the bed, smiling as she unbuttoned her green dress, letting it drop to the floor. Ray pulled at his buttons, undid his belt, and walked toward her. They both had a slight, warm buzz from the drinks at the club. Ray felt as good as he ever had, Aulette didn't know how life could possibly be any better than it was at that moment.

"Hey there," she said as he tossed his clothes to the floor and grabbed her, swooping her naked lusciousness into his arms. They frantically kissed and fell on the bed, laughing and swooning.

"Oh man, oh man," was all Ray could say, and soon they were probing and touching, kissing, and then finally, when neither of them could stand it any longer, he was inside her.

An hour later they were still going at it, sweating, exhaustively euphoric, rhythmically precise in their movements. Ray felt a never-ending energy coming from her—she felt the same from him. The couple hadn't been together in more than a month, and while the letters were nice, the physicalness of their love had no substitute—they always had the highest imaginable level of eros. They didn't talk much during their love-making, and this time they said nothing. Ray pulled back several times just to look at Aulette's face, and then to kiss her, never breaking his movement, sustaining the pace and cadence of their manic, unreal love. When they finally finished—spent and broken, fulfilled and triumphant—Aulette left the bed for a moment, then returned quickly to Ray's arms. He pulled her close and within minutes they were magically asleep.

Following a couple of hours of dead, blissful sleep, they did it again.

CHAPTER 20

May 27, 1965
Cooperstown, New York

The new season was already streaking toward the All-Star Game in Minnesota, and Frank was enjoying it. The Dodgers were in first place, the Yankees were pretty much god awful, and he had just received a stack of the worthless Philadelphia Phillies World Series tickets from the previous fall—their late season choke was being hailed as the worst ever ending to a season. The start of the '65 season had not been kind to Philly, either—the team was falling back to its usual also ran status.

Of all the diamond delights each new season brought, Frank especially liked assessing the talent of the rookie players, and '65 had several new performers who showed great potential for becoming stars and putting together hall-of-fame careers. Willie Horton of the Tigers had the look of a great player in the making, as did Joe Morgan of the Astros and Tony Perez of the Reds. Jim Palmer with Baltimore and Catfish Hunter with Kansas City were two of the top rookie pitchers. Frank made notes on these players and others, and would check them out in five years to see how close he was in his guessing game of greats-to-be.

Since Frank was thinking about greats…two days earlier, Muhammad Ali (Cassius Clay to almost everyone not calling themselves Muhammad Ali) had dropped Sonny Liston with a supposed phantom punch in the

first round of their highly anticipated rematch—screams of "Fix, fix, fix" reverberated throughout the sports world. Frank wasn't much of a boxing fan, but the antics and athleticism of Ali had intrigued him. Everyone, it seemed, had wanted Liston to blister Ali's face—Ali was easily the most hated man in the country—but Frank thought the defending champ would again prevail.

"Get up sucker and fight. Get up and fight." But Liston didn't get up after Ali knocked him on his ass in the first round, at least not in ten seconds. There was now no doubt—none—that Ali was the greatest.

On the baseball side of sports, the real side of sports, the Dodgers had somehow lost to St. Louis, Koufax taking the loss, 2-1. No matter, thought Frank, the Dodgers were still the best team in the NL, and a World Series was surely in their future.

Other baseball news included the Splendid Splinter—Ted Williams was in the middle of an ugly, public divorce. Frank followed the retired slugger as closely in his retirement as he did when Ted was playing, and while he knew the great hitter probably hadn't been the best of husbands, he didn't care. Whatever foibles The Kid brought to his private life hadn't diminished his standing with Frank. The Boston fans would probably always hold their nose when it came to Williams—he was still the greatest in Frank's eyes.

Then there was the matter of the outrageous cough. Frank began coughing slightly at the end of winter, and while he'd had coughs before, this one was persistent and seemingly never-ending. But it faded and disappeared, and as the baseball season took off, Frank didn't give it another thought. As the end of spring came to Cooperstown, the cough returned, smaller in nature, and even less persistent. But it was there, and Frank felt like he could cough constantly.

Lighting another smoke, Frank sat back and fired off another non-news note to Lita Lawson.

Dear Lita,
Hope you are well. I don't have much news, again,
but there are days when I know I'm getting closer.
Ray Cavanaugh is quite the mystery, and I plan on
solving it. By the way, do you have anything new
to share?
Stay in touch.
Frank Aldridge

✑

It was right after the Hall-of-Fame inductions that McMasters got the idea—a Beatles and baseball weekend. The 1965 induction ceremony and time leading up to it had been very boring because the baseball writers elected nobody—they were following a stupid rule that had been adopted after the 1956 election. Voting on recent players only took place in even-numbered years. Frank thought it was one of the strangest rules the Hall had in place and could never find out who the genius was that thought it up.

"Don't they realize people come up here to see *living* hall-of-famers?"

The veterans committee put in Pud Galvin, an old-timer who played in the 19th century, but he had been dead for six decades. And it wasn't that Galvin didn't have the playing record necessary to be in the Hall—he probably should have been inducted years earlier. With more than 6,000 innings pitched and 365 wins, the pitcher had been a workhorse for his teams. That still didn't change the fact that there wasn't a living inductee coming to Cooperstown.

Galvin's son Walter accepted the honor on his father's behalf, and while Frank and McMasters, as well as Johnston and the other guys, tried to give him and the other Galvin family members the "Hall-of-Fame treatment," it wasn't the same. Even finding viable and rare 19th century baseball items and artifacts relevant to Galvin proved difficult.

Sportswriter Hugh Fullerton, who died in 1945, was also honored with the third J.G. Taylor Spink Award for "meritorious contributions" to baseball writing. Writing for newspapers in Chicago, New York, Columbus, and Philly, Fullerton was one of the top scribes who investigated and exposed the 1919 "Black Sox" gambling scandal.

But that was also boring for the two historians. How many newspaper clippings can you arrange on a display board? The usual euphoria and good-time hangover from the ceremony were not there, and in the aftermath of the unusual letdown, a plan emerged to make the summer truly memorable.

It was a couple of days after the induction when both men arrived at their office spaces, and while Frank was a little cranky from dealing with a crying, non-sleeping almost toddler, Ron was unusually energetic. He immediately played side 1 of *Beatles VI* on their record player, filling the stale air of the room with the raucous sounds of "Kansas City"/"Hey-Hey-Hey-Hey."

"I've got it, I've got a plan," he said excitedly in the middle of the song. Frank looked awful, coughed a couple of times, and just stood in the office doorway, shoulders hunched.

"What?"

"I'll tell you what, I've got the plan to save us from the memories of our summer of Galvin.

"Beatles and baseball."

"I'm pretty sure the Beatles don't play ball, or even know what it is," Frank half-heartedly mused.

Ron ignored him. "We can see the Yankees and A's play on Saturday, August 14, and maybe even the next day, too," McMasters announced grandly, sweeping his arms toward the ceiling. "Then we'll go to the concert at Shea Stadium on Sunday night," and he pointed to the record player. "The Beatles concert."

"Why would I want to see the Yankees?" Frank was looking for his coffee cup.

"Why? They suck this year, we'll get to see them lose."

"Let's just see the Beatles," Frank said without emotion. "You know I hate Yankee Stadium."

"I wanna see baseball, too, and that's also how we'll sell it to your wife."

It had been forever since Frank had done anything without someone from his family—wife, a kid, all the kids and the wife—and he really wanted to see the Beatles. He was dying to see the Beatles. Ron didn't have a girlfriend at the time, didn't want a girlfriend. A quick getaway like a trip to the city was an easy endeavor for him.

"Frank, you need to get away from Peggy and the kids. I need you to get away. Let's do this!"

"Not easy, Ron," and Frank ran to the break room to get some coffee. When he returned, McMasters laid his sad face on Frank, did a little pose.

"You should be begging me to go, Mr. Beatlemania," Ron said. "Nowhere Man" was now spinning out on the player. Frank lit a smoke, took a sip of the fresh brew.

"Okay," he said, pursing his lips and blowing out smoke. "I'll bounce it off the wife tonight and see if it has wings."

The trip itself would be cheap—Frank and Ron would drive to the city and stay with McMasters' parents in the Bronx (Frank's mother's place in Brooklyn was too small to stay at). On Saturday the 14th, they would take the #2 subway to Yankee Stadium for the game against the Kansas City A's (the worst team in baseball). It was a relatively short stint on the subway, around 45 minutes. The next day they would take longer, an hour and a half or so, to get to Shea Stadium from the Bronx. They'd spend the night again with Ron's parents and drive back to Cooperstown the following morning.

Now all they had to do was get tickets.

The baseball game would be easy, and even though the grandstand seats were $1.50 each, they didn't care. The Beatles were another story.

The cheapest seats were a $4.50, and the top seats, which is what Frank wanted, were $6.50— somewhat expensive. After haggling over the price with Ron, they finally settled on the $5.50 seats, which were in the lower grandstand of Shea.

"How in the hell are we going to get Beatles tickets?" Ron asked. "It's not like we're the only ones who want them."

Frank had almost ten years in with the Hall of Fame, and in that time, not once had he ever curried a favor from Major League Baseball. He wasn't good at asking for things related to money, and he certainly didn't want to offend anyone or an organization—he decided, with a big push from McMasters, that this was the time to try.

And it was easy. A quick phone call from Frank to the Yankees secured the baseball game tickets, and then another call to Shea ("This is Frank Aldridge of the Hall of Fame. Is it possible for you to help me get Beatles tickets?")

Yes, and yes. "Any particular seats you'd like?"

"Sure, the best you have available?"

"Certainly Mr. Aldridge, we look forward to having you at Yankee Stadium."

She loves you, yeah, yeah, yeah.

For the Beatles tickets at Shea, it was going to take a little more finesse—after about ten minutes of explanations, rules and a little begging, Frank was told by the stadium's marketing director that they shouldn't get him tickets, but since he was with the Hall of Fame, they would make an exception.

"Why you'd want to see those long-hairs, I don't know," the woman told him on the phone, "but we always take care of our own."

The seats weren't the best at the stadium, but they were damn close. After hanging up—"You can pick up the tickets at the stadium"—Frank almost felt as if he was getting the kind of treatment a high-level employee of the Mets might get.

He had done it, completing a hard day's night of ticketing—he and McMasters were set. It was going to be baseball, and the Beatles, a weekend set up to remember, pending the all-important Peggy approval.

᠊ᢌᢓ᠊

The smell of baby shit was everywhere—it was unrelenting with its staying power. The other Aldridge children had pooped with a perfect regularity that was always fragrant in a nasty way, but Molly produced horrendous-smelling shit that lingered, it seemed, for hours. There was a positive to the ugly smells—Frank developed a diaper-changing routine that was second to none. He was able to de-diaper, clean, apply lotion and/or powder, fold on a diaper and pin it with the precision of a highly-skilled surgeon. The dirty, offending article was quickly placed in a mostly smell-proof bucket.

Peggy even filmed a diaper changing event because she knew no one in the future would ever believe how good Frank was at it.

"I'm not changing a diaper," Frank would say," I'm an artist, a superb clean-up artist."

"Another bad joke, Dad," the oldest of the Aldridge children would say.

Frank changed a diaper—it wasn't dirty—when he got home the night the Beatles with Baseball plan was concocted, knowing that any and all angles of persuasion were needed. A quick pick up of toys, an offer to help with dinner, and then he dropped the plan on his wife.

"You're doing what?" Peggy didn't feel like feigning she was happy or indifferent about the trip. It didn't matter that it was only for two days and that Frank would be staying with McMasters' parents.

"What about me?" she heard herself say with just a hint of sadness. "I like the Beatles, too."

"This is McMasters' thing," Frank lied. "I'm sorry, but what would we do with the kids?"

"Exactly, that's why you're not going."

"Really?" He knew that this was the time to drop it, and since he hadn't told her the tickets were already in the bag, he'd let her know about them later. To start a smooth transition, he grabbed baby Molly and sniffed for a diaper change.

"Bingo, poopy butt."

"You're not going," Peggy said, but she knew it was a lost cause. Frank almost never asked to do guy things—his family aptitude and involvement was very high. Still, she wanted to go, too.

Frank changed another diaper, snuggled up to Peggy.

"What do you want me to do so I can go?"

"Take me. Really."

After dinner, after bedtime, Frank grabbed a couple of beers, handed one off to his wife.

"I know this stinks, I know I should take you, but the only reason I can go is because of the Hall."

"Bullshit," and she took a sip, then a big gulp of the Ballantine. That's when Frank started making promises that Peggy knew he had no intention of keeping—more yard work, painting the bedrooms, even taking her to New York for a Broadway show later in the fall.

Four beers later they were having sex—with a condom, of course—and Frank had his go ahead for the baseball and Beatles weekend.

᷍

This digging around in the past for things unknown sometimes left Frank feeling disheveled, even a little lost. As much as he loved baseball and the vast amount of history tied around it, a needed break from the game's patterned history was welcome. Reading continued to be Frank's escape; his latest read was Hemingway's *A Moveable Feast*, the author's posthumously published work, words that he used to tie into the present-day learnings of Ray Cavanaugh.

> *Part of you died each year when the leaves fell from the trees…*
> *you knew there would always be the spring… When the cold rains kept*
> *on and killed the spring, it was as though a young person had died*
> *for no reason.*

Ray Cavanaugh hadn't been heard from in years, which was strange for a ballplayer who'd had a pretty good career. Where to start? Frank always Went back to his original list of known Cavanaugh facts and obvious questions:

Who was Ray Cavanaugh? A left-handed pitcher for the Browns and Senators. Played from 1935 to 1951, missed a couple of years because of the war. He served in the Army. Where was he from? Some shithole town in Kansas. Family? Parents were both gone, siblings unknown. Friends, other relatives, teams he played for? Nothing times three.

The questions always led to the same conclusion—he had to be dead.

The old stadium held the large crowd nicely, more than 51,000 Yankee fans, all of them anticipating an easy win over the hapless Kansas City A's. Frank and McMasters eased into their great seats, ten rows from the field on the third base side and settled in with a beer to presumably watch Whitey Ford move through and put down the puny lineup that the A's put on the field.

That would have been the case if Bert Campaneris wasn't playing for Kansas City. The speedy leadoff hitter went four-for-four, stole a base, scored a run, and knocked one in—by the time the game landed in the bottom of the ninth, the large throng of Yankees' fans were exasperated and already defeated. Ford hadn't been masterful, but he'd been very good, fanning five and holding KC to two runs. New York only scored once, though, and Frank was looking forward to seeing the losing faces of the disappointed fans file out of the stadium.

He forgot they were playing the gold and green clad A's, a team with just 38 wins through more than 110 games—a single, a double, a walk and another single plated two runs and the Yanks walked off with a 3-2 win, much to the chagrin of Frank.

"That was fun," McMasters said as they left the stadium.

"I should have known," Frank said as he lit up a smoke. "Man, Kansas City is bad."

"Time for something else now."

"Forget about baseball, it's time for the Beatles." They made their way to the Subway and back to McMasters' parents place and began the preparations for the music event of the year the following evening.

✍

There were a lot of other acts that performed before the Beatles took the stage—Motown singer Brenda Holloway sang "I Can't Help Myself" and "Sugar Pie Honey Bunch," and King Curtis did "Soul Twist." The crowd was tolerant of the performers, but there was an uneasiness floating around the stadium—everyone wanted the Beatles.

Other opening acts for the show included Sounds Incorporated, Killer Joe Piro and The Discothèque Dancers, and the Young Rascals. Of course they didn't play, but Mick Jagger and Keith Richards were in attendance.

The restlessness of the crowd grew as the Fab Four got closer to performing. Shea Stadium was sold out with more than 55,000 crazy fans, and all of them were ready to scream until they couldn't scream any more at the lads from Liverpool. Frank couldn't hear himself think between the final opening act and the Beatles taking the stage.

When it was finally time for the Beatles to hit the stage, none other than Ed Sullivan made the introduction.

"Now, ladies and gentlemen, honored by their country, decorated by their Queen, and loved here in America, here are—The Beatles!"

It was the last real words either Frank or Ron heard the rest of the show.

As a thunderous ovation swallowed the stadium, the Fab Four, wearing gray military-style jackets, ran to a rickety stage that was placed ridiculously around the second base area of the baseball infield—it seemed miles away from the bursting, rowdy throng of fans. The band positioned themselves on the stage, and after shouting "Hello, hello, hello," to the accolades of cheers falling upon them, they busted into "Twist and Shout."

Then, impossibly, it got even louder.

"What I remember most about the concert was that we were so far away from the audience…. And screaming had become the thing to do," Ringo Starr said of the show. "Everybody screamed." And screamed and screamed, yelled, and then shrieked in earsplitting, non-stop boisterous waves. Nobody heard the music, and it didn't seem to matter. When it became apparent that they wouldn't be able to hear, Frank and McMasters relaxed.

It was a 12-song set, and regardless of the sound problems, it was terrific, fantastic. The Beatles waded through, "I Feel Fine," "Dizzy Miss Lizzy," "Can't Buy Me Love," and "Help," finishing off the night, and the crowd, with a frenzied version of "I'm Down." John Lennon at times played the Vox Continental combo organ with his elbows, playful antics accompanied by laughter from Lennon and George Harrison, moving the crowd to wildly shake the stadium with a thunderous rocking that surprised even Frank.

Cooperstown was a far-away mindset for the two baseball men as they left the stadium. The usual grind of work they loved was waiting, but the spectacle of the concert would stay with them for a good while as they cataloged box scores, statistics, and photos from the on-going season.

Somehow—Frank hoped for and dreamed about it during the drive back to Peggy and the kids as he hummed Beatles' lyrics to himself—maybe a piece of Ray Cavanaugh would fall from the lost legions of his undocumented past into the fold of the search.

Maybe.

CHAPTER 21

November 21, 1942
St. Louis, Missouri

The winter weather was about to descend upon St. Louis, and Ray was not looking forward to fighting the cold—it was still more than three months before spring training, not that it would offer much of a difference in the climate. This year's training season would be different, very unique—because of the war's many travel restrictions placed all over the country, the Browns were going to train just down the road in Cape Girardeau, Missouri, a far cry from the balmy weather of Deland, Florida, the team's location the year before. Just as important as the Missouri weather was the town itself—Ray knew that Cape was a bit backwards in its ways. He also knew that the fans there would be warm and welcoming, and probably pack tiny Capaha Park to the rafters for spring games.

It was almost Thanksgiving and Ray was going home to Kansas, home to see his mother, sisters, and brother. But before taking the short trip there was one important stop that he had put off for far too long—he needed to go and meet with Loretta, and Ray decided today was the day to get it done.

It was late in the afternoon and as he pulled up in front of the house where he met Aulette—Ray contemplated not going inside as he parked his dark green 1941 Chevy coupe. The sun was peeking through gray clouds, the breeze was cool moving to cold, and he was a little scared, a lot nervous. Aulette was inside staying calm, doing a little cooking and preparing her mother for the visit—it was an early Thanksgiving dinner since Ray was going to be in Kansas on the holiday.

"So here he is," Loretta said as he walked in the door. She motioned him in and turned to give Aulette a smirky glare.

"Hello Loretta," Ray said in as pleasant a tone as he knew how. "I'm glad to see you, and," Ray felt the uneasiness of her mood like an anvil falling on his back, "I wanted to thank you again for taking care of me after that beaning."

"Aulette did everything," Loretta grunted back at him. "I was just here, like I am when I'm not working."

"Momma."

"Well, thanks for having me tonight. I'm looking forward to dinner," Ray again said as nicely as he could. Aulette had warned of the cold shoulder maneuvers her mother would employ.

"I just made a meatloaf," and turning she yelled into the other room, "Lonnie, come say hello to Mr. Cavanaugh."

Lightning Lawson walked into the front room, looking a little sleepy, more irritated than anything. He stuck out his hand toward Ray.

"Hi Cavanaugh, how are you?" Ray grabbed his right hand and squeezed it hard, Lonnie squeezed back.

"Stealing any bases?" Ray asked lightheartedly. Lonnie stole three times while Ray pitched when they played against each other two years earlier.

"None as easy as the ones against you," Lonnie said with a smile, and for a moment Ray relaxed. What he didn't know was that Lonnie was not a fan—he disliked Ray, disapproved of Ray being with his sister almost as much as Loretta. But he faked it for his sister that afternoon, and his sister was beaming that Ray was in the room with her family. Ray was fooled—Aulette hadn't told him of Lonnie's displeasure about the relationship, hoping a couple of meetings would take care of the problem.

After 30 minutes of uncomfortable talk—Loretta remained standoffish—the early Thanksgiving dinner started. Uncomfortable chit chat went back and forth during the meal, mostly between Ray and Aulette, with Lonnie chirping in about baseball-related things. The meatloaf was dry with a soggy, cardboard flavor—Ray choked it down, commented on how good it tasted. Loretta stayed silent, her expressions saying more than enough—she grimaced, frowned, looked sad, annoyed, forlorn, and basically unhappy from all sides. When Ray finished his meal—the mashed potatoes were also very dry—he gave Aulette a quick wink.

"Momma, Ray has to be leaving, he's going to Kansas to see his mother."

Loretta looked at Ray and nodded. Taking the cue, Aulette stood, Ray did the same.

"Thanks much for having me," he said to Loretta and Lonnie. "This was nice, I want to take the four of us out to dinner."

"That'll be good," Lonnie said. "Mom, won't that be nice?"

An inaudible grunt left her mouth—Aulette glared at her mother, led Ray to the door.

"Let's talk later, okay?" She grabbed his hand, he grabbed her waist and pulled her close.

"I love you," he whispered, and he left the house, knowing that he'd never be taking Loretta out to dinner.

Returning to Kansas was never on his list of things to do, but Ray received a letter from his sister Sissy asking him to come home for Thanksgiving. Their mother was ill, and while she wasn't sure how sick Maimie might really be, she wrote that she didn't know if she was going to hang on much longer. Specifically, Maimie just wanted to see her oldest son.

The old farmhouse was rundown and in great need of repair, but Ray wasn't going to give any more money. Sissy and Ruthie lived with their mother, still. David had enlisted in the Navy and was currently going through training in Georgia. Sissy was still working at the library, Ruthie was waiting tables at a small restaurant in Topeka.

When he pulled his '41 Chevy Coupe into the farmyard, Ray felt the depression of loneliness swallow him. He should have brought Aulette.

She wasn't embarrassed or ashamed to go to the doctor's office alone and unmarried. Whatever social stigma or shaming awaited her—and it would be considerable, she thought—it would not be acknowledged by her, at least not right away. She was afraid and exultant, anxious and eager, mostly just very much in love with her man and happy to be having his baby. When everything was confirmed, she floated out of the office, took the streetcar back to her neighborhood, and after making some tea, sat down at the kitchen table to write a letter to Ray, the most important note she would ever write, or so she thought at that moment.

> *My Dear Ray,*
>
> *I got the news today so sit down. We are going to have our baby! It is a miracle, and I'm still trying to grasp the realness of me, you, and a baby. A baby! Of course, I know that while we most probably will have a hard, difficult road ahead of us, I know this is the blessing that we deserve. I have yet to tell anyone else, I wanted you to be the first to know. I am flying around in love for you right now. I know this next part will sound funny, but it is not. I feel like I need to constantly throw up. The feeling started a couple of days ago and has not let up. The worst part is that I haven't even thrown up yet, I can't. The awful feeling just stays with me.*
>
> *As for our baby, I'm still not really believing it.*
>
> *I hope you are as excited as I am, even though this is unplanned. But then, nothing about you and me had been planned, and while I know this is going to be the biggest shock to my mother, having you share it will make the hard stuff okay.*
>
> *Please don't dwell on what your dad was, or how little your mother was able to give you. I know that you probably won't share this with anyone in your family but know that I plan to tell my mother and brother. I just don't know when.*
>
> *I love you so, and one way or another, we will be together, be a family in a way that neither one of us has ever been. Our road, the one we'll make for ourselves, is truly as easy as black and white, it will just be a lot harder.*

I wanted to tell you in person, but since you are still down in the Cape, I couldn't wait, and I can't wait for the season to start next month so we can be together.

I love you so, oh daddy to be!

Aulette

Ray read her letter over and over again, fighting off the panic and happy as hell at the same time. He wasn't sure what to do, and since he had no one to talk to about this great moment, he sat down and immediately wrote back to his lover.

Dearest Aulette,

I'm still swimming around your letter, and baby, having a baby will be wonderful! We did it. I'm excited and shaking in my boots at the same time. I don't know how, when or where we can set up house together the way it always should have been, but like I've said before, I'll figure it out, it will just have to be a lot faster.

Send me details from the doctor, what you need to do and so on.

We will be together, as hard as that might be.

I love you!

Ray

✌

It was always something they danced around, never talked about, or just simply ignored. *Negroes and whites were not allowed to marry*—it was a law in the books throughout most of the Southern and Plains states, but it was unofficially the law throughout the United States.

The mixing of races was strictly prohibited—they faced its consequences constantly.

For Ray and Aulette, there was no law or action that was going to keep them apart. While most mulatto children—the uneasy and derogatory term used to describe a mixed-race child—were born outside of wedlock, Ray was determined to marry Aulette, even if it happened after the baby came.

They were in a small restaurant close to Ray's apartment at lunchtime, waiting for their orders. Aulette was sipping a soda, Ray was nursing a cup of coffee. He was leaving later that afternoon for another long road trip—the season had started poorly for everyone on the Browns but Ray—and the thought of leaving her was stressful. Ray took another sip of coffee, then pulled out a small box from his jacket pocket.

"This isn't the way I wanted to do this," he said as he set the box on the table and opened it. "But I can't wait any longer." A single diamond glowed on top of a gold band, lustrous and bright. Aulette started to cry.

"Ray," she said. "Ray."

"I love you, and we're going to get married, someday soon."

She almost jumped up, moved to the other side of the table, and grabbing him hard, kissed him, solid and smooth.

"Yes," she said, "yes. Let's get married."

⁂

Peacock Alley was swinging loud and hard, and elbow room was scarce. Ray and Aulette were situated at a table near the back of the large, low-light main room, and although they were surrounded by other couples and parties, they pretended to be alone. They were holding hands under the table, not talking much. Aulette was nauseous—she had been since the onset of the pregnancy—so she sipped easily at a glass of water while Ray nursed a beer. The sweet, bluesy sounds were having a good effect on her.

"I'll be so glad when this is done," she said as she rubbed her belly.

"The night?" Ray was smiling.

"Night?" she slapped at him. "This baby is going to kill me. I haven't slept through the night in a couple of months. And my bottom always hurts." Ray snuggled closer to her, hugging her with his right arm.

"Hon, you'll make it okay, and we'll get set up somewhere that will let us live together."

"We could live together now," she said, feeling and caressing the engagement ring she wore on her left hand.

"If I wasn't playing ball. You know what a bastard the owner is." He took a sip of beer, turned, and looked her straight on. "I hate this, but here we are, listening to the top jazz in the city, hell the country, and soon enough you'll have the baby. I'll get you a place before it comes so you can finally leave your mother."

"It's not that easy, Ray. She's not going to like it, and she hates you."

"That'll change when the baby comes. She'll want to see it all the time, and to do that, she'll have to see me. I'll make it work, I promise." He leaned into her, kissing her hard on the lips, tightened up the hug.

She responded, kissing back, whispering, "I love you."

When they separated, Ray casually looked off to his left and saw the three men staring and pointing at them, confused, amused, and bewildered looks on their faces.

"Shit, oh goddamn shit."

Three of his teammates, a pitcher and two infielders, were standing, not more than 40 feet away, watching the tender moment between the two lovers in the highly-charged musical atmosphere of the club. What they could have possibly been doing there was beyond anything Ray could imagine. They regularly referred to jazz as nigger music played by coon bunnies and jig-a-boos.

The two infielders were marginal players and had been with the Browns for less than two years each. Both were constantly complaining "about the goddamn niggers in St. Louis"—Ray hardly spoke to either of them. The pitcher, though, was a problem. A ten-year veteran, he was a wily righty who could place the ball perfectly around the plate for two or three innings before getting bombed—he'd won just six games the last season and a half—and was always asking Ray for advice. The three players locked in on the couple, nodded, and said something to each other.

"What's wrong Ray?" Aulette saw fear blanket his face.

"Teammates. Shit." The joy on Aulette's face vanished in an instant, and she started to get up.

"I'm going to the ladies' room."

"No, wait." But she was up and moving, and quickly disappeared into the Ladies Room at the back of the club as the three teammates, almost running, advanced to the table.

"Hey Rock, what are you doing here with the nigger?" one infielder said, looking back to where Aulette disappeared into the bathroom.

"She's kind of chubby," and the pitcher smirked. "Almost fat.

"You look pretty chummy with her. Is she a whore?" Infielder number two said. "What are you doing with a whore?" All three snickered.

The questions, spoken in a mean-spirited jest, rattled Ray, and as his anger started to soar, he tried looking at the floor, then at the back wall of the room. He couldn't think of anything to say, so he said nothing.

"She's fat all right, but not *too* fat. Is it baby fat, Ray? What are you doing with a pregnant nigger?" More giggles.

"We knew you were a little strange, wow." Then the pitcher leaned in, a few feet from Ray's face. "Shit. Did you knock up a nigger?"

Finally, Ray found the words he needed. "Sorry guys, but we were just leaving," and as Aulette walked tentatively out of the bathroom—her pregnant body illuminated by the backlight of the cloak room as she passed it—Ray walked to her, motioned to the front of the club, and they left without looking back at his surprised and startled teammates. He put his arm around her as they left the building.

"Gonna give it to her again, Rock?" infielder number two yelled after them. "Give it good!"

CHAPTER 22

July 11, 1943
St. Louis, Missouri

The two lovers moved through the pregnancy carefully, and while they were able to be together as much as possible, it was never enough. Aulette hid her expectant state from her mother and the school for as long as she could—Loretta didn't talk to her for more than a week after her daughter finally told her. At the Sumner School, no words were ever exchanged on the subject, and Aulette put off any thoughts of what she would do about teaching in the fall—she just wanted the baby to come.

A couple of weeks earlier the two had been seen together at Peacock Alley—as a couple—and Ray had lived in a panicked state ever since. It left Aulette in a poor state of mind, too, but she didn't have to face the players. Ray never mentioned the meeting to the three players, who stayed away from the lefty pitcher—he noticed over the course of ten days or so that almost no one on the team was talking to him.

He didn't care.

Ray tried to keep his baseball sense floating in a workable way, thinking more about Aulette and the baby than anything else. The due date was early August, as far as the doctor could calculate. All Ray wanted was to be with Aulette when she went into labor, making baseball hard for the first time in his life—he could not control the mental aspects of pitching, and while his talent pulled him out a few games, he wasn't close to being the dominant pitcher he had always been.

Aulette Dear,

The season is starting to take its toll on my mind and arm. I'm tired, tired all the time. It seems that the dirty air from all of the stadiums' infield has invaded my lungs for good. I'm always spitting out mud. The end of the season seems to be so far away, and I'll be glad for it to come. The guys on the team are losers. Nobody likes me but I don't care. No one says a thing to me but I know that they despise me, I feel it. So what. Management stays away, the skipper stays out of my way, and even my catcher, the son-of-a-bitch Turner, hardly acts like I'm around. So be it. If I can figure out how to pull it off, I'll leave the game and we will head somewhere and be a real family where no one will bother us.

I hope you are feeling better. I'll see you when I get back from this trip.

I love you,

Ray

᪥

When Ray stepped into the batter's box for the first time, the game with Boston was still tied, 0-0. There were runners on first and second—Collins, the shortstop, had walked, and Glickton, the right fielder who hadn't hit a lick in 10 games, ripped a single to center field. Ray looked down at the first base coach, Bad Bill Billerson, knowing he would see the bunt sign. He thought about ignoring it, then settled into the box and decided that yes, he would sacrifice the runners over. Ray went into his batting stance and stared down the pitcher, ready to turn into his bunting position.

"The nigger lover," the catcher mumbled from his squatty crouch behind the plate.

Ray glared back and down at him, then at the umpire, and quickly asked for time. He didn't get it.

He looked back to the pitcher just in time to watch the ball sail into the space between his right hip and ribs. Ray swerved into the plate and fell on the dish after he was hit, dust puffing up into his face. The catcher pulled off his mask, scooped up the ball lying next to Ray's twisted torso, leaned down close to his face, and snarled at him again, low in volume, but high in animosity.

"Nigger fucker."

Ignoring the pain in his side, Ray popped up and threw a perfect jump punch on the catcher's jaw before he could pull his mask back on, a shot that both stymied and knocked down the pudgy player.

Ray stood over the bully, racist cracker of a backstop, then spit in his face.

"Son-of-a-bitch!" the catcher yelled. "Cocksucker!"

The Red Sox piled out of their dugout, ready to brawl—a few Browns trotted out, ready for nothing, but wanting to get a closer view of the Boston players punching and kicking Cavanaugh. Three hard shots to Ray's face, a couple of kicks to his ribs, and then the infield umpires, who had rushed in when the benches spilled onto the grass, started to pull the players away. The Home plate Blue had ahold of Ray, yanking him up out of the dirt, and pulling hard on his right arm.

"You're out of here. Out!" the ump's face was six inches from Ray's forehead.

"What?" Ray was holding the side of his head with his left arm, and then he felt to make sure his teeth were still intact. They were.

"He hit me! Hit me on purpose!" Ray swirled back around, looking for his manager, who was slowly glancing around the infield, his hands jammed into the back pockets of his gray flannel pants.

"Out!"

The small skirmishes across the front part of the infield around home plate were mostly for show, at least by the Browns, and once Ray had been ejected, the fighting stopped.

"Did you hear what he said?

⊷

Ray only went to the General Manager's office once or twice a year, and that was to sign his contract—actually, to haggle over the small amount of money the bastard wanted to pay him, and then to put his signature on the piece of paper. After his first great season in 1937, Ray started asking for at least $20,000 more than he knew he could get, and two years earlier he knew the old man gave him a lot more than he wanted to. Ray put people in the seats, and when your club loses games—a shit bucket full of games year in, year out—one star player is worth the extra cash, small as it might be.

At least Ray always figured it was that way.

The unexpected call to the office caught him off guard—it came the day after the fight with the Red Sox—and while he could only imagine what it was the old man wanted to talk to him about, in his heart he knew. And it wasn't the fight.

"Ray, I've always liked you, always wanted to give you the extra stuff needed so you could present yourself the way a star needs to, I've heard reports that you were seen in public with a negro woman, a pregnant negro woman." Ray said nothing. "Is that true?" Again, nothing from Cavanaugh. "Is the pregnant woman *your* pregnant woman?" Ray remained speechless, but by now he was glowering at the old baseball man, his eyes locked hard into the faded brown irises of the GM, who continued his questioning.

"Unacceptable. This is unacceptable. You are a representative of the Browns, a representative of St. Louis." And he gave his star pitcher a killing dagger look. "Was that negro with you?"

Finally, Ray spoke. Still very sore from the punches and kicks, he didn't want his GM to think he was hurting. "I play baseball, Mr. Harper. What I do, who I do it with, is my business." He knew that it was a hopeless argument. If he had been holding a baseball, it would've been stuck in Harper's right ear.

"No, it isn't." Harper said slowly, carefully. "Ray, you've always been a wonderful player. I needed you to be a wonderful man, too." Ray stood, thought about spitting on the old son-of-a-bitch's desk, stopped himself. "We're at war, son. War," Harper preached. "Running around with niggers is not the message we want to show the good people of St. Louis during this trying time.

"You disgust me."

Ray stood, and ignoring the small aches and pains running through most of his body, quickly left the small office.

⁓

The clubhouse at Sportsman's Park was almost empty—it was two days before the 1943 All-Star game in Philadelphia, and a week after he'd met with the GM. Ray wasn't playing in the Summer Classic, and he was glad for it. The ballpark, without a bustling, rowdy baseball crowd, always had the feel of a dilapidated structure—the glamor of major league baseball seemed an improbable impossibility at the old stadium. Knowing no one would be around, Ray came to the ballpark to pick up his mail, maybe a couple of personal items. He was flipping through the small stack of fan letters, and hate mail, that had been left in his locker when Dave Paulson, a sportswriter with the Globe-Democrat, strolled in. Wearing an ill-fitting, light-gray pinstripe suit, a big smile busted across his homely face when he saw Cavanaugh.

"Good luck in Washington," Paulson said, still standing close to the entrance to the room. Ray looked over at him, didn't say anything. "Think you'll like DC?" the sportswriter continued with a chuckle. He was almost laughing.

"What?" The comment confused Ray.

"DC. The Senators. Your new team. Think you'll like it there?"

"What are you talking about?"

"Traded. They traded you." Paulson maintained his grin.

Ray was going to the Washington Senators—the Browns were only able to get a couple of mediocre pitchers and a minor leaguer for their star pitcher.

⁓

Dear Ray,

It should be any day now. How I long for the sight of your face, the feel of your touch, the strength of your arms. I am so big I don't recognize myself, but soon, I hope, the baby will be here. I have selected a couple of names for the baby, boy and girl, and wanted to let you know what they are. For a girl I choose Lita, a joyful combination of light and dark, just like us. For a boy I was thinking of Sage, I don't know why. My mother is still cold and I know she will not allow me to be with you. It seems that with the exception of the baby, everyone is against us.

Will we ever be together? Can we be together? I have been so sad these past months. It seems it is all I think about. I've been feeling awful most of the time. I just wish I could throw up.

Lots of Love,

Aulette

Her note filled Ray with his more of his perpetual Washington sadness; he called it the DC blues—love wasn't supposed to be like this. He quickly wrote a short letter to Aulette, focusing on positive thoughts and his remote baby preparation.

Dear Aulette,

There are some mornings when I wake up and I think I'm with you, then I remember I'm in DC and that I play for the stinking Senators. It's just as hard for me as it is for you, the being apart stuff. I'm going out of my head most of the time and trying to pitch with you and the baby in my thoughts is hard, the hardest thing I've ever done. The guys on the team still don't want much to do with me. I hear them talk, I hear their name calling. It's a good thing it doesn't bother me much.

I went to the nearest bookstore I could find and picked out a baby book. I've been flipping through the pages, seeing us in the words and images. It's very nice, and I can't wait to show you.

Stay with this a while longer my dear, and soon enough the three of us will be together as one.

Love and more,

Ray

Book of Baby Mine was a baby book to track the early life of a newborn—filled with advice, poems, musings, love, places to fill in information about a new baby, and sentimental writings, it was a sentimental joy. Ray flipped through the pages almost every day after he purchased the book, reading the passages, finding a way to connect everything with Aulette and his soon-to-arrive baby. He knew she would love it. He would imagine the names Sage or Lita in the lines, wondering about weight, height, and everything else.

> *And long I dreamed in a leafy bower,*
> *My pillow a sweet magnolia flower,*
> *That's why my neck is wary and white,*
> *And fragrant and pure for your delight.*

> *I found a bud on a small rose tree,*
> *And loved it so much that it grew to me.*
> *This sweet little trifle you call a nose,*
> *Is really the bud of a little pink rose.*

Aulette was not prepared when her water broke in the early morning on August 21, and as the contractions began minutes later, she panicked. She was at home, thankfully, and somehow contacted her mother on the phone. The people Loretta worked for were accommodating to family needs, and within a half hour, she was home, and taking her bundled up, ready-to-burst and rattled daughter to the Homer G. Phillips Hospital in the Ville neighborhood, the only hospital available for negroes in St. Louis.

It was a bumpy, hard ride in the taxi for Aulette, and by the time they reached the hospital, she knew something was not right, and as overwhelming feelings of unknown calamity enveloped her, she became very frightened and scared. The panic was understandable—Aulette yearned desperately for Ray. As they made the drive to the hospital, small tears sprinkled down her face as thoughts of him flooded her consciousness.

"Momma, can you get Ray? Can you find him?" and with a ringing desperation, she pleaded, "Contact him? Please? I need Ray!"

Loretta harrumphed an unrecognizable answer to her daughter, ignoring the pleading. Aulette finally stopped talking, held tight to her big belly, and squeezed back the pain. The taxi driver looked back at the two a couple of times.

"Hang on, we're almost there." He got the cab to the hospital as fast as he could, even helped Aulette into the building. Once inside the front lobby area of the hospital, Loretta was able to get the check-in process done without a hitch—the nurse rushed them to a delivery room and Aulette was prepped for birthing. The contractions were coming fast now, and when they checked, she was dilated at 8 cm.

The baby, all were assured, should arrive quickly.

It didn't. Then the pain jumped up, and this time it stayed at the same level for several-minute intervals. Aulette's labor went on and on and on—ten hours. The pain was excruciating, indescribable in the relentless agony it placed on Aulette—the doctor was called in several times, and still—*still*—the baby persisted in not arriving.

"Ray, Ray," Aulette called for most of the ten hours through her agony-riddled pain, crying, and hard-breathing sniffles.

"I want Ray."

The murmurs throughout the room—the doctor and nurses looked at each other with confusion—resolved nothing. Loretta was in the waiting room with the expectant fathers and families of other birthing women, oblivious to Aulette's cries.

"Ray, please," and at one point during the labor Aulette let out a blood-curdling scream, not from the never-ending pain of contractions, but from the emptiness of her broken and battered heart. She went into hallucinations several times throughout the course of the labor, each time imagining that Ray was by her side, holding her hand, dabbing sweat from her brow. She could almost hear his voice....

When it seemed that there was never going to be a birth, a longer, louder, pain-filled gush of noise came from Aulette—a full 12 seconds of screaming—and a beautiful baby girl popped forth into the world, eyes tightly closed, skin shimmering, a small amount of delightful black hair crowned perfectly atop an immaculate, gorgeous face.

The baby only cried for a few seconds.

Carefully cradling the freshly washed and medically checked baby (ears, eyes, heart in order) in her loving arms, Aulette cried with tears from the unholy combination of joy and bitter sadness.

"Oh, Ray…"

❧

It had been a brutal pregnancy. Aulette threw up a couple of times four weeks in, but even though the nausea was unrelenting for the duration of the pregnancy—a perpetual state of needing to vomit engulfed her—she didn't throw up again. Other common pregnancy maladies, however, descended upon her like soldiers going to a USO show—heartburn, headaches, constipation, hemorrhoids, and dry skin. Reassured many times over by her doctor that no, nothing was wrong, it didn't matter. Every sleepless night from horrific heartburn, many painful bowel movements, and pounding headaches kept Aulette in a dismal mood and under her imaginary cloud of doom. Without Ray—she only saw him twice the first four months of the pregnancy, and then not all—the world was dark, cold, and foreboding. She had always felt lonely and alone, but he had removed those feelings. They were back now, brutal in their permanent feel and hold.

Ray knew the time of the birth was approaching. In Philadelphia, he was bombed and out of the game by the third inning. In Chicago, he hit three batters in a row and was removed. Back in D.C., making just this second home start for the Senators, he held on and was going to get a win, but three walks and a hit batter brought home the tying run for the Indians in the eighth, and a bloop single brought in the winning run for the Indians.

As Ray's mind continued to swim around and around the pending birth of his child, he knew that his need to be with Aulette would go unfulfilled. He received a brief letter from her on the 20th, but that was it.

Dearest Ray,

I'm sure your daddy time is almost here, and it can't come soon enough. I'm miserable, but more from being without you than the baby. Come home soon, please? I need you, and our baby needs you. Write back soon.

All my love,

Aulette

For whatever reason, he waited a couple of days to write back.

Dear Aulette,

I'm waiting and waiting to hear from you, it's been a few days since I got your last letter, but I assumed you've had the baby. I'm sorry you haven't heard from me sooner, I was on the road trip from hell, and getting back to D.C. is never fun. I can't wait to get to St. Louis.

I hope to hear the good news soon!

I love you!

Ray

❧

It was the middle of the night, around 1:00 a.m., when the heavy bleeding—massive hemorrhaging, really—started. The baby had been born five hours earlier, and Aulette, exhausted and recovering, easily fell asleep. The baby was in the ward with the other newborns, also sleeping, and from all indications, the girl was perfectly healthy.

But no one was watching Aulette.

She woke up around 2 o'clock in a huge puddle of blood—she was losing it in rapid amounts. When she realized she was lying in her own blood, Aulette began screaming with a frenzied, unrestrained intensity.

"I'm bleeding! I'm bleeding!"

The on-duty nurse rushed into the room, pulled back the covers and saw the large amount of blood pooled around Aulette, soaking slowly into the mattress.

"Good lord." She ran from the room with panic, and soon enough a doctor appeared. He saw the large amount of blood and quickly pulled up her gown. Dr. Gordon Meyers had been a pediatrician for more than ten years, a St. Louis native, and had studied at Howard University Medical School. He returned to his hometown to practice medicine.

"Aulette, Aulette," he said gently shaking her. "Are you in pain?" She barely nodded. "Shock. She's already gone into shock." He did a quick examination of her vaginal area, asked the nurse for more towels, and took Aulette's pulse and blood pressure.

"Her blood pressure is very low," he said, and then Aulette threw up.

"I'm cold," she barely said, shivering after they wiped her mouth and removed the soiled covers. The doctor now did a full examination of her vagina, could not find where the bleeding was coming from.

"Damn. Does she have family here?"

"Her mother, I think," the nurse said. More attendants entered the room, and still the blood flowed from her birth canal, a steady gushing.

"Get her to the operating room, fast," the doctor said, and then Aulette passed out—her blood pressure had dropped to 83/51.

"Stat!"

In the operating area, they positioned Aulette on a table, started an IV, set her up on an oxygen mask, and began to manipulate her uterus to start contractions, which they hoped would stop the bleeding—nothing. And instead of slowing the blood flow, it seemed to be coming even faster. Amid the flustered panic in the room on all sides, a quick counsel among the doctor and his aids determined that a hysterectomy was the way to go, but her blood pressure was even lower now, making any kind of operation very, very dangerous.

Aulette was now unconscious.

Loretta had been found and was again in the waiting room, confused and glum.

"What about the baby?" she kept asking, as if it too, was in peril. Assured that the baby was fine, she thought that also meant Aulette was okay.

"Can I see my daughter?"

"No, not now, and you need to know, it's very dangerous for her."

Loretta sat down, picked up a random magazine, and quietly began to cry. When the doctor came into the room 45 minutes later, as solemn a look on his face as Loretta had ever seen, she half stood.

"Mrs. Lawson?" She nodded once. "I did everything I could, I did."

"What are you…"

The doctor took a breath, looked around the small room, took a few more seconds to focus on what he needed to say. He found the strength to look her in the eyes and spoke slowly.

"We lost her, Mrs. Lawson. Your daughter is gone," and he placed his hand over his mouth.

Loretta slid to the floor, lost in her sudden and overwhelming grief, washed complete with uncontrollable tears.

"I'm so, I'm…I can't believe this happened," Dr. Meyers said. He was about to cry as well. "It was a good delivery, nothing was wrong."

It seemed the walls swirled around and around as Loretta sat on the floor, head in hands, the sound of the nurses' and doctors' voices on the floor were gone. She kept her eyes closed tightly and covered, the images of Aulette dancing through her tattered thinking, her happy smiling daughter with the strength of ten women, resilient in her ways of the world. She's gone, she's dead, how can she be gone? And when Lenny popped into her visions, she thought of him being gone, too.

In the nursery, baby Lita Lawson was now awake, finding a little sight in her eyes, focusing on the world around her, hungry for her mother's milk that wasn't there.

It wasn't an easy decision, but Loretta made it quickly, and like a lot of the choices she made since the disappearance of Lenny, never gave it a second thought. She would contact Ray with a letter and tell him about Aulette. Nothing more. Lonnie even thought he could find Ray and tell him in person, but Loretta was firm in her conviction. She didn't want a white man in her life, and she certainly didn't want to chance losing her granddaughter to him.

White men always got their way.

"Doesn't seem right, mom," Lonnie said as they went over the funeral preparations. "Are we not going to have him here for the funeral?"

"He's been gone for months. No."

"I know Aulette was planning to leave with him after the baby came," Lonnie said, staring hard at his mother.

"Maybe so, but that wouldn't have happened," Loretta said painfully. "No, I would've stopped that."

"I don't like him either—still." Lonnie walked toward his mother, bent down and spoke with an angry matter-of-factness. "We will tell him."

"We will tell him about the death long after the funeral. He's still in Washington anyway."

"Then I'll tell him myself."

But Lonnie did nothing, and after mulling over what to do, Loretta came up with a way to deal with Ray Cavanaugh.

A week later, Ray received a letter from Loretta as he was packing for his next road trip.

Raymond,

This isn't an easy note to write, and no doubt you have been waiting to hear from Aulette about the baby. I have prayed and prayed but still do not know how to write what I must write. I don't have any other way of telling you—Aulette and the baby are gone, dead from terrible complications during the birth. There was a horrible problem during the childbirth and we lost both of them.

My heart is broken. I hope that despite all that happened you will be able to forgive the problems. We have already had services and burial for them—I laid them to rest together.

Please find peace with this news and pray for forgiveness.

Sincerely,

Loretta

In the bottom of the envelope, wrapped carefully in tissue paper, was the ring—Aulette's ring.

He held the gold band in his left hand and read the short, curt note many, many times, pacing the floor of his small apartment. He had been an afterthought for Loretta, nothing more than an obligation to fulfill, but his anger could not shield the crushing grief—Ray could barely breathe, fighting back the tears over and over again, until finally he collapsed on the sofa, face smashed into the blue pillow, uncontrollable sobbing blanketing his body. Sending back the ring was the biggest slap of disrespect.

"No, god no," he said to himself. Each time he read the note, he skimmed it to see if he had misread it, missed something, hoping he would not see the word dead.

But death was always there, and the ring was like a tombstone.

Ray had just one photo of him with Aulette, the two of them standing next to each other with some other people from a club in St. Louis, but it appeared that they were not together, at least not as a couple. Ray always the carried the photo with him, always set it up on the dresser of the hotel room in whatever town his team was playing in. Now he held it in his left hand, touched her face in the photo, and cried, cried until he couldn't cry any more.

The Ink Spots rolled out on the radio then—"Don't Get Around Much Anymore"—and the exhaustive burn of missing her, the loss of her forever, almost killed him when the lyrics hit his face—yeah, he might've gone, but everything was different now, awfully different.

CHAPTER 23

November 15, 1965
Cooperstown, New York

The feel of World War II was still present throughout most of the United States, be it in memorials, postage stamps, movies, or libraries, the memory of what the United States had accomplished on the stage of the world, for the world, was very much prevalent. It had been 20 years since President Truman dropped the bomb on Japan, and 20 years since the USA and Soviet Union had officially started the Cold War. That battle was still raging, loud in its silence, but felt throughout the states nonetheless—baseball moved on as if nothing was happening.

When WWII started, at least for the United States, it was different. President Roosevelt made a formal announcement that the game would persevere, giving the green light, so to speak, for baseball to continue its normal operations for the duration of the war.

"I honestly feel that it would be best for the country to keep baseball going," FDR wrote in his famous letter giving the go-ahead for baseball to keep playing. "There will be fewer people unemployed and everybody will work longer hours and harder than ever before.

"And that means that they ought to have a chance for recreation and for taking their minds off their work even more than before."

So baseball continued throughout the war, but the level of play was different. For the duration of America's involvement in Europe and the Pacific, more than 500 professional baseball players served in America's Armed Forces, which meant the game was less than the best, and in most instances, a lot less. The 1942 through '45 war seasons had been well-documented through the years, honing in on the war effort slogans and service performed by the players —stuff like 'baseball goes to war,' 'the stars chip in,' 'doing their part,' and on and on—the players lent their names and faces to the US Armed Services when asked. The game's executives, ever the salesmen, praised the President for allowing them to still make a buck from non-war related activities.

"Baseball feels highly honored that Mr. Roosevelt has chosen to regard our game as such a vital asset to popular morale," Clark Griffith, president of the Washington Senators said of the decision to keep baseball's doors open.

"President Roosevelt's letter has clarified the entire baseball picture," Larry MacPhail of the Brooklyn Dodgers told the Chicago Sun-Times. "The needs of the government are paramount, but I believe baseball can contribute a lot in these times."

As he looked through the massive amount of WWII baseball files the Hall had available in its research library, Frank Aldridge was somewhat surprised to find almost nothing on Cavanaugh.

But he kept looking. He finally found a small newspaper article in the *Washington Post* announcing that Cavanaugh had left the Senators to join the army.

CAVANAUGH ENLISTS

Newly Acquired Pitcher Leaving Team Plans to Join Army

Washington---August 29. The Senators' lefty Rock 'n Fire Ray Cavanaugh will enlist in the US Army. Effective immediately, he is no longer with the team, trading in his baseball flannels for army green.

"I just couldn't wait any longer to help with the effort," Cavanaugh said in a statement released through the team.

"It's time to do my part for the country."

No other details were given for Cavanaugh's upcoming service. It is expected that Tim Reeves will take Cavanaugh's spot in the Senators' pitching rotation.

It was everywhere, the war, and it was with everyone. As the 1943 season clunked to a slow end, Ray knew it was time to make the decision—he was going to enlist. The daily pounding of grief on his chest and shoulders, coupled with the unbearable concentration of pain in his heart and head, had sabotaged his season—he couldn't have cared less. On the first day he pitched after learning about the deaths of Aulette and baby, Ray hit the first four hitters he faced, hoping that the home plate umpire, the youngest on the crew, would quickly toss him. It took a pitch aimed at the fifth hitter's noggin to finally get him out of the game.

The next morning, he informed his manager, Ossie Bluege, that he was leaving the Senators to join the army and help the war effort. A former ballplayer and umpire, Bluege was trying to make a run at the Yankees for the '43 pennant, which was the main reason the club acquired Cavanaugh.

In his first season as the Senators' manager, Bluege was not happy that his new pitcher was bailing before the end of the season. Overtaking the Yankees was a longshot at best, but they didn't have an angel's chance in hell without Rock 'n Fire Ray.

"Have you talked to the owners yet?" Bluege asked when Cavanaugh met with him.

"No, I'm telling you."

"This isn't the way you should do this. I know you're struggling with your control and all, but why not wait till the end of the season?"

"I'm going, now."

"Look, Griffith and Richardson will not like this." Bluege said, and he was right. The club's owners had hoped this was the year the Senators could finally move past New York, the war be damned. Adding Cavanaugh to the pitching staff was a big deal.

"I'm enlisting, if not today then tomorrow," Ray said. "I'm no good to you right now anyway."

"You need to talk to the owners."

"You do it," Ray said. "They haven't shown me the time of day since I got here." Bluege was visibly angry now, standing up and pointing at Ray.

"Goddamn, I knew you'd be a loser. And I didn't want you on my team," he screamed. "I know what you are and what you've done." There it was, the negro thing dropped without really saying it.

"You think I wanted to be on this team?"

"Nobody wanted you, you goddamn sonofabitch. Nobody!"

Ray left the office, then the stadium, and he thought, baseball for good.

The US Army induction center in Washington was a throng of patriotic energy, bustling with noise, high hopes, a few solemn moods, and massive amounts of highly infused, surging testosterone. All the men at the center were eager to join, anxious to kill for and defend the United States. A few were visibly scared, but in a good way. The unknown horrors of war were still months away for most of them, and the mythical fantasies of becoming a hero-soldier were very much present. A lot of officers wandered the building, looking at the new men, smiling while also looking tough. The outcome of the war was still very much in doubt, and to the best abilities of the induction officers, every new man was made to feel that his service would make the difference in taking down the Evil Axis of Germany, Japan, and Italy.

Ray went through the induction process in a fog, paying little attention to the other newbies—tests, a physical, more tests, and finally, at the end of the day, his papers processed and complete. At least he thought so. While the other men were finalized and done, Ray was told a couple more items had to be checked out.

After being told to wait in a restricted area for more than hour, an old captain appeared, smiling.

"Are you Raymond J. Cavanaugh?" the man asked.

"I am." Ray tried to sum up what the captain was about, but found that hard to do with a highly-decorated uniform jacket draped nicely over his shoulders. The captain was holding papers and Ray figured he was going to get a final run through before finding out where he was being sent. He was wrong.

"Raymond Cavanaugh? Are you the baseball player?"

"Yes."

"Rock 'n Fire Ray? With the Senators?"

"That's me." Ray was a bit embarrassed. None of the other inductees were asked those kinds of questions, and while a lot of the news services and the major leagues liked to promote the enlistment of baseball players, that wasn't anything Ray wanted. Anonymity was his goal.

"You're a helluva pitcher, aren't you?" Ray just nodded slightly, looked at the floor. The captain continued, still smiling. "Look, I'm going to be putting together a team at Fort Riley, that's where I'm headed, a team of major leaguers. I've got some of the Cardinals lined up to play—Joe Garagiola, Lonny Frey, Al Brazle, and some others. A few of the top minor leaguers, too. How would you like to pitch for the team?"

"I joined up to help the fight, you know, kill Germans or Japs, maybe both."

"What happens in the U.S., the home front, is just as important. Keeping up the standard way of life, you know? Important. And, Mr. Cavanaugh, baseball is, as you more than know, a part of that."

"I didn't enlist to play ball."

"Yes. But that's how you can help the fight."

The World War II training camps were the catalyst used to transform civilians into military men. New service men faced rigorous physical conditioning—drilled over and over in the basic elements of military life and trained to work as part of a team. They learned to operate and maintain weapons, took tests to determine their top talents, and learned specialized skills—paratroopers, antiaircraft teams, desert troops, and other unique units received additional instruction at special training centers.

Ray got none of this type of training. Instead, he was cycled into the Army's baseball rotation of major league players, sent off to Fort Riley in Kansas to play for the team there, and to play exhibition games around the country against other service teams.

Ray did get a gun, an M1 Garand; it was never used in combat, of course, and he barely fired in it practice. For all the patriotic, save-the-world fervor that covered the United States, it was strange to see so many men content to sit out the fight and instead organize, promote, or play baseball. Ray was certainly not content—he had hoped to go overseas and die, so broken was his will to live.

It was common for the top service teams to have past, present, or future major leaguers at every position. Both the Army and the Navy had outstanding teams at several of their installations around the country. There were Navy outfits at the training centers in Norfolk, Great Lakes, Bainbridge, and Sampson, New York. The Army had teams at the Seventh Army Air Force, Fort Riley, Kansas—this was the unit Ray played with—New Cumberland, Pennsylvania, and the Waco, Texas, Army Flying School. The Marine Corps had clubs, as did the Coast Guard. And there were a lot of very good teams stationed along the West Coast.

That was the war for Ray, playing the same high-quality baseball that he had played before enlisting. The games were competitive, and stadiums were almost always packed—more than 60,000 filed into Cleveland's Municipal Stadium to watch a game in 1943—and the money raised for the war effort was huge. Ray pitched a lot for the Fort Riley club, and usually he pitched well—he felt no stress to perform well, and so he signed autographs after the games, posed for photos, and glad-handed the fans there to give their money to the war effort. Most of the players on the Fort Riley team left him alone, but occasionally he'd hear the whispering of a "nigger fucker" comment, but always off to the side.

He ignored them.

A couple of times he thought his service would finally end, but his value as a baseball player stopped his commanders from signing the papers to send him back to the Senators. So it was—Ray appeared in a couple of newsreels for the good of the war effort, and even helped with a big bond drive in D.C. when the Fort Riley team played at Griffith Stadium. FDR was at that game, and as Ray shook the president's hand, he thought of how much Big Jack hated the man.

It was his best moment of the war.

On D-Day, while Americans and the rest of the Allies hoped and prayed for the big break out and advancement in the war, Ray was playing baseball. On V-E Day, as the world celebrated the end of Nazi Germany and the end of the atrocities perpetrated on mankind, he was playing baseball, on the day the bomb was dropped on Hiroshima, he was playing baseball. Even on V-J Day—the war was finally over—Ray was playing baseball.

At the end November, 1945, baseball-battered and down-trodden with the preposterousness of the army, Ray got his papers, receiving an honorable discharge—honorable for pitching, a discharge for keeping his mouth shut, papers to let him return to his miserable, melancholy civilian existence with the Washington baseball club. He returned to D.C., checked in with the Senators' front office to make sure he still had place with the team, and began to ready himself for the upcoming season. Washington was holding spring training in Orlando, Florida, for the first time, and much to his surprise, Ray was looking forward to going to the warmer climate and playing baseball in the sunshine state.

At times Ray's military service was the perfect balm for his grief—regardless of the baseball playing, the army still had strict, never-varying routines. Breakfast, workouts, small details of non-baseball work, and even scheduled publicity training for how to deal with the war-time newspapers and radio stations. Schedules for everything, and you better be on time—most importantly, thinking was not required, or desired.

Through all the fervor of the United States war machine, during exercises, meals, or before and after a baseball game, the specter of Aulette would appear from nowhere, crushing him. A couple of times he would imagine her voice rising above the buzz of the crowd as he was on the mound, her sweet, calming tune of words, telling him it was okay.

But it never was.

Too many times he would lay in his bunk at the base, Aulette swimming around his brain, keeping him awake. Sometimes the baby would be with her, or Loretta. When he'd doze off, he'd have dreams of playing ball with Lonnie, against him, striking him out to win a big game. Big Jack also invaded his middle-of-the-night reveries, yelling at him to hit Lonnie Lawson in the head, and he would jerk awake. Other dreams had Big Jack screaming at him about how bad he was, running at him with a bat. The worst was always seeing Aulette and the baby, and then waking up with more grief than he ever thought possible for one man to absorb.

Like the constant presence of heartache, army baseball was always waiting for him in the morning.

∽

Mixed in with the WWII files were a few things on the Negro Leagues. Frank was surprised to see them, and he ended up spending more time flipping through those files, clippings, and magazines than he thought he would. The world of black baseball was fascinating—a parallel universe of the sport, a universe that he was always told was lesser than his own. Somehow, he knew it wasn't.

When Frank came across a couple of WWII pieces on Lonnie Lawson, he stopped looking at the other things—there were a lot of items from 1944—and sat down. He pulled out a fresh pack of cigarettes and quietly read the articles about Lawson at his desk, chain smoking as he gulped down coffee.

⁓

It didn't take much dot connecting by Frank and McMasters to figure out that Lonnie Lawson was Lita Lawson's uncle, which meant that Lita was a negro—half, it would seem—and the reckoning of their own misconceptions about what was and wasn't acceptable in the world was laid open for examination.

"I think it all makes sense now," McMasters said, looking at the WWII pieces on Lonnie. "It's the baseball connection—it has to mean something."

"Probably."

"Do you think she hid this from us on purpose?"

"Of course. She must have been afraid we wouldn't help or that it would look like a scam."

"What are we going to do?" McMasters dropped the article, picked up a photo of Lonnie.

"Nothing, not a goddamn thing. We're going to pretend we don't know anything and find Cavanaugh, that sneaky son-of-a-bitch," and he lit a cigarette. "That's what I promised I'd do, and we're doing it."

McMasters smiled and nodded his head. Sometimes—not often, but sometimes—Frank would surprise the hell out of him.

"Good," was all he said.

CHAPTER 24

July 17, 1944
Port Chicago, California

He should have been more afraid—scared of death, really—than he was. Everyday Lonnie Lawson pulled long, physically brutal shifts handling bombs, bigger bombs, and other arsenal of all sorts, moving and loading them onto the munition ships. It was unskilled labor—grunt work, actually—the kind of jobs the Navy pushed readily and happily to the negro seamen and seamen recruits. For Lonnie, the work wasn't the worst part—he knew he would never see action in the Pacific, would never be sent out on an aircraft carrier, battleship, cruiser, or even a mine warfare vessel.

He was going to be landlocked, forever pushed to the docks because of skin color, relegated to nothing more than menial tasks. Stewing in his own anger the first few weeks at Port Chicago, Lonnie tried to figure out how to get out of his service commitment, or at the very least, get away from moving and loading the bombs. He quickly learned it was a useless pursuit. A lot of the negro men had been trained at the Naval Station Great Lakes to fight on the oceans, and not a one was performing the type of duty they trained for or envisioned doing before starting their tours. The Navy sent Lonnie to San Diego for training, and he too was quickly disappointed and disgusted—he wasn't going to be a sailor, he was going to be nothing more than a grunt, a cook, a janitor—a highly-trained step-and-fetch-it boy.

With the war in the Pacific going full throttle, the need for never-ending munitions was extremely high. The loading officers had been vigorously pushing their men to move the explosive cargoes quickly, striving to load 10 short tons per hatch per hour. It was an incredibly unrealistic goal, but the junior officers placed bets with each other in support of their own 100-man crews—called "divisions" at Port Chicago—and coaxed their crews to load more than the others. The enlisted men were aware of the unsanctioned nature of the bets and knew to slow down to a more reasonable pace whenever a senior officer appeared. The good fun of the bets might have been okay, but there was no system at Port Chicago for making sure officers and men were familiar with standard procedures for loading. Safety regulations were posted at a single location at the pier, and no enlisted man at Port Chicago had ever received formal training in the handling and loading of explosives into ships.

Most of the officers had no training, either.

⁘

His words had been succinct and spoken with a sense of conviction.

"I'm going to enlist," he told his mother.

Lonnie played ball during the 1943 season, but with the '44 season still several months away, he couldn't hold back his need to become a part of the war effort. A patriotism he didn't realize he had kicked in, and he wanted to be a part of the United States effort to curb and stop the evil engulfing Europe and the Pacific.

It didn't matter to Lonnie that he didn't have to join the fight—negroes weren't expected, or wanted, to help with anything. The black communities in most of the northern cities accepted their much lesser role within the confines of their segregated society and made their own way, but increasingly, third-class citizenship (or no citizenship in reality) was no longer acceptable. Lonnie had always taken for granted that he would never play Major League baseball and it had never bothered him before. He had enjoyed one of his best seasons in '42—he played in both Negro League All-Star games in Chicago and Cleveland—but because he had played in a few exhibition games against major leaguers, he knew he could play with them, and he also knew he was better than a lot of them.

After bouncing around to several different teams after the Stars folded, Lonnie landed in Cleveland and began to play the best overall baseball of his career. He was hitting more home runs, too, making spectacular plays in the field, stealing bases at will. And while he was happy to be playing for the Buckeyes, he began to resent not being in the Majors, and it affected his game. The end of the season brought a calmness to him that he hadn't felt in a while, but with the war raging on, he made the decision to jump into the fight.

The army didn't hold much interest for him—he didn't want to march through mud hauling killing equipment and wondering if he'd be ambushed on a beach or in a forest. The thought of being at sea, however, appealed greatly to Lonnie. He knew nothing of the oceans or water, and he could barely swim. That didn't matter. He had a romantic vision of the water, the oceans, and braving the seas to advance the war effort.

It was the Double V signs posted around the black neighborhoods in St. Louis and other cities that was the final catalyst igniting Lonnie's previously nonexistent patriotism—the death of his sister had left him wrestling with emotions he never knew he had. Aulette always filled a large gap in his life, and without her he struggled to find the daily meaning that always helped move him forward. Baseball had always been enough before she died—in the months since, it made very little sense, and while the pull to join the fight became overwhelming it made little sense, too, until the "Double V" popped up.

The "Double V campaign" was a slogan and drive for negro Americans to support the United States war effort in Europe and the Pacific—for democracy abroad—but more importantly, and with greater emphasis within the black communities across the United States, it was a drive for true equality for Negroes at home. The Double V refers to the "V for victory" signs that were prominently displayed by countries fighting "for victory over aggression, slavery, and tyranny." The slogan was prompted by a response to the letter, "Should I Sacrifice to Live 'Half American?'" written by 26-year-old reader James G. Thompson, a negro worker at the Cessna airplane plant in Wichita, Kansas, to the African-American newspaper *Pittsburgh Courier* on February 7, 1942. Pitched as "Democracy – Double Victory, At Home – Abroad", the Double V campaign highlighted the risks negro citizens took fighting in the military campaign against the Axis powers while at the same time being denied their rights as full and complete citizens within the United States.

As a black baseball player, Lonnie had seen many things his all-black neighborhood didn't have to put up with simply because there were no whites around—segregated toilets, restaurants, and constantly facing the collective dismissal of not being regarded as a complete person, let alone a citizen. Double V made a lot of sense to him, and he hoped that his efforts in the fight against the Axis would translate into good things for the negro at home.

A small, unknown town about 30 miles north of San Francisco, Port Chicago was the solution that the Navy was looking for to keep up with the vast amount of ships coming into the area to be loaded with munitions for war. The Naval magazine was constructed in 1942 after the base at Mare Island was unable to keep up with the demand. From the Port Chicago's main pier, seaman worked their asses off on long shifts transferring bullets, depth charges, artillery shells and monstrous 1,000- and 2,000-pound bombs from train cars to the dock, and from there into the holds of waiting ships.

It was grueling and incredibly dangerous work.

It was also the type of menial labor that almost always fell to the black recruits—the segregated U.S. military liked it that way. Lonnie became one of 1,400 negro sailors at Port Chicago who worked in the 100-man crews, all under the supervision of white lieutenants. The biggest problem with the crews wasn't the segregated troops, it was that they had minimal training as dockworkers—no training in the handling of high explosives and munitions. And despite the hazardous cargo, the Navy placed an emphasis on speed above all else. The negro laborers were given a target goal of moving ten tons per hatch per hour—professional stevedores at Mare Island averaged just 8.7—and the officers rewarded or punished their men based on results.

Speed was king.

The commanders would pit one division against the other, and arguments over what division was beating the others happened frequently. If the recruits voiced concerns about handling such volatile, dangerous material, the commanders waved them off with the same explanation—most of the bombs lacked detonators.

There were 102 men from the Sixth Division on the dock that evening preparing the *SS Quinault Victory* and *SS E.A. Bryan* for the loading of explosives, which would begin around midnight. Flammable fumes from the ship's partial load of oil fuel floated in the air, which was common. Nine Navy officers and 29 armed men were on hand to watch the preparations, and after that the actual loading of the munitions onto the ship. In the water, the ship's giant propeller was slowly moving, churning at the water in an almost invisible pace. At the tracks, the men were having a difficult time removing the munitions from the rail cars because, as always, they were packed too tight.

"Jesus fuck," one seaman said of the bombs, "these things are smashed tighter than fat sardines in small cans. Shit."

Nobody laughed.

As one of the men who had already loaded many, many ships since coming to Port Chicago, Lonnie was trying hard to not think about the work. Explosives had always scared him, but this was far beyond anything like a box full of firecrackers. He always thought of the "good" the bombs would do and how many would be killed to save American lives—the typical war propaganda the Navy bestowed on the men when they began their munitions duty.

"I wonder how many this stack will kill," Lonnie said to one of the other men on duty who helping him. "A hundred? A thousand?" The men giggled slightly, yet nervously, and carefully placed the load on the dock. It was ready for placement on the ship later that evening.

※

At around 10:18 p.m., July 17, 1944, a metallic-type of noise with rending timbers sounded across the port—it could have been a falling boom or almost any large object on and around the port. As soon as the noise dropped, an eruptive blast rocked the pier—about seven seconds later a thunderous explosion went off and rippled across the entire pier area—the majority of the SS E. A. Bryan detonated in a fireball that was visible for miles. Chunks of glowing hot metal were flung more than 12,000 feet into the air as the Bryan was completely destroyed. The other ship, the Quinault, was blown out of the water, torn into several sections and tossed in various directions all over the port.

The fast, colossal destruction of Port Chicago was massive and complete.

The pier, boxcars, locomotive, rails, cargo, and of course, the men, weren't just blasted into pieces, they were disintegrated into oblivion. The barracks and other buildings at the port, as well as much of the surrounding town, were severely damaged. Shattered glass, jagged metal, and undetonated munitions rained down on the area, causing even more injuries among military personnel and civilians, although no one outside the pier area was killed.

⁂

The knocking sound was soft, yet firm. Loretta opened the front door and a somber looking young man adorned in a Western Union uniform, cap tilted slightly to the right with brown hair protruding on the sides and front, stood before her. He had a look of surprise on his face, not realizing until the door was opened that his customer was a negro.

Loretta saw his outfit and her knees buckled.

"Loretta Lawson?" the man asked. She nodded, and he removed his cap. "Ma'am, I have a telegram for you from the Navy." He tried to hand her the small piece of paper as she started to sob.

"Please," was all she could utter, pushing it back toward the man.

"Ma'am, this is for you."

"I, I just...," she took a deep breath, and with great urgency and sorrow, pleaded, "read it." Then she stepped backward and sat on the floor, looking up the man from Western Union, hoping he heard her.

"We're not supposed to do that." He wanted to leave, wanted nothing to do with the negro woman.

"Please," followed by more sobs.

The man unfolded the telegram, skimmed it, then stopped and refolded it.

"Don't you know how to read?" the man said. Loretta just stared at him. "Look, I, we can't…don't do this. Take it." When she didn't respond, the man dropped the telegram on the ground, turned and left. Loretta sat unmoving, watched the man leave and cried for several minutes. She finally reached out and picked up the telegram, stood, and crept with miserable movements to the sofa. After wiping away tears on both cheeks, she read the note.

THE SECRETARY OF WAR DESIRES ME TO EXPRESS WITH DEEP REGRET THAT YOUR SON LONNIE LAWSON SEAMAN USNR WAS KILLED IN ACTION IN THE PERFORMANCE OF HIS DUTY AND IN THE SERVICE OF HIS COUNTRY ON 17 JULY 1944. THE DEPARTMENT EXTENDS TO YOU ITS SINCEREST SYMPATHY IN YOUR GREAT LOSS. ON ACCOUNT OF CONDITIONS, THE BODY WAS NOT RECOVERED AND CANNOT BE RETURNED. LETTER TO FOLLOW.

REAR ADMIRAL JACOBS THE CHIEF OF NAVAL PERSONNEL.

Loretta finally found the strength to stand, wadded up the telegram, and threw it at the front door. She paced throughout the house for almost 30 minutes, crying, lost in thoughts of her son that she didn't realize she remembered, stopping to look at pictures of Lonnie and his sister placed throughout the living area. Finally, she went upstairs to where the baby— her granddaughter—was sleeping. It was almost time for little Lita to eat. Loretta gently woke up the girl, cuddled her warmly, and took her to the kitchen.

The follow-up letter that described the tragedy at Port Chicago, Lonnie's duties, and the probable cause of the explosion arrived a couple of weeks later. It was filled with denials, apologies, and great commendations for Lonnie Lawson's service to his country. It also stated that if Loretta needed anything, they wanted to know, and would be glad to help. Posthumously awarded medals would also be arriving soon. All told, 320 men—226 of them enlisted negroes—died at the explosion with 390 military and civilian injuries added to the mix of tragedy.

Loretta never read the letter, and when they arrived, threw away the medals.

CHAPTER 25

October 23, 1946
Hillman, Kansas

The downtown area was bustling and busy, people swarming up and down the sidewalks, looking in store windows, grabbing a bite to eat— soon enough they'd be standing in line to buy a movie ticket. While most of the autos parked along Main were pre-war models, there were a couple '46 Chevys mixed in with the others, even though they were nothing more than revamped '42s. It was an impressive looking small town—the post-war years had started a renewed prosperity in Hillman. There were a couple new clothing stores, two new restaurants, a second movie theater, and new gas stations at both ends of downtown.

Ray turned his '41 Chevy coupe into a parking spot in front of Rambler's, one of the new downtown diners, and turned off the engine. He hadn't been to Hillman since his mother's funeral during his tenure in the army, and now, more than ever, the small town's slow vibe was very foreign to him. If his sister hadn't pleaded with him, he wouldn't have come this day.

Kansas was still Kansas, unfortunately.

ᔑ

His mother's funeral had been surreal in many ways, changing the land-scape of his personal place in the world—any last connection Ray had to his hometown died with Maimie. He had given up his roots in the town years earlier, of course, but he was hoping to get a better sense of what he was and where he might go from the services to commemorate his mother's life, especially since it was in the middle of the war.

Not a chance.

The usual parade atmosphere around his return was gone at the funeral, replaced by a standoffish snubbing he had seen once before, when the Browns found out his girlfriend was a negro. When he saw the whisper-ing and pointing, the kids getting ready to run to him and say hello, but then pulled back by sneering parents, he knew—that is, they knew about Aulette, however that happened.

When the service ended and Maimie was in the ground, Ray handed off $40 each to his sisters, the same to his brother, hugged the girls, shook David's hand, and left the town to go back to the preposterous world of army baseball.

"Good riddance, Hillman," he said to himself when the town was in his rearview mirror.

❧

"I need something," Ruthie said to Ray on the phone two days earlier. "Will you come home? Please?"

"I can send you a few dollars, if that's it."

"No, I'm having problems with a couple of guys."

"Shit. Who?"

"You don't know them but they think I'm a, I'm a..."

"Christ, Ruthie."

"I know, but I'm scared all the time," she said with a nervous, pleading voice. "Please?"

Ray agreed to come to Hillman and see if he could help. Two men had been harassing her, throwing dollar bills at her, and asking for sex in front of a lot of other people, and one of them had assaulted her, ripping off her dress at night in one of the downtown alleys before she got away, screaming with wild hysteria. Ruthie was now afraid to go anywhere or do anything. Sissy couldn't help, of course. David had moved to Denver and was disconnected from the family.

"Do you know their names?"

"Yes, and you do know them."

"Who? Who in the hell is bothering you?"

"The Smiths."

"Son-of-a-bitch. You didn't do something with them, did you?"

"Just come home, okay?"

The two men were brothers—Claude Smith, the oldest, and his brother Elmer. Claude had been Ray's friend years before, and had tried, unsuccessfully, to woo Myra Hooper after Ray left her—she tried him out, didn't like him, and he didn't like that. After a few years of moping and whining about her, he decided to go after Ruthie. Elmer came along for the harassment ride, probably thinking he would get laid, too.

Ray stopped his car and stepped onto the sidewalk, took a look up and down the block. He figured out where he was going, walked past the new restaurant and went into the Perfect Pocket, one of the popular beer joints and pool halls in Hillman.

The brothers were there, almost like they were waiting for him, playing eight ball and drinking. The juke box was blaring out Erskine Hawkins "Tippin' In," and the two brothers were hopping around the table with uncoordinated movements to the smoothness of the popular song. Ray went to the bar, got a beer, and moved toward the two men, who still didn't see him. The song ended on the juke box, but seconds later, the tune started up again—Claude and Elmer let loose a wild guffaw.

"Fifth time in a row!" Elmer laughed.

"Tip it!" Claude yelled, and the two took a big swig of their beers, then clanked their pool cues.

As Ray stopped for a moment to watch the foolery of the brothers, he heard a couple of whispers behind him.

"It's him, Cavanaugh," the oldest of the old men playing pool on another table said softly. "The fucker."

"Nigger fucker."

"What's he doing here? He ain't got to be here, why is he?" Then more whispering that he couldn't hear.

Ray turned around and got a glimpse of the soft-speaking men, but he didn't recognize their haggard-looking, bumpkin faces. When he looked back at the Smiths, they were looking at him.

"Ray fucking Cavanaugh," Claude said with a little drunken disgust.

"Cavanaugh," Elmer said with a slight amount of trepidation.

"Hello boys," Ray said with an angry tone.

"What are you doing here, Rock?" Claude said. He pulled out a cigarette and lit it.

"I'm here to see my sister," Ray said. "She's been having problems with a couple of assholes."

"All I did was fuck her a couple of times," Claude said, backing away. Ray was two or three inches taller than both brothers, and probably weighed a good 20 pounds more.

"Is that all?" Ray sat his beer down on the pool table.

"Why are you really here?" Claude blew smoke at Ray, who ignored it.

"Let's sit down, boys. I just wanted to see you." Ray pointed to an empty table, and the brothers stared at each other, shrugged, and sat down. Ray, remaining very calm, talked slowly.

"How are you Claude? It's been a long time." The brothers relaxed—it was Ray after all, and they immediately fell into their hometown comfort zone.

"I've gotten a few calls from my sister about you two. Whatever it is you're doing, stop."

"She's such a bitch, Ray."

"She's my sister," Ray said with a lot of emphasis on the word sister. "You've scared her pretty good."

"That was the point. She's a whore, Rock. Remember?"

Ray stood, didn't say anything, slowly forming a tight fist with his right hand.

"You've been gone a long time, Rock. You still fucking niggers back east?" Claude asked with a light laugh. "Are you?"

"How could you stand it?" Elmer chimed in. After collecting his thoughts a bit more, the younger brother took a deep breath, said with what he considered a matter-of-fact tone, "A nigger? Niggers? You are a stupid bastard. A goddamn nigger. You know, everybody in this town hates you. We all know what you did."

It wasn't much of a fight—lasting just under three minutes—and afterward, Ray was surprised at how much blood was on his hands. He knew he broke Elmer's nose, hurt his ribs, and probably gave him a concussion, too, but he didn't realize how much of his blood he had spilled. Claude had crimpled down after taking one good punch to the jaw, blathering and whimpering like a dying hyena. The brothers were caught off guard by Ray's quick ambush, and even though he hadn't been in a fight in years, the feel of the bullying blowhards' boney flesh on his knuckles hurt in a very good way.

Leaving the pool hall in a hurry after the beating, Ray was certain the city police would show up—how could the owner not call the cops—but nobody called, and nobody showed up. The Smith boys had been notorious with their antics for a long time in Hillman—harassing women, stealing small amounts of money from people and businesses, food, or even pilfering gas. Ray's simple beating of the two was a welcome sight for the few people in the pool hall—he knew it wouldn't take long for the rest of the town to hear about it. And even though he was greatly disliked in Hillman, Ray also knew that a lot of people would be happy the Smiths had finally gotten a comeuppance.

The major leagues didn't know it yet, but a black man would be on their fields of play the following season. Jackie Robinson had played for Brooklyn's top minor league club in 1946, could have played for the Dodgers that season he was so good. But he had to wait, *prove* that he could maintain a level of play—Ray followed him when possible, thought it was ridiculous that he was still at Montreal, but marveled at the small tidbits of information that was written about his talent.

After playing against a few of the best negro players before the war, Ray knew what they were capable of doing on the diamond. He also knew that it might be one of the hardest things the country ever did—integrating baseball. Except for a few men in and outside of the game, no one wanted it.

No one.

Sometimes Ray would fantasize about having some of the top negro players on the Senators—pitchers like Hilton Smith and Gentry Jessup, hitters with the power of Josh Gibson and Buck Leonard. Those were just a couple of the players—the Negro Leagues had a large number of very talented players, players who would dominate in the majors.

Which was why it wasn't happening.

Ray also thought of how good Lonnie Lawson might have been, his speed taking control of games on the bases, enabling him to get to balls in the outfield that looked like sure hits. And thinking of Lonnie brought back Aulette—she was always close to the top of his thoughts—and then the melancholy would break out, and with that, the seething anger. Aulette and the baby were buried together, at least he figured the baby was with her—and while he wasn't able to find a record of the baby's death, he assumed that either it was stillborn or it died immediately. Just thinking about it ripped his insides apart.

On his long drive from Washington to Kansas, Ray finally did a little research and found where Aulette was buried in St. Louis. He had never truly said goodbye, and as strange as it seemed, he also wanted to say hello.

He figured that she was buried in Greenwood cemetery, the largest black graveyard in St. Louis, and he was right—Aulette Lawson was laid to rest on August 27, 1943. He arrived at Greenwood, and even though the map marking the locations of the graves was very poor, he was able to find the general location of her resting place. After searching and circling the designated spot for more than 30 minutes, he finally found her marker.

AULETTE LAWSON

BELOVED DAUGHTER
BORN SEPTEMBER 22, 1917
DIED AUGUST 22, 1943

AN ANGEL ON EARTH

He sat on the grave for more than hour, humming "Moonlight Serenade," crying on and off, and finally, as he got to leave, kissing the ground and stone.

"I should've been with you," he said. "Forgive me, forgive me," and as he stood to leave and finish his trip to Kansas, Ray turned back just ten yards from the grave, gave it one final look.

"I'll always love you."

∽

Ray drove out to the farmhouse to deliver the news to Ruthie that the Smith brothers would no longer be bothering her.

"You beat them up?" Ruthie didn't believe him. "By yourself?"

"I know. But I did," and Ray held up his right hand to show her his bloody knuckles. "I need to clean up."

"Oh, Ray," she said with a touch of sadness, but she was smiling.

After making him a nice dinner, Ruthie talked a little about the hardship of being on the farm.

"I hate it out here. Can we sell the place? I want to move to Topeka or Lawrence," she said. "Sissy wants to live in town, too."

"Sell it, I don't care. You and Sissy can have the money, just give some of it to David."

"Really?"

"Go ahead. Call the real estate office tomorrow and set it up."

"Will you?" she asked, sounding helpless. "I wouldn't know what to do."

"I'm leaving soon, but I talked to them when we sold the land. They should have everything ready to go, but I don't think you'll get much," and Ray walked over to the hutch off the kitchen, opened it and pulled out some papers. "Here," and he handed them to Ruthie. "These are the papers you'll need." Ruthie couldn't believe it was going to be that easy.

"Thanks, Ray."

"I don't need to come back to this place, so you and Sissy can move on."

An hour later he left the farmhouse for the final time and drove to Kansas City. He hadn't been able to go to hardly any jazz clubs while he was in the service, and since his movements with the Senators the previous season were watched closely—they wanted to make sure he wasn't screwing negro women—he'd only been able to sneak into two clubs. Kansas City's music prowess was just what he needed to shake off the depression of Hillman and the Smith brothers.

The vibe of Street's Blue Room was heavy and vivacious—Ray sunk into his seat, got a whiskey to sip on, and fell into the rhymical tones, enjoying the solitude that the music provided. It was a great way to finally say goodbye to Kansas and the trappings of family that he never liked.

CHAPTER 26

August 30, 1963
St. Louis, Missouri

She NEVER STOPPED looking and searching for clues, hints, little pieces of evidence—anything—that would help divulge the identity of her unknown father. The question had never stopped burning deep within her core, and on this day, it was an unrelenting blaze on her brain. She was forever haunted, it seemed, by her mother's ghost for not knowing who he was, a permanent emptiness, a punishment, for her failure to learn the truth. Occasionally, she caught Loretta in a good mood and dropped the question on her—no matter how many times she asked, no answers came. Loretta, who had long ago refused to share what she knew with Lita—other than the fact that yes, he was white—never changed her mind.

"I can't tell you anything," the old woman had said to her granddaughter years before, the same as she had three months earlier. "I don't know who he is, where he is. Most likely he's dead," and she always added, "Hopefully."

"Won't," Lita said.

"Won't—what?"

"Why won't you tell me? You know who your father is, mom knew her father. All my friends know, even the people I don't like know." Lita, like every other time they talked about her father, fought back sobs.

"Why can't I know?" she asked again.

Loretta simply stopped talking, like she always did, preferring to apply the silent treatment to Lita instead of sharing what little she knew of

Aulette's romance with "Rock 'n Fire" Ray Cavanaugh. The thoughts of her daughter with the awful baseball player still upset her, still left her wreathing in the anguish and pain for the awful loss of her daughter.

Lita, as she had determined years before following Aulette's death, would never know about Ray.

❦

It had been a couple of months since Lita buried her grandmother. She found Loretta in the early morning—her grandmother passed peacefully in the middle of the night from an undetermined cause. And while Lita wanted to cry, knew she should be crying, it didn't happen, not that morning, not the next day, not at the funeral. Dealing with the burial specifics, working through the details of Loretta's death was not something Lita wanted to do. She had gathered the paperwork, the bank information, title to the house, everything that had anything to do with her grandmother's life was in a little steel box that she found in the hall closet on the top shelf. There were other things in the box, envelopes holding other envelopes, a small photo album, and old coins. Before Lita could get lost in the details and contents of the box, the church stepped in and helped with everything needed to arrange the burial of Loretta.

The pastor, with all his wonderful, judgmental sincerity, told Lita that he was certain the pain of Loretta's death would soon pass, with the glowing help of Jesus, of course. A rotund, strong man, the pastor now had slightly graying hair and perpetual bad breath. He did provide the comfort she needed, and while Lita knew in the end he would expect a nice donation, a small, very small contribution, would be all that the church received.

She certainly never forgot about, nor forgave, the advances he had thrown at her five years earlier, the dreadfulness and shock of the revered man's attempted assault and rape. The pastor never made amends, and since Lita never told anyone, he moved forward—she always assumed he found another girl—and she went about her life.

❦

The truth about who her father was went to the grave with her grandmother. Lita knew he was a white man and nothing else. She didn't know his name, where he came from, what he did, and most importantly, Loretta never told her about the connection the man had with her mother. When she was old enough to understand what it was, she thought it had to have been a rape, that her mother was a victim the way she almost was.

With Loretta's death also came a strong and newfound resurgence of missing the mother she never had. Aulette's death was explained to her as nothing more than something that went awry, an unavoidable medical abnormality, like it was a tornado or an earthquake.

"They tried and tried to save her," Loretta told her many times when they talked about Aulette. "They couldn't do anything. I couldn't do anything."

Lita always accepted the explanation—now she felt maybe Loretta hadn't told her everything, just as she never told her about her father. Maybe, if she could find her father, find this person who might have raped her mother, cheated her, or just screwed her, and then deserted her—maybe some answers might follow. Perhaps Aulette didn't know who he really was—the questions that were always there within her mind had tripled since Loretta died.

But what if, Lita wondered, what if he loved her mother? Visiting the cemetery, her mother's grave, wasn't something she ever did, but with Loretta's passing, Lita soon found herself at Aulette's graveside, mourning her, loving her, searching for things she couldn't find. Asking questions. It was a cloudy day, but cooler than usual when Lita walked through the rows of headstones and found her mother's resting place.

"Did you love him?" She touched the simple stone, caressed her mother's name, and a forceful surge of direction and meaning ran through her heart.

What if she could find her father?

❧

It was in a small envelope with a photo of Aulette at the bottom of the steel box, hidden from itself, possibly Loretta hiding it from herself. A baseball card. Sitting at the kitchen table, Lita slid it out of the packet and gingerly held the card, stared at it with the wonder glaze of a baby when it first recognizes a parent's face. It was a posed shot of the player from the middle of his chest up—a steely-eyed, rugged-faced man stared out at her from the card, looking tough-as-nails, incredibly handsome in a harsh way. The man was wearing a dark cap with an overlapping SL logo.

The name at the bottom of the card below the picture read *Ray Cavanaugh*.

Lita looked at it for two or three minutes, gazing at it with awe, fascination, perplexed anger, and joyous sadness. She looked to see if she shared any kind of facial similarities—perhaps, maybe their mouths were similar, she couldn't tell—or if the shape of his eyes rounded out to anything like hers. Lita tried and tried to determine if this was the man, if this hard-edged looking ballplayer could really be a part of her origin, if he could possibly be her father. Then she turned the card over—it had an off-white, cardboard color to it with black type—and she read about the picture of the man on the front.

---

203.   RAY CAVANAUGH
"Rock 'n Fire Ray"
Hometown – Hillman, Kansas
Pitcher - St. Louis Browns
Throws: Left Bats: Left
Height: 6' 1" Weight: 180 lbs.

A hard-throwing, left handed farmboy, Cavanaugh topped the majors in strikeouts in 1939, fanning 288 batters. He also led the American League in wins, E.R.A. and hit batsmen. As for the future, the sky is the limit for Rock 'n Fire Ray, and the Browns are counting on big things from him. Leading the St. Louis Americans to a first-ever trip to the World Series would be ideal, as Cavanaugh strives to become the top pitcher in the Majors.

PLAY BALL — AMERICA
This is one of a series of 250 pictures of leading Baseball players. Save to get them all.
GUM, INC., Philadelphia, Pa. Printed in U. S. A.

Lita got up from the table, turned on the radio, looked at the card again. The magical voice of Sam Cooke floated from the General Electric receiver, and for a couple of minutes, she sat still, took a long breathe, and reveled at how the man could sing a story, in this instance, a tragic one—Frankie and Johnny.

She flipped through the family atlas, checking every town in the state of Kansas—Hillman didn't exist, at least in this book. Lita looked at the card again, and even though she fought to sustain them, a few sobs burst out, and then she completely lost control, wailing to herself for several minutes. How could her grandmother have kept this from her all these years? What had this man done to her mother? She thought of the possibility of rape again, and that sent an awful shudder up her backside, accompanied by more tears.

The next morning, a Saturday, Lita walked over to the neighborhood grocery store to get a doughnut and a newspaper. She was leafing through the paper, dropped a couple of pages, and when the Sports section landed on the top, the idea struck her. She had been trying to think of ways to find out about Ray Cavanaugh, and the headline on the sports page of the *Post-Dispatch*—"Cards Hope to Make a Run"—gave her the inspiration she needed: She would write to the Sports pages of a few papers—they would have to know where this man was.

After going to the library to get the addresses for mailing information, Lita sent letters asking about Ray Cavanaugh to all the St. Louis newspapers, one to *The Sporting News*, the *Washington Post*, the *New York Times*, and *Chicago Tribune*, just for good measure.

A couple of her letters were never answered—and a couple were answered very rudely—and that's when she decided to quit telling people she was a negro. It most likely killed any type of help she could expect to get.

The Sporting News, however, was different. They didn't have any current information on Cavanaugh, but it was suggested in their return note to Lita that she contact Frank Aldridge at the Baseball Hall of Fame.

"Frank is an expert on most things baseball," the note said, "and if anyone can help you find Ray Cavanaugh, or might know how to get a hold of him, it is Frank. Good luck."

For the first time in her short search for the old ball player, Lita felt a sense of hope. She carefully crafted a short, nice letter to the Hall of Fame—no mention of being negro, just in case—and while the weird-looking letter 'c' on the typewriter made her want to junk the letter and instead send a handwritten note, she didn't. As she finally finished typing the note, Peter Paul and Mary were playing on the radio—"Oh, the answer, my friends, is blowin' in the wind."

The simple musings of hoping an answer was forthcoming swept through her with the song, and after finding a stamp, she placed the letter in an envelope, wrote the Cooperstown, New York address across the front, and left for the post office.

⁓

Two days earlier, Dr. Martin Luther King had delivered a speech for the ages, an oration that Lita was sure would prove to be an iconic moment in the history of the country, so powerful were the words, and so perfectly were they delivered to a country desperately in need of a guiding hand to move the masses from the wilderness of segregation and racism to the unity of single-minded togetherness.

Dr. King had splashed hope across the hearts and minds of most Americans. When Lita coupled his words on racial justice with her own dreams—her dream of finding her family legacy—they meant even more.

"I say to you today, my friends," King said from the steps of the Lincoln Memorial, "that in spite of the difficulties and frustrations of the moment, I still have a dream...

"We cannot walk alone. And as we walk, we must make the pledge that we shall march ahead. We cannot turn back....

"In the process of gaining our rightful place we must not be guilty of wrongful deeds."

Lita recited the end of the speech to herself many, many times—she hoped to speak the words upon learning of her family heritage and how it would feel.

"Free at last! Free at last! Thank God Almighty, we are free at last!"

⌘

Lita always felt as if her mind was cluttered and overloaded, but it never affected her high level of achievement at school, and her high grades not only got her into Harris-Stowe State University, she also earned a scholarship. She enjoyed the school and finally put together a semblance of a social life, making a few new friends from her classes. While Lita hadn't officially declared a major, she was leaning toward teaching—the thought of having her summers free was appealing to her.

And then there was the man problem.

Lita had moved back and forth between a couple of boyfriends, but neither one of the men stuck with her. There was the constant mulatto problem—"A lot of white blood, huh?"—that always popped up. She dallied around with sex, but there was always something missing, and without a complete mental connection with someone, she couldn't enjoy herself— and then there was the worry that she would never enjoy herself, or worse, that she would get pregnant.

Finding her birthright, her true family name, became the driving force in all that she did.

CHAPTER 27

May 6, 1951
Washington, D.C.

"Have you ever tried to throw a spitball?"

"No, no." The question pissed off Ray immediately—it caught him off guard, actually—and he looked at his pitching coach, an old man who in his time was a mediocre arm just good enough to have a cup of coffee with the Braves. Now he was trying to help Ray overcome a horrific start to the season—he was hammered in his first two starts—and keep the veteran pitcher from a destiny date in the bullpen as a mop-up man.

Or simply released.

"Relax, Ray," the coach said. "A lot of good pitchers throw a spitter, and not just the ones at the end of their career. Preacher Roe, for instance." The Brooklyn pitcher had been a winner throughout his career, and while Ray had always heard rumors that the left-handed pitcher threw wet balls, he never gave it much thought.

"I don't need a spitter," Ray said as he spit on the dirt.

"You need something," the coach said as he packed a wad of tobacco into his right cheek. "A lot of something."

"Fuck it," Ray mumbled, and he dropped the ball that he was holding. "I think maybe my arm is a little stiff," but he looked away from the coach as he said it.

"You want to stay in baseball," the coach said, more as a statement than question. "I've helped a couple of guys learn this pitch, and I can teach it to you."

"You think I've never looked at it? They were throwing it on the Browns when I was a rookie."

"And they threw it before that, and they'll be throwing it in 50 years." The old coach spit, a tobacco juice-laced lugi that kicked up the dust on the ground when it splashed down. "Do you want to stay on the club or not? This is coming from Bucky." Bucky Harris was the Senators' manager, a long-time baseball man who spent most of his playing career with Washington—he was the playing manager on the Senators' only World Series championship team—had kicked around baseball ever since, most recently winning the World Series as the Yanks' field general in '47. If Harris wanted Ray to throw a spitter, then Ray had better learn.

❧

By the end of the 1950 season, the mental game of baseball deserted Ray, lost in the wilderness of age with his fading physical talent. The previous three seasons had slowly drained the speed from his fastball, the ache and strain of time had dulled the sharpness of his curve. The end of the 1948 season had ended smoothly enough—he won his final three starts to finish with a winning record, broke even the next year, and had a losing mark in 1950, the first of his career.

When he reported to Spring Training in Orlando to prepare for the 1951 season, however, Ray felt great, at least physically. He had worked hard in the off season at staying in shape, running almost every day, stretching his arms and legs, doing pushups and sit-ups—everything but lifting weights, the taboo workout for all baseball players. He even got a little pitching work in with some college kids at Howard University.

But when he landed in Orlando, he had nothing.

Throughout the month of training, Ray got bombed, blasted off the mound in almost every outing. He looked horrible, and even though he was penciled in as the number two starter on the pitching staff, he knew he was in trouble. In his final spring appearance, he found a little life in his fastball, got his curve breaking with a strong sharpness.

It was an anomaly.

When the Senators broke camp, Ray's confidence was good—he thought he was ready to pitch for the duration of the season. In his first start, he lasted just four innings before allowing seven runs and afterward, he was sure his arm was dead. There was nothing on any of his pitches, and while he felt no real and sustained pain, he knew something had to be wrong.

His second start was even shorter, eight runs in three innings, which prompted the meeting with the pitching coach.

❧

The spitter had been illegal since 1920, but that didn't mean it wasn't used. Seventeen pitchers were grandfathered in, allowed to toss a spitball until they retired. For all the other pitchers, getting caught with an illegal substance while pitching—artificial spit and the like—meant an automatic ejection and a ten-game suspension. The rule was obviously well known, and for the most part, followed.

At this point in the season—in his baseball career, actually—Ray didn't give a damn about rules.

❧

"The thumb, and the thumb alone, directs the spit ball. The saliva on the ball does not make it drop. In fact, the saliva does not affect the ball in any way," one of the greatest spit ballers of all time, Jack Chesbro, had said of the pitch. "The ball must be moistened simply for the purpose of making it leave the fingers first and thumb last. All curves and all balls leave the fingers last. By moistening the ball, the fingers slip off first and the thumb last. The thumb does the trick on the spit ball and does it well."

Ray tried it Chesbro's way, and for all he could figure out, he might as well have stuck his thumb up his ass. He couldn't "direct" the ball, deliver it with velocity, and even though he tried and tried, the goddamn thumb direction didn't work.

Luckily, there were other sources for the spitter.

"The spitball, which is probably the most deceptive ball that a batter ever struck at, is thrown at medium speed," the great manager of the Giants, John McGraw had said of the pitch. "If thrown fast it loses its effect." That was perfect for Ray since his fastball was clinically dead, at least according to the coach. "If it is too slow," McGraw continued in the old newspaper piece Ray found in the Library, "it will break too soon and will probably hit the ground before it reaches the catcher." Ray was already dropping hooks in the dirt too soon, so maybe no one would notice.

"To throw a spitball," McGraw said in the article, "wet the first and second fingers so the ball will slip away, instead of rolling away. It will be difficult at first to control the ball, and the beginner is apt to be discouraged because of his wild throws."

Ray tried it on his own for a while, using his spit. Nothing. It was hard to control the ball just to get it to the plate, let alone make it dip and move. He was ready to give up.

As a last gasp attempt, he decided that he'd just wet the ball and let it slip out, direction be damned. It was an approach similar to what Dizzy Dean had talked about in another article Ray found. Diz was another pitcher whose arm died on him, but he never used a spitter in games, or so he said.

"You don't need much saliva on the ball," Diz said of the pitch he tried to throw. "You hold the ball like you was going to throw a fast ball, with two fingers on the top of the wet section. The slippery top sort of shoot-slides out of your hand, and the ball spins with a forward motion. The pitch breaks in or out. The bottom falls out of the throw and it drops dead when it reaches the plate."

Ray tried this, and goddamn if it didn't kind of work. But, and this was the most important part, how in the hell was he going to hide the wet spot on the ball?

Finding a comforting solace in reading was something Ray never wanted or expected in his youth, but as he'd moved through the years virtually alone in his self-made, protectionist isolation, books gave him a sense of well-being he found nowhere else. He always grabbed a bestseller whenever he was in a store that sold them, and while there were some books that wouldn't hold his interest for more than ten pages, there were some that brought sadness when he finished them.

Ray tried to read *From Here to Eternity*, James Jones' epic novel about Pearl Harbor and World War II, but the almost 900-page book didn't hold his interest. Since Ray had received a bit of a celebrity treatment during the war, reading about the fictionalized and mostly unrealistic brutality in the service was something that he couldn't and didn't want to relate to.

He fared better with other current books, *The Disenchanted*, *Joy Street*, and *The Caine Mutiny*, all bestsellers. He also satisfied his love of Raymond Chandler, finding a copy of *The Little Sister*, a murder piece about a woman from a small Kansas town who hired Philip Marlowe to find her missing brother. Of course, Marlowe quickly finds himself tangled in a web of drugs, blackmail, and murder—good reading all the way around. Ray particularly liked how Chandler depicted Kansas.

"Manhattan (Kansas) is a small town. It has to be. Only half a dozen places in Kansas are anything else."

His favorite book of the season, though, was *Behold, Thy Brother*, by Murrell Edmunds, a baseball novel with a racial undertone that Ray had never found before, let alone read. The story was about a team fighting for the 1945 pennant, but it needed more pitching to make a real run for the flag. The owner's liberal son had a solution—adding a star black pitcher to the roster—and he makes a deal adding the talented hurler to the team. The racist manager refuses to use the black player, but circumstances finally fall into place and he has no choice—the black pitcher wins the pennant-clinching game for the team.

An excellent read.

The book also made Ray think of how the real team owners had put forth the stupid, hideous notion that negroes could not pitch at the major league level—"They don't have the proper intelligence necessary to sustain the amount of know-how it takes to be successful on the mound for a big-league team," one jackass owner had said on record. The high level of racism in supposedly smart men was astounding—but then the high-level of racism in all people was equally surprising. Ray knew the real reason—if a lot negroes "infiltrated" the game, the white fans would stop coming.

Through the first couple of weeks of the 1951 baseball season, just 15 black men had broken the "color barrier" placed around the game by the owners—Jackie Robinson started with the Dodgers in 1947. Only three of those players were pitchers, and two of them had been with the same team. The worst of the slowness was this: ten of the 16 teams had yet to integrate—Ray assumed it was because they were waiting for the black experiment to blow up and go away.

The Senators were one of those teams waiting—no negroes were on Washington's roster, again. Ray didn't know of any potential prospects, either. His old team, the Browns, had been active in the beginning, signing Willard Brown and Hank Thompson in 1947, but none since.

✦

After getting pounded again in his next start, Ray got serious about the spitter, and worked on it daily before his next start. After devising a simple plan to hide the saliva, he was ready to try it out in a game—one of the most important factors for using the pitch was to disguise it by working it together with some of his normal mannerisms on the mound. He decided that he'd rub his leg a couple of times every inning, and that would also be the indicator to his catcher that the pitch was coming. Before each inning, he'd load up on chewing gum to keep his mouth wet—his natural saliva worked well when he threw the pitch, and it also dried well between pitches.

He worked up a routine to get the saliva on the middle finger of his left hand, usually by doing nothing more than walking off the mound between hitters and pitches, and pretending to fiddle with the ball. He always thought he was being incredibly obvious, but the pitching coach told him that he didn't see anything that a lot of other pitchers weren't doing.

"It works, putting it on the middle finger and pretending to wipe it off on your pants." Ray went through a long series of repetitions—step from the mound, spit to the finger, wipe the pants, twice. Then he would shake off the catcher, twice again, and offer up the unholy pitch to the batter. Spit, pitch, repeat.

The Philadelphia Athletics were the first team to get his wet pitches—Ray won the game easily, 5-3, going the distance with nine strikeouts, by far his high mark of the season. He left the field that afternoon with a self-satisfied invigoration—he was so good at pitching he could learn to cheat in a matter of days. Next up were the goddamn Yanks—he was going to enjoy spitting out a win over them.

THE END OF THE ROAD

Ray Cavanaugh Faces Key Career Choice
Rock 'n Fire is Now Just a Fizzle
Spitball Suspension Looming

By Clifford Kach, Jr.

The Sporting News

The angry face and chin-buzzing pitches are still ample in supply, but the fire-inducing speed attached to the fastball is but a distant memory. The angles, ups and downs, inside and outside trajectory of his pitches have also been misplaced, and when he tries to muster a piece of his former talent, Ray Cavanaugh now fails, and fails spectacularly.

The Rock 'n Fire king of the mound is more like a court jester, and the transformation has been swift.

"He can still pitch, I know he can," Senators' manager Bucky Harris said of his old lefty. "Cavanaugh has a great competitive nature. He's going to figure this out."

One thing he did figure out was how to throw a spitter, a pitch he seemingly mastered between starts. In the span of five days, Cavanaugh went from giving up 26 runs in his first four starts—in only 12 innings—to throwing a complete-game win over the Athletics, allowing just two earned runs, and ringing up 11 Ks.

In his next start against the Yanks, Cavanaugh again was looking like his old self, and that was the problem. Yankee skipper Casey Stengel called for a quick study of the ball, and it was determined that Cavanaugh was spinning wet pitches. He was given a warning, and five pitches later, he was booted from the mound and sent to the showers. Afterward, Cavanaugh was defiant with outrage over the removal and accusation.

"I didn't do a thing, nothing," the veteran pitcher said. "I don't understand how or why they listened to Stengel. The only reason he tried to make that stuff up was because I was going to beat him."

This wasn't made up. Cavanaugh was caught wielding the wet one, and it was also suggested he was throwing one in his outing against the Athletics.

"I know he was throwing spitters," the Athletics Eddie Joost said. "I've been hitting against him for a few years and I've never seen his pitches dance like that."

With the ejection from the game, Cavanaugh is automatically fined $250. He is also facing an automatic suspension, probably for ten games.

"I don't get it," he said of the fine and the possibility of missing playing time. "I worked out a few problems with my pitches and delivery and I get this. All because the Yankees didn't want to lose to me. Again."

Commissioner Happy Chandler, who has been fighting his own battles with the owners over his contract renewal, made no comment on Cavanaugh. Baseball's top man might well-serve himself if he brought down a harsher suspension. American League President Will Harridge had no comment.

Regardless, the loser here, without a doubt, is Cavanaugh. Whether or not he can return from the suspension and again wield his former type of fire is yet to be seen, but the best guess is that he'll again struggle.

The rocks have piled up on him, and there isn't any gas left to start a fire.

❧

An unknown teammate left the issue of *The Sporting News* in Ray's locker— Ray figured it was either the second baseman or one of the racist relief pitchers. He read most of it, couldn't believe the shit Joost had said—that little son-of-a-bitch couldn't hit Ray's underhanded tosses.

The article left him feeling pissed and moody. He had given up reading about himself a few years earlier—the ugly rumors about his private life were always placed perfectly in between the lines of almost every piece done on him, vicious in a non-written way. He hated every fucking writer, every piece-of-shit asshole who would piss his pants from just catching one of his pitches, it would hurt their hand so much.

But this time was different. The stakes had been planted around the league and all the years of winning, winning when most pitchers would have given up because their team was so bad, meant zilch. The blackballing Ray received in 1943 was always contingent upon him losing his pitching powers—eight years later, spitball be damned, the blackballing was going to be finished.

In the middle of the suspension—he was supposed to start in six days—Ray was called into Harris' office. When he arrived, the manager was gruff and unpleasant.

"I got the word today and thought I might as well let you know, get it over with," Harris said. "The club is releasing you."

Ray was speechless.

"I want you to know I agree with the decision, that I asked for it."

"Really," and Ray felt his face going red. "This is for throwing a spitter, something *you* asked me to do?"

"You're a real problem, Cavanaugh, always have been. And while this *is* about the spitter, I think you know it's about everything else, too. I'm tired of making up shit for you."

"Making up shit? What are you talking about? I bust my ass for this shitty team and your shitty managing."

"Just get out. Clear out your locker before the team starts coming in."

"I want to talk to Griffith." Ray knew the owner hated him, too, but he wanted to give him a final 'fuck you' as well.

"That ain't happening. Now get out," and Harris motioned to the door. "Just leave, goddammit."

"I know what this is about, don't think that I don't," and Ray spit on the floor.

He left the office, the stadium, and after every team passed on him over the course of the next couple of weeks—he thought he might get a nibble from a Pacific Coast League team, but no—he left baseball. By the middle of the summer, Ray Cavanaugh, for the first time in his life, was running through life without the rudder of baseball to steady and guide him.

⤙

If only Aulette was with him.

They had dreamed together, talked often about life away from baseball, life together as a normal couple within the "boundaries" of society. It had been eight years—he cried sometimes just thinking about her. Ray drifted through the rest of the summer, laying low, hitting a couple of the DC jazz clubs periodically, but even listening to the blues didn't filter away his own despondent and lost feelings.

Then there was the unforgiving permanence of grief from losing a child, and while the weight of Aulette's loss was heaviest, the sorrow of the baby dying—whatever the specifics were—was unimaginable on many different levels for him, so much so that he rarely had any comprehension as to just how deep his pain drilled into him. He didn't know if it was a boy or girl—and for not finding out he never forgave himself. His short time in St. Louis on road trips with the Senators might have allowed a confrontation with Loretta, but he knew that on top of Aulette, she also had Lonnie's death to walk around—he stayed away from her.

A couple of times after being released he'd call a woman friend, take her to dinner, screw. It was a simple walk-through of life's motions for Ray, fulfilling a need, and while he always assumed the women knew they were nothing to him—he liked them okay—he never gave second thoughts to their feelings.

Sex never cured his blues—maybe that was a good thing.

For more than a year, Ray stumbled around DC, not knowing what to do, where to go. He contacted the front office of the Browns and inquired about a radio broadcasting job—hell if Dizzy Dean could do it, then he could, too.

The Browns never returned his calls.

Before the start of the 1952 season, he again reached out to a few Pacific Coast teams—the Hollywood Stars, Los Angeles Angels, and Portland Beavers—nothing. Other cities, teams, and potential opportunities were nonexistent—and that's when Ray decided to move on from the game.

From his small DC apartment, he read, tried to work out when possible, even looked up old teammates. But he had no friends in the game, and no one wanted anything to do with him. But there was the radio and he still loved to roll with the newest sounds. There was also the chance to watch TV, but he never did.

Tony Bennett had a song from the year before, and of all the things he listened to, of all the different melodies, good and bad, this one brought him down, back into Aulette—"I only live for your love and your kiss… And I can smile, because of you."

When he started thinking about how his dad died, he knew that if he didn't start to move forward, he never would.

⌇

A road trip to Chicago with a woman he barely knew started the summer of 1953.

"We will have a grand time," the woman said as she snuggled, naked and happy, next to Ray. "We can spend a lot of time on the lake, go shopping—do this," and she kissed his chest.

"I've been to Chicago," he said.

After two days of her kissy-face, handsy, lovey-dovey ways, he left her at the hotel on Michigan Avenue, snuck away in the early morning, and rented a car—he wasn't going back. He originally planned to drive to Kansas City, spend a week taking in the jazz clubs, then head west to Denver, maybe find a starting point there.

When he found himself driving toward Comiskey Park, the smell of baseball lured him to stop. He took in a game—White Sox versus Red Sox—and by the third inning, his emotions got the better of him. He missed baseball, he missed the game. Still, he left before the end and headed north, found a place to stay, and the next day, as the White Sox left town, the Cubs were starting a series at Wrigley. He purchased a bleacher seat, had a beer and watched the Reds destroy the Cubs' pitcher, Johnny Klippstein.

✍

Since baseball, for whatever reason, had closed its doors on him, the aimlessness that he had fought against for so long remained. He had enough of his savings left to last him quite a while, and after finishing off a beer at a small diner off the downtown area, he made the decision that he was going to live in Chicago.

The next day he found a small studio apartment and moved in. After a couple of expensive long-distance calls to DC, he was able to arrange to have his few items shipped to him.

Ray started driving around the city, up and down Michigan Ave., back and forth between the two ballparks, through the Northwestern campus up north, and to Lincoln Park Zoo. He tried to look all over the city, driving to parts known and unknown, places he was always told to stay away from—the more he looked, the more he liked.

The Beehive Lounge and Hi-Hat were visited frequently throughout the first few months in Chicago as Ray buried his stakes into the city's fertile and rich cultural experiences. He loved the many musicians' easy talents that were spread across the jazz venues—their considerable abilities dulled and enhanced his struggling sense of well-being.

As baseball stayed in his rear window and his sight-seeing jaunts throughout the city helped him learn more about his new, hand-picked home, Ray started looking around for ways to make a living. One of his driving tours landed him in the Cleveland Heights neighborhood, and sitting there on a nice corner lot in the business district was a hardware store, still open for business. Ray didn't know it was up for sale—he would find out when he went inside, and one look was all it took.

A couple of months later, after securing a loan, Ray had himself a new business that was in no way related baseball—just the way he wanted it.

CHAPTER 28

The large, black-and-white photo that hung on the living area wall of the aged, two-story house looked older than ever; a ballplayer kneeling with a cocky-yet-cautious smile as he held a well-used bat over his right knee. St. Louis was embroidered in block letters across his grayish shirt, and a dark cap was tilted slightly to the left on the head of the handsome young man.

"Lonnie Lawson – 1939," was written neatly on the print at the bottom.

Lita stared at the old photo almost every day, then she'd sit down and look at the photo of the smiling, glowing woman stationed on the corner of the sofa table that ran across the back wall of the small living room. She loved the look of her mother, but didn't know very much about her; while Loretta was never forthcoming on any substantial information or stories about Aulette, she had talked and talked about her ballplaying son.

"He was a hero; to me, your mother, the whole city," Lita heard her grandmother say many, many times staring at the picture on the wall. "He was going to be a major league ballplayer when he returned from the war. Oh yes." And that's when Lita would bait her grams, always asking the same question.

"Was he better than Jackie?"

"Jackie? Robinson?" And the old woman would smile, shaking her head slightly. "He was great, yes. Lonnie might have been better." With that explanation, the one Loretta usually extended to her granddaughter, Lita would fall back in her chair or slowly sigh, imagining with all her creative ability a scene of the speedy Lawson sprinting across the outfield grass, diving desperately for the ball and snagging it an inch from the turf to win a game.

"Lita, honey, I wish you could have seen him play. It was a joyful thing."

"Me too, Gramms." Somewhere in the conversations about Lonnie, Lita would throw out a reference to her mother, hoping to snag a piece of elusive information.

"I wish," and Lita would sigh heavily, "I wish that my mom was still around." Sometimes the mention of Aulette would blow over Loretta's graying hair, and sometimes she would just leave the room. But usually the old woman would scowl as gloomy sorrow washed over her, and fighting off tears, she would mumble, "Yes, yes," and move her small feet into the kitchen.

Most of the time Lita would remain silent, letting her grandmother's bitter silence go unchallenged. But not always.

"If you won't talk about my mom, maybe you can tell me about my father." This always resulted in glowering, angry stares from the old woman, followed by hours of silence. When Loretta's wall would finally drop—usually the next day—she would act as if nothing had happened, and then prepare Lita's favorite food for dinner; fried chicken and chocolate cake.

"Eat it up, honey," and Lita would thank her, eating very little of the chicken and almost all the cake.

❧

The man elicited so many different feelings within her—Lita thought of the word "swoon" when thinking about her emotions stirring from hearing Sam Cooke sing, but that was much too simple. He didn't just move her—he stirred her inner passions, his dreamy voice floating easily to and through her. Watching him on TV, Lita marveled at the way Cooke did his little glide-dance with an easy energy when performing "Twistin' the

Night Away." With his slower melodies, Sam would stop, sometimes sit, and reverently tell the song's story with his magnificent singing and handsome face—what a wonderful world it was when Cooke shared his voice.

Every time Lita heard Sam Cooke's dreamy, near-perfect vocal tones, she didn't think there was any way he could be a real person. How could a man's voice enthrall and capture her emotions so cleanly? With each release of a new song of his, Lita would rush to the drugstore to purchase the 45 rpm—with each new record, the never-ending wait for the next one to come out started. Lita's high school years were filled with Cooke and his music—she bought every Cooke 45 she could find and listened to them over and over until the lyrics were burned to her memory. When she was able to finally purchase a new record player, Lita bought a couple of his albums, including his latest, *Ain't That Good News*. The album included a powerful piece, "A Change is Gonna Come," a song that Lita never imagined would stir her emotional sensations over and over again—every time she heard it, it was like the first time.

"My change is coming," she told herself frequently, and she would think of Ray Cavanaugh and the big what if of him truly being her father.

But her obsession with Cooke never dropped off. She constantly searched the TV listings to watch the singer—she had missed one of Cooke's appearances on "American Bandstand" and was upset for a week. She saw him on "The Tonight Show," "Wink Martindale," and others. The singer even made an appearance on "The Jimmy Dean Show."

Sometimes her grandmother would sit down and watch Cooke with Lita.

"I like him," Loretta said every time they watched Cooke together on TV. "Look at that smile." It was a good feeling for Lita, a rare moment of a shared warm feeling. The old woman even had a Cooke favorite song, "Wonderful World." Lita liked "You Send Me" and "Chain Gang," but really loved "Twistin' the Night Away," and would dance by herself to the song.

"Puttin' my troubles on the run!"

Lita had never been much of a baseball fan, but the discovery of the Ray Cavanaugh baseball card after Loretta's death pushed and pulled her toward the game. Almost overnight, Lita became an avid Cardinals fan, and she quickly found a favorite player—the Redbirds' speedy left fielder, Lou Brock. Following a sluggish start to the 1964 season, St. Louis acquired the outfielder from the Cubs in June, and the team began to dig itself out of its slump. Lita went to her first-ever game in July—she loved that the team's best players were negroes. She saw the Cards' best pitcher, Bob Gibson, perform masterfully on the mound as he struck out 10. Brock stole a couple of bases in the game and the team's center fielder, Curt Flood, made a rally-killing catch as the Redbirds secured a win against the Pirates.

That was it, Lita was hooked. While she liked all the players on the team, it was Brock who stole her new-found baseball heart.

"He has buckets of potential, and then some," Cubs' coach Buck O'Neil told the *St. Louis American* in a story shortly after Brock came to the Redbirds. "When he gets going, I think the fans in St. Louis will fall in love with him."

Lita certainly did. Watching Brock play—running in the outfield, hitting doubles and triples, stealing bases with fierce speed and determination—she liked to imagine that her uncle Lonnie played much like Brock, and that he would have also starred in the majors.

For most of 1964, the United States simmered with an overflowing, volatile sparking fuse of protests, large rallies against the chaining repression of racism. Northern cities tried unsuccessfully to quell any and all types of racial upheaval and dissents, while the states across the south fought vigorously to tamper down and kill the increasing number of civil rights protests and maintain their status quo of the racist Jim Crow laws. In Mississippi, three young men, Freedom Riders, had traveled to the state to help negroes register to vote. They never left, being abducted and murdered on June 21. Their bodies weren't found for more than six weeks—the appalling and ghastly crime would come to define not only the summer's racial rage, but proved to be a marking point in the civil rights moment.

For Lita, the murders of the three Freedom Riders were a numbing reminder of what the world, her world, was. The demonstrations throughout the States meant little to her—she didn't expect anything to change, and for good reason. When she was 12, Emmett Till, a 14-year-old negro from Chicago, was brutally murdered in Mississippi—it was as heinous a crime ever perpetrated on a teenage negro boy, as least one that was fully reported by the media. Till, who was visiting family, had supposedly been "disrespectful" to a white woman. He was abducted from his great-uncle's home a couple of days after the "incident," and three days after that his body was found in the Tallahatchie River. Till's young, cheery face was brutally beaten and mutilated to an unrecognizable pulp—he had also been shot in the head.

It was an unspeakable crime, a beyond gruesome action that left negroes across the country greatly shaken.

And yet, his murderers, the woman's husband and half-brother, were fully acquitted by an all-white jury. Emmett Till became one of the first true icons of the civil rights movement, a symbol to fight everything evil about the South, indeed, most of the country. But for Lita, he was simply the first in a long list of lessons learned—don't trust white people, least you also become another dead negro statistic. The Freedom Riders were the newest lesson sprung from the hate of racist Mississippi.

Almost 10 years after Till's murder, not much had changed.

✺

In the middle of the country's racial strife came a soothing salve that would uplift the country's oppressed for years to come—the Civil Rights Act of 1964. It was a momentous law that banned discrimination based on race, color, religion, sex, or national origin. The new law also prohibited voter registration requirements, as well as racial segregation in schools, employment, and public accommodations.

President Kennedy originally pushed for the legislation in 1963. After Kennedy's assassination, President Lyndon Johnson took up the cause to make the bill a reality. Following a long battle in the U.S. Senate, he signed the Civil Rights Act on July 2, 1964.

"Let us close the springs of racial poison," President Johnson said as he put his signature on the paper that created the new law. "Let us pray for wise and understanding hearts. Let us lay aside irrelevant differences and make our Nation whole."

A couple of weeks after the Act became law, protesters in St. Louis tested the strength and validity of what the new law supposedly meant for black workers everywhere in the United States. The Gateway Arch, a soon-to-be glowing symbol and image of the city, was about a year away from completion. Set on the banks of the Mississippi River next to downtown St. Louis, the arch was going to be 630 feet of glimmering, polished steel—a landmark next to none.

What was there to protest? None of the construction workers were negroes. Not one.

Two men—one black, one white—shimmied 125 feet up the north leg of the arch to "expose the fact that federal funds were being used to build a national monument that was racially discriminating against black contractors and skilled black workers." Protesters on the ground were demanding that at least 10% of the skilled jobs on the project go to negro workers. After four hours on the arch, the two men came down and were promptly arrested for trespassing, peace disturbance, and resisting arrest.

What came of this protest? Nothing immediately, but eventually the federal government started enforcing equal employment opportunities on federally-funded projects and jobs. Lita thought the two men were brave, but she also knew their actions would be fruitless—weren't all civil rights protests?

Sam Cooke was coming to St. Louis!

Lita was ecstatic, and no matter the cost, she was going to go. If she had to get an extra job, go without food for a week, it didn't matter. Sam was her man and she would be there.

As it turned out, while the ticket price was very expensive—the best seats were 10 and 12 dollars—Lita decided to dip into her modest savings to cover the cost. She bought one for herself and her friend. The concert was at Kiel Auditorium, a venue she'd never been to before. In the weeks leading up to the concert, Lita purchased a new outfit, shoes, and had her hair styled. It might have seemed silly, but she wanted to look her best—what if Sam looked her way?

A near sellout throng of fans crowded into Kiel Auditorium, the depression era building where Cooke would sing his magic.

He didn't disappoint Lita, or any of the other thousands in attendance, dancing, smiling, dropping his sweet vocals on the crowd with great energy and affection. In addition to Cooke, Jackie Wilson also performed at the show, along with several other groups and singers. But there was little doubt as to who ruled the roost at Kiel—Cooke was fantastic. Lita never felt as alive as she did throughout his strong, smooth performance; the man could sing.

Cooke performed two sets, starting off with "The Best Things in Life Are Free," and ending the night with "When I Fall in Love." He also performed "Blowin' in the Wind" and "If I Had a Hammer."

The night was perfect, almost as good as the day she received the note from the Hall of Fame telling her they would try to find Ray Cavanaugh.

∾

The small headline that ran across a couple of columns at the bottom of the *Post-Dispatch's* front page seemed nothing more than an apologetic afterthought by the papers' editors:

SINGER SHOT TO DEATH

Star Was Searching for His Companion

LOS ANGELES (AP) — Sam Cooke, a Negro Singer, was shot and killed early today by a woman motel manager. The police said he had kicked in the door of the manager's apartment and was struck in the chest by one .22-caliber bullet.

The article stated he was gunned down with a single bullet, wearing only a topcoat when he received the mortal wound. Supposedly, Cooke accused the manager of hiding his female companion who was with him at the hotel. The rest of the details were straight out of a mystery novel—why was Cooke at the hotel? Who was the woman he was with? Why did he assault the manager?

It was seedy, dirty, uncomplicated—Cooke's murder was bland and crazy at the same time. A back-alley, depraved killing, almost like he had it coming. It did not seem real; the story in no way seemed to be about the greatest singer in the country. But it was—Cooke was portrayed as a villainous negro.

Just another bad, dumb, worthless negro getting what he deserved, right?

It had been five weeks since the concert in St. Louis, and Lita had listened to his albums every day, lived the albums, sung the songs, breathed the music. Reading about the unthinkable murder spurred more sorrow in her heart and soul than she thought possible. Lita cried for two days, played "A Change Is Gonna Come" over and over, then "Twistin'" and her other favorites.

The joy of the music evaporated, and the reality of the hollow, lost triumph of Cooke's life covered her, causing even more sadness and depression.

∽

White people—specifically white men—scared her. Lita had an ever-present fear that she would have to deal with them, one way or another. Her dad—Ray Cavanaugh, yes?—was a white man. Should that fear extend to him? Would it? Lita had pushed the rape fears—she now felt she was not the product of a rape—to the side, and imagined Ray and Aulette were in love.

He could still be a bad man. But a lot of the negro men she had met and had encounters with were bad, too. Lita had a different feel about everything going on in her life—Sam Cooke's death and the lost promise of his talent reset her desire to meet her dad. She *would* know where and who she came from.

Sam Cooke was gone, but her new love, baseball, had given her the Cardinals. Following the lead of Brock and Gibson, the team stormed back to win the 1964 pennant, and then held off the Yankees to take the World Series. Baseball took the sting out of the bad year.

She had heard very little from Frank Aldridge, but it didn't matter. She wrote him a note, out of turn, again thanking him for his help. Lita hoped that the note would spur the baseball man forward in his promise of sleuthing for the old ballplayer. When she quickly received a return note that said yes, the investigation was moving, relief and anticipation set in together. She was going to meet her dad, she was now convinced.

It had been a long time coming—her whole life, in fact—and she really felt it for the first time. Change would happen. At last.

CHAPTER 29

February 8, 1966
Cooperstown, New York

Frank hacked out a whopper of a 40-second cough that left him exhausted and scared. The croupy, loud barks were happening frequently—several times a day—but he was always able to make them stop, either by lighting up or just drinking water. Finally, when he could no longer regulate the coughing—cherry cough drops and other drug store medicines had no effect—Frank gave in to his wife's wishes and promised to see their family doctor.

"I don't feel sick at all," he said to his wife, but his throat was raw from the coughing.

"Just go, go." Peggy was sitting on the couch in their living room, in the middle of changing a particularly stinky diaper. The baby was giggling and kicking, oblivious to the nasty smell.

"Here," she said, handing the highly-soiled diaper to Frank, who again started coughing. "When's your appointment? This is getting old." A high-level of irritation coated her voice as it left her mouth.

"Tomorrow, right before lunch," and he coughed again, kissed his wife's cheek and after depositing the poop bundle in the bathroom, left the house to walk to the Hall.

Rock 'n Fire was waiting for him.

It was a bit chilly—a thick throng of clouds had descended on upstate New York, and there was a light fog hovering in the crispness of the morning. Frank breathed in the late winter air, coughed once, and lit another cigarette.

At his desk, he sipped coffee and again read over his Rock 'n Fire notes—the who, when, where, and why of the old southpaw hurler. Either nothing made sense, or everything did. Frank went back and forth over the life, what little he still knew of Ray Cavanaugh, and imagined the man was sitting in prison, crippled, or dead.

The morning was an uneasy one for Frank—McMasters was late getting in, the items they were expecting didn't show up—autographed balls and uniforms from 1938 and 1939—and the topper was receiving more "I don't know anything about Rock 'n Fire" letters from sportswriters around the country.

From Cleveland he got this note:

> Dear Frank,
> Good to hear from you, but sorry, I don't know a thing about Cavanaugh, other than he was, to put it nicely, a real asshole. A couple of the old timers here said he was tough to talk to, kept to himself.
> I wish I could be more help. If you do find out about him, I'd like to know. I'm betting he's dead.
> Sincerely,
> Bob Baldwin

From the Minnesota Twins, who took forever to get back to him, he got this note:

Dear Mr. Aldridge,

Thanks for your note and inquiry concerning what information we might have on Ray Cavanaugh. I wish I had better news for you, but almost all the items we had when the franchise was located in Washington were not brought to Minnesota. All I could find out is that most of it was thrown away, for whatever reason.

Sorry we could not be more help, good luck in running information on Cavanaugh.

Sincerely,
Jerry Nestors
Media Relations
Minnesota Twins

The *Omaha World-Herald* replied with this:

Dear Mr. Aldridge,

In regards to your request for information about Ray Cavanaugh: I have looked through our morgue several times and in several different areas. All I could find were a couple of articles about Cavanaugh: 1) when he almost killed another player in 1933 with a pitch to the head, and 2) an article about the man he hit 20 years later, and how he has had a miraculous life, no thanks to Cavanaugh. I thought we might have a few other things, but no. I have enclosed copies of the articles for you to add to your files.

Sorry we couldn't be of more help.

Sincerely,
Leon Larson

Sending inquiries to the radio stations proved rewarding—a couple of the best things Frank and Ron received on Cavanaugh were from KWK in St. Louis and WJSV in Washington, DC. Both stations had recorded interviews with the lefty pitcher.

From KWK in St. Louis, Frank received this note:

Dear Mr. Aldridge,
We know the collected information on the game's
great players of the past is important. Thanks for
contacting us, we're happy to give you this tape
recording we made with Cavanaugh in 1939, which
is generally regarded to be his best season. If we
happen to come across anything else we'll be glad
to send it your way.
Best,
Francis Dracken
Station Manager, KWK

Frank perused the transcript that came with the recording as McMasters ran to find a tape player. It was a fascinating interview, a real peek into the persona and mindset of Cavanaugh in 1939, and he was hopeful that some small clue to his life today might have been present when he was pitching for the Browns.

McMasters returned with a player, loaded the tape, and as Frank fought off a small cough and lit a Winston, the two men listened to the long-ago voice of Ray Cavanaugh, who sounded congenial but a little rough, polished, but still a little country. Frank marveled at the confidence the young pitcher conveyed. The interviewer was Johnny O'Harra, who was one of the station's broadcasters for Browns games.

O'Harra: We're talking with Ray Cavanaugh, the Browns great lefthander. Glad to have you on the show, Ray.

Ray: Thanks, I always enjoy talking with you.

O'Harra: Let's get into the talk and see what's up in the world of the Browns this week. So—you finally, and I know this isn't fair, you finally have a less than good performance, a few days ago against the Tigers in Detroit.

Ray: (Chuckles a little) Well, yes, they had my number for most of that game. Greenberg, what a hitter. Did I have any strikeouts in that game?

O'Harra: You did, but only six (another chuckle). The other stat you were low on was hit batters—none.

Ray: Okay, I know a lot of people around the league, a lot of my fans, even, think I hit batters on purpose. Let me say for the record, that's a bunch of applesauce (again chuckles). I don't hit batters on purpose. I know a lot of opposing teams think I do, but sometimes the pitches get away. They really do.

O'Harra: You've denied hitting batters for years—why so many of them season after season? And have you ever tried to better your control?

Ray: I could improve it dramatically if I didn't throw inside pitches, but I also wouldn't win very many games or strike out very many batters. I've been fighting this allegation for my entire career, and I wish it would stop. I want to pitch the Browns to the pennant, and for that to happen, I need to throw inside. If we were in first place, instead of last, I don't think you'd hear anyone, at least here in St. Louis, complain about hit batters.

O'Harra: As for throwing inside, where did you learn how to do it? A specific coach in the minors?

Ray: I had a coach when I was pitching for the Topeka Senators, yeah, a while ago. He taught me how to go inside consistently against lefties and righties both. The trick is, and I'm giving away a secret here, is don't be afraid to hit them. Make them be afraid of you. Once he taught me to understand that and make it work, well, here I am.

O'Harra: I'm afraid just talking about you throwing inside (more chuckles). Okay. As this season heads into the final two months, what do you think the Browns can accomplish, and what do you hope to contribute?

Ray: This has already been an all-star season for me, playing in the all-star game at Yankee Stadium and all. As for the team, I think the club can turn it around a little bit. Our record is pretty bad, but we're much better than the numbers, I guarantee it. If we can push out some wins, we'll move to next year with high hopes, ready to move up in the league. And if the boys behind have hot gloves and hot bats, well, I'm looking forward to it.

The rest of the interview was Cavanaugh talking about some of the other players on the team—pretty bland stuff, all buddy-buddy teammate things, but presented in an insincere manner. The interviewer signed off telling the fans to come out to Sportsman's Park for the current home series.

A day later, a tape from station WJSV in Washington, DC, arrived; it was another interview with Cavanaugh. After all the newspaper probes and requests, all of the sure-thing queries that led to nothing or nothing new, the two tapes showed Frank more about Rock 'n Fire Ray than almost anything else.

Dear Mr. Aldridge,

We appreciated receiving your note asking for anything we might have on Ray Cavanaugh. I went through our old broadcast records and was able to find this interview we did with him in 1949 or so. I've included a copy of the tape with this note, and while I don't think we have anything else, I'll certainly let you know if I find anything. Good luck with your future searches.

Sincerely,

Nathan Commons

Sports Director, WJSV

The interviewer was none other than Walter Johnson, the greatest-of-the-great pitcher for the Senators—he was also a native Kansan—transitioned into the radio booth after his pitching and managing career ended. The tape quality of the recording wasn't as good as the one from St. Louis and was missing the first part of the talk. Cavanaugh sounded angry from the first word on, and the "I'm the greatest pitcher" attitude that was in his tone ten years earlier was noticeably absent.

Johnson: …why you did that. So, as you work on your pregame preparation for the next series, the Yankees are coming into Griffith Stadium, what do you want to do?

Ray: I've never worried about individuals on the Yankees, I always look at their entire lineup. Their manager, Casey Stengel, has put together lineups that are hard against lefties, and he will stack the order with as many right-handers as possible to face me. I pitch to all of these guys differently, of course, but it's not like they have anyone as good as Josh Gibson was in their lineup.

Johnson: What about DiMaggio?

Ray: Joe is getting older, and he just came back what, a month ago? I always pitch him tough. And like I said, if you concentrate on any one man in that lineup, three or four other guys will kill you. They are tough, top to bottom.

Johnson: I know you'll pitch them the right way. A couple of other things, and I think the fans want to know about this, you've been kind of vocal about the Senators adding a negro player to the roster. Can you talk…. (interrupted)

Ray: Look, Walter, we need help, as you know. There are 30, 40, maybe a hundred negroes available that would help this club. I'm not joking around, either. You think Jackie is the only black man who can play ball? Or Doby? Doby kills my pitching, and I haven't really had a chance to pitch against Jackie. We might lose 100 games this year. I hate losing, but I hate stupidity, too. Our owner needs to…

That's where the short interview ended, Cavanaugh cut off for what had to be considered outrageous remarks for the time. Frank and Ron were quiet for a few minutes after listening to the tape, and Frank realized that whatever had happened to the pitcher—the war and other things—had affected him more than most of the other baseball players, maybe more than most Americans.

There were a couple of other stragglers of inquiries that had come back long after the original request was sent out—they, too, like almost all the entreats, bore no Cavanaugh fruit. There were still more answers to come, hopefully, and Frank remained hopeful. The rejection letters, McMasters name for the returns that had nothing, were numerous and still growing. Frank started a new file and the no-news notes were approaching 50.

"How can no one else know this guy? Why don't they know?"

"They knew him," McMasters said, "and it seems he was just as nasty off the field as on it, or at least in his later years, that was how he was seen."

"The thing is, no one cares about him. No one. Seems very strange, almost as if he wanted it that way. But really, who wants that?"

෴

The doctor's appointment lasted much longer than he anticipated, but he didn't think about it too much. Weight, height, blood pressure, a quick look at his throat and ears.

"I'm going to prescribe some stronger cough medicine, something that not only will stop the cough, but it should also knock out whatever it is that's causing the cough."

"Okay."

"How's the throat? It looks a little raw, but not bad."

"It's not great, but it's still there," Frank said. Then he let out a little, suppressed whoop.

The doctor was getting ready to leave and write up the prescription, but on a whim, at least it seemed that way to Frank, he decided to x-ray Frank's lungs.

"It's better to be check everything because I can't find anything," the doctor said. Trying to remain calm, Frank shrugged.

"Sure, Doc."

The doctor took some blood and urine, then sent Frank over to the hospital for x-rays. It was a somewhat slow process overall—it didn't feel right to Frank. When the tests were done, Frank felt pretty good—the coughing had virtually stopped. On his way home, he decided that it must be nothing more than allergies.

◧

Through all the coughing troubles, the comfort of the Beatles was still with him, and along with baseball, remained one of the best things in life. The newness of each album, the evolution of their music, amazed him—how could they get any better? They always did. The health problem he was facing would work itself out, and the song "We Can Work It Out" became a kind of anthem for Frank—at the end of each refrain, Frank would sing off key with great exaggeration, a poor, non-musical improvisation, "Go to the doctor!"

◧

When Frank and Peggy were both called into the doctor's office three days later, he thought nothing of it—she was petrified. They waited about 20 minutes before being ushered into the doctor's personal office at the back of the medical building. A couple of diplomas on the wall, a few medical knick knacks, a picture of the wife and kids, and a signed baseball adorned the small room. It felt comfortable. The doctor was prematurely gray—Frank knew he wasn't very old—but he had the mannerisms of a much older physician. Peggy was holding tight to her husband's right hand, squeezing it, really, afraid to look at the doctor's face.

"Thanks for coming in, I know you're busy," the doctor said. "And I thought it best if your wife was with you."

"What's up, doc?" Frank let out a muffled chuckle at his joke, Peggy squeezed his hand harder, gave him a stern look. The doctor started talking, a pained look in his cheeks, saying a lot of medical terms neither Frank nor Peggy had ever heard before, and then he eased back to normal verbiage. Frank didn't hear anything until he heard the word, the "C" word.

"You have lung cancer," the doctor finally said.

Peggy began to cry hysterically. The doctor rubbed his temple trying to suppress the pain of delivering the catastrophic news, leaned forward and spoke softly.

"I could do a little walk around the issues that you have running through your body, but it's pretty bad," the doctor finally said. "Very bad."

Frank couldn't move. As Peggy kept crying, Frank slowly lifted his head and focused on the coffee cup sitting on the back edge of the doctor's desk, a plain white mug, empty. He looked at the doctor, empty eyes, speechless.

"It is advanced," the doctor said. "I'm not sure what, exactly, we can do for treatment."

Moments later, Frank leaned back in his chair as the weight of the world's looming mortality shifted on his back, and spoke.

"But I have a chance, right? A chance?"

"It is very advanced, Frank, advanced," the doctor repeated, and Peggy cried a little louder.

When the couple finally left the office, they were holding hands. Peggy was still sniffling, Frank had a shell-shocked mask on his face, the trappings of death poking at his mind.

Before getting into the car, he kissed her gently on the lips and touched her left cheek.

"I'm sorry, Peg." She grabbed Frank, pulled him into her arms, and squeezed with all the strength she had. After holding his hand on the short, silent trip to their house, Peggy went straight to their bedroom, sat uneasily on the bed, and started to cry again.

An hour later, she was still oozing tears.

CHAPTER 30

May 22, 1966
Cooperstown, New York

The postmark on the upper-right corner of the envelope said Chicago, dated four days earlier—it contained a simple note. Harold Titus was finally answering Frank's letter from more than a year earlier. Weak from small amounts of back and forth pain—and useless medication—but excited with a burst of emotional vitality, Frank tore open the envelope and quickly studied the letter.

> Dear Frank,
> Forgive the tardiness of this return letter, I've been busier than usual, plus trying to find anything current on Ray Cavanaugh proved impossible. But I was not to be deterred!
> I remembered that my friend Stanton Walters, who used to write for the Chicago Defender and now for the American and a couple of magazines, might know something about Cavanaugh, for whatever reason. I contacted him, sent him your information, and I think you will be hearing from him soon.
> Good luck with your search, and thanks for thinking of me. See you at the next induction, if I'm lucky.
> All the Best,
> Harold

For the first time—he still couldn't believe it—movement on the Cavanaugh front! Feeling better than he had in weeks because of the news, Frank excitedly called McMasters to his office and showed him the note.

"I've got him, we've got him, I just know it," Frank said with bubbly enthusiasm. "Ray fuckin' Cavanaugh, come to daddy."

"Walters," McMasters said as looked over the short letter. "I've read some of his stuff. He's good, and I bet you're right." He left the office and returned with a box, plopping it on a chair.

"I've been waiting for this day—looky at what I found stashed away in the catacombs," and he pulled a gray-flannel jersey from the box, a big, brown number 28 trimmed in orange on the back, St. Louis in block letters on the front, and handling it like it was the shroud of Turin, held it out to his boss.

"Cavanaugh's shirt from his no-hitter."

"Fuck," was all Frank could say. He took the jersey, held it, caressed it, took a whiff of the numbers, and then handed it back to McMasters. "His no-hitter? We've had that all along and nobody knew?"

"Well, as you've said many times, he played for a shitty team that doesn't exist anymore."

After holding it high to the ceiling, Frank slipped the old jersey on over his shirt and tie, zipping up the front.

"Kind of ugly, as baseball jerseys go," he said. "But this is special. Let's get this on display with some of the other pre-war stuff."

"Here's the game ball," Ron said, pulling an old American League horsehide from the box and flipping it to Frank. Then he pulled out a brown cap and tried it on, striking a goofy pitching pose. There were also a few newspaper clippings in the box and a glossy photo of Cavanaugh in his standard pitching pose.

"Yeah, we're putting this stuff in an exhibit." Then Frank placed the ball on his desk, took off the jersey, lit up a smoke, and read over the note from Titus again.

⸜

Two days later, the true celebration happened—a letter arrived from Walters. The two historians, giddy with glee and boyish delight—Frank felt almost perfect after reading the text—had to contain themselves within the confines of the office and library. Rock 'n Fire Ray Cavanaugh was suddenly very much alive, breathing, and most certainly visible on the lonely horizon of lost America.

> Dear Mr. Aldridge,
> My name is Stanton Walters, and I'm a writer at the Chicago American newspaper. I also write for several other publications, but I'm primarily a baseball writer and have been covering the game since 1937. I recently received a note from Harold Titus at the Chicago Tribune asking me if I knew anything about Ray Cavanaugh, and that you are trying to find him.
> Because I am still fairly active within the Negro community here in Chicago, I came across a little league coach named Cavanaugh. I did not know his first name, but after a couple of simple inquiries, I found out it is, in fact, Ray Cavanaugh.
> I have not talked with this man, he does not give out his personal information. However, the director at the little league headquarters passed along how I could get a hold of this Mr. Cavanaugh. If you think this might be the former ball player, here is his Chicago address:
> 5707 La Salle Street
> Chicago, IL
> If you need someone to talk to him or go to this residence, I'll be glad to help the Hall of Fame in any way that I can.
> I hope this letter finds you well and enjoying the current baseball season.
> Sincerely,
> Stanton Walters
> Chicago Defender

Walters knew his baseball, was a pitcher in high school in the early 1930s—he faced discrimination and racism on the field, and while he was good enough to pursue a pro career, like all other negroes, was denied the chance because of his skin color. Forgoing an attempt with a couple of Negro teams, he chose college, and after earning a degree at Delaware State, Walters embarked on a career in journalism. He landed at the *Chicago Defender* following graduation, and after that wrote for several newspapers and magazines, had a couple of books published, and was currently penning great copy for the *Chicago American*. He was a helluva writer, and as soon as Frank saw his name, knew he should have been contacted with the initial group of inquiries sent out.

The envelope had an official Baseball Hall of Fame logo in the upper-left corner, and seeing it surprised Ray. He had never been to Cooperstown before, and while he had at one time dreamed of being inducted into the hallowed Hall with baseball's other great players, he hadn't felt the need or pull to examine baseball's self-glorified and mythic past since he joined the army. There was nothing there for him he always figured, nothing that baseball's history offered—save for Jackie Robinson and Larry Doby honors and maybe a few other items—that was remotely interesting to him. Baseball had long considered itself the National Pastime, but Ray knew it never really was. And with his own "unofficial ban"—he never received even ten percent on the Hall of Fame ballot—Cooperstown hadn't been on his watch list for a long, long time.

It sat alone on the table for a day, then Ray threw the letter on his kitchen countertop with a couple of bills—he considered throwing it away. There could be nothing inside the official envelope that would be good, and he imagined they were asking about Ted Williams—that would be okay—or Casey Stengel, maybe wanting to ask about the genius of his move in the spitter incident.

After a couple more days, he picked it up, looked at it front and back, and as he started to crumple it for the trash can, he changed his mind and opened it.

Dear Ray,

If you are Rock 'n Fire Ray Cavanaugh, read on. If not, throw this letter away.

For the past couple of years, I've been trying to locate you, and upon finding you (hopefully), I knew that sharing the information I have would not be easy. The best way to do this is just to throw it out there: I was contacted by a woman who claims to be your daughter, and was asked to help find you. Her name is Lita Lawson. If this is new news to you, my apologies for how I've presented it.

Let me give you the little information that I know.

I had to do a lot of homework on this search to find you. It's almost as if you left the planet. I checked the story, and Lita Lawson was born on Aug 21, 1943. Aulette Lawson is listed as her mother and the father is listed as unknown. I also searched the death records in St. Louis and found that Aulette Lawson died the following day.

Also, Aulette is listed as a negro.

If any of this is viable at all, I ask you to write me back. I have found Lita's story to be believable as she was told by her grandmother that she didn't know who her father was, and the unknown was used to keep his family away.

Lita always thought her grandmother knew who her father was.

It also seems her grandmother was not happy about you, the thought of you. I'm sure this is all quite like a bomb has been dropped on you. But Lita wants to meet you, more than anything else in the world.

Think about this, what it means, and if you are, most assuredly, Lita's father. I can set up a meeting if that is something you would consider down the road. Please let me know if you think this is true.

Sincerely,

Frank Aldridge

Baseball Hall of Fame

It was a joke, a prank of the worst magnitude. It had to be.

Ray didn't believe a word of the letter, not for a second. Who would tell him he had a child that he didn't know about? What kind of a fiend would casually write a letter telling him he had a daughter—a daughter who had been dead before ever being alive—and she was looking for him? The unmitigated gall of the information typed on the paper brought anger, and then tears. He spread out the years past in his mind and couldn't figure out how he would have missed this—except he was in DC, then Aulette died, and he joined the army, the fucking army. By the time he was a civilian again, this was a long-ago story that he was trying to forget, that he would never forget.

Who was this Frank Aldridge? How did he know about Aulette? The name Lita? St. Louis? He even had the dates correct.

What if it was true?

As she did often in his thoughts, Aulette swept over him as he turned the radio on and started to quietly cry. The Outsiders were rocking on the station, and somehow their words struck him the right way—time wouldn't let him deny that the letter was real.

She was breathless, and then panic rushed through her body. Lita couldn't breathe for 15, 20, was it as long as 30 seconds? She finally closed her eyes, dropped to the floor and was able to inhale, several times in five seconds, and when the light-headedness subsided, she stood, picked up the letter from Frank Aldridge, and read it again.

> Dear Lita,
> I have the answer you've been waiting for: I found Ray Cavanaugh, and he is alive. I can hardly believe it, it's been so long.
> I have written him a letter, explained everything to him, and hopefully I'll hear back soon. This is what we've been waiting for. If I don't hear back from him I'll figure out a plan of action, but for now, know that he is alive.

Send me your thoughts and other questions. I know
this is a short note, but I wanted to let you know as
soon as possible that he is alive.
Sincerely,
Frank

As the initial anxiety from reading the letter subsided—she wasn't
expecting good news—jubilation swept over her. She had a father, he was a
baseball player, and most importantly, he wasn't a rapist—and that's when
Lita danced about the old house, singing. She knew he was her father—no
further proof was needed, as far as she was concerned. Lita also felt that
the man, Ray, would probably feel blindsided to know he had a daughter,
but so what? Then there was the awful possibility that he wouldn't want to
meet her—would that happen?

She had heard stories like hers before, a child finds a long-lost parent,
only to be rebuffed and spurned, ignored. It could happen, and with those
thoughts came a mild depression—she pushed back on by telling herself
that at least he wasn't a rapist. But maybe he did rape her mother—and
that scared her, too.

Lita quickly wrote back to Frank, again thanking him, and telling him
that she would be waiting with a great amount of hope.

✎

The handwriting was sloppy and the ink smeared across the words on the
paper, left to right. Frank coughed loudly and spit into the trash can by his
feet as he cleared a space on his desk to place the letter. Even though he had
read it several times, he found it hard to register what it said—a problem
he was having more and more—so he kept re-reading it.

Mr. Aldridge,

That was some letter I received from you. I am still in shock over the
news that I might have a daughter. I have had a hard time figuring
this all out but it seems to be true. If you don't already know I was
told the baby died with its mother. After all these years to find out

that she is alive and has been looking for me is wonderful. Of course I want to meet with Lita. If she is my daughter it is the best thing.

Thank you again for finding me, it seems you had a hard time. Well I'm still here.

Tell the girl that I am willing to meet and let me know the details of how it will work.

Ray Cavanaugh

He was really alive—the goddamn, left-handed son-of-a-bitch was alive, and he had written back. No denials, no threats, nothing but a warm feeling emitted from the page. Frank shook his head, coughed again, and lit a cigarette. After all this time—almost three years—and it was as simple as this?

✧

The Chicago that Ray Cavanaugh moved to was as racially conflicted as any major city in the country, probably more so. The large strip on the South Side—known as the Black Belt—was the landing point for most of the new families who came to the city and became the major living area for the negroes. As new residents migrated and moved to Chi Town, a life many negroes never thought possible materialized, and the new lives, charged with new meanings and hope, also spawned the rise of a thriving, black middle class, new businesses, culture—music and literature—sports, and politics exploded across the south and west sides.

It was that vibrant community that drew in Ray and ignited his desire to live there.

But the area was also plagued with a persistent, daunting racism, poor schools, and demoralizing segregation in the housing market—as a result, overcrowded slums became the norm for living arrangements for most black families. The city was complacent in its non-help to improve the area.

A strong civil rights movement in the early '60s produced many large protests against the gross segregation of the schools and other poor conditions. Those protests, and the other blights that keep growing and growing within the black community, eventually brought Dr. Martin Luther King, Jr. to the Windy City in January of 1966 to launch a campaign for open housing. He got a nasty taste of northern racism—much more than he had expected or was ready to deal with—when leading marches in all-white neighborhoods, and was met with viciously-violent responses. King was hit in the head with a rock during a march.

Because he was white, Ray was able to easily pick out his home in the area—if anything, he was discouraged from living in the "problem" area of the Heights. Ignoring the real estate concerns and advice he received, Ray found a nice little two-bedroom that was close to his new store and bought it.

Sweet home Chicago.

∾

In January, Ted Williams was voted into the Hall of Fame—he received 93.4 percent of the vote and became just the eighth player elected by the Baseball Writers on his first appearance on the ballot. What Frank couldn't fathom, what he would never understand, is why any writer wouldn't have voted for him. There was the stupid adage that players needed to wait, no one was worthy of first-ballot inclusion in the greatest hall of fame in the world.

Frank thought that kind of thinking was silly, horseshit nonsense.

The notion that great, deserving players should have to wait a year, or years, to be included as a great, memorable player among other great players, was insane. A lot of self-respecting writers would dupe themselves into the waiting game, thinking it was an okay method for voting in players—it was one of the things Frank tried not to dwell on. He really felt Ted would not get in on the first ballot, so great was the baseball writers hate for him. He was glad he was wrong.

For the last few months Frank and Ron had been assembling display items for Ted and Casey Stengel, the other new member of the Hall. There were a lot of items for Stengel—uniforms, gloves, and balls from his playing days, lineup cards as manager, but there wasn't much of a magic feel to Casey's stuff—of course, Frank still loathed the Yanks.

Williams' stuff was different.

The Hall had collected many, many Splinter items—the 1941 All-Star game home run ball, a bat used in the final game of 1941 as he finished with a .406 batting average, jerseys and caps, photos, and a uniform from his service as a pilot during WWII and the Korean War, game programs, magazine covers, and other "artifacts" of his sensational career. Frank also had a few of Ted's famous quotes highlighted on large display plaques. This was his favorite, of course:

> *"A man has to have goals - for a day, for a lifetime - and that was mine, to have people say, 'There goes Ted Williams, the greatest hitter who ever lived.'"*

It was a great display of both men, one that truly conveyed their baseball greatness, one that the large number of visitors during the induction would love. One of the best things Frank found was a photo of Stengel and Williams together, a rare thing for a Boston player and Yankee manager. Ron wanted to make a sign for one of his favorite Stengel quotes, the guiding light for all the induction weekends throughout the years.

> *"Oldtimers, weekends, and airplane landings are alike. If you can walk away from them, they're successful."*

It was an impulse purchase when Ray picked up *Paper Lion*, the book by George Plimpton, who pretended to be a backup quarterback for the Detroit Lions so he could write about it. The book was okay, and the way Plimpton related his story and time with the Lions was entertaining. But when he read about how sports and personal gratification can mix together different meanings for athletes, Ray was able to juxtapose it with his past and present, surprisingly, at the same time.

> *"The pleasure of sport was so often the chance to indulge the cessation of time itself—the pitcher dawdling on the mound...savoring a moment before committing themselves to action."*

—George Plimpton,
Paper Lion: Confessions of a Last-String Quarterback

That was where Ray was now—that moment before, the precious seconds in front of an action. It was a strange feeling this time—in games he'd feel the rush of adrenaline before each pitch, then again and again and again. This one moment, this simple motion of dropping off a letter, nothing more than raising and lowering his arm, the ridiculousness of the action was going to find something he never thought he had—he was going to value its memory.

The mail drop box on the street corner in front of the coffee shop was where he mailed all his bills—it was where he was taking the letter to the Hall of Fame. This man who contacted him, he didn't understand the rationale behind this search, and while he still didn't trust what he was doing, he did it anyway.

Whatever it meant, he didn't care. The past had called—Aulette had summoned him, it seemed—and he was going to answer.

∽

When he first realized his love for Aulette more than 25 years ago—god, the lost, hard time from the relentless agony of loss—he fought it. He looked beyond the wonder of her and saw the world around them, the unaccepting, the uneducated—the cruel stupidity of ignorance. He had grown up with it, watched his old man revel in unholy joy of negro hate, and goddamn if he didn't almost fall into it, too.

Baseball, for all that it wasn't to him, had always been his savior—it was baseball that got him out of Hillman, baseball that allowed him to meet Aulette, and now baseball, after taking away his life, might possibly breathe some soul back into his empty chest. The contemplation of what he didn't have set with him most days. He never had another woman in his life—he had sex with a few—but he never felt much for them.

Baseball started to give back to him as he began coaching the boys, but he didn't understand the significance of how it added a little hop to his step. When he'd decided years earlier that he would choose Aulette over the game, she protested.

"I want to be together, not make you leave the game," she told him more than once. "Let's do both." Ray knew that was always impossible, especially so in his baseball world. And it was that world that separated them, kept him from being with her when she died.

Now, all these years and tears later, came a letter from the Hall of Fame—baseball, it seemed, was calling with reparations.

CHAPTER 31

June 2, 1966
Chicago, Illinois

The lock slipped into itself easily, securing the back of the shop—the front door had already been bolted shut. Ray ignored the uncomfortable heat from the late afternoon sun and walked to his red, '61 Ford Galaxie. From the rear of the small parking lot he glanced at the back of his hardware store, *Tremendous Hardware*—everything looked fine. He slid behind the wheel, started the car, and steered his way toward the Cleveland Heights neighborhood park.

Baseball was waiting for him.

The two fields he helped build four years earlier had changed the landscape, not just of the physical area, but also the mentality of the neighborhood's people. The diamonds were truly the boys of the community's best friends—when the kids weren't practicing with their teams, they were fooling around, playing sandlot ball, or home run derby. Ray had done a small fundraiser five years earlier, petitioned the city, threw in several thousand dollars of his own money, and even helped build the two ballparks.

He named the two-field complex, complete with pitching and batting tunnels in addition to other workout areas—with the approval of the city council—Pete Hill Park, after the great outfielder who had played for the Chicago American-Giants in the Negro Leagues from 1911 to 1918.

"I mean, why not Bibb Falk, Eddie Collins, or Gabby Hartnett?" one the council members had asked at the meeting finalizing the park funding. "No one knows who this player is anyway."

"Yes, they do. He was a tremendous player, more than worthy of this." Ray was tired of explaining black baseball to the elected officials.

"This wasn't an easy sell, even for a negro neighborhood."

"It's the right thing, and I know the name will sit well with everyone," Ray said as diplomatically as possible.

The funding passed by one vote, and Ray got his ballfields for the Cleveland Heights' kids. And on this day, as he drove to the fields, his team, the Stars, would begin practicing in preparation for the end of the season league playoffs.

The fact that Ray was in the windy city at all was still like a dream. It had become the landing spot he needed, a home base. One of the worst things about being "blackballed" by baseball was that even if no one knew who he was, they "knew about him" in most of the major cities. The "spitter incident" was the last thing the American League office needed to effectively end his career, and while Ray should have at least been considered for the Hall of Fame—he was unofficially marked by the baseball writers as a cheater—he never was. And in DC, he was friendless and drifting, and stayed in the Capitol much longer than he should have.

He ran through women, ran through money, ran from life in general—Chicago, maybe because he was trying to give back a little, changed everything for him. The hardware store in Cleveland Heights not only afforded him the chance to meet new people, at least on a non-personal level, it also gave him the chance to earn trust, and he worked hard at it, especially among the negro community.

The slowness of acceptance—was he just another greedy, racist white man trying to exploit the community?—and then baseball, little league baseball, rescued him. The few girlfriends he had were inconsequential— sometimes he would have sex, but when he did, that would usually end the relationship. So, he focused on the store, spent a lot of time with the kids on his baseball teams, and filtered in and out the things that gave him small notions of happiness.

~§~

During the summer of 1965, Ray had been able to get Buck O'Neil, the great Negro League manager who was now a coach and scout for the Cubs, to come and talk to Ray's little league team. It wasn't easy—amiable as he was, Buck still liked to have an introduction from someone connected to both parties. Ray had been struggling with his boys, unable to connect mentally with the team—they needed a talk from someone who had answers that he didn't have—Ray thought of O'Neil.

"I know who you are," Buck said on the phone. "I think I've heard a thing or two about you."

"Well, whatever it was, it doesn't have anything to do with this—I want you to talk with my team of 11-year-olds in Cleveland Heights."

The line was silent, and Ray was afraid Buck was about to hang up on him. He was wrong.

"Okay, Mr. Cavanaugh. I can hear and feel your sincerity. Sometimes I don't. When can I come by?"

~§~

So. Ray Cavanaugh was alive, responsive (it seemed), viable. The letter Frank received from him was direct but guarded, and that was easily understood—he was told the baby, his baby, Lita—was dead with her mother, his lover. The man wanted to meet Lita, and while that was a joyous thing, many questions popped up that Frank hadn't originally thought through, but one question in particular had left him stumped:

How were they going to meet? And where?

Frank also wanted to meet these two people—after his long paper trail pursuit, there was a real need to see the union of the lost family. While he wanted to be a part of the reuniting—no, it was more of an initial togetherness—how could he do it? And how could he be with the two of them in case something went wrong?

The cancer had drained all his natural living energy, and it also stole any kind of notion he might have had to travel—hell, it sapped every ebb of his being on most days—he knew he couldn't do it. Had the finding of Cavanaugh happened just a few months earlier, he would've driven to St.

Louis, picked up Lita, then taken her to Chicago, to Ray's doorstep. Or if he trusted them, 100 percent, he could have Ray travel to St. Louis, or Lita to Chicago, on their own, and be done with it.

Nothing is that easy.

"Do you think she's his daughter?" Peggy asked after all the kids were in bed.

"At first, I didn't, not really. But I was being stupid."

"Yes," she nodded at him.

"I think, even without looking at everything I've found about this guy, it's easy to determine that she is," Frank said, almost apologetically.

"I knew she was when you first told me about him," Peggy said. "Who would send out a letter like that if it wasn't true, or think that it was true?"

"It makes no sense, though. Why didn't he know?"

"No sense. But you're making it happen." Frank went into an uncontrollable cough, eyes watering complete with body spasms to go with the loud hacking. And of course, the pain. He sat back, took one long awful sounding cough, and stopped, at least momentarily. Peggy walked to him, stroked his hair, picked up the glass of water and handed it to him. After taking a drink, Frank stood up and walked to the front of the room.

"This guy. This ghost of a man, this pitcher who has shunned his baseball past," and then he coughed again.

"Why don't you have both of them come here?" Peggy said. "A kind of baseball union."

"That won't work. Why would they do that?"

"To see you." She stroked his back.

"Why don't you go for me?" Frank said. "You could meet Ray at the airport in St. Louis, or at a hotel, and go meet Lita."

"You need to do this, Frank. Ask them to come up here. I think it's the only true way to pull them together, a real start."

The next morning, feeling the brunt of pain breaking him, Frank made it to his office and with Ron's help, wrote to the father and daughter, one letter for both of them.

Hello Lita and Ray,

I think that we are almost here, or there, with the end in sight. It has been a long haul for me and Lita. Ray, I have been searching for you almost three years, Lita has been looking for most of her life. As I've written before, no one seemed to know anything about you, where you were, and so on. I'm very happy that you answered my note, very happy also that you want to meet Lita.

My question for both of you is this: Would you consider coming to Cooperstown for the meeting?

I know it sounds strange, but I want to meet both of you, feel like I should meet both of you in person. This is the problem: I'm very sick, quite sick, and I don't think I'm going to get better. For that reason, I can't come to see either one of you; travel is pretty much out of the question for me. I've talked this over with a few of the people I work with, and my wife, and if it is possible for you both to do it, coming to Cooperstown would be the best thing all the way around for me, and Ray, it would be especially good for you, too.

It will be a long trip for both of you, but coming to my town, to the Baseball Hall of Fame, would make the special meeting eventful, especially for me. I've picked out the day of the hall of Fame inductions, July 25, as the day. It is always a wonderful day and time here in Cooperstown, filled with nostalgia, wonder, and strange as it might seem since it is the past that is celebrated, the hope of tomorrow, a way of looking forward to things that aren't yet here.

Again, I'm sick. If either one of you need any kind of financial assistance to make the trip, let me know, and I can make arrangements through the Hall to help.

How about about it? Lita, I know you've waited a long time for this, but the induction day is coming up on us fast. Ray, as I studied your career and found out more and more about you, coming here, not just to meet Lita, but to resurrect your place in baseball, would be a wonderful thing to do. Sharing it with her should make it even better.

I'll look forward to hearing from both of you, and soon.

All the Best,

Frank Aldridge

Baseball Hall of Fame

✍

When the boys saw the Cubs' cap on Buck's head, they stopped playing catch. Ray called them over to the bleachers, and for the first time in a while, they listened. O'Neil strolled to the front of the seats, grabbed a bat off the ground and smiling his great smile, started talking after Ray introduced him to the team.

"Boys," Buck said to the young players, "there ain't nothing you can't do, nowhere you can't go. Follow your dreams—let them take you as far as they can. But remember, hard work walks together with dreams.

"Your coach was a great player, you need to know that, and he worked very hard to get to the majors. That's what he wants for each of you."

As O'Neil kept talking to the boys, Ray thought of his old man and the long, ridiculous workouts he made him do, the yelling, the screaming— "Fuck it, you'll never be a player"—the old barn, and the stupid tire target. If it had helped him, made him tougher, it also purged him of a lot of feelings. It always felt like abuse—everything his dad did felt like abuse—but somehow the baseball work was worse and less at the same time. As Ray bowed his head and thought of the worst of his old man, O'Neil perked up a little.

"This game, I love it," Buck said. He took off his cap, scratched his head, and leaned forward to make his point. "If you love it, give it your all, do your best. I gave this game everything I had, asked for nothing but the chance I earned, and it gave back. Life is like that, too."

The twelve boys were mesmerized, hanging on every word. The Cubs were a big deal, bad as they were, and the kids, because they were all black, knew of Buck and his work with the team. At the end of his short speech, Buck dropped the bat, and looking each boy in the eyes, finished with his topper.

"Always love your teammates—they're the ones who got your back."

When practice officially started, Buck watched for a few minutes before leaving, giving Ray a firm handshake as he left the field.

"Good group of boys, good group. I know they'll make you proud," and Buck spread his sweet smile to Ray and gave a hearty wave as he walked to the parking lot.

⋘

When did he first hear the long hairs? 1963, or was it '64? Didn't matter, it seemed like they'd been around forever. Every time Ray clicked on the radio, it was the Beatles—"yeah, yeah, yeah?!?"—their stuff was always playing, over and over. Ray noticed that while the songs were never the same, the *sound* was constant. He'd never heard anything like them before, and maybe that's why he didn't like the foursome from across the pond. When he thought about them for any length of time ('Who wants to hold hands?'), he felt that—of course!—he hated them, and did not understand how anyone liked them. He'd take any one of the big bands from 20 years earlier over the British group—they played real music.

Then he heard "Twist and Shout"—it was pretty good.

When he heard "This Boy," he thought he might cry, and that was it. Ray pulled the Fab Four into his music soul, and while they never fully replaced the sounds, passions, and feelings he had for the music of his youth, they had a special place in all things he held close to his heart.

Could the Beatles, like the other new things in his life, really help him put all his troubles behind him? Ray hoped so.

⋘

Lita was beside herself with happy, surging anxiety.

He wanted to meet her!

When she was able to pull her thoughts into one place, her first thought about the letter was, 'Where in the hell is Cooperstown?' Lita knew it was a long distance from St. Louis, a trip that would not be easy for a young, black woman. She couldn't afford to fly, didn't want to take a bus. Could her 1959 blue-green Chevy Impala make the trip without breaking down or blowing up? The car had been steady and solid for her since she got it the year before—traveling alone was her biggest concern.

"You're really going to go alone?" her closest friend asked many, many times. "Alone?"

Lita didn't want to make the trip by herself, but knew that was the only way to meet the man—her dad?—and the historian Frank Aldridge.

After checking the date on the calendar, picking up a road map at the Mobil gas station, she plotted the trip, calculated the time it would take, and figured out where she could spend the night. After checking her savings account, Lita determined she could make the trip on her own without help from Frank Aldridge, but she needed to buy a suitcase for the trip. Baseball was giving her father back to her—going to a baseball town to meet him seemed almost like a fairy tale to Lita.

It was a long time coming.

CHAPTER 32

July 25, 1966
Cooperstown, New York
Early Afternoon

Even though the room was warm and humid, Frank was cold, shivering under his blankets as he fought to control the pain running through most of his body. His breathing came in short gasps that were seconds apart—the normal intake of air hurt too much. He'd been in the hospital a few days, and despite the denials from his wife and doctor, Frank knew he'd moved into the early stages of his death watch.

He wished he was already gone—his lungs felt like flattened, hardened pancakes, the stabbing aches dispersed from them was immense. Each day brought new feelings of agony, remorse, more visions of lost opportunities and love. Peggy had spent most of each day with him since he had checked in, but he'd only seen the kids once, and that was killing him, too. But each day Peggy would walk in with a smile, give her husband a firm hug, and read a couple of notes the older kids had written to him.

"You're the best dad. I miss you. Come home and buy me ice cream."

"Get better daddy."

"I love you."

Through the pain of breathing, Frank was able to squeeze out a few tears over the notes. Peggy didn't stay long this morning—she instinctively knew that he needed to be alone, so she was taking the kids to help with a birthday party in the late afternoon, and getting the four kids squared away by herself was a large task, especially with two-year-old Molly.

"Peg, play *Rubber Soul* for me, okay?" Frank asked as she readied herself to leave.

"Side 2?" she asked, walking to the table where she had set up his small record player.

"Yes, that side." Peggy put on the album and turned back to her husband.

"Do you have the radio set up for the speeches?"

"Yes," Frank coughed out. "WDOS is broadcasting, so at least I can hear them." Peggy walked back to the bed, kissed her husband, and left the room.

As the Beatles filled the room, and Frank fell back to a near sleep, the music drowned out the stabbing aches, easing the relentless pain. The soothing voices of Lennon and McCartney moved into "Wait" as Frank finally fell into painful dreams.

Today was the day of the Hall of Fame inductions, the day Frank was supposed to meet Ray Cavanaugh and Lita Lawson—and Ted Williams— the day he'd been waiting for, the day he'd long envisioned and planned for when the meeting was finalized. It was also the day he'd dreamed about since he first drove into Cooperstown 11 years earlier, the day that he'd be there to help celebrate Teddy Ballgame's induction.

Only he wasn't.

⌁

A throng of almost 10,000-plus baseball crazies and dignitaries were jammed around the east side of the Hall-of-Fame building in Cooper Park, waiting for Ted Williams and Casey Stengel to talk about the greatness of their careers. It was a little overcast, humid and very warm, and the reserved excitement in the buzzing crowd had a polite feel—the two baseball greats were highly deserving of the honor about to be conferred on them, and everyone was anxious to hear their words.

Off to the side of the presentation platform sat Ron McMasters. He was looking around the crowd, searching for faces he didn't know. He didn't like being alone—he had never done a ceremony or anything else without Frank—and he did not have the easy-going personality to hang with the old ballplayers. That was always Frank's thing. But he felt the excitement of being there to watch and listen to Ted, and he also had his little Kodak to snap a few shots for his boss to see.

Williams was introduced to the crowd, and as the Splendid Splinter advanced to the heavily microphoned podium amid a loud ovation, it was easy to see he was genuinely moved, a rare share of emotion from the great player. He placed the notes for his speech on the stand and started talking in a humble tone.

"I guess every player thinks about going into the Hall of Fame," the Splinter said as he looked over the crowd. "Now that the moment has come for me, I find it difficult to say what is really in my heart. But I know it is the greatest thrill of my life. I received two hundred and eighty-odd votes from the writers. I know I didn't have two hundred and eighty-odd friends among the writers. I know they voted for me because they felt in their minds and in their hearts that I rated it, and I want to say to them: Thank you, thank you all from the bottom of my heart." The crowd broke into applause, and Williams paused, scratched at his face and took it in.

"Today I am thinking about a lot of things. I am thinking about my playground director in San Diego, Rodney Luscomb, my high school coach, Ross Caldwell, and my managers, who had so much patience with me—fellows like Frank Shellenback, Donie Bush, Joe Cronin, and Joe McCarthy. I am thinking of Eddie Collins, who had so much faith in me—and to be in the Hall with him particularly, as well as those other great players, is a great honor. I'm sorry Eddie isn't here today.

"I'm thinking of Tom Yawkey. I have always said it: Tom Yawkey is the greatest owner in baseball. I was lucky to have played on the club he owned, and I'm grateful to him for being here today.

"But I'd not be leveling if I left it at that. Ballplayers are not born great. They're not born great hitters or pitchers or managers, and luck isn't a big factor. No one has come up with a substitute for hard work. I've never met a great player who didn't have to work harder at learning to play ball than anything else he ever did. To me it was the greatest fun I ever had, which probably explains why today I feel both humility and pride, because God let me play the game and learn to be good at it.

"The other day Willie Mays hit his five hundred and twenty-second homerun. He has gone past me, and he's pushing, and I say to him, 'go get 'em Willie.'

"Baseball gives every American boy a chance to excel. Not just to be as good as anybody else, but to be better. This is the nature of man and the name of the game. I hope some day Satchel Paige and Josh Gibson will be voted into the Hall of Fame as symbols of the great Negro players who are not here only because they weren't given the chance.

"As time goes on I'll be thinking baseball, teaching baseball, and arguing for baseball to keep it right on top of American sports, just as it is in Japan, Mexico, Venezuela, and other Latin American and South American countries. I know Casey feels the same way....," and Stengel, sitting next to Williams on the stage, hammed it up a little at this point, comically motioning Ted away from the mic as the audience laughed. "I also know," Ted continued, laughing a little himself, "I'll lose a dear friend if I don't stop talking. I'm eating into his time, and that is unforgivable. So in closing, I am grateful and know how lucky I was to have been born in America and had the chance to play the game I love, the greatest game of them all, baseball."

The large audience broke into wild applause as The Kid stepped away from the podium, giving way to "The Ol' Perfessor," Casey Stengel. As it was, Williams needn't have worried about the time—Casey talked and talked, then talked some more, telling stories and reminiscing about everyone he'd had the pleasure of playing with and for.

"I chased the balls Babe Ruth hit," Stengel said during the speech, "and we couldn't play on the Sabbath, that was the day for the preacher to collect." And then he talked about balls knocked over his head in the outfield, reminisced about teams, towns, money, where he lived, talked about managing, and who he played for. As much as any one man could, Stengel laid out his life in stories, talking nonstop for more than 20 minutes. It was, as always, a great time when Casey pontificated—laughter filled the spaces around the Hall. Nobody enjoyed Casey's speech more than Ted, who put on a pair of sunglasses and took over Stengel's chair on the stage.

"I want to thank everybody," Stengel finally said to the crowd as he ended his talk. "I want to thank my parents ... and I'm thankful I had baseball knuckles and couldn't become a dentist."

McMasters took a shot of the two players, separate and together, wishing Frank could be in the shot, too.

When the speeches concluded, Frank used all the energy he could muster, sat up, and reached over to turn off the radio. Then he took a drink from the glass of water positioned next to the small receiver, thought briefly of Cavanaugh and Lita, wiped a tear away from his left eye, laid back gingerly, and fell asleep.

CHAPTER 33

July 25, 1966
Cooperstown, New York
Late afternoon

The small downtown area of Cooperstown, a couple of blocks of simple two and three-story buildings, was dedicated almost completely to the National Pastime. The town, even as it was bursting at the seams with the thousands of rabid baseball fans this day, had a familiar feel to Ray. Forget about the beautiful, majestic, and rolling landscape that led travelers into the village, scenery so splendid it could evoke disappointment leaving it to enter Cooperstown. Coupled with the feel of Otsego Lake, whose edge set cleanly off the downtown area extolling an air of strength and calmness, the hamlet was like nothing he had ever experienced before. But it was still small-town America—even with all the baseball extras—and flashes of Hillman shot through his head nonetheless as he saw the structures along Main Street, images quickly followed by sparks of his dad, mom, and the rest of his goddamn hometown.

And then he thought of Aulette.

His brain had worked overtime on the long drive—he spent the night in a motel outside of Buffalo, finishing the trip to the small hamlet that day. He had almost timed it perfectly, pulling into the town an hour and a half before the scheduled meeting. He went through the roller coaster of his life several times on the drive, never coming to the end—baseball was with him again, in a different and better way—Ray shook off the melancholy vision of his past hardball life and took in the new surroundings. The town was pulsating with a vibrant excitement—Hall of Fame inductions will do that. The ceremony and speeches were finished almost an hour earlier, and even though some of the celebration after parties and gatherings were already under way, downtown Cooperstown remained radiant in its baseball glory. A couple of signs were prominently displayed in merchant windows—"Welcome Casey and Ted!" Ray thought of the times he beaned Williams, remembered Casey challenging the umpires when he was experimenting with the spitter.

"I've seen that pitch too many times not to know that he's throwing one," Casey barked at the umpire after a particularly juicy pitch floated passed a Yankee hitter. Ray smiled at the memory, especially since he calmly spit at Stengel's shoes as he walked back to the dugout following the riff with the umpire—the subsequent suspension that followed the encounter killed the fondness of his best Stengel recollection.

Ray didn't have an invitation to any of the parties or other events, and why would he? There were plenty of formal get-togethers of all living Hall-of-Famers and former players who could make the trek to Cooperstown, plus parties thrown by the locals, and small events by other ballplayers and baseball people. Ray wasn't invited to anything except the "meeting", and that's the way he wanted it—seeing old players was not something he ever wanted. But the instructions from Aldridge were haphazard at best—meet the young woman outside the Hall around 4:00. Frank noted—promised in his note, in fact—that he would be there, too.

After driving his '61 Galaxie up and down the side streets looking for a suitable parking spot, he finally gave up and parked the car several blocks away from the downtown strip. Ray walked through the neighborhood from his car to Main Street, and since it was just 3:15, he strolled up and down the block a couple of times, looking in the windows of the shops, watching the other people, checking out the baseball souvenirs in a couple of stores. A couple of times he stopped, pulled the ring out of his pants pocket—Aulette's ring—and gazed at its simple beauty. When he looked at his watch, it was 4:08.

Where was the girl? And where was Frank?

❧

The last black person Lita saw was in Ohio in a grocery store, just before she crossed into Pennsylvania. She had the letter from Frank, the instructions on how and where to meet, her road map—she didn't believe it was really going to happen, and the closer she got to Cooperstown, the more she doubted the realness of the meeting. But Frank's letter had been deliberate enough—she was going to meet Ray, and Frank, outside the Hall of Fame at 4:00. She kept wondering why the date of the Hall of Fame ceremony was picked, and why she had to drive halfway across the country. What if this was a gigantic joke? A fraud? Was this Aldridge man for real? What if *he* was a rapist? She had doubted his sincerity many times, especially when he was so slow to send her letters.

But he found Ray Cavanaugh. And Lita was certain, more than ever, that he was her father.

She was constantly saying prayers during the trip, not for anything in particular, and she certainly didn't think answers were coming, didn't believe in the power—for the duration of her trip to Cooperstown, however, she would hold her breath, pray for a little help and strength, then pull into a gas station hoping to be served.

She always was.

❧

Frank was listless and in a painful half sleep when the tall, handsome man walked into the hospital room. He was wearing a dark plaid sport jacket without a tie, and his tanned face carried a solemn but friendly look.

"Frank Aldridge?" he said stopping a few feet from the door. Frank opened his eyes wide in recognition of the voice, half sitting up in the bed.

"Ted? Ted…Williams?"

"Yes, yes that's me." The Splendid Splinter broke out his famous smile and pulled the chair that was next to the wall over by the bed and sat down. He extended his hand toward Frank.

"I'm Ted Williams."

"Ted," Frank whispered through his pain as he shook the hand. "Ted, Ted. I'm Frank," and McMasters shot through his heart as he knew instinctively that it had to have been his protégé who arranged the meet-ing. The stabbing ache and agonizing grip of pain the cancer had on him notwithstanding, Frank pulled back the tears he wanted to cry and smiled at the newest member of Baseball's Hall of Fame.

"I heard you were a big and important guy at the Hall," Williams said. Then The Kid leaned back in his chair, presented his comfortable face to Frank, and the two men began to talk quietly about baseball and other important pieces of life.

∾

Getting Ted Williams—The Kid was swarmed over with many requests for his time while in Cooperstown—to meet up with Frank was no simple task. Getting a minute of face time with Williams was harder than it should have been, but McMasters' persistence—phone calls and more phone calls—paid off. When he finally got to talk to the Hall-of-Fame slugger after the speeches, he showed him the folder with all of the shitty writers' articles and that "Frank keeps most of these out of your file." When he was filled in on the cancer, Ted didn't blink.

"Let's go."

McMasters wandered around the grounds that surrounded the Hall's building after dropping Williams off at the hospital, looking at "dignitar-ies" and other special guests, hoping to spot the young negro woman or the old pitcher. He never saw a negro, and most of the guests were older men, blending into one another in an uneasy way. He stayed at the designated meeting place on the side of the building for more than 30 minutes before walking across the park and looking back down the street.

It was in vain—he never saw Lita, missed picking Ray out of the large, indistinguishable crowd.

∾

As the last of the celebratory induction crowd disbanded and made their way across and out of the downtown area—people were either leaving Cooperstown, heading to after parties in various parts of the town, or just milling around the ceremony platform—Ray rose from the bench he was sitting on, looked down the street at the Hall of Fame building two blocks away, and started to walk to toward it. Maybe the whole thing was a long, awful, ridiculous joke, a prank played by the Hall or even former teammates. In the past, rage would have taken over, but this time sorrow called his name, and he answered. As the blues of loneliness crept up his backside to cradle him, radio music from one of the small downtown cafés filtered into the hot and humid summer air above the buzz of the scattering baseball fans, and the sound of The Vogues' upbeat song, "The Land of Milk and Honey," fell over him. Ray stopped and took it in—'Yes,' he whispered to himself, 'I've lived bold and hard. I hope this *is* the land of milk and honey.'

He started walking again, sadly humming the tune while looking at the women in the street, the men, and a few kids yelling with joy for no reason. As he got closer to the Hall's building, he looked once more at Aulette's ring, and when he glanced up, spotted a woman sitting by herself on a bench about block beyond the other side of the building, head low, elbows on her lap holding something with both hands. Ray stopped and watched as she sat up slowly and wiped at her eyes, looked at the object she was holding, and as she turned her head and looked in Ray's direction, he saw the light-caramel skin of her face and arms, and a strong, feminine jawline in the outline of her dark hair. He walked closer—their glances locked and Ray saw the lost, forlorn aura around her dark, riveting eyes—she was clearly crying. His feet stopped moving and he stood motionless, yet jittery, staring across the boundaries of time. Ray pulled in emotions long dead, and then breathed, it seemed, for the first time.

Lita slowly stood up, smiled weakly, again wiped at her face, glanced at the baseball card, then looked at him straight on—she knew it was true.

Ray envisioned Aulette's beautiful smile as the timeless echo of her sweet voice rolled over and through him.

"I love you so, and one way or another, we will be together, be a family in a way that neither one of us has ever known."

With one colossal inhalation, Ray's heart soared with more delight than he had felt in decades—Main Street melted away from his vision, and he began walking quickly to her before breaking into a slow run. As if she'd seen it a thousand times, Lita instinctively knew the gait of the old ballplayer, and she watched his eyes soften as he drew closer to her—yes, it was him.

"Daddy?" she said loud enough for him to hear, and again his heart jumped. Ray said her name a couple of times before reaching her, and as tears dropped over their cheeks, father and daughter embraced tightly, crying with the uncontrollable and joyous elation of their unknown love for each other reborn.

Free at last.

EPILOGUE

Sport Magazine
September 1966

The Return of "Rock 'n Fire"

By Stanton Walters

One of the game's most intimidating competitors, he made the beanball a big part of his pitching skillset. Baseball forgot about Ray Cavanaugh, but he remembers and still loves the game. "I have no regrets about my career," he says. "Baseball will always be who I am."

I f you look closely at the man's face, you can almost see his vicious, competitive nature in action, how he needed to fire a baseball at high speeds toward unprepared batters. There was always much glee in his deep blue eyes when the batters flailed helplessly at his speedballs, never an ounce of remorse when a pitch got away and plunked a hitter in the ribs. That part of his life is now gone, but it is still very much with him.

"It was a good time," 'Rock 'n Fire' Ray Cavanaugh said of his baseball career with the St. Louis Browns and Washington Senators. "Pitching was my life. Baseball was my life."

What a baseball life it was.

The hard-throwing southpaw amassed 182 wins and 1,953 strikeouts to go with a 4.02 E.R.A., all while pitching for sub-par clubs.

He also hit 308 batters, the major league record.

"I guess some hitters were afraid to face me, but so what? It was a big part of my game."

There are many stories about Cavanaugh and his penchant for beaning batters. Some players were so scared of getting hit that they struck out with three quick and feeble swings. Others would duck and sway in the box, almost daring the lefty to throw at them. There is one tale of a young second baseman in the Texas League who soiled his pants when a pitch from Cavanaugh whizzed close to his head. Several times throughout his career he was accused of throwing at hitters, serving multiple suspensions for hurting opposing players.

"Did I ever throw at a hitter on purpose?" Cavanaugh mused. "Hell, yes."

His career ended 15 seasons ago, and since then he has had very little to do with the major leagues or his former teams.

He found a nice landing spot, though, and likes the direction his life has taken.

Hardware Heaven

For a Kansas farm boy, the big city seems to be a strange place to live, but for Cavanaugh, who never did the natural thing throughout his playing days, returning to the farmlands in the heart of America was never an option.

"There wasn't anything there for me," he said of his hometown, Hillman, Kansas, which is located between Topeka and Kansas City in the eastern part of the Sunflower state. "My family is gone, and I haven't lived there since 1934 or so."

These days his life centers around his hardware store in the Englewood neighborhood of Chicago, something that he never anticipated. But an opportunity to buy the store arose eight years ago, and Cavanaugh jumped at the chance. Looking at screws, plumbing parts, and yard equipment is a far cry from the baseball diamonds he once pitched on, and that's the way he likes it.

"I'm pretty comfortable here," he said of his current life. "It's been pretty good."

His store, *Tremendous Hardware & Supplies*, does a nice business, and also employs five negroes.

"It's a great place, this neighborhood. I like the people, and I think, for the most part, they like me. I learned the hardware business pretty fast, but I found that being nice and earning trust with customers was the best thing I could do to be a success in the business."

The transition wasn't the easiest.

"I'm sure that many of the people didn't think a white man would do right by this area, but that was my plan," Cavanaugh said of his business. "I wanted to make myself a part of Englewood. I love this place, and I love all of the new friends I have."

A Great Baseball Career

Cavanaugh hurled the horsehide for almost 14 seasons, usually for poor and struggling teams. He always had championship stuff, but most of his teammates did not.

"The World Series? Sure, I wanted a championship, to win a championship, but it wasn't in the cards," the old left hander said. "I played ball with some great guys, a few not-so-great guys, and okay organizations.

"But still, I think my career was pretty good."

A pitcher's pitcher, Cavanaugh had an arsenal of pitches and placement that many other big leaguers were envious of and wanted. He had true "Rock 'n Fire" stuff—hence the nickname that he's had since he first started playing the game. The numbers added up to championship-like results, but Cavanaugh never had the teammates to produce a winning record for their teams, let alone to make a pennant run.

"There were a couple of seasons in St. Louis when I thought we might have something, but boy oh boy, the Yanks would always come to town and hand us our hat," Cavanaugh said with a sad smile. "I got 'em more than they got me, though. Check it out."

He did. The record shows that his career mark against the Bronx Bombers was a very good 27-18 with an E.R.A. of 3.88.

"They tried to trade for me several times," Cavanaugh said of the Yanks, "especially when I was with the Browns, but they never offered anything even close to what I was worth." And then the smile faded. "That's why I always wanted to beat them."

One of the best games Cavanaugh pitched was against the New Yorkers, a 1-0 one-hitter in 1941. The Rock 'n Fire stuff was sizzling that day as the lefty chalked up 14 strikeouts.

"Yeah, I remember that game. I think I hit DiMaggio in the leg," he said with a chuckle. The *best* game of his career, though, had to be the no-hitter against Detroit in 1940.

"I only struck out six or seven batters that day, but everything they hit was either a simple pop up or an easy grounder," Cavanaugh remembered. "I don't think the fielders had a tough play the whole game."

A life-long bachelor, Cavanaugh does have some regret about missing out on a family.

"My dad taught me how to be a ball player, but not much else," the old pitcher said with a touch of sadness in his voice. "To be honest, sometimes I think I made a mistake, but I always followed my heart when it came to matters of family, women, and love. Marriage is something that never was a real possibility for me. But you know, I had baseball, or at least baseball had me.

"And my dad always told me to do stuff my way. That's what I did."

While Cavanaugh does not have his own family, he isn't without support from other relatives.

"I recently found a family member I'd been estranged from and it's a good thing," the old left hander said. "I didn't know what I was missing," and then he added, "They'll be coming to Chicago soon."

Earning His Name

Baseball has always been keen on nicknames—Rube, Cool Papa, Scoops, Candy, Wahoo Sam, Double X. The Wild Horse of the Osage. And, of course, Babe. It's one of the things that make baseball fun, endearing, and memorable. For Ray Cavanaugh, his nickname was a big part of him and his athletic prowess. The question that many fans wanted to know but never really asked during his playing days, was where did the name come from, and who gave it to him?

"My dad started yelling it at me when I was a kid—'Rock 'n Fire Ray, Rock 'n Fire!' From there, the rest of the town started calling me Rock 'n Fire Ray whenever I pitched. But the name really came from my grandpa, and I'm pretty sure he got it from watching a negro ballclub in Topeka play. He used to say it to my dad when he was a pitcher for Hillman. From there, my dad yelled it at me. My grandpa yelled it at me, too, but he died when I was still a boy."

When he joined the Topeka Senators in 1933, the local paper already knew the nickname, and they used it a lot.

"I don't remember a time when I wasn't called 'Rock 'n Fire,'" Cavanaugh said.

A Humble Start

Cavanaugh began his professional career close to his hometown of Hillman, Kansas, playing for the Class A Topeka Senators. The lefty earned his 'Rock 'n Fire' stripes that first season, whiffing 244 hitters—he also beaned 44 batters.

"Every time I hit a guy, the league (the now defunct Western League) wanted to suspend me, fine me, keep me from pitching," Cavanaugh said of his first go-around in the minors. "My manager was Alex Butterfield, a tough baseball man, and he backed me up all the way. I only missed one start." The old pitcher smiled at his recollection.

After two-plus tremendous seasons in the minors—Cavanaugh also pitched for the Browns' San Antonio Missions club—the Kansan earned his way onto the Browns roster in the middle of the 1935 season. His major league debut was outstanding; Cavanaugh struck out 10 Washington Senators in a 3-2 win, and the lefty quickly settled in to begin what would become a stellar career. He won 12 times that first year, and in 1938 and 1939, won 18 and 20 games.

"Baseball creates a craving for more and more, and the more I won, the more I wanted to win. But boy, a couple of those Browns teams I played for were terrible."

His Washington teams weren't much better. Three of his Browns' teams lost more than 100 games, and twice the Senators did the same. When St. Louis finally won the pennant, Cavanaugh was gone, traded away to D.C. He also served in the Army during WWII. Sometimes he thinks about what might have been if he pitched for a different club, but overall, he has no regrets.

"The best days of my life were in St. Louis, and I really enjoyed the people there. I learned a lot about myself, life in general, even about baseball," he said with a somber smile. "I was happy to serve my country during the war, and Washington was good to me, too."

Still Attached to the Game

When Cavanaugh isn't helping customers find the right pipe fitting or hammer, he's on the little league ball diamond a few blocks from his shop, helping the local boys learn the game that he still loves. Almost all of the kids he works with are negroes.

"They don't have too much, the kids who live around here,"

Cavanaugh said of his coaching. "But they want to play ball. I sponsor a couple of teams each summer, and I like to coach. It keeps me invested in the game, and it also gives me the chance, at least on this level, to help the eventual future of the game.

"I love working with the kids. The thing about the boys in my neighborhood, they are hungry to learn. Being with them has brought back my own memories of how hungry I used to be to play."

Coaching the young boys also fills the void of not having his own children.

"I never really thought of it that way, but maybe," Cavanaugh said of his little league instruction. "I just knew that if I didn't step up, then these kids wouldn't get to play baseball."

The old lefty has been involved with the kids for about seven years. But despite his new life away from the big leagues, Cavanaugh recently ventured to Cooperstown and the Hall of Fame to rub elbows with some of the men he used to play against, most notably Ted Williams.

"The Hall of Fame ceremony was great, a lot of fun. I saw a

lot of old players I hadn't seen in years. And ballplayers are always ballplayers, no matter what."

It wasn't really a return, so to speak, of Cavanaugh to big league baseball, but it was the first time he'd done anything connected to the major leagues since he hung up his spikes in 1951.

"Baseball got me here, and now baseball, with the kids anyway, keeps me going," he said. "I know it might be hard to believe, but I don't miss playing. I would miss working with the young players."

Know this: Baseball misses the likes of Cavanaugh, and while there hasn't been a player remotely resembling him since he retired, anything and everything he does for the game moving forward should be well-received. It's good to reminisce

the pleasures of baseball's past—a lot of players like Cavanaugh tend to fade away quickly, as he did, easily lost in the constant newness of each baseball season as phenom rookies surge across the green diamonds of ballparks around the country.

Baseball always begins, again.

The game endures, and just as surely as the collective memories of our fandom dissolve into one another, sometimes the long-gone luster of fire from an old, hard-throwing lefty slips out of the dark shadows of forgotten stars and recaptures our passion, unquestionably and completely as the baseball heroes of tomorrow always resurrect the game.

Welcome back to baseball, Rock 'n Fire Ray, welcome back—we've been waiting for you.

ABOUT THE AUTHOR

An award-winning author who has written 13 nonfiction books on sports, Mark Stallard makes the jump to the world of fiction—*Rock 'n Fire* is his debut novel. With degrees in English and Journalism from the University of Kansas and Wichita State University, plus a Master's degree from Baker University, Stallard has also written for numerous newspapers and publications, including *The Wichita Eagle* and *Baseball America*.

He is a full-time writer living in Kansas City.

A NOTE FROM THE AUTHOR

Dear Readers,

Embarking on the long journey that brought *Rock 'n Fire* to life proved to be a twofold challenge for me: I had no clue that the book would take more than 10 years to complete and I wasn't even sure if I had a story to tell—in the beginning all I knew was where the story would end.

Well, kind of. But let me tell you, it was a great trip, regardless of how long it took to complete. Piecing together the historical aspects of the novel proved challenging—inventing a small town rooted in the numerous parts of the country's systemic and overt racism was especially hard. There is no such place as Hillman, Kansas, even though I've visited it many, many times. Almost every other location in the book exists, even if the names are different, and there are some names that are real but attached to imaginary places.

I was faithful to many parts of the historical record, both in baseball or otherwise, but everything is fiction. Several characters were obviously real, and while I took liberties with what they may or may not have done, it is important to remember that as depicted in this book, they are fictitious—don't waste your time looking up dates, times, places, or even players. Their use is purely and completely fictional in the novel.

There is one major issue I'd like to cover—my use of racial slurs—the N-word, the most offensive word in America that will not die, the grossly hateful utterance usually coupled with the evil intent that has stained our nation's soul for centuries. After much reflection, I decided to use it and other words as openly and freely as they were spoken in the time periods depicted throughout the book. That meant throwing the N-word around as casually as one might use the word "man" or "ballplayer." It isn't something I took lightly, but to fully and realistically show the world as it was, the N-word is used as it would have been over the long arc of time that is covered in the story.

Sadly, I know it is still widely used today. I hope that someday, the word and feelings attached to it will be gone, allowing the United States to truly be a land of equality both in spirit and the law.

If *Rock 'n Fire* has ignited your imagination, invoked emotions and thoughts about where the United States has been and what it can become— good. As you moved forward during the long trip to Cooperstown, I hope you enjoyed the ride.

Thanks for reading,
Mark